Advance praise for *States of Motion*

"Stories can feel too careful, built rigidly around a single moment when the other shoe drops. Not these: Laura Hulthen Thomas fearlessly drops whole closets full of shoes, one after another, in these generous, spacious stories. She makes room on the page for all the complexities of real life."

— Caitlin Horrocks, author of *This Is Not Your City*

"You will engage with these characters from the edge of your seat, as Laura Hulthen Thomas reveals their constant state of motion between memories of the past and present complex circumstances. Their futures remain uncertain. Yours may, too, after you read their stories."

—Lolita Hernandez, author of Making Callaloo in Detroit (Wayne State University Press, 2014)

"The stories in *States of Motion* are a revelation: harrowing, tender, full of moments of everyday unease and menace. Laura Hulthen Thomas is a master at rendering characters undone by what life has thrown at them and by what they're capable of doing in response. As with the very best fiction, the results are both surprising yet inevitable, and we are amazed, again and again in these stories, at what can be contained in the human heart, and at what can spill out. A debut collection not to be missed."

—CJ Hribal, author of *The Company Car* and *The Clouds in Memphis*

"*States of Motion* shimmers with a quiet lyricism that transforms the stuff of ordinary life into pure magic. Laura Hulthen Thomas's stories remind us that we are flawed and fragile and loving and dignified, and that every human moment contains the possibility of heart-wrenching beauty. What a lovely book this is."

—David Haynes, author of *A Star in the Face of the Sky*

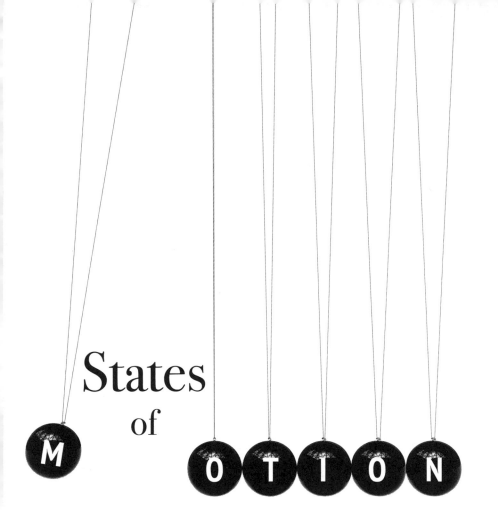

States
of
M OTION

Stories by Laura Hulthen Thomas

Wayne State University Press
Detroit

ISBN 978-0-8143-4314-2 (paperback)
ISBN 978-0-8143-4315-9 (e-book)

Library of Congress Control Number: 2016959424

Publication of this book was made possible by a generous gift from The Meijer Foundation. Additional support provided by Michigan Council for Arts and Cultural Affairs and National Endowment for the Arts.

Wayne State University Press
Leonard N. Simons Building
4809 Woodward Avenue
Detroit, Michigan 48201-1309

Visit us online at wsupress.wayne.edu

For Ron

Contents

Acknowledgments

Bringing a book to life possesses a life all its own. I owe this life to Annie Martin and all of the dedicated staff at Wayne State University Press. My deepest gratitude also goes out to Kevin McIlvoy, Susan Neville, Megan Staffel, and C. J. Hribal for their guidance on early drafts of these stories. I am indebted to Lolita Hernandez for her forever wise and generous counsel and support. Dr. Geoff Murphy provided crucial background for Emily's story, and any errors in science and the details of a laboratory scientist's critical work are my own. My mother, Carol Church, is my first and best storyteller and lifelong inspiration. And all my love and thanks to the very best stories of all, my kids, Meg, Nathan, Bennett; and my husband, Ron, who have been with me every day, through every word.

I'm so very grateful to the editors of these journals for publishing the following stories: "An Uneven Recovery" in *Novella-T*; "The Lavinia Nude" in *the Cimarron Review*; "State of Motion" in *WomenArts Quarterly*; "Sole Suspect" in *Midwestern Gothic*; "The Warding Charm" in *Art Saves Lives International Magazine*. A monologue version of "Adult Crowding" was performed at the Mix Studio Theater in Ypsilanti, Michigan as part of *Suspicions: An Investigation of Monologues*. An excerpt of "Adult Crowding" appeared in *Synesthesia Literary Journal*.

An object at rest stays at rest and an object in motion stays in motion with the same speed and in the same direction unless acted upon by an unbalanced force.

Newton's First Law of Motion (Law of Inertia)

O powerful love! that, in some
    respects, makes a beast a man, in some other, a man
    a beast.

Shakespeare, *The Merry Wives of Windsor*

The Warding Charm

The day *he* came back, Emily was in the driveway, squatting in a gravel pen she'd built to capture ants. A black line streamed over her bare feet on its way to the nest in the corral's center. Sometimes she would squeeze a few in the calloused patches between her toes. Abundant ants, restless to reach home. Their single-mindedness made them easy to trap.

He saw her, of course. She was in plain sight and made no move to hide. Under his arm he carried a floppy-eared gray rabbit like a football. His special-for-her gaze rested on her as it always had, although they hadn't seen each other *since*. Emily was twelve, a late bloomer, her mother called her. Straight hips, hard shallow breast-buds. The training bra snagged her nipples. Her mother had scolded her to wear it that day, grow up, dress *appropriately*, but Emily refused. The chafing stung, and anyway what she wore couldn't ward off his evil doings.

He walked past her up the drive, strode up the cement steps to the concrete porch. What was he doing here? He'd promised not to come back if she didn't tell. Well, she hadn't, she'd kept her word. He scratched the rabbit between the eyes. She hated that he was still handsome. The pale skin like blank paper. The deep-black hair curled at his neck. The mustache trimmed in a neat patch over his red lip like an inkblot. Shouldn't he be ugly after the ugly thing he did? *They did.* Maybe that was why he still appeared to the world as handsome. Maybe it wasn't to be thought of as ugly if she was now a part of him.

A single knock summoned her mother to the door. She opened the screen and parted her lips as if tasting every word he spoke. She always breathed through her mouth. *Chronic sinusitis* was what Emily had been told was the matter with her mother. Gunk made her breath stinky. Impossible to kiss her, hard even to stand near her when she spoke, yet *he* stood fast at the threshold. To hide her red, swollen eyes she was wearing her thick shades, the reflective Jackie O disks Emily would one day realize were fashionable back then. She cried all that morning, seized by one of those sudden jags that made Emily talk long and frantic. Her mother had finally kicked her outside. Now *he* was staring into her pitch-black lenses at his own reflection, commanding her attention.

Emily couldn't hear them, but she was convinced he was telling her mother the whole story. Well good. She'd be released from her promise not to tell. Her parents would quit nagging her about her sulking. They'd quit squelching the talky bursts that followed her silence, those hour-long stories she'd weave, one thought rambling to another like mismatched beads Emily was determined to string into something pretty. If he always intended to tell, why hadn't she gone ahead and done it first? What was the secrecy for? Why attach rules that only she was expected to obey, as if he were nothing to her but just another parent?

The strong line of his shoulders shifted as if he might hug her mother, comfort her over the bad news about her daughter. Emily wanted to run to the porch then, touch some part of him. Some clean part. Like his arm, the one curled around the rabbit. She waited, hopeful and grieving, for her mother to fetch the gun and shoot him dead. Grandpa's Mauser rifle hung over their mantel, the one he'd taken from a German soldier's corpse on the field of battle. That's how her mother always described the trophy, *taken from a corpse on the field of battle*. Grandpa was a hero. He'd known how to fight a war and what to take from the battlefield after a triumph. Her mother was a hero's daughter. She would know these things, too.

The sun whitewashed the gravel, frosted the cement porch with a glaring light. Through the sharp gleam the rabbit changed hands. The soft gray ears grazed her mother's chapped knuckles, red rimmed knobs like her eyes under the shades, like her nose's rosy bulb.

Emily turned her attention to the ants. She chose a jagged-edged gravel fragment studded with mica. The chunk was big enough to cover the line of ants marching over her foot's flat table. Still, she was selective. She squished hard enough for the stone to cut her skin. Slow, thick blood trickled over the crushed ant. The line scattered, fell back into order, skirted the dead body like a stream's current around a boulder. She'd remember this moment in high school biology, and again as a postdoc researcher, as her first glimpse of instinct's unmerciful march.

The screen door clapped shut. Emily didn't understand why her mother would take the rabbit except maybe she didn't want to hurt it when she shot him dead. His shadow joined with hers. They were touching again down here at the gravel. Oil and sweat spoiled the clean air. Emily didn't look up. With the sun behind, his face would be black. Nothing to see.

Emily shifted her bare feet in a sprinter's starting crouch. When her mother fired the Mauser, she would have to scoot out of the way fast. Emily had to keep him in the driveway while her mother got the gun. She let the embroidered neckline of her peasant blouse fall open a bit. Bait for the catch, but she wished now she was wearing that bra.

His shoe knocked over one of her gravel walls, on accident or maybe on purpose. The ants scuttled to the break.

"Hello, sweetheart." His voice special, as if they'd parted just the day before, although *since* the winter had disintegrated into this warm sticky spring.

Did he want to hear her voice? His was the same. A dip in his tone like the even swoosh of a swing. She shrugged.

"How are you?" He sounded hurt at her silence.

It was good that she could hurt him. When would her mother get out here? She mumbled, *"Fine."* From the apple tree in the front yard a bird trilled two notes, hi-lo, probably a chickadee. She was memorizing bird calls that spring, something else to do when her mother sent her outside besides play with the ants. Were the blossoms out by then? Could she also hear bees buzzing at the pink-tipped blooms, their faint kazoos piped through the air like wax paper pressed to toothcombs? Beyond the apple tree and a row of lilac bushes the lawn sloped to the dirt road. His rusty old truck was parked on the shoulder's grass. He hadn't pulled into the drive, maybe afraid he'd hit her on accident even though she was right there in plain sight.

His shadow shifted. His arm melted into her head. "I brought you a bunny for a present. I remember you said your hamster died."

Oreo died a long time ago. She was too old now to miss him anymore, too old to want another small creature. Rodents were for kids who didn't know anything about what made a good pet. What Emily wanted now was a dog, the bigger the better. A cuddly gentle breed but with a huge barrel chest and fangs. Terrifying on the outside, loving on the inside.

Maybe he was remembering only that she'd told him about the hamster, and the telling made the death seem recent. He cleared his throat. "Bunnies are stronger. Not so susceptible to every little thing. They make good pets. I asked your mom if it was OK just now. Do you like bunnies?"

Emily hated bunnies. When she was a kid, *The Velveteen Rabbit* had scared her to death. Instead of comforting the sick boy, burning up with scarlet fever, the parents took away his favorite stuffed toy and banished him to the seaside. Any normal kid would die outright from such cruelty, but the boy had gotten better, so maybe it was all right. But why burn all of his toys while he was gone? Why not just spray them with bleach like her mother used to?

"I guess I like them," she said.

He approved of her reply. "Lots of girls do."

Their shadows drew apart. The ants abandoned the opening he'd kicked, streamed back to the nest.

She glanced up at the porch. The door was still closed. Maybe her mother was having trouble loading Grandpa's rifle. Keep him here, hold him fast. Still, her hand crept to her blouse and scrunched it closed. Willed the door to open, the same door she'd opened to *him* when she was home alone and wasn't supposed to let anyone in but he was there to fix the furnace, her dad had called him to come right away, *he said*, so Emily wouldn't freeze to death, and he had a toolbox and she'd flirted with him, she *had*. Plenty of times when he hung around drinking beer with her father, she'd wandered into the den or onto the deck, pulled her bare legs up to her chin for him to run his gaze over. Met his eyes boldly. She didn't even blush. Once they'd held hands when her father was in the kitchen fetching more beer. Wasn't she old enough to know exactly what she was doing? When she showed off her new bikini to her dad last summer, flashed a grin over her shoulder, her dad laughed and said, "My goodness but a girl is never too young to flirt." He meant to tease her. But Emily took him seriously, trusted his judgment of girls like her.

"Do you want to know what's special about this bunny? Other than it's for a special girl?" His voice dropped to the special tone he always used with her. The deep secret music used to thrill her.

She mumbled, "I guess."

He squatted down to her level. He wanted her to look at him. She searched instead for the ant stragglers. "It's not a tame one from the store. It's wild. I caught it."

How he'd managed *that* would be another string of terrifying imaginings she'd spend years trying to quash.

He touched her chin, tilted her gaze to his. Friendly eyes, black as sunglasses, why wasn't it hard to look at him? Maybe she was braver then she thought. "It's not easy to catch a bunny and not hurt it so it can't be a pet to anyone."

"OK."

"So you can feed it anything. Because it's used to eating what it can find. You don't need to go to a special store to get special food." His long nail nicked her chin when he let her go. He'd cut her in her other places maybe on accident, maybe on purpose. "It was hard to do. To catch her."

A repetition of a fact she was expected to remember. She was meant to be grateful. "Thank you." She tried to sound ungrateful.

"I'll come back sometime. Help you feed her."

He knew the family had a gun, he'd asked her dad to tell him the whole story once. Why wasn't he scared to show his face here? A bird's lithe shadow, maybe a chickadee, flitted over the gravel. Emily selected the ant milling over his toe. The shoe's leather crown wrinkled under his crouch like ripples of brown water. She rubbed the worn leather with the gravel as if she were polishing the shoe. When the ant was crushed, he wet a finger. Familiar, the sound his tongue made. He used his water to wash away the ant, then dabbed the blood on her foot.

"That's cruel, sweetheart," he said.

She dried her foot by wiping the gravel chunk along her cut. "I know."

"Like tearing the wings off flies. I knew a kid who did that. He was bad news."

Emily knew a kid who had pulled the wings off a monarch butterfly, and a girl, too, but she didn't tell him that.

"This is how you get rid of them." He stood up, nudged the nest's mound with his shoe. Fine grains cascaded into the hole like sand sliding through an hourglass's throat. "See? Easier that way. But it won't keep them away for long."

She looked up at the black hollow of him, his silhouette cut out from the sunshine like a paper doll. He might have blown her a kiss good-bye, she couldn't see. He walked down the drive, disappeared into the day's glare. The motor sounded as rusty as the truck.

Emily went after her mother to tell her she'd missed her chance to shoot him dead. The house was still, as it often was because of her mother's condition. The day's glassy brightness made the familiar rooms caverns, or maybe her eyes refused to adjust to the gloom. On the dining room table, the bunny was dumped in the old hamster cage. It filled the space like a fat aunt in a parlor. The water dispenser was empty. The shavings smelled of mold. Emily went to the den. Above the mantel, huddled in the flagstones, the Mauser lay on its pegs. The grainy blond wood stock and barrel gleamed as if her mother had chosen to polish the gun instead of use it. Her mother knew how to shoot this gun. Once she'd pointed it at Emily's dad during the loud fights they used to have before the sinusitis became *chronic*. The gun wasn't loaded, on accident or on purpose. The trigger's hollow click made her dad laugh, like her mother was playing a joke.

So by the looks of things her mother hadn't disappeared inside the house to prepare to defend her daughter. Doubly bad news, because this time he'd left with a rule change. He planned to come back.

He must mean for them to be lovers.

And since, after what he'd told her, her mother hadn't shot him dead, she must mean for this to happen.

Down the hallway a light burned. Her mother's bedroom door was closed. Emily rapped lightly. "*Mom.*" Cracked the door to see a mound of blankets burying her on that bright warm day. The sunglasses stood rickety on uneven earpieces as if she'd bent them on her way to her room. A bottle of pills to treat her sinuses lay empty on its side near the lamp. One of her *hard stuff* bottles stood next to the pillbox, the cap screwed on neatly. Beer was all her father ever drank. He left *the hard stuff* to *my lovely wife*, he always said. Emily could never tell whether he was joking or not. Her mother kept her bottles in her nightstand, some in her sewing cabinet, never in the kitchen. Emily wondered if her dad knew how often her mother replaced those bottles.

Her mother must have gone to sleep to escape the news of her daughter's *defilement*, a word Emily had read in a tale. A heaviness in the air, the sour scent of resting up before facing the truth, but whom would she confront upon awakening, *him* or her daughter?

Anyway her mother wasn't going to be a hero.

The first order of business was to fill the water dispenser and carry the rabbit to the garage. No animals in the house. After the hamster died that became the new rule. She slid the cage on a low shelf tucked in dust and gloom. When her father pulled into the garage, his fender would graze the bars, hide the animal from view.

Then back to the ants to await her mother's awakening.

●   ●●●●

Not only did her mother survive *his* visit that day, he never even confessed; but the blistering memory of her mother's deep sleep made hard and fast truth out of childish supposition. Such news would make any mother want to kill herself, Emily reasoned. Sometimes heroes did that, absolved the family dishonor by taking their own life. It was how Emily forgave her mother for not shooting him dead. The real truth was that her mother had already swallowed those pills when he came to the door. He'd interrupted her long slumber, not caused it.

For years, Emily thought her father's desperate attempts to awaken her mother when he found her that evening, his frantic call for an ambulance, her mother's confinement to her bed for weeks after she came home, *proved* he'd told. When her father yelled at her, *why didn't you call for help?* Emily thought immediately of how hard and sudden *he* had grabbed her in the furnace room. *I couldn't*, she tried to explain, which made her father furious. She understood his rage, shared it, even. Couldn't she have gotten away somehow before he knocked her to the concrete floor and it was too late? But her father was forgetting that no one had been home, so what difference would her struggle have made? At the time it didn't occur to her that her father meant, *help your mother.* Emily assumed that by then her mother had told her father about the defilement, that they were all dancing around the same unspeakable thing.

As the weeks dragged on and her parents never mentioned him, Emily never dreamed of bringing him up. It was about that time that she approached Officer Friendly in school when he was warning the class about drug danger. Officer Friendly called his talk D.A.R.E., which to Emily sounded more like an invitation than deterrence. She didn't make herself at all clear. She mixed up the telling of *him* with how he'd then tried to kill her mother. When the officer looked concerned, Emily's teacher stepped forward. *Suicide attempt.* Everyone in the class could hear her stage whisper. Officer Friendly patted Emily's shoulder kindly, embarrassed for her. Not that Officer Friendly's reaction mattered, not really. What worried her wasn't justice, just keeping *him* away.

One last faith, that if she fed the bunny exactly as he'd instructed, the rabbit's health would ward him off. During her mother's hospital stay, when Emily was left alone in the house for him to come for her any time he pleased, she loaded the cage with all of the vegetables she hated. Limp salads pickled in vinegar, mushy cooked carrots, slippery canned green beans. She fed it sweets, too, bits of fudge and cookies. The rabbit's belly bulged. It forged guarded, knowing black eyes and a sly way of moving as if anxious for the day it would outgrow the cage and return to the wild. Emily never knew if it was male or female. Did she know how to check at her age? Of course she knew. She must have refused to learn the sex, and she'd forgotten he had called it *her*.

Why didn't she release the monster in the yard before her father discovered it? When Emily came out to feed it one evening, her father had set the cage on the station wagon's hood. By then the enormous belly pressed through the bars. The rabbit's eyes were narrow and short-sighted from the chronic gloom. The orange light from the dusty garage window startled it. It shied from the sun, pressed its flab tight into the cage's corner. "Where did it come from, Emily?"

Emily told. Waited for his reaction at being reminded of all the trouble. Did Dad blame *him* or Emily for her mother's condition? Well, now the rabbit was the charm to find out.

"How thoughtful of him." Her dad smiled, the first pleasure she'd seen in weeks, months really. Not since her mother had pointed the Mauser at him and he'd laughed. "I didn't know he'd been by. Too bad we've been out of touch. A pet will be a nice plaything for you, won't it?"

She nodded. Except how was a rabbit supposed to play? But she didn't say this out loud.

Her father gave her the uneasy look he'd been casting at her lately, like he wished he didn't have to talk to her at all. "Your mother's illness is hard, isn't it, sweetheart." He said this like a fact, not a question she was expected to answer.

She did anyway. She allowed as how it wasn't all that hard because her mother slept so much.

Her father disapproved of her attitude. She could tell because he petted the bunny's floppy belly through the bars instead of petting her. She wanted to scream, *don't give me away*, because what else could his pleasure mean at *his* gift?

"I hope you said thank you."

She curled her fists at her hips. At least she didn't have to lie about that.

"I'll build your bunny a cage out back, honey. Animals need light, a roomy place to live. You shouldn't have put it in the garage. They're like us, Em, OK? Animals need what we need. The basics, anyway. Understand?"

She did understand.

Her father scratched the rabbit on the silken crown, rubbed a finger between its dim crafty eyes. "After your mother is all better we'll give a call, invite him over to dinner. Thank him properly for thinking of you."

That was how a timeline was established for his return.

The magical notion that keeping the bunny fat was her warding charm vanished with her father's pledge. Emily stopped feeding the rabbit. The animal's slimming took longer than she imagined. After a week it was still huge. It drank greedily when Emily filled the water dispenser. It butted its crown against her palm, licked at the sweat and dirt between her fingers. The longer the bunny kept its fat, the more affection Emily came to feel for it. Because it didn't change appearance, it couldn't be in pain, she reasoned. Its refusal to suffer was a show of loyalty.

Or a sign that her fear of *him* would never show.

• ••••

Her father's pledge to invite him back meant her parents had decided to restore her honor by giving her away, like a village girl to the bandit who'd defiled her. Would they braid her hair with flowers, dress her in white, parade her through town as if the arrangement were a wedding, not a sacrifice? Her mother's suicide attempt was a necessary response to *the field of battle*. No one would blame Emily directly for her mother's enduring despair. But giving her to *him* was an atonement that made sense.

That these assumptions were fantastical and irrational, that such cruelty contradicted her parents' competent, if sadly distant, treatment of her, never crossed Emily's mind. The imagination she possessed. The fear she carried. The tale she spun of the village girl and the bandit, handsome to all the world, his villainy shown only to her, was a way to cope with impulses she didn't understand. Crushing the ants. Starving the bunny. Her missing appetite for food, for friendships, for the normal passions other girls her age were pursuing with clumsy single-minded quests for affection. A hero was her last hope, but no way would he show up in time.

One sweltering day, it must have been late June, Emily climbed the attic stairs to rummage through some boxes. What had she been looking for? She couldn't recall anything being worth enough to her that summer to leak sweat, dizzy and disoriented, in the dismal heat. She must have gone after some long-forgotten obsession, a little-girl doll she suddenly wanted to play with again, a book she wanted to reread. She found instead a box marked *Eagle's Nest*. Inside was a photograph of her grandfather sipping wine on a marble terrace, a lead-gray sky blending with the mountains behind a caramel-brick chalet. Grandpa had bright-blue eyes, but the black-and-white photo erased their color, made everything in the photo look like stone. He was squinting at the camera the way he used to squint at Emily before he died. Angry and scared, warding her off as if *she'd* caused his stroke. Her mother explained Grandpa didn't mean to look that way, he didn't even recognize Emily anymore. The wine glass in the photo was still full. She flipped it over. *Damn fool Hitler's damn fool wine 1945* was scrawled on the back.

From a wad of yellowed tissue paper Emily pulled a red marble chunk, dull as old blood. Folded neatly underneath the marble were two satin dresses dimpled with stains. The hems rustled on the pine floor when Emily held them up to her shoulders. In the pale light of the bulb dangling from the ceiling, the crimson and lavender silk shone like wildflowers.

She set the dresses aside and pulled out a thick handkerchief. Wrapped inside she found five cigar-sized torpedoes capped with steel. Maybe they were toys, since real torpedoes were enormous. The close, dusty air was getting to her. Her sweat dripped onto the crimson dress draped over her bare toes. She wiped her neck with the bodice and took out another tissue-wrapped packet. More photos, but the paper was sturdier than photographic paper and the pictures on the cards were larger than Grandpa's snapshots. One showed Hitler with his head squished between a naked woman's fat, round breasts. In another, Hitler's stern salute collided with the mud-brown saucers ringing a woman's nipples. The women's arms were draped around Hitler's neck. Their wide-mouthed hungry grins leered down on his greasy, tousled hair. Why was Hitler dressed in uniform when the women were naked? But *he* hadn't undressed either, with Emily. He'd torn off her sweatpants and unders, scrunched her shirt around her neck to choke her. All he'd done to his own clothes was tear open his belt and unzip his jeans.

More cards, decorated with foreign words. One cartoon was split into two panels. In the left panel a tired soldier hunched behind barbed wire. The bodies of fallen soldiers hung limply from the tented wire fence. In the right panel a naked woman in a fancy room brandished a champagne glass and snuggled on a man's lap. Outside the window behind her nude shoulder, the Eiffel Tower's black skeleton shone starkly on the white paper. On the table next to the armchair was a photo of the tired soldier in ordinary clothes kissing the woman. The man she was snuggling with now wore ordinary clothes. He'd wedged his hand between the woman's spread legs. The woman's lips curved around the champagne glass as if she were enjoying her drink and that hand didn't hurt a bit, but Emily thought she saw pain in the woman's flat inked eyes.

Emily thumbed through the drawings. Soldiers with naked women flung over their shoulders like sacks. Soldiers bumping into naked women from behind, the women bent double to the ground. Black soldiers squeezing fat white breasts. Foreign words unfurled like triumphant banners over the scenes, showy script, fancy exclamation points. Warnings or celebrations? Impossible to tell.

The last card showed a pretty village girl framed by plump blond braids. She was lying on her belly, elbows propped under her chin, dainty slippers crossed at the ankles, a daisy stem tucked in her smiling lips. Behind her stretched a field thick with wildflowers and grass. Above her unfolded a clear, empty sky. The girl's expression was peaceful, happy in that daydreamy way, maybe because she was the only girl in the bunch with her clothes still on. But what was she dreaming about? The empty sky offered no clue. Emily rubbed at a smudge above the girl's head. Held the drawing up to the bare light bulb to inspect the dirt. Smack dab in the blank empty sky the ferocious snarl of a soldier grinding on top of the girl jumped out at Emily. His hairy, muscle-roped hands choked the girl's white neck. Her pretty dress was torn to shreds. The plump braids flopped into her gaping mouth. Her legs wrenched like broken toothpicks under the soldier's thrusting. The daisy she'd been chewing on lay crushed beneath her arm.

Emily cried out and dropped the card. The soldier and the suffering girl winked out of sight. The village girl was alone again with her happy dreams and the wide empty sky. Her defilement lurked above her, hiding in wait for the next ray of light.

Emily fought back tears. Why did Grandpa have these wicked, dirty cartoons? Had he fought the Germans to rescue these poor women?

She laid the cards next to the toy torpedoes. The steel tips gleamed in the dim light. The rafters creaked in the heat. A moldy smell like her mother's breath seeped from the satin dresses. *He'd* done some of these things to her, things she thought had never been done to any girl. But if what they'd done could be drawn, they must be common things, nothing special, like that village girl with the daisy.

She picked up a torpedo. Why would Grandpa have toys in this box, toys he'd never given to her?

She glanced back at the cards, picked out one with a grinning soldier ramming into a woman's behind. His gun was slung over his shoulder. It looked like Grandpa's Mauser.

She pressed the torpedo's sharp tip, studied the deep impression it dimpled in her finger. Too small to be real torpedoes, but were they just the right size to be bullets for a big gun?

The field of battle stretched before her as if a magic carpet had flown straight to her feet to take her there. If she dragged a chair to the mantel, she could easily reach the Mauser. Her sleeping mother wouldn't hear a thing. The fat muumuued neighbor lady wasn't out today on the back deck sipping Tab, settling her hawk's eye on Emily, poor thing, playing all by herself while that sicko mother neglected her. Their overgrown lawn bounded a stand of oak trees, and the trails through the woods led to abandoned cornfields. She could easily spirit the gun away.

She knew where *he* lived and could walk there.

Emily piled Grandpa's treasures back into *Eagle's Nest*. Except the dirty photos. Those she tucked in her sundress pocket.

Lugging the gun proved the real chore. Emily could barely lift it over the hooks. A peg caught the trigger guard, almost sent her tumbling to the carpet. She was awkward, bony-weak, as if hammered to life on a worn-out anvil. The gun was almost as long as she was. But Emily managed to get it out of the house and drag it across the yard to the protected path without being discovered. She didn't dare think about how she would heft the gun once she had him in her sights.

She was tromping through the cornfield, the Mauser bumping along at her heels, when she burst upon a girl smoking in a clearing. The new girl, Dinah, the one who'd pulled the wings off the monarch butterfly. Dinah's bare toes were buried in the furrows. The cigarette dangled from her hand, ashing on a mound of dried husks.

She shared none of the surprise Emily felt stumbling onto her. Her gaze rested on the barrel poking from Emily's fist. "That's not the way you carry it."

The same calm assurance she'd shown over the butterfly's torture. At her feet, a filament of smoke unwound from the husks.

"It's heavy." Emily drew the gun to her chest.

"Are you shooting with the boys?"

Dinah's hard curiosity raised a wrinkle of feeling Emily would come to realize was attraction. She thought Dinah had said *at the boys* until a shot rang out, followed by a metallic plinking on tin. Whoops drifted through the cornrow's slats. She shook her head.

"Can I watch you shoot?"

"There's nothing to watch."

Dinah appraised her skinny arms, her flat, plain body. Sizing up whether Emily was capable of doing anything interesting. She must have liked what she discovered. She pulled on the cigarette, held the cloud in her lungs, an abrasion Emily could almost feel. She dropped the butt, ground the husks with her bare heel. The smoke curl winked out. "No reason I can't tag along, then."

She might need help loading the gun, was Emily's thinking. She allowed Dinah to trail her, said nothing when Dinah lifted the Mauser's stock as if they were village girls hauling the water bucket home. When Emily wound her way toward the boys, toward the wrong way out, Dinah nudged her east, the rifle her rudder.

His house was isolated on the outskirts of town, a cobblestone plunked down in stark presuburban Southeast Michigan fields not yet thought of as real estate. The girls crossed a dirt road to wade through a grassy field scorched from the heat. A flatbed farm truck sped by. Gravelly dust skittered along the road in front of a white concrete apron. A short road divided the opposite field, ended for no good reason in the middle of the corn. She would learn later that the unfinished street was the beginning of a new subdivision, but on that day the nowhere road seemed like an abandoned mistake.

When the truck rattled past, Dinah lowered her end of the rifle to bury the weapon from sight, but out there, back then, no one would question the sight of a gun in a field filled with pheasant, not even if girls were carrying it. Their rustling traipse through the long grass should have raised a bird. By now a flash of green and gold, a glorious pinwheel against the broad white sky, should be casting a shadow on the girls. But the sky stretched empty and clean like a yawn's void. His house and a clump of oak trees behind, leafy branches woven like an emerald tapestry, were lonely bumps on the horizon.

He was unlikely to be home, Emily realized, too late. In her girlish view of summer's unmoored routines, she hadn't thought that he'd be at work. Like her father. She'd hauled the Mauser all this way for nothing. Sweat streaked her back and heels. Salt burned her eyes. She'd have to face Dinah now. Admit to poor planning and the narrow vision of the imagination where deeds are foolish descendants of impulse.

But then there he was, behind the cobblestone house, walking across his clipped grass into a wildflower carpet partly shaded by the oaks. Sunny buttercups, royal-purple dragon catchers, white aster parted under his boots. Daisies popped their golden eyes as he passed. Crimson clover tongues brushed his legs. He waded carelessly through the color as if sloshing upstream. He looked ridiculous, padded in a full bodysuit of whitewashed armor. With a helmet hat, black mesh lumped at his neck. Why was he so protected? Had he sensed she was coming for him like those crafty bandits in the tales?

Dinah touched her bare shoulder. "That him?"

Emily nodded. That Dinah would know *he* was the one Emily was after did not strike her as strange. Already she took for granted Dinah's divining her heart.

"Don't hurt the bees."

"What?" Emily brushed the sweat from her eyes. The sun glanced off the flowers' bright colors. Thick perfume rolled to her on the humid air.

Dinah pointed. A tall column of stacked boxes rested on pallets in the oak glade. That's why he was dressed the way he was, it was stupid of her not to realize. That he would be a keeper of bees jarred her, that he coaxed honey from them! He'd been as ruthless with the ants as she had. He'd filled their mound with a casual swipe of his shoe. He'd handled her with cold ferocity too, smothered her without snuffing her out for good. How could he tend bees?

When he reached these hives, would he withdraw a comb, drip the honey on his fingers, smear the sweet on his lips? Of the parts of him she'd known, his mouth had not been one.

"Do you know how to load this thing?" Dinah's voice floated to her from a distance.

Emily took the handkerchief from her pocket, unwrapped the bullets. The sharp torpedo-tips would rip through that suit; they'd rip through anything. She handed the rounds to Dinah.

Together they figured out how to work the bolt action by removing the pin. The rounds chambered perfectly. Five shots. But after the first he'd run away, or run toward her, snatch the weapon, turn it on her. She had one chance at the upper hand.

"You're too far away," Dinah warned.

Emily couldn't move closer to him. She couldn't move at all. She hefted the gun, settled the silver guard into her shoulder's bony cave. The stock lodged smoothly under her arm. Harder to lug the gun than to raise and aim. She felt light, steady. A cold band tightened around her belly like a strap of ice.

Dinah placed a hand on the barrel as he lifted the beehive's lid and pulled out a frame. "You won't hit anything from here anyway. Wait until he's away from the bees."

Emily pressed the trigger. Dinah's hand flew from the barrel. The kick knocked Emily backward into the grass. The gun landed above her head. The silence baffled her, as if the gun's report had sucked in all the air. Instead of *him* she faced the sky, fringed by grass, the sun a bright, shimmering bauble.

"Jesus." Dinah was pulling on her dress strap. "That was really *close*."

Emily rolled to a crouch, peeked over the grass. He was facing the field, rooted fast, the bees swarming like sunspots on his white suit and gloves. Emily scrambled for the gun as he turned to replace the frame, dusted, carefully, the bees from his suit as if picking at stray threads. Emily stood up. He started toward the girls. When he reached the wildflower patch, she raised the gun. But she hadn't chambered the next round. Perhaps he knew she wasn't ready to shoot because his stride was calm, measured.

Dinah tugged her. "Heaven's sake. Come *on*."

Then they were running through the field, the gun bumping behind, the grass slapping at their legs. They flew across the dirt road, hightailed it down the nowhere street, plunged into the tall cornstalks at the concrete's end. Emily didn't realize she was crying until Dinah stopped, grabbed her by the shoulders, and forced her head to her knees until she caught her breath. The dizziness cleared. The sudden brightness showed Emily she'd been running in darkness, on the verge of passing out.

She looked up. Dinah's dark damp hair was with sweat. She was grinning at how easy it was to get away with anything. "You OK?"

Emily nodded.

"What did he *do?*"

There might come a time, later, not to lie. "He stole something."

"You must really want it back." Dinah helped her straighten up. "Did you see how fast he ran? That stupid hat just *flew* off him."

Emily frowned. "He wasn't running away."

"He sure was. All the way to Detroit." Dinah picked up the Mauser's barrel. "Come on."

"But he was coming *after* us."

"Are you kidding? The only way he'll come around you again is to give your shit *back*. Let's go."

The trek through the cornstalks dimmed the white glare, brought the day back into focus. The dry crumpled stalks, Dinah's ivory skin against her dark tangled hair. The gunstock's smooth, soothing grain, the sharp bite of husks scraping her legs. She'd be cut up from this adventure like a regular girl playing an ordinary summer. She tugged on the gun to get Dinah's attention.

"Hey. What do you care about bees?"

"What's that mean?"

"How are bees different from butterflies?"

Dinah stopped, planted her feet in the dirt. "Did you bump your head or something?" She stared at Emily a moment and then grinned. "Oh. That. You too?"

"Me too what?"

"Fooled you, that's what." She turned on her heel. "That butterfly was already dead."

"Oh." A trick. No wonder she'd been so cool. Emily felt disappointment when she should have felt relief. "Why'd you do it, then?"

"Not the first time I've been the new girl. I know how not to get hassled. Let them think you'll do anything. But don't think I'd ever hurt even a butterfly." Dinah stopped at the edge of the field and grinned at Emily's expression. In the clearing beyond the stalks, the boys' whooping rose over a hollow tinny plink. "You're so *provincial*, Em. You've got guts, though, I'll say that for you." She stepped into the clearing.

Emily hung back. "I don't want to."

Dinah turned, stretched out her hand. "This is your alibi. Come *on*."

• ••••

Dinah pulled Emily out of the stalks. Under a maple tree on the far side of a grassy clearing, three boys stood in a loose circle around a skinny, wolfish shepherd dog. The dog's legs shook like wobbling stilts. Light-brown fur tufted the dog's bony ankles. A dented soup can glittered on the summer-singed grass near a rifle propped against the maple's trunk. The boys were high-school age, old enough to be plinking with .22 rifles, anyway. Emily didn't recognize any of them. She didn't think Dinah did either, which didn't stop her from dropping Emily's hand and walking right up to join their circle. Emily hung back at the cornfield's edge, clutching the Mauser's stock.

"Your dog looks sick. What's wrong with him?" The skinny dog snarled at Dinah. She reached out calmly and scratched behind his ears. Bits of fur rubbed away under her touch. The coarse hairs scattered on the thin breeze. The dog whined and snapped at Dinah's hand. She snatched her fingers away in time and stood fast, unafraid, or pretending to be.

The tallest boy, a blond with a kinked scowl and bright blue eyes, kicked the dog's ribs. The dog howled and shrank from Dinah as if she'd been the one to cuff him. "Nothing's wrong with that dog." He pushed past Dinah to gape at the Mauser. The other boys followed him. The one with wire-rimmed spectacles had a white capture-the-flag scrap of cloth stuck in his jeans pocket. The other was bulky in the chest and arms, farmer's muscle. A farmer's sun-soaked squint crinkled his eyes. He wore a flannel plaid work shirt. Sweat soaked his collar, except it wasn't so hot here in the clearing. The maple leaves shielded the sun, and the breeze held a shaving of coolness. Anyway, Emily felt the cold.

"That's a German rifle." The blond boy was standing right in front of Emily but didn't look at her. Her sundress had slipped low, was barely covering her chest. Dinah had broken the strap she'd tugged on to get Emily to run from *him*. Emily hadn't noticed her bared skin until the boy failed to.

"It's not real." Spectacles reached out to touch the stock. Emily stepped back.

"It's real, you dodo," the blond said.

The farmer said, "Bet it doesn't shoot."

Dinah stroked the dog's trembling back. It tolerated her touch, too afraid now, or tired, to snap at her. "I'll take that bet."

The boys all looked back at her as if seeing her for the first time. The blond looked twice. Ran his gaze down her dark, wind-tangled hair; tight black tank top; long, pale legs. Dinah tossed a careless sexy look back at him like a casual volley.

"If you're so eager to bet, you know it shoots." The blond turned back to Emily. Absorbed the gun with the same hunger he'd absorbed Dinah.

"Bet you my friend can blow away your crummy tin can with one shot."

Emily flushed, shook her head at Dinah. Dinah gave her the same look she'd lobbed at the blond. A natural flirt, but Dinah knew how to pick the right targets, not become the target.

"No way." The blond studied Emily, dismissed her pinched, plain face. Too timid to say a word to a pack of boys, let alone shoot a big gun. "She doesn't even know how to *hold* it."

"*She* knows exactly how to hold it. Wanna bet?"

"What do you wanna bet?"

The farmer noticed Emily's flush, her nervous, shifting feet. "Leave her alone, Rick."

"This old dog." Dinah's grin was sheer brightness, but Emily, watching her play with the dog's ears and thinking of the butterfly trick, saw the hard muscular curl along her clenched jaw.

Spectacles curled a fist around the white kerchief in his pocket. "That's a stupid bet."

"Whoever owns this dog is too stupid to take care of it right."

Rick walked over to Dinah, shadowed her with his chest. Dinah's glassy, teasing smile never wavered.

After a moment, he relaxed. "You got a dog of your own to bet?"

For a moment Emily expected Dinah to offer up the Mauser, but she must have sensed that her command over Emily's alibi did not include the gun. "I've got a pack of my stepdad's Hav-A-Tampa Jewels and some SweeTarts."

"I don't smoke and I'm pronated to cavities." Rick laid a hand on the dog's head. The shepherd's knees locked like tree knots. The farmer and Spectacles joined him to ring Dinah.

Being penned didn't seem to bother her in the least. "Prone."

"What?"

"*Prone* to cavities." Dinah slipped her hand into her short's pocket. Popped a SweetTart in her mouth and rolled it on her tongue. "Plenty left for you boys." Flecks of spittle gleamed on her lips.

Rick stretched a finger to her bare wrist and tickled his way up her arm. *Itsy bitsy spider*, Emily thought he whispered. She lodged two fingers in her mouth, whistled sharply. From an oak on the other edge of the clearing, a bird trilled back. A sparrow, probably.

Startled, the boys turned to Emily. Dinah and the dog didn't flinch.

Emily took the wicked, dirty cards from her sundress pocket and held the packet out.

Rick mumbled something, *"Fucking sped,"* and crossed the clearing to take the packet. The boys crowded around as Rick unwrapped the tissue and flipped through the cards. Emily expected them to laugh at Hitler squished between the naked woman's breasts, or grabbing the woman's tit on accident, but the boys didn't so much as crack a smile. Although he drank up the images greedily, a flush crept up Spectacle's neck. The farmer glanced at Emily uneasily. Rick looked back at Dinah, who teetered on tiptoe behind him to see what Emily had dragged out *now*. She answered his questioning look with an arched brow, *see what I mean about her?*

Behind glinting lenses, Spectacles took in Emily's flat chest, her broken dress strap. He was thinking she wasn't at all like any of the grown women being defiled in the pictures, but what would he say if he found out that she was exactly like them?

Rick wrapped up the cards and stuck them in his back pocket. "You're on," he said.

Emily stepped to the middle of the clearing.

Dinah swiped up the soup can from the grass, looked around for a stump or a rock to place it. "Where do you set this thing up?"

Rick grinned. "Right on this old dog's back."

The farmer crossed his arms. "Come on, Rick. Leave them *alone*."

Rick cuffed the dog and held out his hand. Dinah handed over the can without a word. A low whine rumbled from the dog's throat when the soup can touched its back. Bleak black eyes fastened on Dinah.

"No way did you shoot that can off this dog's back." Dinah glanced at Emily uneasily. So Dinah had nerves after all, she wasn't always the cool girl. Well good. Emily chambered the round calmly. The bullet's click rang out like she'd already plinked the tin.

"Guess you'll have to take my word for it," Rick said.

Emily knew by the dog's terrified lockjaw that the boys had shot at it, all right. Controlling that much fear took training. "Take it off," she said. Too loudly. Her voice echoed off the trees.

Rick grinned. "The mute speaks. Bet's off, then."

"I'd watch that mouth, sport." Dinah stepped away from the dog, her bright eyes on Emily.

Emily hefted the Mauser. Still a struggle, but it pillowed in her shoulder's hollow naturally. "Take it the fuck off or I'll shoot *you*."

The farmer made for the oak tree. Spectacles laughed at him. "What the fuck, man. She can't even hold it up all the way."

Emily aimed at the empty space beyond Rick's elbow. The recoil knocked her flat again. This time the rifle's boom filled her ears. How had silence swallowed this roar when she'd shot at *him*? The boys yelped and scattered. *Shit.* If her father was home by now, the noise would bring him on the run. Not for a moment did she think that she'd actually hit anything. In her fantastical view of guns, a wild aim was destined to miss.

Dinah's loose, tangled hair blotted out the sun. She was grinning. Even with the sun behind her, Emily could see every detail of her wide smile and shining eyes. Dinah admiring, the one joy of that summer. But her hands were shaking as she grabbed the gun and helped Emily to her feet.

The dog was still frozen in place. The light brown rings around its ankles quivered. The can was nowhere in sight, and the boys had fled to the clearing's edge. Spectacles looked ready to dive head first into the withered cornstalks.

"Jesus Christ." Rick's voice cracked.

"You're an asshole," the farmer said. He was staring at the poor shivering dog, so Emily couldn't tell if he meant Rick or her. She deserved it. Her own knees were shaking as badly as the dog's. What if she had hit this dog, or Rick? Or Dinah? What was wrong with her that her impulse to shoot had obliterated any thought of harm?

Dinah turned to Rick. "Pay up, twinkle toes."

"Shit." Rick left the oak tree's cover, came out into the clearing. "My dad's gonna go ballistic."

"What does your dad care?" The farmer's watchful, wondering gaze never left Emily.

"Socks is his fucking dog."

"Socks is a fucking cat's name, man."

"Fuck you. I didn't name it." Rick snapped his fingers. The dog limped over to him. "At least it's got a name. Fucking farmers never even name their shit." Rick pinched the scruff and hauled Socks over to Dinah. "All yours, beautiful, but don't your crazy-ass friend here deserve the prize?"

Dinah clapped the Mauser barrel back and forth between her hands. The dog leaned into her leg. "Seeing you shit-scared was her prize, sport."

Rick shook his head. He mumbled, "*Sped,*" and dug out the wicked, dirty postcards to give back to Emily.

"Keep them," she said and turned on her heel.

"That's one sick girl." As Emily slipped into the cornfield, one of them, probably Spectacles, spoke just loudly enough for her to hear. Maybe on accident, maybe on purpose.

Dinah caught up with her a few rows from where Emily would take the path through the trees back home. Emily heard the Mauser bumping along before she saw Dinah burst through the stalks. Socks trotted at her bare feet.

"Well, Em, there's more to you than meets the eye." Dinah gave her back the gun. "Guess you have your alibi. They'll never forget that as long as they live. Where'd you get those crazy pictures, anyway?"

Now that she had the Mauser back, Emily's one thought was to get it up on the pegs before her father came home. The stalks' shadows splashed the dirt furrows in front of her, the air was dense with pent-up heat, but it could be any time of day. Emily had no sense at all of how long it had been since she stumbled upon Dinah on her way to *him*.

Socks came up to her and sniffed her hand. Emily touched his bony head. Tears rose to her eyes, the sting so unfamiliar she couldn't for a moment understand why the dog's ruff was blurry. Nothing had made her cry since before *him*. "You shouldn't have made me do that."

Dinah grinned. "Now that's an interesting perspective on the day's events."

But you did, she wanted to say. Emily was nothing but a joke to those boys, right up until the moment she fired. They didn't believe the old war gun would actually fire, or that a girl like Emily could shoot it. But Dinah had known and let her go through with it. She'd even risked her own hide. Emily might have just as easily shot her on accident as Rick or that poor dog.

Dinah was studying Emily with her already familiar appraisal, half-teasing, half sizing up, *you're so provincial, Em.* "That asshole's right. You won this dog fair and square. But you don't look like you have it in you to take care of him." Her voice dropped, softened. "Do you, Em? Maybe you need to be taken care of, too."

Socks shook his head and loped back to Dinah. Emily wiped her eyes. Suddenly she wanted to be rid of this girl. She wished she'd told her to fuck off in the first place. Sharing *him* with Dinah was dangerous. So was Dinah's bullshit sympathy, stupid and mean after egging her on to shoot. "I don't want that scrawny old dog," she said coldly. "I already have a pet."

Dinah shrugged. "Good thing I want him, then. See you around, Em. Be careful."

Dinah slipped through the stalks, Socks at her heel, feathery tail swaying in an almost-wag. She was heading east, back toward *him*. For the first time, Emily wondered where Dinah lived. Perhaps he was her neighbor and Dinah hadn't said a word about it, which would be her typical sleight of hand, wouldn't it?

After she'd hefted the Mauser back on the pegs and returned the chair to the dining set, Emily grabbed a fistful of the rabbit food her father had bought. She ran to the pen behind the garage. The bunny was lying on its side. A slow shudder rippled through its slack belly as if it had been popped. Emily had mistaken for fat these empty rolls of fur. How could she have missed this wasting, the dull varnish on the eyes? She bit off a piece from a pellet, held the chip close to the mouth. The rabbit nudged her hand gratefully before nibbling the food.

Had the warding charm turned out to be her superstition about the rabbit's health or her damn fool's stunt with the Mauser? Maybe it was fattening that bunny right back up or maybe it was her clumsy potshots after all, but when her father called later that summer as promised, *he* refused to come to dinner.

The way Dinah stuck to her from that summer on, admiring her and teasing her and forever pulling her into clearings made her believe that Dinah could tell her what the charm was, if only Emily would ask.

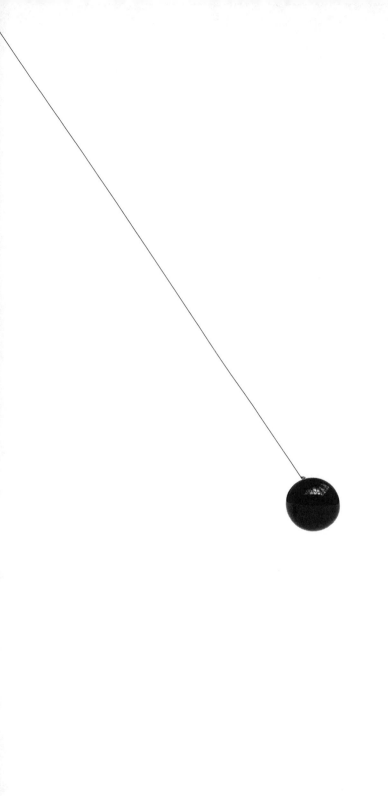

Reasonable Fear

Maybe for other couples there was something to the idea that confession made a marriage stronger. But it wasn't working out that way for Dan Rilke and his wife.

To start with, she accused *him* of inflicting the bite.

When Julia hollered from the bathroom, Rilke was just settling down to sleep for the day. He'd come off a grueling shift, and exhaustion was messing with him. A tussle with a wife-beating thug kicked off the long night. The man had a history of run-ins with the county sheriff's office, should have been put away a long time ago and save everyone a lot of hassle, the poor wife most of all. The woman involved was tough and true, which Rilke admired. Typical township type; someone he remembered vaguely from high school as one of the fringe gals who hung out in the shop wing with the automotive tech guys. She was giving it back so good that when Rilke first arrived on the scene he was confused as to who was beating on whom until he saw the kink in her nose and a bloody smear above her lip. Even so, Rilke had to threaten to cuff her to the oven range to make the arrest on her husband.

Just after Rilke processed that individual, he was called to a gruesome pileup on I-94. Wrapped in a thick veil of fog, the bodies of a young woman and her two little kids clung together in a minivan's mangled remains as if the mother had managed to hold her daughters close in their last moments. The semitruck driver walked away unhurt. Rilke spent the rest of his shift cleaning up this horrifying proof of fate's lopsided rules. Hours later, the bodies still haunted him, and the cut on his arm, courtesy of some whacked-out kid he'd arrested a couple of weeks back, was oozing again. So maybe he wasn't as prepared to be patient with Julia as he might be if he had been scheduled for a night off.

He grabbed the badminton racket he kept handy to deal with the bats and hustled to her. Julia, hair streaming, nude skin soft and puckered like loose silk, was peering at her mouth in the fogged mirror. Steam swirled thick and foamy around her lovely body. She never used the fan when she showered, which was why the ceiling above the shower head was dimpled with mold. Rilke threw the switch, startled her with the motor's sudden static. Her lip was swelling fast. The stark bathroom light paled her, or else fear had drained her color.

"Look," she demanded. This while covering her mouth with her hand so he couldn't see any damn thing.

He tried to grab her hand away to inspect, but she shook him off angrily. "Well, let me see it, then." He should have minded his tone, but he was pissed that she was mad. They'd been married long enough that Julia acted like every little setback was his fault somehow, even the things that happened when he was nowhere near the problem.

Julia eyed the racket and punched his arm near the cut. Not lightly, either. "There's no bat in here. Did you do this to me?"

Rilke almost laughed, but in fact they'd made love before he left for his shift and he'd been passionate. It had been months since she'd made overtures. Last night when she'd downed a beer and joked with him a bit, he'd been attentive to possibilities. Until the bat problem, their physical connection had always been sustained and intense, her body the reliable wonder of his life. But when Rilke adopted an arm's length response to the bat situation, the lovemaking stopped.

Julia was waiting for his reply as if the question were a serious inquiry regarding harm he might actually inflict. He choked back the laugh impulse to consider carefully whether he'd kissed her too hard last night and accidentally clamped down on her lip. From the bedroom, the fan he used to drown out wakeful daytime noises hummed steadily under the bathroom vent's static. He was still holding the racket. If she believed he'd hurt her, she should be screaming at him, *fuck you Dan*. Instead she surveyed his clumsy, confused stance blankly. Her arms lay slack at her hips. Her lips were parted, coddling their tenderness. Her breasts swayed, the dark nipples hard in the stir of cooling air. He propped the racket behind the bathroom door, crafted deliberate movements, kept the timing slow.

She took his silent maneuvering as assent. "You did do this. You *bit* me, Dan." She moved on him then. Got in his face, her breath bitter with sleep and coffee. Another of her habits. She brushed her teeth after she showered. Complained that toothpaste soured the day's first coffee.

He couldn't have done it, he decided. He'd barely touched her mouth. "Let me *see*."

"See?" She thrust her mouth at his. Her teeth snagged his lower lip as she gave him a hard shove.

He staggered back. "Jesus, Jules."

"Like it?"

He swiped at the pinprick of pain, surged hot at the dot of blood on his thumb. "You want me to like it?" He struggled to keep the volume down.

"Sure, Dan. Sure I do."

"Come on, Jules."

"Because I love it so fucking much. Especially the part where I go to work looking like this."

"Don't you think if I had done it you'd have felt me?" he asked mildly. Her color was back. The flush in her cheeks splashed down her neck. Her breasts brushed his T-shirt, her hip grazed his bare leg. It hadn't been so long ago that he would have felt moved, *entitled* by her anger to pull her into him, make love on the tile. Their dustup would be a coda to the previous night's passions. Maybe other couples possessed a more equitable rhythm to their marriage, but they'd always played lopsided. This inequity was what Rilke loved most. Julia's *fuck you Dan* blazed the same joy as her body opening to him. But touching her now felt like a violation, and then there was the sudden confounding problem of his desire leeching from him the closer she drew.

She reached behind him. Switched off the bathroom fan. "Don't you think if you hadn't you would say so?"

Which unnerved him a bit. Did he want her to think he'd hurt her? "Will you let me *see*?"

He pulled her to the vanity light, a bit too rough. She didn't protest the manhandling like she should. He tilted her mouth, spotted an inky red streak leeching from two tiny puncture holes. Knowing how she'd react he didn't want to tell her. But she'd need the shots and antivenom, too, and soon with those streaks, so it wasn't a fact he could conceal.

"A bat bit you."

Her eyes widened. Wonder on the first wave, not dismay. "But how could it? I never saw it happen."

"I don't know, Jules. Maybe the one we chased out yesterday got you and we're just now seeing it."

She made a low, harsh sound and drew away from him. He fetched clothes for both of them, and her coat. Bundled her up although the autumn air was not yet very cold. She let him maneuver her arms into her coat sleeves like a little girl. Her unsettling wariness kept her manageable.

They were almost to the car when she stopped in the middle of the drive and clamped a hand on his arm. "It must have bit me in my sleep."

The yawning horror in her eyes was so steeped in repulsion that for a moment he thought she'd finally guessed his dreams, *seen* what he was doing to her in his unspoken heart. The fear that seized him bubbled a laugh, which at first he could have passed off as a hiccup. But then the fit had him. Once it started, he knew he'd never get it under control. She stood there exasperated, frightened, *poisoned* for Chrissakes, while Rilke laughed it out in hoarse, honking gulps. The noise drew that loony drunk Gary Handelman from next door onto his front porch to stare at the couple with his usual greedy nosiness.

After Rilke was released and had wiped away the tears, Handelman offered a three-fingered wave. To this day Julia's sympathy for that busybody's wounded hand irritated Rilke. She smiled gratefully, waved back as the old man shuffled inside his house to mind his own business. Julia settled a bleak gaze on Rilke which suggested an outlook that *from now on* anything he did was bound to be unacceptable, unforgiven.

● ●●●●

Julia'd been on Rilke for months to deal with the bat infestation. She even blamed his work on the siding as the instigation of the problem. Rilke had assured her many times during many arguments that the bats must have nested in the attic for years, well, months anyway, before he'd ripped off the rotted board and batten and installed the HardiePlank this past summer. It was true he'd rushed the job. Rilke had chosen the last week of August to tackle the project and couldn't hold the heavy boards in the blazing heat. So after his shift he nailed like crazy all morning to beat the sun's arc past the maple canopy that sheltered Rilke until just about noon. The work cut into his sleep, made him cranky and uptight. Late in the week, Julia served him sandwiches and silent resentful looks and not much else. But he'd finished quick, done a decent job. Painted in record time, too, the jay blue that made the house pop out from all the others on their street.

Julia had admired his work for all of two days, until the first bat wheeled out of the bedroom closet straight to her golden hair, dug its hairpin talons into her scalp, beat at her with leathery wings. Rilke had walked in on her running in tight circles between the bed and the dresser, cuffing the bat. The wings' dry swish flapped in time with the click of Rilke's old flip alarm clock. The bat's weak squeak and the watery slap of Julia's sweaty hands had raised Rilke's hackles. He'd grabbed her arm, a bit too rough because she was a bit crazy and wouldn't stop running around the damn room. Working the bat's fisted claws out of her hair was like coaxing tangled thread from a needle. He trapped the creature with the badminton racket and let it loose outside.

The very next day, another bat wheeled to her golden head, guided by the sonar of her lovely scent. More bats followed, and more trouble for the marriage. Each encounter left her drained and fearful and ready to heap the blame on him. Julia remained convinced his disturbance of the siding had summoned the bats. She came to view the siding job as some plot of *stiflement* on his part. That's what she'd called it, *stiflement*, as if replacing worn siding that had been low quality in the first place with something durable and fireproof wasn't basic responsible maintenance on a house. Anyway, *stiflement* wasn't even a word. He'd pissed her off when he pointed that out. *You're dodging the issue with semantics*, she complained. If she could get a word like *semantics* right, why couldn't she get *stifle* right, was his response.

A response he would change now if he could.

Instead of cracking wise he should have hugged her and stroked her and soothed the trouble away like he'd always done. Instead, her fear made him want to fuck her. Which he would never do in real life, take advantage of her weakest moments, so as retribution for his terrible desires Rilke endured disturbing half-formed dreams where he forced himself on her. He would watch with clinical detachment her mouth gape open, stuffed with soundless cries, silver beaded tears sliding down her flushed lovely cheeks. He would bury his hands in her golden hair, seize a flapping bat, choke the life from the creature as he came. In some dreams he withdrew and came on parts of her body he would never violate that way, not ever, during their waking love.

It never occurred to him to wonder why, in their years together, he hadn't *known* she was so afraid of bats. In a loving marriage such as theirs, such an ordinary fear should never have been a secret.

• ••••

The bite brought on a fever, three days of chills and hallucinations that changed some assumption between them that the bat problem was a temporary irritant, one of many a happy marriage would endure. After the fever abated, Julia made it clear she would no longer suffer Rilke's soft stance on the infestation.

"If you won't kill them, I can't go on living in this house. With you. Do you understand me, Dan?"

They were standing in the hallway below the attic access as if she expected him to climb up right then, just off a shift. Had she been up all night waiting to confront him? He understood her, he said, and proceeded to tell her some of the truth, that there was no way to eradicate the bats for good.

"Fuck you, Dan. You never even try. Set traps. Poison them. You don't do fucking *anything*. Why are you ignoring this?"

"I'm not ignoring this, Jules." He didn't point out that any and all options for temporary shelter—like his mother's farmhouse on Scipio Township's outskirts—also had bats. Like every other southeast Michigan house, because weren't bats as routine a pest as rats and roaches?

"You've shot two people as part of your fucking *job*, and you can't deal with some bats?"

Those shootings were in the line of duty, he pointed out. Plus, he hadn't *killed* anyone. What Julia didn't know was that the second incident had pulled Rilke probation. Two weeks ago, some punk farm kid had tried to set a light pole in the Costco lot on fire. Never mind that the metal pole was noncombustible and the kid was using a butane lighter. Rilke spied him crouched at the lamp's base flicking his Bic intently like he'd just discovered fire, not tried to start one. A simple warning situation, but when Rilke approached, the kid freaked out, pulled a knife, sliced Rilke's arm. Lunged again after Rilke sidestepped, so he'd had no choice but to disable him. The boy was out of his mind by the time the ambulance arrived, writhing and hollering despite Rilke's efforts to calm him down, kicking around ineffectual and outdated insults like *pig* and *fuzz*. The EMT had to strap him to the stretcher while the kid thrashed and cursed like Rilke was his whole problem. Obviously high on some stupidity-enhancing substance. The bullet only grazed the kid's knee; Rilke never fired unless he was certain of his aim.

Later the physical evidence, not to mention the EMT's statement on the boy's condition at the scene, supported Rilke's response as reasonable and necessary. Plus, he'd needed stitches on the arm wound, which turned out to be deeper than it looked and still wasn't healing up right. But the kid was only fourteen, and an Adler, one of the township's old farm families. Some grumbling ensued. Some complaints were lodged about the use of *excessive force* against a *harmless prank* and a *mere boy*. If anything was excessive, it was these baseless accusations, offered up like they were damn evidence by folks who weren't even there. But to be on the safe side of community sensitivity, Rilke spent a couple of nights on desk until the inquiry ruled him justified. The national mood toward cops these days made such caution necessary, he had to admit. Recent unhelpful and chaotic protests in Chicago over routine policing errors, committed by overextended cops doing their best despite deep cuts in resources and personnel, were igniting distrust between the law and the public. No use crying over the deal. Managing, hell, *protecting* the world as is, not as one wished it could be, was the greater part of effective policing. He was just glad the Adler kid was well-known as a dismal punk. Since the incident occurred in the middle of his night shift, not one member of the whining public saw Rilke ignore the damn blood pouring down his own arm while staunching the undeserving kid's bleeding leg.

Seeing as the marriage had passed the point of routine loving sympathy, Julia hadn't shown much concern over the arm either, so he'd left out much of the incident's detail.

"I'm not asking you to *kill anyone*. I'm asking you to exterminate vermin. And speaking of line of duty." Julia was shouting now, more like her old self. Drawing too close, tapping his chest, the hot curdled breath steaming him up. He waited to feel the old normal hunger for her anger, or perhaps it was normalcy he craved. "Here's the line I'm drawing over being bitten in my fucking sleep, when I don't even know it. OK?"

He gave her a push with his shoulder, just enough to get her to back off. "Why don't you take care of it, then?" Really an unfair attitude on his part. The deal between them had always been that Rilke took care of her in the million ways men took care of women like Julia.

Seeing as Rilke had never once suggested she take care of anything except him, Julia hesitated. She pressed her back to the wall opposite, the rosebuds on her loose blouse blending with the girlish floral wallpaper she'd chosen for the hallway. Her wariness sparked. Maybe she'd suddenly become aware that he was still in uniform, still wearing his gun. Her angry summons to the hall the moment he opened the door had disrupted his after-work routine of shedding his gear before seeing her. Weapons didn't usually bother Julia one bit, so her attitude confused him. Maybe his hand had dropped to his hip when she began shouting at him, some stupid cop instinct in response to amped-up drama.

She rocked on the balls of her bare feet. Surveyed him as if he were a distant occurrence she couldn't quite make out. Her voice softened. Her lovely certainty dissolved. "You *know* I'm really phobic of bats. You *know* we had them growing up, and they scared the shit out of me, and my dad was too much of a drunk fuck to get rid of them. He used to laugh at me, Dan. Don't you remember?"

Rilke didn't remember her house having bats, a memory lapse he chose not to share with her at that particular moment. What he recollected about their teenage years was thrashing it out in her cramped kitchen with her bastard-of-a-father while Julia and her mother hollered at his back and her tiny towheaded brother Steven stood with his thumb rammed in his mouth. Before long Rilke found himself craving these scenarios, the thrill of fear and helpless anger put into motion, a feeling he'd later experience as the joyous backswing of a strenuous arrest or a victim's gratitude. "I *do* remember, Julia," he responded promptly. "I'll see what I can do."

Right then, he scouted the attic for the nest. He checked the rafters for cracks, inspected the roofing seal. Like a damn scaredy-cat he pulled his gun on a quivering shadow that might be a bat clinging to a moldy mattress but turned out to be a trick of a flickering bulb's uneven light. Later he called Critter Control for an outrageously high quote. For a few days more, he made a show of attentiveness to the problem, which Julia guessed to be all and only show.

She must have complained about the problem to Handelman, because before Rilke knew it the old man showed up to huddle on the porch with her. Handelman suggested a one-way door, which he offered to install gratis. Julia promptly informed Rilke she'd gone right out and taken care of the problem just like he'd suggested.

Typical of Handelman's busy-body outlook on their marriage to jump at the chance to interfere. Last spring Rilke had caught the old man peering into their bedroom from his bathroom window. To keep the peeping-tom shit to a minimum, Rilke installed blackout blinds. He'd told Julia the blinds were to help his daytime sleep. Julia loved the man, so it reflected well on Rilke to keep Handelman's behavior a secret. Back when they'd first moved into the house on Peachtree Court, Handelman was the damn one-man Welcome Wagon committee, carting over a six-pack and a bag of peaches. By the wounds on his right hand, Julia recognized him as her first real-life hero. The right thumb and index finger ended in stumps at the knuckles. Soft pink scars ran the length of his palm and up his arm like lacy cobwebs. Injuries from an electrical accident at one of his rental properties some years back. The details were the one aspect of the man's life he didn't go on about to anyone in earshot, but Julia remembered the incident. Although her bastard-of-a-father owned his crummy house, they lived down the street from a slumlord cluster of sketchy homes. The electrical accident killed a little girl living in one of those rentals. Handelman lost those fingers trying to save the little girl's life.

Seeing as Julia's regard was the one luxury he hadn't yet pissed away on drink, Handelman offered to install the one-way door at Julia's earliest convenience. Which turned out to be the very next day. On a late October afternoon, Handelman set to work with the single-minded purpose Rilke knew Julia would admire. Her happiness at the activity, far and away more enthusiastic than what she'd expressed over Rilke's grueling labor on the siding, made it impossible for Rilke to object to the old man's infiltration.

After two days of diligent sawing and hammering that completely disrupted Rilke's sleep, Handelman announced the bat door was ready. On Rilke's night off, a full hunter's moon on the rise, Handelman set up the folding chairs, Julia set out the beer, and they both set to watching the exodus. From the back porch, Rilke watched Julia and the old man stretch out their legs on the backyard grass, looking like kids sprawled in the short beach chairs. The moon's first crimson light lit the gentle valley of Julia's lap. They pulled on their beers and chatted away like old and best pals. Rilke surveyed the gable near the chimney where the door, neatly trimmed, swayed in the light breeze. Cutting a hole in the HardiePlank must have cost Handelman some effort, but the wretched old man had done a neat job of it, Rilke noted with, he had to admit, unreasonable consternation.

Well, he shouldn't be so hard on the man, even if he was a pain in the ass. In his own way, Rilke owed his happiness to Handelman. At the time of the accident that had killed the little girl, Rilke and Julia, in their junior year at Lorch High, weren't yet dating but Rilke was in love with her, all right. He was adrift in that lonely, anxious limbo of being so deeply in love he knew he'd have to endure her certain rejection because he couldn't keep silent any longer, he couldn't. Julia was beautiful and popular. Rilke was just a fat kid in field hand's plaid. He lurked in the back of every class, tongue-tied with classmates who ridiculed him as a farm kid. Her rejection was a sure bet. Still, it couldn't be helped. Even hearing *no* meant possessing a fleeting part of her, at least. He spent agonizing weeks building the nerve to approach her. He analyzed every moment he saw her alone for declarative potential, not that she was alone very often. Girls like Julia were always fucking *populated*.

Then, on a cold winter's afternoon when he was cutting behind the school to the parking lot, he stumbled upon her huddled in the shop wing's courtyard. No coat, the lack of protective foresight he'd come to recognize as a typical consequence of her emotional impulses. Chewing gum ferociously, teeth snapping like a farm jack's clicking. Crying soundlessly behind her pale hand, hiding tears no one was around to see. *Jesus Christ.* Those tears, terrifying and lovely, had stopped him in his tracks. How had clumsy, brooding Dan Rilke then summoned the presence of mind to bundle her in his Carhartt jacket, stroke her golden hair, rope his arms around her as naturally as if they were already lovers? Her fragile, willowy limbs molded to him. Holding her should have felt like ferrying one of his mother's precious china cups to the dining table. *Don't you dare drop it, Dan.* But her cuddle was determined, instinctual, her body a perfect fit to his. *All right.* He felt her strength when she clutched his waist, the ripple of muscle her weeping raised along her back.

She'd stammered out how the little girl she babysat was electrocuted the night before. Storm winds had ripped live wires from the girl's home right in her path as she was running indoors to take cover. She described how the landlord had lost part of his hand, almost his *whole arm,* trying to save the girl by pushing the wires away with a tree branch. Which promptly conducted the current that injured him. Which outcome the landlord should have *known,* Rilke almost pointed out. Julia was as choked up about the man's heroism as she was about the little girl's death. *He risked his life to try to save her,* she repeated. Not exactly true, in Rilke's view. The tree branch was a half-assed panic move, bound to end badly. But he held his tongue, held her tight, gave himself over to the thrill of her body tucked so perfectly into his. He said all the right things, soothing words he conjured out of some untapped reservoir of nurture. She dried her tears and wiped her nose on his farmer's plaid. She asked if he would drive her home. As they walked to his pickup, the biting wind froze the shirt's tearstain. Her ice clung to his bare chest. Helping her out of the truck, walking her to her crumbling stoop, accepting back his jacket now unbearably laced with her mint gum and grief, were the most difficult acts of his life.

The hope of men Handelman's heroism had illuminated for Julia had bathed Rilke in the same glow. From that very moment, she attached her hope to him. They were married straight out of high school.

No matter the straits the bats had landed the marriage in now, the decrepit old man was in no way a rival. Rilke's tick of jealousy was some other emotion entirely he didn't care to investigate at that moment, brooding on the porch, staring at the curve of Julia's lips ringing the bottle's mouth. So he strolled out to join them. Opened a nonalcoholic beer to be sociable. "Any action out here yet?"

Handelman caught Rilke's glance at Julia's leg relaxed against his knee. The old man knew exactly what Rilke was getting at, but Julia maintained her usual cluelessness, or maybe she was playing dumb on purpose to rile him up.

"Is it time?" Her lovely voice was hushed. Rilke's jealousy at her awe almost drove him to grab a real beer from the cooler. Maybe he should get good and drunk for once during the bat show, if the fucking door even worked.

"Wait a bit." Handelman drained his beer. "The dark will bring them out."

The dusk gradually dropped its gloomy mesh. Julia's silent anticipation was a continuation of the night's descent. Handelman respected her by keeping quiet for once. Her leg cuddled Handelman's knee. Neither acknowledged their unconscious cradling, although Rilke felt their contact crawl along his skin like the air's fast cooling. Back when Handelman's peeping had riled Rilke up, he'd looked up the old incident report from that electrical accident. He discovered multiple complaints from the tenants about the electrical service. Seen in *that* light, Handelman's delay in fixing the problem had resulted in the little girl's death. The report didn't substantiate criminal negligence, and the tenants would have been too poor to sue. The injury to his hand was really a testament to how easily he'd gotten off.

Handelman broke the silence. "Almost there." Although it was too dark to see it clearly in the eave's shadow, Julia watched the one-way door, lips slack, eyes held wide.

Jesus Christ. The drama in the man's tone. Rilke should take him down a peg right now, tell Julia all about the peeping and a few other things about her hero Handelman, wipe that happy look off her face once and for all.

A rustling seeped through the door like faraway voices. The first bat emerged, wheeled up and away. The air rang with slapping wings. The door swept open, swung shut, the steady rhythm of an orderly escape. Once freed, the bats glided up to the moon as if Rilke's attic had all along been a holding room for the night sky.

Julia laughed. Looked at Handelman with the gratitude she used to bestow upon Rilke after he'd stood up to her father or saved the cost of a plumber with an effective repair or any of the million ways, lifesaving or petty, he'd taken care of her over the years. She slipped her hand into the palm of Handelman's bad one.

"Thank you." Rare vocabulary for her. Handelman heaved himself from the minichair awkwardly to fetch more beer. The man was blushing, for Chrissakes.

When the door was still for the duration of another beer's consumption, Julia told Handelman she had something for him and hiked to the house. Handelman diligently avoided Rilke's glare as if evasion were a sworn duty.

"Worked like a charm there, right, Gary?" Rilke moved to the beer cooler, stood a bit too close to the man, the tactic to put a troublemaker on the defensive while sniffing out cause.

"I find it usually does the trick, Dan." Handelman fixed his bleary gaze just past Rilke's shoulder. "Tried to make the door blend in with your siding."

"Real nice job you did."

"Give it a couple of days to let out the stragglers and I'll seal that right up for the lady." Handelman popped open another beer. The suds bubbled up the bottle's neck. The old man licked the head before it streamed down over his hand. "Unless you'd rather do the job your own self."

The man's drunkard odor lurking under the beer's malt was downright sulfurous. Rilke took a step back. Every time he dealt with Handelman, Rilke was grateful he wasn't enduring his papa's last stages. Shackled to drink, that wormy rot inside. Wishing a man dead was kid stuff, which hadn't stopped Rilke from wishing it on Papa plenty of times even as an adult until last year his wish came blessedly true. Handelman was tempting Rilke into similar mean and childish thoughts, and from the smug look of the man, he knew it, too. "I'll let you handle it, Gary, seeing as you started the job."

"I'm glad for the chance to do something useful for you folks. I'm real attached to Julia. Seeing as Lainie and the grandkids live too far away to visit."

Seeing as Lainie didn't want to have a damn thing to do with her poor-excuse-for-a-father anymore, which Rilke had every sympathy for. "Yeah, Gary, I know how attached you are to looking in on us."

"I try my best to keep tabs on you folks." Handelman swallowed noisily. Clueless or sly, either one.

"Like from your bathroom there."

Handelman didn't bat an eye, or maybe the flutter in his gobbler's throat was some *stiflement* of reaction. "Seems like you got right down to correcting those privacy concerns, didn't you, Dan?"

"Some correction was called for, Gary."

"Glad I can take a shit now without you folks bearing damn witness."

That remark deserved a *fuck you* if anything did, but Julia returned balancing a white paper lantern and a stick lighter in her hands. Wouldn't do to abuse Handelman in her earshot no matter how deserved. Julia heaping the blame on Rilke for any rudeness would be automatic. "Help me out with this, Dan."

Rilke took the lighter from her.

"No, Dan, the *lantern.*" Julia showed him that march of her chin.

"Well, *tell* me what to take, then. I'm not a mind reader."

"That's for sure."

Handelman said, "Is that one of those things you light up and they float off?"

"It's a wish lantern," Julia said. "You make a wish and then you launch it. And then your wish comes true."

Well, the old man would rather have another six-pack or a check for his troubles, Rilke would bet. Wishes were wasted on men like Handelman. On Rilke, too, but Julia knew that. She wouldn't expect him to play this silly game.

Julia hustled Rilke to the middle of the yard and instructed him to hold the thin rice paper careful and still while she bent to light the fuel cell. Warned him not to crush the lantern by accident, seeing that he was generally rough and klutzy with delicate objects. When the cell wouldn't light, Handelman hovered at Julia's shoulder to give unneeded instruction.

The breeze picked up, ruffled the lighter's weak flame. After another try, the lantern glowed at last. Julia stepped back. "OK, now, when Dan lets go, we all make a wish."

Rilke would stake cash on Julia's wish. That the problem of the bats was forever solved.

Handelman's wish would breathe life into the girl he'd failed to save from electrocution.

Rilke's wish was automatic and childish and mean. That, after Handelman sealed the one-way door for good, a bat or two would remain in the house.

"Let go, Dan." Julia's voice reached him from a distance. He blinked, startled that she stood so close, smelling of cut grass and beer. The fuel cell's heat warmed the rice paper against his hands. The thin bamboo frame shone black and skeletal through the lantern's pale glowing skin.

"You have to let go." Julia punched his arm near the cut. Not lightly, either. Handelman grinned.

Rilke clapped his hands together. The lantern crumpled. The bamboo collapsed, projected a satisfying snap like a wishbone's break. The fuel cell sputtered. Rilke crushed the smoking cell with his boot when he dropped the mess onto the grass.

Julia drew away from him. A door slammed roughly from the neighbor's yard on the other side of Rilke's tall back fence, an invisible impatience. Rilke waited for Julia's *fuck you Dan*, her tough and lovely heat.

If she felt angry, she wasn't about to show it. Her voice was low, like it had been in the hallway. "Should I be afraid of you, Dan?"

Handelman retreated to the cooler, drained the beer in progress, opened another.

Rilke pushed the lantern's ruins around the grass with his boot.

"Why?" was what she demanded next. He had to admit some right and reasonable answer was called for under the circumstances, but he wasn't feeling very right or very reasonable at the moment.

"Wishes are kid stuff," he told her. A response he would change if he could.

Handelman shot him a look as he tipped back the beer bottle that communicated a sly recognition of the unproductive behavior men struggled to hide inside out of pride. Or sadness. Or the desire to remind the folks who needed reminding that good-natured reliability was not a matter of temperament, but will.

Or maybe the old man was gloating a bit over the marital trouble. What would Julia say if she knew that old man's hero act was nothing but a fraud? Serve both of them right. He longed to tell her, right then, on the spot.

Julia's *fuck you Dan* lay in reserve in the house. She emerged with another damn lantern. Tasked Handelman with the holding this time. Lit the cell on the first try. She took the lantern and offered the glow to Rilke. Her blond hair captured the light like beaded fireflies. A rustling sounded from the direction of the eave. One last bat. Or a mild breeze ruffling the maple tree leaves at the side of the house. Or Rilke's own breath coming hard and audible although he couldn't feel the air. He held out his hands, grateful for her second chance.

"I was saving this one for our anniversary," Julia said, and let go.

A nimble wind took the lantern straight and high before a draft dipped it down behind the chimney's silhouette. The light dimmed only for a moment until the lamp rose above the roofline, steady and bright as the hunter's moon, caught a steady current, rode the night to the vanishing point. Julia tracked the flight's bright trail. The glow shrank to a pinprick soon enough, but an illumination from somewhere—a neighbor's back porch, Handelman's bathroom window—set her blond hair and her white flowing blouse afire.

Rilke had married a beautiful and a strong woman, in every way his match and mate.

He was struggling to keep her and losing that battle. He didn't understand the nature of the struggle or when trouble had jumped him or why. He could have easily installed the one-way door. He could have released the lantern with the wish lodged deep in his heart, that he could save her from everything she feared the way he used to do.

"Did you make a wish in time, Gary?" Although she was looking at Handelman, Julia's sweet tone was cocked full bore at Rilke.

The old man nodded, a sly maneuver of the chin.

Rilke knew a few things for certain. Among them that Julia had made her wish in time, and that this wish no longer concerned the bats' fate.

● ●●●●

Rilke never would know if Julia and Handelman would be granted their wishes, but his mean wish about the one-way door's effectiveness sure as hell came true.

A week after the exodus, a bat wheeled into Julia's hair right there in the hallway. The creature's high-pitched screeching pierced the house, woke Rilke from one of his violent dreams so abruptly he couldn't tell at first whether the squeaks were dream-sound or real. The moment Rilke freed her, Julia ran from the house. After Rilke released the bat out back he found her crouched on Handelman's knobby pine stoop, cradled in the old man's cottony arms, weeping her soundless unnerving cry. Her poppy-red shirt shook with her sobs like a darting bird. Handelman was holding that look of triumph. Rilke's mismanagement of Julia's fear had transformed Handelman from a drunk, withered loner to a strong man holding tight to another man's beautiful wife. That he could harbor jealousy over Julia's girlish hold on her childhood hero; such was the spectacular bungling of Rilke's own fear.

Julia's hair, still tangled where the bat had clung, shrouded Handelman's wounded fingers in gold. From the court, a door creaked. Grace Smith stepped out to check her mail, lingered at the box, gaped at the huddle on the fragile porch across the street.

Rilke had to pry Julia free. Handelman's wormy fingers left dimples in her skin. Her lip was still swollen a bit from the bite and the shots. He wanted to kiss the tiny wound hard right there, suck and swallow the cries she kept from him.

"Come home," he said. "Please."

She came home, all right. Straight to the bedroom to pack a bag.

Rilke stood insubstantial in the doorway while she filled her case and clicked the locks shut. Handelman's sour-milk drunk's odor wafted from her skin and hair as if she'd bathed in the old man. Now was the time to tell her about Handelman's cowardice, how he'd *caused* that little girl's death, for Chrissakes. He should have told her. He'd never understand what misfiring protective instinct silenced him. Maybe he sensed that undermining the old man at that particular moment, when she was fresh from his touch and comfort, would drive her away for good.

Julia stood in front of him, not too close, gripping the case. "Will you move out of my way, Dan?"

He didn't move out of her way. Instead, he confessed.

He told her how one evening, when Rilke was fourteen, on her way out to the store his mother had told Rilke to fetch Papa because the slop sink near the furnace had backed up and if he didn't unclog it a fire might spark so it couldn't wait till morning. Rilke tried to snake the drain himself to avoid the chore of dealing with Papa. He was holed up again in the guest cottage at the back of the property, across Scipio Road beyond the cornfield. Tying one on, as his mother would say. Rilke was ten years old before he understood his mother wasn't referring to Papa's boot laces.

The blockage wouldn't budge. Rilke was soaked in gray water. The old furnace spit like it was already drowned. He shop-vac'ed the water that had spilled on the concrete floor and sprinkled kitty litter to wick moisture. The cat had gone missing weeks ago, but Rilke couldn't bring himself to get rid of her things just yet. He felt the hiss of the furnace like breath on his neck. He was worried to leave the situation for the hazard it posed, but he'd only be away a moment.

He'd crossed Scipio Road at a run. Trudged through the line of pines and the fallow field. The papery bones of old husks crackled under his work boots. The guest cottage shimmered under a half-yoke moon. Rilke was sweating when he arrived breathless at Papa's door to parry a tentative knock.

His mother had told him to *never open the door* when Papa was holed up in the one-room cottage, advice Rilke had always accepted as good common sense. When Papa didn't answer, Rilke rapped again. Listened carefully, heard only uninformative murmurs and rustlings, and then a come-in grunt. Rilke pushed open the door to find Papa sprawled spread-legged on the bed with a faded quilt bunched over his head. The raw flame from an unshaded lamp bulb lit Papa's bare arms. The tidy room gleamed cleanly in the bare light. Buffed brown shelves glowed like shoe polish. The urethane streaks on the oak floor were burnished to a slick icy film. Even in his rubber-soled boots, Rilke could skate to Papa if he wished. Papa peeked at him. Flapped the quilt's bright edging with a peek-a-boo gesture that might have been playful coming from another man.

"What is it, Son?"

Rilke cleared his throat. "The utility sink's clogged, sir."

"Snake it, then."

"I tried." From his slurry of vowels, Rilke determined Papa was far gone already. Whiskey's musky odor plumped the air. A bottle stood on the kitchenette counter, half empty and open in a permanent state of access, the screw cap tossed aside. Rilke pressed against the doorjamb. His vision hooded. Papa rolled from the bed, stood up, shook the shivers from his legs one at a time. The crisp snap of denim rattled the room. "Mama thinks it's a hazard." Rilke hoped Papa would achieve the sense of his mother having sent him on this errand rather than Rilke relying on him for help. "Water's leaking to the furnace."

"Shouldn't be leaks from a clogged drain. You check the pipes for faulty seams?"

"No, sir."

"There's your leak, then." He glided to the counter, lifted the bottle. Papa's size could take Rilke's breath away when he wasn't guarded against the basic intimidation the man posed. In matters of farming, Papa was cursed with incompetence. But the tireless work he performed had built up a rigid grid of muscle in his arms and chest. His height was nerve-racking, too, his girth outgunned by the limber stretch of his limbs. Papa looked like no one else, his mother had said once. Like rubber-band balls had been pinched together to form his flesh. When drunk, his eyes shone with old-timey brimstone. They flashed at Rilke over the curved rim of a shot glass as Papa swallowed a colorless stream without a single bobble of the throat. Blame was about to be laid, for the faulty seam, for overlooking the real cause of the trouble. Rilke braced for it.

Papa refilled the shot. "Shut the damn door, Son. You're letting the heat in."

It couldn't be any steamier outside the cottage than in. Humidity poured from Rilke's skin, now that he'd sweated out his run. His T-shirt reeked of sour gray water and the pus of his own perspiration. And Papa was holding out the shot to him. Dryness tatted Rilke's tongue. He fought the instinctual impulse to run as hard as he could home.

Instead he shut the door.

Took the shot. Tipped back his head and tossed the whiskey down his gullet the way Papa had done. Choked like a baby on the sting of it, a sensation he hadn't foreseen. The losers at school drank themselves sick every weekend, but Rilke had never touched a drop of alcohol in his life. They weren't a family to discuss issues, but the one unstated principle of the house was that while Papa sober was no saint, Papa drunk was Papa ruined, the alcohol itself being the tip of that scale.

Papa laughed at his babyish gagging and clapped him on the shoulder. "Better chase that cough." He poured him another shot full.

Rilke drank in the manner of the first, all at once with a rigid swallow. He found Papa was right about the sting yielding to a pleasant burn against his throat's leather. His vision cleared in the light's incandescent crown. A motor hummed unevenly, an earthy rumble that clotted his hearing, confused him for a moment. Once he'd located the sound, it would be the wonder of the rest of his days how he hadn't spotted her the moment he'd opened the door.

The lost cat lay purring on the oak floor behind the stainless garbage pail.

Rilke cried out in joy to see her tail wrapped around two tiny kittens cloaked in fragile flakes of snowy hair. They blinked at him with nearsighted, crystal-blue eyes. The bigger of the two was decorated with his mother's tiger striping between the pink, translucent ears.

Papa usually drowned unwanted kittens while they were still hairless. For a moment, Rilke was impressed by Papa's love for him, that he'd not only found the lost cat but had spared her and her kits' lives. He should have assessed at once that the cat was protecting so few kittens.

He resisted the cloudy impulse to slide on his knees across the icy polish and take the cat in his arms. Instead he faced Papa, wedged a silly grin, raised a film of babyish tears. "Papa. You found her." He did nothing to prevent the gratitude from seeping through his voice.

Papa was drinking as Rilke spoke. Once he'd drained the shot, he eyed the cat. She flicked her tail and roped it around her kittens. "Like hell. Snuck in here dragging her litter. Took up residence, didn't she." He spewed another harsh bubble of laughter. "Got 'em down to two."

Down to two.

A gruesome subtraction. Rilke felt a bit stupid, a bit confused. The room tipped. Surfaces gleamed, a brittle riot. The cat warbled an off-key purr and then a hiss.

Papa strode to the pantry closet, pulled from it a heavy-handled metal broom, moved swiftly on the cat.

Papa's muscular back blocked Rilke's view. It seemed to him that the cat maintained her broken-motor purr under the broom head's wet, steady slap. The kittens fled sightlessly to the corner by the bedside table and cowered, their glassy sight too immature to see the obvious shelter of the dark space under Papa's bed. A wail, thin as gruel, yawned wide and entered him. Rilke became aware of blood pooling between Papa's heels. He hadn't noticed until then Papa's bare feet, the thin yellowing toes, the rough, chipped nails. Papa grunted. Effort or ecstasy, impossible to tell.

When it was over, Papa swiveled on the balls of his yellowed feet. His features protruded off kilter, his body too bright, like his skin was another of the room's gleaming finishes, and he was advancing on his son. Rilke awaited his own beating with eyes closed against the crumple and the blood and the kits in the corner, crystal-gazed and shuddering. Breath wadded with whiskey dabbed his neck. More laughter unfolded. A hiccup at first, and then a horrifying honking riptide. Rilke opened his eyes. Papa slung a taut arm around his shoulder, not as a fatherly gesture but to keep from falling down under laughter's gale. His droopy eyes ran with cloudy tears. His belly and chest flexed against Rilke's arm and hip. They were almost hugging, which Rilke couldn't ever remember hugging his father before. The narrow space between them reeked of grain and gray water as if Rilke's own foul odors were leaking from Papa now. A sound rose from Rilke's throat, something painful that he only recognized as laughter by the fat rude sound of it. Papa watched the fit take him with a drunkard's crafty glance. Just like that he quenched his own laughter the way he tossed down a shot full of drink.

"Save me the trouble of the drowning then, Son."

And he'd handed Rilke the metal broom, the head dented and dinged, the bristles speckled with blood.

What happened next was very confusing, and Rilke never would remember it just right.

He knew he'd picked up a dish towel from the kitchenette counter.

He knew he'd lifted the kits to the towel, maybe to bundle them against the blows, maybe to protect the floor's satin polish.

He knew he hadn't been able to throttle his laughter in the efficient way Papa had.

And he *knew*, when he'd finished the telling, that it was a fatal misjudgment of the marriage ever to admit to Julia what he'd done.

He was still floating in the doorway of the bedroom, aware that he was blocking her way out; aware of her awareness of his body's barrier. Her poppy-red shirt filled his vision. She settled a wary gaze on him which suggested an outlook that *from now on* anything he did was bound to be dangerous.

To mitigate his error, he added, "So I can't ever hurt an animal again. On purpose." As if the cruelest act of his life was merely by way of explaining why he had failed to deal with the bats.

She set down her case. She grasped his arms.

Her response might be bestowing compassion and understanding. She'd witnessed more than a few of Papa's behaviors. Ever since they began dating, their bastard fathers had bound them together in a protective pact. But in his stupidity and confusion he could not decipher her. The kindness might be carrying the terrifying caution she held toward him lately. But her lips, still tender from the bite, were parting in a kiss. He awaited the grace of her mouth and limbs. From the hallway, the baseboards hummed. He should feel hot. He should feel her grasping hands. He should feel the grace of sensation.

Miraculously, she did kiss him.

Rilke peeled away his papa's rubbery crawl on his flesh and kissed her back.

She relaxed under the pressure of his mouth. *All right.* He drew in her breath, sticky and curdled from that morning's sugared coffee. Fit to her as he'd always done. It made sense that her body would melt into his as if nothing had ever caused any trouble between them. He ran his tongue gently over the tiny swollen mound on her lip, the bite so healed he barely felt it.

He barely felt it, too, when she bit him hard, nearly plumb through the skin. Jerked her head back, ripped open a cut like she was carving meat. Rilke knocked her back, swallowed a lukewarm lump of blood. Julia went down hard and silent against the bedstead.

"Jesus, Jules." Rilke snatched her up by her arm, hauled her to her feet. Dribbles of blood sprinkled and vanished into Julia's poppy-red shirt.

She wrenched her arm free. "God dammit, Dan, get off me."

Rilke stepped back, grabbed a T from the dresser top and stuffed it hard against his weeping lip. Through the open blinds, he saw Handelman standing at his bathroom window, messing with something on the sill, pretending not to gawk. "Come on, Jules."

"Come on, what? So you did some stupid shit with your fucked up dad once upon a time so now you get to act any way you please?"

"I don't get to act any way I please." An obvious statement if there ever was one. Maybe it came out crybabyish. The T was muffling his voice, messing up the necessary tone to manage this situation.

"Am I supposed to feel sorry for you, Dan?"

"Wouldn't hurt," he said evenly. A response he'd change if he could.

Julia hit his arm. The blow mashed the cut that stupid farm boy had carved into him. His wound wasn't healing as fast as Julia's bite. She probably knew that, too, when she aimed for the cut. "Do you know there are piles and piles of bat shit in the attic? That I can't sleep at all anymore because I'm so damn frightened? Then you get to sleep every minute you're home, and don't give me that crap about your biorhythms."

Rilke set down the T on the dresser to rub his throbbing cut. He let blood weep down his chin to see whether she'd make any damn move to *help* him, for Chrissakes. "I don't sleep every moment I'm home."

Julia was staring at his arm, not his lip. "You shot that kid for no good reason, didn't you. I know how good you are at subduing people. Were your *biorhythms* off that night?"

Rilke took up the T again to mop his chin. "How do you know what's in the attic?" he asked quietly. "I thought you were afraid to go up there."

"Gary tells me it's a real mess. He says you didn't flash under the eaves when you did the siding, either, so we've got mold now, too, while you sleep all day and shoot children at night, and why did I only hear you'd been on probation from the damn secretary?"

Rilke curled his fists. "You never even asked about my cut."

"Gary said you didn't get nearly what you deserved for hurting that kid."

"Is that what Gary said?" Rilke glanced out the window. Handelman had vanished, no doubt to gloat or make the call on Rilke to report some bullshit domestic when *he* was the one with his lip chewed off.

"So excuse me if I don't give a shit about what you did to some cat once upon a time."

"It was a kitten." Rilke let his gaze drop to her lip. "Here's the whole problem, Jules, which is what I'm really trying to tell you. I didn't bite you. But under certain, ah, conditions, I could. So it's important to avoid establishing those certain conditions in the first place. For your own good, I mean."

Well, that statement didn't come out as he intended. Julia tweaked the T. The sleeve flipped up, slapped his nose. "So what are you telling me, Dan? That you're just dying to beat me to a pulp for my own good, just like your itty bitty kitty?"

Through her baiting a fresh horror dawned. For the first time, Rilke understood how her bastard-of-a-father must have felt when he'd gone after her. The impulse seized him, to squeeze the throat's tender hollow peeking through the poppy-red collar. But the bad moment passed and she probably didn't even really know what she was saying she was so worked up.

As to her question, he certainly wasn't about to dignify *that* with an answer. He sucked on his lip. She adopted a defensive stance, light and steady on the balls of the feet. Ready to flee or to come at him with everything she had, just as he'd taught her when they were still only kids.

• ••••

At the start of his shift that night, Rilke parked in the Costco parking lot to tamp down his agitation. His lip was still throbbing, and when he wiped his mouth blood smeared the back of his hand. Julia's bite had opened a ceaseless flow. No amount of cloth and Kleenex had staunched the wound. He'd managed to control the flow long enough at the station so he could get on duty instead of being ordered to the urgent care, but if the damn thing didn't quit bleeding soon he'd need stitches all right. Plus, he'd have to explain to his mother both the reason for the bleeding lip and the reason Julia showed up on her doorstep with a packed bag. Rilke didn't know whom he would throttle first, his wife or hero Handelman, if he could *act any way he pleased.*

Rilke turned over the engine, peeled out of the Costco to pull into the Burger King across Jackson Boulevard. He'd been too upset to eat that evening. Time to pick up a coke and burger, stretch his legs, get mind and body together, get through this shift. On his way to shutting the car door, he fished a napkin out of the glove box to press to his flowing lip.

He swung open the Burger King's glass door. Above him a bell tinkled a thin high note.

"*Hey man hey what the fuck?*" A tall skinny punk had a weapon trained on Rilke by the time the door breezed shut.

"OK, son, OK." Rilke showed the kid the hand not clenching the napkin to his lip and quickly assessed the scene. The teenage girl behind the counter was keeping it together pretty good. Black uniform, oversized name tag he could almost read from where he stood. A pretty sweep of blond hair tied with a black ribbon. Her hand was thrust deep in the register drawer. The other hand clutched the rim of the countertop, knuckles shining. Rilke gave her a slight nod as she locked eyes with him and then stared at the soaked napkin. Her relief at the sight of the law melted into fright as if a split lip diminished his competence, or maybe she was afraid the punk had beat him up before entering the store.

Rilke looked past the girl to the kitchen's gleaming metal surfaces. All clear. The fry cooks had slipped away, then. Better for incident management, but Rilke felt a surge at the craven fact of the girl left alone.

The dining room, too, was empty, and now that he had the scene straight he could assess the boy. The kid was far more frightened than the girl. Dark eyes bulged from puffy purple bags. Skinny and insubstantial under a loose navy sweatshirt and baggy jeans. Judging from the physical aspects, the boy was in no way prepared to deal with unexpected trouble in his ill-conceived plan. A boy out of his league. A vulnerable boy. An unreliable boy.

Which made the fact of the weapon much more dangerous.

A more seasoned hood would have gauged Rilke's uniform before making so much as a twitch with the gun in his direction. A hood would have kept it trained on the girl until Rilke moved his ass out the door, but this hapless kid was aiming right at the bloody napkin as if Julia's bite constituted the whole threat.

The damn napkin muffled his voice at a critical management juncture. "Let's calm things down here, son, and lower that weapon." The napkin's tail flapped with his breath.

"What, man?" The boy's arm was shaking. The barrel jerked like a bumper car.

"Lower your weapon," Rilke repeated. He raged at Julia's distant bewitchment that was keeping his blood flowing. And he was livid at this kid's skinny scared face and the jerky fingers curled around the trigger. If it came, the shot would not be a deliberate extermination of a man or the law, but an accident of nerves during a half-assed robbery.

The kid's next statement was downright infuriating. "How do I do that?"

Rilke felt a laugh bubble. Shit, was he going to honk it out right here? The girl's expression pleaded with him to keep it together, subdue this individual, be her fucking *hero*, and then a movement at her waist startled him. A head of hair. Two heads, then three. A panicked eye peeked over the counter's rim. *Jesus Christ.* The customers and cooks hadn't abandoned this girl. The punk had corralled them, and now the eye narrowed and bobbed like it was going to vault over the counter in a desperate show of bravado and get everyone shot. The honking bubbled out of Rilke, great gales of spillage that wrenched a pain in his gut, and the eye widened and ducked back out of sight and the counter girl stared at him as if she might just laugh, too.

The napkin blew from his lip. The girl screamed. The boy followed the napkin's flutter with the barrel, stupid kid, and, as Rilke went for his weapon and the kid shouted, *"No don't I'll shoot,"* but didn't mash the trigger as a half-assed amateur would, Rilke saw that the gun was missing the magazine.

Even with the kid's hand low on the grip, Rilke should have seized on this crucial fact at once, and he would have, too, if it weren't for the bite's everlasting seep. Now it was a straightforward matter to say a calming word, seize the unloaded weapon, quiet the girl, call it in. *I know how good you are at subduing people, Dan.* Procedure was what Rilke intended as he moved on the boy, but even before his hand clamped down on the gun and wrenched the skinny wrist he knew he was moving too fast and blood was filling his mouth again. *Jesus Christ,* Julia had fucking cursed him to bleed forever and the sharp crack of the boy's bone set the girl off screaming like she'd been shot and she crouched down on the floor with the customers and cooks and they all rocked and screamed and the eyes rimmed the counter and the boy hollered, *"Stopmanstop it's not loaded,"* but there was cause for reasonable fear and imminent danger of harm because the boy wouldn't *couldn't* let go of the gun.

Sometime after the incident, Rilke would think he overheard Handelman joke to Julia that her hickey had sure saved Rilke's butt because the bleeding lip proved Rilke's claim the kid had resisted, but then again maybe Rilke really heard that half-assed crack in one of his terrible dreams when he was tucking a bat between Julia's legs and the creature was glowing white with lacy wings, and in the ecstasy of their bodies' join Julia took the dove-bat in her hand and set it free; and this time when Rilke released the kid and drew his weapon he sure as hell wasn't going for the kneecap, and maybe in time he would dream that the beautiful girl behind the counter rose up, took wing, rested her tender hand on him in time to mess up his aim.

State of Motion

The first launch was perfect, their plane a wood-bellied sparrow fluttering at the apex of the school gymnasium's domed ceiling before surfing the curve, winging steadily down. Terrence's landing was an expertly piloted drop to the waxed oak floor. Two and half minutes in the air. That time aloft put Moor's fourth grade team easily in medal territory for the Wright Stuff event. But on his turn at the controls, Conner piloted the plane straight into one of the chrome light fixtures dotting the dome. He wiggled the joystick frantically. The tail shuddered, but the nose remained buried in the fixture's bowl. Terrence yanked the remote control from Conner. Moor cursed under her breath.

"Don't swear, Mom." Conner's admonishment was reflex.

"Sorry, hon. Terrence, don't grab the controls. All right?"

Terrence scowled. He unnerved Moor with his spooky inborn talent for all things competitive. She avoided his pout and stared at the ceiling. They'd need a ladder. She'd have to find Will, the school custodian, if he was working this late.

He was, she remembered.

They'd made love that afternoon in the custodial closet ten minutes before the bell rang. He'd told her he'd taken a double shift, knowing she'd be bringing her Wright Stuff team to the gym that evening for their test flight. But she'd hardly shaken off his shine to pay attention to Conner's animated after-school chatter. She couldn't see him now, with her son and his plane needing rescue.

No, she'd get Kay to help, Terrence's mom, who was meeting in the cafeteria with the Ann Arbor District Science Olympiad committee. Kay was their school's head coach. Although she was already an event coach for Wright Stuff, Moor had volunteered to pull double duty to assist her. Almost at once Moor had come to hate dealing with the woman. Kay was aggressively competitive in that American-working-mom way that made Moor instinctually petrified.

"Terry, quit it!" Conner said as Terrence revved the motor. The plane whined as a wing dipped sharply over the fixture's rim. "You'll break it!"

"It's broken anyway."

"Terrence," Moor said. "Don't be rough with the remote."

"It's not broken." Conner jogged to stand directly underneath the plane's squirming tail. "I think it's in one piece."

"You busted it. You can't steer. I kill you on piloting."

Moor took the controls before Terrence could jam the joystick into reverse again. "Terrence, don't say kill, OK? Great, sweetie," she called to Conner. "Maybe there's a way to save it."

Just then a pop echoed in the dome like wet-snapped bubble gum. A shower of azure sparks bubbled up from the fixture. The plane shuddered and burst into flames. Two fiery balls rained down fast toward Conner, who, true to his nature, wasn't looking up anymore but was answering Moor's encouraging words with an elaborate plan for scaling the dome and plucking out the plane; was, true to his naïve nature, completely oblivious to the harm hurtling his way.

And Moor couldn't move.

Even if he had interrupted his narrative to look up, Conner wouldn't have darted out of the way. He'd watch with curiosity as the flaming comet hit him square between the eyes. He had no instinct for self-preservation. Moor's own threat instinct was on a hair trigger, but when real catastrophe struck, her constant coil of tension had the bizarre result of immobilizing her. Whenever Conner really did get hurt, or Ivan had another bout of lung congestion, a stubborn holdover from a childhood infection that hadn't been treated properly in a Soviet hospital, Moor felt an elemental aversion to their distress. She found injury and illness revolting. She never could bring herself to scoop Conner up and kissed his boo-boos, or hold Ivan's hand as he gasped, could barely keep her own breathing sound.

She never could form the words *it'll be OK*.

Her craven aversion to suffering peaked that past summer when their dog unexpectedly died. Boxer devoured a nest of rabbits he unearthed from under the deck and soon after began to bloat. Moor, pissed that he'd scattered miniature paws and shell-pink guts all over the backyard for Conner to see, at first didn't recognize the urgency of his swelling gut. But when she heard gurgling and keening from the backyard, and he wouldn't come when called, she'd realized it was bad, and the familiar fear filled her. She'd actually *hid* in her closet, pretending to clean it. Finally, Conner asked if Boxer was going to be all right and shouldn't she take him to the doctor? And Moor had called the vet's office for help before fetching a baseball bat and venturing outside. She was convinced the dog would maul her in his final excruciating moments. She didn't know why. Boxer had been a gentle soul all his life. She had no reason to fear him. Except for tearing the bunnies limb for limb, he'd never so much as chewed a table leg.

When she found Boxer under the fir tree, stiff, stomach distended, eyes rolled back in his skull, she'd gripped the bat tighter, rooted to the grass. The dog had dragged his stone-heavy body to the farthest point of the yard to die. He was wedged between the tree trunk and the fence post, as if his last thought had been to escape, not death, but Moor and her bat. It was Conner who crouched at the dog's side and patted his head. Then an emergency tech from the vet's office had driven up, lunged past Moor, dropped to her knees beside Boxer, and covered the dog's slack black lips with her own.

This stranger is kissing life into my dog, and here I stand with this bat, Moor had thought gauzily. After it was clear Boxer was dead, it was the tech who sobbed, and Conner who cradled Boxer's floppy ears in his lap.

Her shame ran too deep to tell Ivan exactly what had happened, so she stuck to the facts Ivan would easily digest. She told him the cause of death was suffocation, that the bloated gut crushed the dog's diaphragm. She described Conner's bravery and compassion in holding on to Boxer's paw while they'd hauled the boulder-heavy body into the tech's van. That she'd helped the tech carry Boxer was a minor victory of the will, at least. Although if she'd admitted wielding a baseball bat while a stranger locked lips with their pet,

Ivan would be the one person to understand her. He'd been ruined by violence. He understood confounding reactions to fear. But such acceptance of the worst in each other had, by degrees, eroded their marriage. And it wasn't good for Conner to have parents who never tried to stoke a bravery in each other that must, somewhere, still reside in their souls.

"Neat," she heard Terrence breathe in awe as one of the fireballs sputtered and died and the one heading for Conner's hair flared hungrily.

"Hey, buddy—watch out." Suddenly Will was at Conner's side, gently nudging him out of the way. Moor hadn't noticed Will enter the gym until he rested his hands on her boy. Conner looked up just in time to see the fireball extinguish as if snuffed out by an invisible breath. A fairy dusting of ash settled in Will's fair hair.

"Wow," Conner cried. "Mom! Look what happened to our plane!"

"We are fucked," Terrence said.

"Terrence, don't say fuck," Moor said, although it was the same curse Conner had chastised her for a few moments before. The flakes of ash in Will's hair drifted to the waxed gym floor. She stared at his easy grin as if through glass, sharp and glaring, far from her. Will ruffled Conner's hair and came to her. On his feet were the tangerine Crocs she'd given him. Her first gift to a man in years; Ivan and she had ceased exchanging presents long ago. Will was a die-hard Detroit Tigers fan. The Crocs' orange color matched the lurid tiger-striped shirt she'd uncovered a few weeks back while stripping off his slate-blue custodial shirt. A joke, but he'd worn them every day since, although the Crocs' clown toes made him stumble on the stepladder. He had to slip them off whenever he was fiddling with something in the ceiling.

"Jesus, Moor, you're white as a sheet." Will slid an arm around her waist. Was he going to kiss her in front of her son? She pushed him away.

"Don't do that," she whispered. His skin was hot. He reeked of bleach.

"You look like you're about to pass out."

"My son almost burned to a crisp."

"Not even close." Will was standing too close to her, smiling wide. He always did, even after school in the crowded hallway. His happiness at seeing her was sexy, even as she imagined the other mothers taking note of the way he allowed his arm to brush hers as he passed, carrying that big sweeper or a bucket of tools. He teased her openly her with frank black eyes. As blond as he was, he ought to have blue eyes, she often thought. The contrast startled her, as if his features belonged to two different people with clashing complexions.

"Goddamn it," she said. "How are we going to rebuild that plane before Saturday?"

"Don't swear, Mom," Conner said. And Terrence said, "I have No Bones About It and Circuit Wizardry and Water Rockets practice, plus soccer and my piano recital this week. There's no way I can build another plane."

Will laughed. "Plus eating and sleeping really crowd the schedule."

Terrence scowled at him. "We eat pizza at practices."

"Why don't we ever order pizza at Wright Stuff, Mom?" Conner whined.

"We eat healthy at home, don't we, sweetie?" Moor struggled to relax. It didn't help that Will was lingering instead of figuring out how to make that fixture safe for the Science Olympiad. But he was in no hurry to leave her. He was thinking of her, as she was always thinking of him.

Thinking of their trysts in the custodial closet, which wasn't a closet at all, despite the plastic identifier on the door, but a large concrete-block room lined with shelves of disinfectant and mop heads and the detritus of broken school equipment. Several times a week they hurried to make love before the final bell. They would stand against the open section of wall next to the spare mop handles. Sometimes the handles cascaded down as they came, and the clatter would make them collapse against one another, breathing hard, legs weak, almost falling down themselves; and then that long metal rod he used to change out-of-reach light bulbs would roll around and hobble them both, and they'd laugh themselves to tears. She would stroke his fair hair, stiff like heaps of fine wire, before burying his lips in hers. Laughter was as sensual as sex, she had rediscovered, if she had ever discovered it. She and Ivan had never laughed much together.

"I always get pizza after Wright Stuff practice," Terrence boasted. Conner looked as crushed by this taunt as he was about the plane's incineration.

Kay burst noisily through the double doors from the cafeteria. "What's that smell?" Her high voice echoed in the cup of the dome. No detail of sight or odor ever escaped Kay.

"Our plane burned up," Terrence announced.

"That's weird. What'd you do, pilot it into a socket?"

"I didn't do it. Conner did." Terrence jabbed his finger at Conner's flushed face.

Moor bit her lip. "Obviously an accident. Not Conner's fault at all. Kay, we have a safety issue here. We'll need to move the event outdoors, I think."

"Against the rules. This event has to be held indoors." Kay planted herself under the fixture and peered up. She was tall, with shoulders wider than her hips and long, athletic legs. Her auburn hair streamed down her back like a windswept swirl of maple leaves. She was a knockout. Moor couldn't understand why Will didn't attach his gaze to Kay the way all the dads did whenever she entered the room, but Will was one of those rare men who didn't allow fantastic looks and a great body to trump an aversion to character. "How the heck did it catch fire anyway?" She leveled a bullet-glare at Will. Moor knew that look. She'd received it many times over the last few weeks. "The bulbs seem protected to me. Possibly a short in the wiring?"

It was more than just the happy assignment of blame Kay was fixing on Will. Kay knew all about their affair.

"Maybe it was Conner's precision aim," Will said.

"Conner's an idiot. I kill him on piloting," Terrence muttered.

"Sounds like a freak thing to me," Kay said.

"Kay, it's a hazard." Moor began to tremble. She sensed in Kay the same potential for violence under duress she'd feared in her sick dog, but in Kay's case a bat wouldn't be any comfort.

"Will, do we have a *legitimate* hazard here?"

Will shrugged. "I agree it was a freak thing. I don't think there's anything to worry about. But I'll check for a short."

Moor stared at him. The danger was obvious. Why was he downplaying it?

Conner moved to Will. "Are we going to get disqualified because I ruined the plane?"

Will ruffled Conner's hair. The gesture was so affectionate Moor almost cried. "No, buddy. You just have to build another plane. Anyway, not one pilot in a million could have made that beauty soar so high."

Moor swallowed as Conner beamed up at Will. "I would like to address the safety issue further." Her voice shook embarrassingly.

"I don't want to take this to the committee if it's a fluke," Kay said.

"It's their job to provide a safe environment for the events."

"Mom." Conner tugged at her sleeve. "It's no big deal. I'll let Terry pilot my turn on Saturday."

"You bet you will."

"Terrence, it's not OK to be rude," Moor said. "And Conner, that's not the issue. We get two flights, one for each of you to pilot."

"But I'll be rebuilding the plane. Come *on*, Mom. I promise the plane won't catch fire again."

"Moor, if you feel that strongly, then by all means feel free to speak to Linda. You can catch her now, if you want," Kay said. "But maybe there's a work-around we can find. Will, any solutions come to your mind?"

A traitorous look of thoughtfulness crept into Will's expression as he threw his head back to examine the fixture again. "I could wrap some chicken wire around the base and protect the bulb that way."

"Great solution," Kay said. "I think we've solved it, Moor."

Moor glared at Will as he winked at her and padded away in his tangerine Crocs to fetch his tools. Kay watched them archly, smug that Moor's lover was an elementary school janitor.

• ••••

Why had she told Kay about the affair? Moor berated herself as she drove Conner home through an unexpected fog, thick as cotton batting, that forced her to creep the car along the side of the road. Had it been some impulse to brag, as Kay bragged about her engineering PhD or her most recent salary bump? Was sleeping with Will Moor's biggest accomplishment? She'd never know what spasm of misguided ego had made her tell.

Anyway, they'd been drunk. A month ago, the Science Olympiad work had overwhelmed them both. Getting busy parent-coaches to schedule practices had been a pain. Then a coach melted down during a Science Jeopardy practice when the buzzers malfunctioned. That's what happens when parents volunteer to coach an event just to get their kid on the team,

Kay had complained. Moor had wondered why on earth anyone would
volunteer otherwise.

"They have to be committed to the *event*," Kay had responded. "Not
just to their kid."

So they'd met at a bar to toss out names for replacements. Not a real bar,
but the one attached to the family restaurant where she and Ivan always took
Conner; where, while waiting in the lobby to be seated, Moor would stare
through the glass doors at the crowds of the unattached as they drank and
flirted and cheered at whatever sports contest was on the big screen. She and
Kay had talked through the Olympiad business. Kay assigned Lola Hughes
to coach Science Jeopardy.

"She won't lose her cool. She's used to managing twenty-five computer
techs. Anyway, now that she's a stay-at-home, she's completely underutilized,"
Kay noted.

As they drank, Kay, as usual, segued into bragging points about her job,
about the upcoming multimillion-dollar contract and the need to fire so-
and-so next week for nonperformance, and Moor had asked, "How do you
do it? The work-family thing? I mean, I struggle with a part-time schedule,
and my job isn't nearly as stressful as yours." Moor worked as a liaison for
Russian émigrés at a social-service organization. What had started as a volunteer position years ago quickly became a part-time job because of Moor's
native Russian and natural sympathy for the sad circumstances that brought
the émigrés to America. These days the stories more often concerned financial ruin than state persecution. Ivan was far less sympathetic to her work-re-
lated conversations than he used to be, when the traumas had to do with
honor, not greed. Moor herself found it harder to tolerate the sad stories, but
not because her sympathy had slipped. She knew most of the émigrés weren't

equipped to compete, having never been bred to it the way Americans were. Despite their high hopes for their futures here, Moor knew they would never regain even what little they'd left behind at home.

"Tom and I are fifty-fifty," Kay said.

Tom was Kay's husband, a low-key guy who drank brandy and scrubbed dishes every time Moor visited Kay's home for a meeting. "You are? I mean . . . what does that mean?"

"Fifty-fifty split at home. Chores. Terrence's care. Dealing with the school, with our folks."

"Well." Moor, loose by then, had spoken without thinking. "How do you keep track, through charts?"

She was joking, but Kay had brightened as if Moor had pegged the system exactly. "Chore lists. Broken down by task and due date. We keep our spreadsheets in a family binder. Great organizational tool."

"Shit."

"Terrence is by far our most complicated chart. Especially right now with his four Olympiad events."

"Ivan and I are most definitely not fifty-fifty," Moor said. "I don't think Conner would trust him with his care chart."

"You have to insist, Moor." Kay had leaned across the tall table. "You have to make it clear to Ivan that if you are going to work outside the home that the income partnership you create in the professional sphere demands absolute equality in your domestic partnership. Anything less and you're just selling yourself short."

Or selling Conner short, was Moor's reflexive thought. On the rare occasions she asked Ivan to fix Conner a bowl of cereal in the morning, they both pouted through their morning routine; and, Moor hated to admit, their reaction pleased her. She didn't like Ivan caring for Conner in those personal ways. He performed them as mere tasks. Not that Ivan wasn't a good father. He loved Conner. He simply expressed that love through a specialized band of interactions—minilectures on the physical properties of things, or the discipline of self he practiced so carefully. It was Russia in him. Severe, touched with sadness. Moor felt a sudden tipsy impulse to defend him.

"Fifty-fifty's not for Conner," she answered, swerving from Ivan's presence in the conversation.

"You've got to train Conner to accept it."

"Or I could have an affair." She'd blurted it out. It made no sense to say it. Another glass of Shiraz appeared. Moor hid behind the curve of the oversized glass.

"Are you?" Kay's eyes narrowed. Moor shrugged. "You are!"

"I'm fucking the janitor."

Everything about the vulgar way she'd said it was false. She was in love with Will. And although there was not a thing in the world wrong with being a custodian if that's all he ever could be, he'd *chosen* it. He'd been an electrician with a successful business. Successful until one big client had welshed on one big job. He could have started over, if the recession hadn't tanked the construction trades. But he'd seen the custodial job posting, and he'd leaped at the opportunity for security.

"The blond guy who works afternoons?"

Moor nodded.

And Kay had pursed her lips together, lifted her beer. Her obvious surprise seeped to smugness as she took a deep pull from her longneck and surveyed Moor as if she'd tumbled a few more notches down the ladder of success; as if her competition-allergic kid, her part-time job, her ninety-ten with Ivan, her rash choice of lover, cast her forever in the rubbish heap of underachievement.

Dammit, what was I thinking? Moor navigated through the sheet of fog tensely. Tonight that same clandestine smugness had radiated from Kay's bearing as soon as she spied Will. Why hand her all that power?

She felt Conner's fears, of the weather, of the rusted sedan's wobbly creep, sink into her bones. "Don't worry, sweetie. Almost home."

"Can we rebuild the plane in time?" They'd constructed the plane from a National Olympiad mail-order kit. The kit Moor had allowed Terrence to assemble with token assistance from her son. The thing had been so expensive she hadn't wanted to order a backup.

Kay would have gone ahead and bought the second one, damn the budget, and built it at once as a back-up. While angling Tom for that fifty-fifty split on the construction checklist.

"Of course. We'll get Papa to help."

She wished the mention of Ivan would reassure him, but Conner slouched and stared out the window at the opaque white shroud pressing the glass.

●　●●●

Her affair with Will was energy and inertia in equal balance. She felt this most strongly whenever she was confronted with a moment when she might confess to Ivan once and for all. For months she had thought her affair was playing out the physical law Ivan was always explaining to Conner, that all objects resist changes in their state of motion unless acted upon by an unbalanced force. Passion, she'd hoped, was her unbalanced force. Yet it turned out she'd created a way to stay put permanently, unless she *did* something.

And she was rooted to her spot.

Particularly on a night of crisis like this, the evening after the fire in the dome, when she was hunkered down at the dining room table with Conner seated at her elbow. Ivan was isolated in the den, absorbed in a pile of work, and she knew she'd have to pull this off without him despite the fact that in training and temperament he was far more suited to rebuilding the Wright Stuff plane. A dispirited heap of wood, thin plastic sheathing, glue, and toothpicks for detail work confronted her. She'd picked up a couple of cheap hobby shop kits, some cast-off material from the local scrap store. She'd thought at the time she'd done a good job selecting what they'd need, but the debris before her was more upsetting than the ashen remains of their first little craft.

Ivan should be at the table. He never let up on his relentless attention to work. It was Russia in him, this overkill of conscientiousness. He'd begun his career in aeronautics, trained in Novgorod. Twenty years ago aeronautics had been the leading edge of Soviet technology. But when he'd emigrated, it had taken him five years to catch up with the young American engineers who developed more expertise as undergraduates than he'd done working as an engineer in a top Soviet facility. He was perched precariously in America where he'd been secure in Russia, and the hard work, and the long path, and the sense of inferiority he'd carried through it all made his intense focus his only defense. He'd reached as high as he would ever go in his profession. He wanted only to remain where he was, never sink, never advance.

But he didn't need to work so hard anymore, Moor often pointed out, usually when there was something on the table that Ivan should rightfully handle.

She'd volunteered herself, not Ivan, for the Science Olympiad, she told herself firmly as her resentment bubbled. If she was in over her head, it wasn't Ivan's fault.

Conner sat patiently, chatting up possible methods of attaching this stick to that scrap. It would never be won, this battle against inertia. She couldn't even move Ivan from the den to the dining room table. She sighed and watched Conner's plump hands rummage through the mess. "How about these, Mom?" He held up two sticks that almost looked like wings.

"Here's the glue. Give it a whirl."

He attached the wings to a fat body constructed from two flat pieces of wood affixed end to end. Fashioned a propeller from three smaller pieces and a rubber band. Moor helped him attach plastic sheathing to the wings, and they went outside to the deck for a test flight. Conner nudged it airborne with a gentle flick of his wrist. Immediately the plane banked a hard right into the bushes. The plane collapsed on impact. Wreckage pocked the yew's flat top.

"We'll never get it to work on time!"

"Don't overreact, sweetie. It's our first try."

"Terrence is gonna kill me!" Conner's voice shook. Tears streamed down his round cheeks. He cupped a hand to his brow to hide them from her, a man's gesture.

"Conner, Terrence is not going to kill you." She laid a hand on his shoulder.

"You don't know him!"

"Yes, I do. The little asshole doesn't know how to behave. It's just an expression he uses. He doesn't mean it."

"Don't swear, Mom." He stared at the wounded plane. Not once had he reminded her that she'd promised him help from his papa.

"Come on." She grabbed his hand and walked him through the house, down those two steps into the den as if descending into a pit. Ivan was hunched over a manual, his sagging shoulders forbidding humps in the dim light. When he raised his head, his full beard hid the annoyed curl of his lips from Conner, although Moor saw his expression plainly.

"We need your help with this plane," she told him in her firmest nonnegotiable tone.

"I have a deadline."

"So do we. The Olympiad is this Saturday."

Ivan rested a broad hand on Conner's shoulder. Moor burned when Conner flinched. "Son, I would love to help you tomorrow. Tonight, it is impossible."

"Sure, Papa."

"I've got to do a test flight tomorrow night."

"Moor, it is difficult for me."

"You can get up early tomorrow to work. Besides, this won't take you long. You loved model planes as a kid. Shit, you *designed* planes for a living, once."

"Mom." Conner winced. "Don't *swear*."

"Once upon a time," Ivan said gravely. But he hoisted the manual and his notes—Cyrillic script, she saw, he still organized his thoughts in their first language—onto a side table. You'd think it was a funeral, Moor thought bitterly as he shuffled after them to the dining room.

But she had to hand it to him. At the sight of the detritus, his mourning transformed. He took in the materials with a thoughtful eye and sat elbow to elbow with Conner while sifting efficiently through the junk. Moor poured herself a glass of Shiraz and leaned against the doorjamb to watch the rare sight of Ivan ignited and Conner absorbing his spark. Before long they had the frame constructed.

"Will it fly, Papa?" Conner asked.

"The laws of physics can be counted on if we meet their requirements. There are forces at work that, if we respond to them correctly in our design, will make flight certain."

"What's physics?"

"It is the study of force. Matter, and energy, and motion."

"Like flying?"

"Like flying."

"What are the forces of flying?"

And Ivan smiled, a crimson pucker beneath his whiskers. "We have four. We have lift, and gravity; and thrust, and drag." By then Ivan had covered the wooden ribs with plastic sheathing. He held the plane level, ran his long fingers from the nose to the tail. "And we must balance all of these forces to achieve flight. This is called equilibrium. The wings will give us lift, to counter gravity."

"Here're some wings." Conner plucked two flat pieces of balsa wood from the jumble. Moor watched him hold the wings steady while Ivan glued them in place, and suddenly she remembered how Will had ruffled Conner's hair affectionately, the gesture so natural it seemed Will performed it unconsciously. Will had called him buddy and Conner had drawn close to him, also unconsciously.

Ivan's sole endearment was *son*.

By the time she'd finished her wine, they'd moved to the deck for a preliminary run. Ivan showed Conner how to launch the plane at the best angle to catch the wind under the wings. The plane glided gracefully, vanished in the dark.

"You see." Ivan sounded pleased. "All forces working together."

Conner nodded. "But what about the controls?"

"Just simple wiring for the remote. And now, run out to the big pine and get your plane. With this breeze it will have gone at least that far."

Conner bounded from the deck. Ivan settled his arm around Moor's shoulders. "You're happy with the job we have done?" he asked quietly.

"It makes a difference to him when you get involved."

"It's you I want to reach."

"You should have signed up to coach an Olympiad event." She said it lightly, but Ivan dropped his arm to his side. "You'll come on Saturday afternoon to watch him?"

"I will be in the office all morning. I will try."

Conner appeared in the splash of light spilling from the back door. "I found it! It went all the way to the end of the yard, near the fence. You know, Mama. It landed right where we found Boxer. Remember?"

Moor swallowed. "I remember, sweetie."

"I wish we could get another dog."

"You're all the puppy I can handle right now." Her stock answer, which provoked his stock exasperated grin up at her.

"Come on, Papa. Time for the controls."

"In a moment." They watched Conner dart into the kitchen, clutching his plane. Ivan slipped his hand into hers. Moor suppressed an instinctual pulling away. "You think this competition is right for him? Being an eager learner is enough, I think."

Moor gave in to her impulse and took back her hand. "He needs to learn how to be eager to win."

"He'd be that already if it were in his nature."

"That's not true. Our natures were fucked over by the time we were his age."

"There's no cause to swear," Ivan chided.

Moor shook her head. He should know all about the fragility of temperament. Ivan's nature had been changed by what he'd seen; Moor's, by what she hadn't.

As a boy in Leningrad, Ivan had been out for a walk with his grandfather when a man in a glossy mink hat dragged Dedyushka into an alley and stabbed him with an ice axe. Just like Trotsky, Ivan had tried to joke when she was still just a volunteer at the agency and it was his sad story she was absorbing. Although it was against protocol to touch, she had taken his hand lightly in hers. He showed her the petal-shaped scar on his collarbone where the axe had slipped and pierced his wool coat before he'd managed to sprint down the alleyway and hide behind a dumpster. The man in the glossy mink hat had kicked Dedyushka's corpse and then disappeared. Blood poured from Dedyushka's eye like an accidental leak. He'd reached out for Ivan, but Ivan couldn't move from his hiding place. He'd listened to Dedyushka call his name, and then stop calling for him. He'd watched as the body was discovered and removed. For three days he ate discarded bits of sausage and potato before a garbage collector discovered him. Even then, he'd come out swinging a broken mop handle, cracked the trash man's knees.

Because they were holding hands, she'd told him her story. She was six years old, living in Moscow. She'd heard something break, so she'd gone to the living room. She would always remember the crystal ring of shattering glass and wonder why she'd never found the shards of whatever had broken. The front door was closing. No one had cried out. Except for that first crash the scene was soundless. Yet she knew Mama was on the wrong side of the closing door. She'd approached, and the man must have heard her stocking feet gliding on the oak, because he burst back through and was upon her, fist raised high, angry amber-streaked eyes glittering, and she'd understood that the fist would crush her no matter where she tried to move. So she stood perfectly still. It's what bunnies do, Mama had told her once. Even when trapped in plain sight, they freeze. In stillness lies safety.

It worked.

The man's fist unclenched. The amber-streaked eyes widened. She never would understand their expression, although the eyes lived in her still and her adult perspective should have deciphered their mystery by now.

The door had closed, Mama on the wrong side of it. Was the abduction an affair or an assassination? Was the amber-eyed man a lover or a jailer? Papa never would say. They'd moved to America, re-created a life. Papa had died silent. Parkinson's. Immobile at his end.

She knew as little of her mother's crimes and passions as Ivan knew of his dedyushka's, but then, in Russia finding answers never was the concern. Leaving forever the place where retribution was the sole portion of justice preoccupied anyone who witnessed the imbalance between *why* and vengeance.

"Not everyone sticks to their natures to get what they want," Moor said as a cold breeze fluffed Ivan's beard.

"No. But we could at least wait to see what he wants."

"I don't think we can wait." Anger bloated her voice. "And I don't think we should be giving him the message that it's against his nature to compete."

"Being eager to win is not the same thing as being a successful competitor, Moor."

This was the moment, Moor thought suddenly. Not to confess. Confessions were bids for attention. What she wanted was momentum. Will wasn't about wanting. He was about doing.

But just then Conner ran up to them, trailing wire like tendrils of wisteria, eyes shining, and the impossibility of her situation reverberated in the high happy notes of his voice as he urged Ivan to *hurry up*.

• ••••

On Friday afternoon, Will pulled her playfully into the custodial closet and propped his head on a bleach bottle to kiss her between her legs. Moor hung on to the legs of a tippy metal shelf that rocked in time with her rhythm. The steady ping of shaking objects made her laugh as she came.

Afterward Will cradled her head in his lap, the strands of her fine hair catching on his callus-laced fingertips.

"I almost told Ivan about us last night," she said on impulse.

"Time we came out of the closet?"

"I'm serious."

"Why didn't you?"

"Conner interrupted us."

He didn't answer at once. When he finally spoke, she couldn't read anything into his voice. "What do you want to tell him?"

"What we're doing."

He laughed. "Good thing Conner interfered."

"Meaning we don't really know what we're doing?"

"We know exactly." Will kissed her, upside down. The stubble on his chin scratched her nose. "We just aren't certain we want your husband to know yet. Are we?"

"You aren't, I guess."

"I like our secret."

"How secret is a janitor's closet?"

"I always lock the door." He grinned. "Even that's not necessary. No one wants to go where the cleaning supplies live."

She looked up at him. Topsy-turvy. His even teeth where his eyes should be, his hair hanging down in a straight blond fan, the folds of his brow burrowing into his skin as deeply as a smile. She sat up, dizzy from gazing at the dislocated pieces of him. "Do you have anyone to tell?"

"My ex-wife."

Moor stared at him. She'd no idea he was divorced. What a relief it was to know so little about him. "There's an ex?"

"She left me after the business failed. Guess she didn't want to fuck the janitor, like some high school chick."

Moor flushed. *I'm fucking the janitor.* Had Kay told him about their conversation in the bar?

But he flashed his wide-open smile and kissed her deeply before releasing her into the hallway. As she waited, she thought of Conner packing his backpack right then, perhaps enduring a shove from Terrence, recoiling from the confident curl of Terrence's lips as he whispered, *I'm gonna kill you tomorrow.* Sweet Conner with a fallen mother who tomorrow would thrust him into the line of competition fire while secretly longing for her lover, and this was what felt like motion to her; like living, like love.

The bell rang, and although Conner was old enough to be embarrassed by her eager greeting, he sank into her hug, nestled his cheeks in the folds of her coat. The door to the custodial closet opened, and Will strolled out, tripping over his tangerine Crocs, exchanged with her their private look, brushed her hip with his arm as he tousled Conner's hair; and she wished she could stay in that closet until the Olympiad was over.

• ••••

The morning of the Olympiad passed in a suffocating crush of neon team T-shirts, banners and bullhorns, keyed-up kids to corral, video cameras affixed to parents' faces like metallic noses. In between escorting teams to competition sites, overseeing the homeroom, and comforting the third grade team when their Straw Tower collapsed on the fourth story, Moor hurried to the dome gym to watch the Wright Stuff competition. She was dismayed to see plane after plane hug the dome's curve and land smoothly at the edge of the Puff Mobiles track.

Just before lunch, dejected at a particularly amazing pair of two minute flights, she spotted Will's orange Crocs and amused grin lurking by the bleachers, watching her. Although Kay was nearby, Moor chanced a little wave, which he returned with a salute. She'd be damned if she cared whether Kay caught the public flirtation.

But she tore her attention from him at once to brood. Conner just couldn't compete with those lifts and landings.

Terrence could.

Maybe Terrence should pilot both turns. After all, Conner had provided the foundation for the win by rebuilding the plane. It was enough, Ivan would say. If he were here. She watched a girl wearing a droopy, concentrated frown bring her craft in for a smooth landing. Over the chaotic din of the gym, Moor heard the click of the judge's stopwatch, and the ghost of Ivan's low, disappointed voice: *You think this competition is right for him?*

She sighed. Time to round up Conner and Terrence for a quick slice of pizza before their time slot. Terrence would pilot both runs. She wanted that medal for Conner.

Just then she spotted Kay with Will. He was piloting a wheeled bucket with a wood-handled mop that she recognized from their closet. Kay was pointing out a mess at the entrance to the cafeteria. Some kid with an attack of competition nerves probably lost his lunch. She watched as Kay wagged a slender finger at the polished gymnasium floor. The fast flight of her lips Moor recognized as another tiresome lecture. As if Will needed her direction for a simple mop job. Will shrugged. Kay pursed her lips, and there it was; that smug glow, that hand on the bell curve of her hip. The farthest thing from a real friend Moor could have, wielding secret authority over Will's mop, and job, and heart.

Over pizza, when Terrence insisted he take over Conner's turn and Conner nodded eagerly, a dab of red sauce smearing his cheek like a gash, Moor shook her head, *no*.

• ••••

At one o'clock, she thrust the remote into Conner's sweat-soaked palm and murmured an encouragement she did not feel. She'd decided that Conner would make the first run. Then Terrence would know how much time he'd have to make up to win.

Terrence placed the plane on the taped X at the judge's feet for preflight inspection. The judge, a serious young dad with narrow glasses framing a narrower face, lifted the body with his pencil, saw that the wheels were attached securely and to spec, tapped on each wing with his eraser tip, made a note on his clipboard. Terrence scampered back to Conner's side. He snaked his fingers between Conner's to flick the remote on. Moor suppressed the urge to slap his hand away.

"You sure you want to fly it?" Terrence said.

"Mom, do I have to?"

"You'll do fine, sweetie." Moor stroked his chin. Conner looked panicked as the judge gave the thumbs up to begin.

In the circle of spectators lining the ropes, she saw Tom, Terrence's dad, flash them a grin. Next to him stood Kay, arms crossed, watching Conner taxi the plane. Conner looked ready to burst into nervous tears. Kay looked ready to leap over the rope and yank the controller away. Moor felt her stomach lurch, and then she saw Ivan, his steady eyes on Conner. She raised a hand to wave before she realized Will was standing next to him, practically touching shoulders. What on earth was Will doing, approaching Ivan that way? Had they spoken?

But of course she was being ridiculous. Their pairing was coincidence. They'd never even seen each other before.

The plane lifted smoothly from the waxed floor, a wonderful takeoff. Terrence whooped as the plane scudded high into the dome, wings dipping, tail bucking like a barnstormer. Moor glanced at Conner. His face was pinched and pale. He bit his lower lip as he tried to tame the crazy trajectory, nudge the plane into a landing curve. But the plane looped at the top of the dome, brushed like a drunken moth against the light fixture that had doomed the first plane. The motor whined as the plane bobbed and sputtered. Any second it would stall, crash to the floor, and they'd be disqualified. Moor felt her throat constrict.

"Come *on*, give it to me!" Terrence hissed at Conner's shoulder.

"Terrence, cut it out," Moor snapped.

"Mom! It's gonna crash." Conner jammed the joystick.

"I'm gonna kill you if it does."

"Don't say kill, Terrence," Moor said as the plane lurched, pirouetted nose down, and snagged in a light at the base of the dome. No chicken wire around the bowl. Will hadn't caged all the bulbs.

Conner stood mortified, the controls slack in his hands.

"Jesus Christ," Terrence groaned. "You are such a loser."

"Shut *up*, you little fucker," Moor snapped.

Conner stared at Moor aghast, two tears scuttling down his cheeks. "Don't swear, Mom," he whispered. "*Please.*"

Ivan stepped over the rope and walked briskly to Conner's side. "It's OK, Son," he said as Conner hid his tears behind his hand.

"Of course it's OK," Moor said. "He didn't do anything wrong."

"I lost the competition."

"I knew you would," Terrence scowled.

"Don't be obnoxious, Terry." Tom and Kay had joined the group. Tom cut his son off with a heavy hand on his shoulder. "Apologize to Conner."

Kay interrupted. "What a bummer. I thought Will was going to rig those fixtures, Moor." Her gaze was matter-of-fact. "Guess he dropped the ball on that one."

"Maybe he didn't feel covering the lower bulbs would be necessary."

"You'd know." Kay shrugged.

"Look, Will's got a long hooky thing." Conner pointed. Will was poking at the plane with the tall iron tool he used to adjust the height of the basketball backboards. "If he gets the plane out and it's OK, will the judge let me do it over? Terrence can pilot my turn."

"The rules say you get one shot," Kay said.

Conner's shoulders drooped. Moor's cheeks burned. "We can ask the judge, sweetie," she said, and was embarrassed to hear her voice tremble.

"Do you think so, Papa?" Conner looked anxiously up at Ivan.

"In competitions, they do not often make exceptions, Son. But." Ivan met Moor's eyes, saw her distress. "It is always acceptable to ask."

"I'd rather accept the disqualification," Kay said. "Since I'm on the district committee, it isn't cool for me to request a do-over for my son's benefit."

"The plane's cooked anyway," Terrence added.

"Terry." Tom squeezed his shoulder. Terrence rolled his eyes.

"Let me see." Conner darted to Will's side and tugged at his belt, talking a blue streak. Moor sighed and crossed to take Conner's hand.

"Can you get it?" she asked Will quietly.

The muscles on his neck strained as he guided the hook. "A ladder would help."

Moor told Conner not to jaw Will's ear off and jogged toward the exit. Kay waved her down. "What's up?"

"The custodian wants a ladder."

"I'll go," Tom offered.

"Moor can do it," Kay said. "She knows right where it is."

Smoldering, Moor headed for the door. To her dismay, Ivan followed her. She didn't stop to wait for him. "This is too bad for Conner," he said when he caught up with her in the crowded hallway.

"I don't need your criticism."

"I am not criticizing."

"You didn't think this was right for Conner. You didn't support my doing the Olympiad at all."

"I support everything you do for our son."

"Bullshit."

They had reached the closet. Ivan caught her hand. "There's no cause for swearing."

She snatched her hand away and pushed open the door.

The ladder was leaning against the tippy metal shelf she'd hung onto yesterday afternoon with Will's lips pressed to her. She flushed as Ivan retrieved it. As he lifted the ladder it knocked the shelf, upsetting the container of bleach Will had used to rest his head.

"Jesus. Can't you be more careful?" The bleach rolled across the concrete to her feet. She kicked it against the wall.

"Moor," Ivan said slowly. "When did you become so angry with me?"

He was standing before her, hefting the ladder with one arm, the other slack at his side. She looked at him and saw what she always saw. Exhaustion, and that wariness he wore. *I fuck the janitor right here on this floor.* It was time to say it. Ivan was expecting it.

"I'm not angry with you," she said instead, and turned away.

When they returned to the gym, Will was leaning against the iron hook, resting his arms. The judge huddled with Kay, Tom, Terrence, and now Linda, the district committee chair. Conner tugged at Will's shirt when he saw them. Will ruffled his hair and flashed him a reassuring grin. Moor's eyes filled with tears.

Ivan handed Will the ladder. By now Will had guessed who Ivan was, of course. "Thanks," he mumbled as he rammed a metal leg into the gym floor. A divot dimpled the waxed surface. Irritation shadowed his brow.

"Moor, we've been discussing a do-over for Conner's turn." Kay gestured for her to join the group. "Linda doesn't think we can bend the rules here."

"Is it really bending the rules, Kay?" Moor said, voice trembling. Linda was as tough as Kay, a divorce attorney who shouldn't have a spare minute to run the entire Olympiad but managed the job brilliantly anyway.

"According to Don here," Linda nodded at the judge, "the rules on disqualification are clear."

"Pilot error," Don said.

"I knew it," Terrence broke in. Tom shook his head warningly.

"Well, Kay. I don't think it's exactly a case of pilot error," Moor persisted. "Didn't I point out the hazard posed by these lights during our test flight the other day? I think I even suggested a different venue for the event."

"Will was supposed to fix that problem."

"So it's the *janitor's* fault." Kay arched her eyebrows at Moor's cool emphasis on the word. "You said yourself he dropped the ball."

"Moor's got a point there," Tom said.

Moor glanced at Ivan. True to his nature, he wasn't paying attention to the squabble. He was watching Will stretch tall on the stepladder, a stocking foot balanced on the top platform, and reach into the fixture with the long iron hook. Conner climbed up onto the second step and threw back his head, sandy hair winnowing at his neck as he lobbed instructions up to Will. The plane wiggled, nearly free.

"Ivan." Moor tapped his shoulder. "Can't you add anything to this discussion, please?"

"He took off his shoes," Ivan said. "Why would he do that?"

"What?" She took in the tangerine Crocs nested on the gym floor. "He can't wear those on the ladder. They make him trip."

Ivan turned to gaze at her, a wonder in his eyes.

Suddenly a bolt of blue light seared the air. Ivan croaked, "Conner!" as their boy sailed backward onto the floor. Will flopped down nearly on top of him. The iron rod soared, struck the oak with a gunshot clatter, the hook split neatly in two. The smoldering fork ripped a black, meandering scar into the floorboards as it scudded crazily across the gym.

Screams filled the dome. In the swirl of confusion, Kay triaged calmly with Tom. "Go to our homeroom," she instructed him. "Kaylee Tyne's dad is a doctor. Her event's at two ten, so they're up there waiting."

Tom ran off. Kay darted to Conner. At Moor's elbow, Terrence burst into hysterical tears.

As Kay knelt next to Conner, he sat up slowly, rubbing his head. Together they crawled toward Will. Moor backed away, sick with repulsion. The swollen, panicked keen echoing in the dome couldn't pierce the glass that trapped Conner and Will, kept them sharp and glaring, far from her.

She watched Conner lace his fingers in Will's hair while Kay tipped his chin up, pinched his nose, and rested her lips on his.

Moor had to find a way to break through the wrong side of the glass.

But as a crowd of parents ringed the catastrophe, Moor knew she would never move, and when she clenched her fists against her trembling, she realized Ivan's hand was clasping hers, clammy, immobile, rooted to their spot.

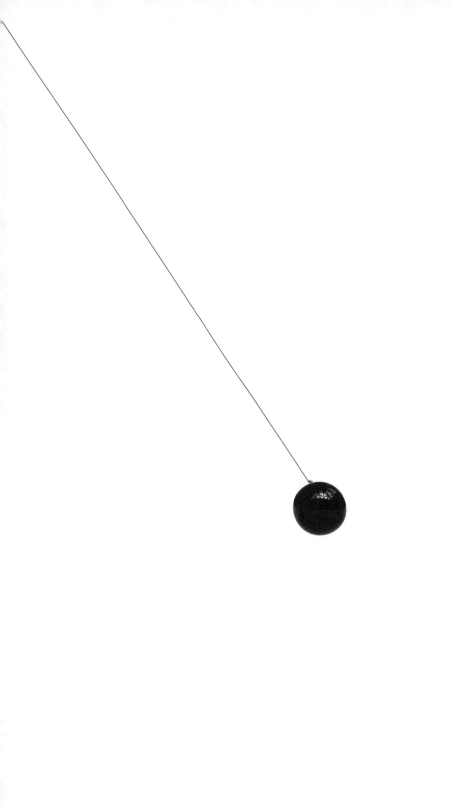

Adult Crowding

The Gold Star driver's education sedan, a real tin can, needed a tune-up. A rattle behind the glove box was unnerving the student driver at the wheel. She pulled up to the stop sign east of the Brecon strip mall and brushed away a strand of golden hair curling at her eyelash. She clamped her hand back on the wheel, fielded a glance at Jerrell's clipboard, wondered if he'd note her failure to keep her hands at nine and three o'clock. When he was a student driver, Jerrell had learned to position his hands at ten and two o'clock. Another rule he'd had to unlearn as an adult. At ten and two an airbag's force would ram the driver's arms into their face. Who knew that such a minor adjustment in position meant a driver walked away from a crash unhurt? Most of what Jerrell knew about driving he found out was either outmoded or just plain wrong when he trained at Courtesy Driving School. Earned his wings, Ruth liked to joke before her decline, back when his mother still could crack one.

Then again, Tammy might be staring at the blood he'd smeared on the student assessment sheet. Ruth had sure done a number on him, just when he thought she was plumb out of her dirty tricks. Jerrell dabbed at the oozing punctures stippling his hand with the towel he'd grabbed from Assisted Living. Snapped open the glove box to hunt down a Band-Aid. "Turn right at the Big Boy up there, about a half mile down."

He'd given her plenty of time to anticipate the turn, so Tammy's choppy acceleration through the stop Jerrell first took for nerves, not confusion. Pretty Tammy was a real Betty-and-Veronica type. Tom-Dick-and-Harry sat slouched in the back seat, eyes wide and wary. Mr. Salisbury. Jerrell always referred to the young men as mister, just in case they needed the reminder about who was boss in the driver's training instructional environment. But a young man's cockiness usually evaporated in the Gold Star car. Jerrell chalked up the humility to the situation, not anything about Jerrell's demeanor. No, the men just wanted that license fast, no hassle. The first step toward getting out of this town. Deflating the blowhards sure made the job easier to stomach. Jerrell's change from construction manager with Southeast Michigan's largest contractor to driver's ed instructor began as a desperation move during the recession but was looking more and more like a permanent career shift. At least he'd traded up on dealing with assholes.

Jerrell dug out a Band-Aid and slammed the glove box shut. Tammy flinched but kept her hands firmly on the wheel. "Mr. Jerrell? Where's the Big Boy?"

The Big Boy was now the Palace, home of finer family dining than the

Big Boy ever was. At times the places of Jerrell's youth still seeped through the town's canvas.

"Well, it used to be the Big Boy." With his uninjured hand he pointed to the restaurant's steep purple roof just past the Dairy Queen Brazier, which had always been the Brazier. Like the Speedway gas and Jackie's Tavern at the four corners, some businesses had escaped the state economy's rip tide. The A&P, the Farmer Jack, the Shanghai Shack, all had gone bust. Although the Shanghai Shack was history because the Chinese immigrant family had relocated the business to a strip mall in liberal Ann Arbor. Not that Brecon wasn't liberal, in the small town sense of the word.

"Can we get an ice cream for the ride?" Mr. Salisbury asked.

Jerrell tore open the Band-Aid and pressed it to the punctures. The deep impressions circling the wounds were filling with purple. He could just make out a bracket's smug dimple smack dab on each tooth mark. No wonder his hand hurt like hell. Dr. Frank's office was open until five on Wednesdays; Jerrell ought to know. Best to drive Tammy around a bit so he could cool off before paying the good doctor a visit. "What did we learn about driving distractions in unit six, Mr. Salisbury?"

Salisbury slumped in his seat. "I was only kidding. My dad says eating while driving increases your chance of a crash by 80 percent."

"Doesn't the textbook say 65 percent?" Tammy was bearing down fast on the Brazier.

"Watch your speed, young lady."

Tammy dutifully slowed to the posted limit. Salisbury piped up, "That's the number of *near misses* caused by eating while driving. Right, Mr. Jerrell?"

"Any type of distraction is to be avoided behind the wheel." Jerrell stared out the window at the Dairy Queen's squat barn-red roof and impassive row of shining glass windows. He hadn't even understood what a brazier was until he was these kids' age. He'd only been to the Dairy Queen once before he could drive there himself, pay for his own damn burger and fries. Even that one time, a special occasion, Ruth only allowed him to order the smallest ice cream on the menu.

"Will eating and driving be on the test?" Tammy cruised past the Brazier. On the other side of the DQ lot, the Palace's parking lot was hopping. An elderly couple, bundled in bulky coats and sweetly holding hands, was hurrying in the front door for the senior special of the day. Tammy was still failing to signal the turn ahead.

"Signaling turns will be. Left blinker, Tammy, don't forget."

"Are we doing the highway today, Mr. Jerrell?" Was the boy eager or nervous? When the young men's voices dropped their octave, it became harder to tell genuine bravado from the tough guy act. Mr. Salisbury looked to be a reluctant tough at best. The hoodlum jacket was a size too big. The leather puffed at the shoulders, shrank his round head to a pale, tiny globe. The slicked-back look didn't achieve the desired effect, either. A boyish nest of unruly curls bounced along the pizza-pie pimples on his brow. The small-town young these days were so very harmless. And, well, so very *young*.

"That's for next time, Mr. Salisbury."

"Where are we going today?"

Nervous, Jerrell decided. The childish persistence was a give-away. Mr. Salisbury had a habit of bobbling over the center line. His overcorrections mashed the wheels to the curb. Mr. Salisbury might turn out to be one of the rare few who failed driver's training. "Thought we'd stick to town today. That OK with you, Mr. Salisbury?"

The kid nodded, curled his hand around the door handle. Frequent stoplights would work to his advantage. The white, even smile flashed in the rear view mirror. Lucky kid to have that smile. Luckier still if it stayed that way.

Jerrell positioned the rearview mirror to Tammy's view. "Adjust your mirrors before you begin driving, remember. Swing a left at the golf course." He'd take Tammy out of town a bit before circling back to the four corners in the heart of downtown Brecon, if the dinky village could be said to have a downtown. Or a heart. Give the hand some time to settle into a dull throb, because the way it was howling now made Jerrell want to punch Dr. Frank right in the pickets.

"Did you know that the force of a crash can wrap a golf club right around a guy's neck?" Mr. Salisbury offered.

"That would never happen." Tammy brought a finger to her lips to perform a dainty nibble at a hangnail. "Right, Mr. Jerrell?"

"It did, though." Mr. Salisbury popped a fly over Jerrell's reassurance that no, such a thing could never happen.

"*How* do you know?"

"My dad's a crash-site investigator. Sees all kinds of bizarre shit."

"Let's watch the language," Jerrell suggested. His glance into the back seat held the embers of a warning. Mr. Salisbury grinned, blister white. Hard to tell whether it was the curry-favor type of smile or the wise-guy preamble to more trouble.

"You're seeping." Tammy hung a left past the greens without signaling.

"Left blinker next time, young lady. Don't forget."

"Your *hand*, Mr. Jerrell. You're *seeping*. What happened?"

Jerrell studied the wound. Blood had soaked through the Band-Aid.

He wondered how Tammy could have seen it and kept her eyes on the road, since his hand had been tucked in his lap. Under the clipboard. Which meant she'd scrutinized his lap. Jerrell clicked open the glove box. Rummaged for another Band-Aid and a packet of Kleenex. No future in thinking about where a little girl's gaze might rove during her driving maneuvers. "Just got hung up on something sharp there. Watch your speed."

"Did you know that in a crash a Kleenex box can kill you if the sharp edge hits you in the temple?" the backseat peanut gallery informed them.

"That would never happen." Tammy's nibble was more doubtful this time around.

"Can so. Killed this one guy. Dad said it was a freak thing."

Tammy glanced at Jerrell's tissues. Jerrell tucked the packet between his knees, under the clipboard. Swabbed the blood, crisscrossed another Band-Aid over the first.

"Dad said anything can kill you if it hits your temple dead-on," Mr. Salisbury added.

"I don't think we should be talking about car accidents during driver's training. Right, Mr. Jerrell?" Tammy applied the brake, glided to a four-way stop. Already they were in the suburbs. The threshold between town and country in this flat patch of Michigan farmland was a matter of a couple of miles. Modest ranch homes lined the private cul-de-sacs cut rudely from long-fallow cornfields. An abandoned cobblestone farmhouse stood near the intersection, the weed-choked driveway shaded by maples just shedding their crimson leaves. Traffic was backed up behind the Gold Star sedan. Tammy was waiting for Jerrell's instruction. Which he'd failed to give, fooling with his hand. He rode out a wave of rage over Ruth's nasty decline, Dr. Frank's chintzy orthodontics, the blood dribbling from the second Band-Aid's tan edge.

"There are no accidents when it comes to transportation. Only crashes." Mr. Salisbury leaned forward, gripped the back of Tammy's headrest. "My dad says someone's always at fault."

Jerrell couldn't agree more.

• ••••

Before this decline, Jerrell could make short work of Ruth's care. Between sessions he'd pull up to Brecon Heights Assisted Living for a quick dash in. *Need anything, Mom?* He'd have to sort the errands from the complaints. *My legs feel like pin cushions, Son, I'm so fuzzy in the head, I have my taste for butterscotch back so bad.* So during the next instructional run he'd grab a bag of Werther's, the only obtainable mercy on that list.

But with this decline there were mercies of the body to perform, rituals just shy of washing the dead. That's what the Assisted Living Staff was calling his mother's condition. This decline. Like this and that. Like there would be *this* decline, and then there would be *that* decline. The Assisted Living Staff would only do so much for Ruth, and Jerrell did the rest.

This decline meant stiff, painful limbs to massage, groans of pleasure to endure under the sensual relief of his hands.

This decline meant thrush. Jerrell would thrust his fingers into his mother's mouth to clear the cottony fungus so she could swallow. Ice chips under her tongue soothed the inflammation. Despite the gruesome infection, Jerrell came to realize that he found her mouth comforting in ways he didn't care to investigate. Like her baby's-milk breath, sour and new. Like the last thing she would ever give him was this tenderness. Maybe make up for the mother she'd never been, or the son he'd failed to be, their chicken-and-egg, their covenant. Also the warm sensation distracted him from the hope that *this* decline would turn out to be *the* decline.

Yesterday the Assisted Living Staff told Jerrell this infection might be resistant to the usual treatments. The Assisted Living Staff blamed the thrush on the morphine, but Jerrell had his own ideas about the cause. He'd looked it up, had goddamn *confirmed* that the braces could be, were very *likely* to be, the wellspring of the trouble. Metal complicated the mouth's environment, he'd read. One obtainable mercy was to have the damn brackets removed. Yet another was a refund.

Today, before he left Ruth to meet Tammy and Mr. Salisbury, the situation had escalated. The mucus lodged in Ruth's throat like a jellyfish. Clearing the goo and scrubbing his hands at the kitchenette sink was a long, painstaking process. After he was clean, Jerrell filled a Dixie cup full of ice chips and pulled a hard chair from the dinette to her bedside. As he slipped ice under her tongue, he let his fingers linger in her mouth. Her irritated gums pillowed the gleaming brackets. He had to be careful around the unmoored wire dangling from her left molar. The braces made the swabbing and the icing a surefire hazard. Yesterday he'd nicked his palm on the wire. He'd taken up pliers himself, tucked the wire back into her cheek's soft pouch. Yet another reason the braces had to go. Dr. Frank was no longer returning Jerrell's calls about his mother's oral health and welfare, so a visit to the man's office was, in Jerrell's view, unavoidable. Anyway, the student drivers never minded a midsession break, he reasoned. The kids could grab a soda at the Lucky Drug while Jerrell took care of business.

A quickening of his mother's parchment eyelids startled Jerrell mid-icing. He pulled his hand from her mouth.

"I feel like a zombie." Ruth blinked at him as if he were a puff of air, the looking-through he'd always hated.

"What, Mom?" Jerrell had heard her perfectly. But Ruth's spiritual and moral outlook did not include the possibility of the undead, so her statement was odd.

"I feel like a zombie."

Well, that could mean anything. She could barely move her legs. She complained constantly about her sizzling nerves, live wires under her skin that ignited sensation but not movement. Or morphine could be the zombie. This decline involved liberal, even dangerous, levels of morphine. The Assisted Living Staff had cautioned against accidental overdose, but the caution had been given with that clinical boredom he resented, as if to say *don't be too careful, might be doing her a favor.* Any accident was all up to Jerrell, was what they seemed to be saying.

"Come again, Mom?" Jerrell pulled the chair closer, looked deep into those periwinkle eyes. Hammered metal was her usual expression, but she was soft today, fuzzy, addled. A film on her gaze, her limbs dopey and slow. Good things come in threes, had been his thinking there. So did death. Not that Jerrell was superstitious. But she'd barely spoken in a week, so if she said one thing three times, well, that could be a sign.

But she wouldn't say it the third time, only looked at him placidly. Like she used to watch his silent weeping, satisfied he was keeping quiet after she decked him for his smart mouth. *Mama's little man.* Back then messing him up had been her only joy. Maybe she was just screwing with him now for old time's sake.

Jerrell stood up. One of Ruth's Hull Collectible treasures, the Sad Eyes puppy, mooned over the wadded Kleenex and pill boxes scattered on her bedside table. The baseboards hummed. Geriatric humidity wafted from the slats, reeking of rose water and rubbing alcohol. Jerrell took up a tissue. Wiped a rivulet of cloudy water from her chin. "Want a popsicle, Mom?"

"Butterscotch, Son." A command. A plea. Hard to say anymore what she was really trying to tell him. The blue bird clock on the kitchenette wall chimed the hour. Another of those damn Hull Collectibles she'd worried would never make it to Assisted Living in one piece. Ruth especially treasured her Swan Planters, a horrifying duo trumpeting from the sofa table, enormous brown bills held high like military buglers, open backs filled with sparse sprigs of dried flowers where the internal organs would be. Jerrell had carried in each bird under Ruth's anxious watch from her old green recliner he'd placed by the apartment's only window. He'd positioned each swan so the light wouldn't catch the jagged fracture line where the bills were glued to the downy white jaws. His mother did not like to be reminded of Jerrell's hoodlum stunt. Cared more for the collectibles' welfare than his. He'd never liked that schmaltzy crap, anyway. Used to scare him as a kid. Who was afraid of puppies and swans and tiny birds daisy-chained around a clock face? But the exaggerated features had upset him when he was, himself, tiny. He still cringed at the puppy's droopy eyes, those trumpeting swan bills like trippy clown feet.

Jerrell crossed to the refrigerator. The clock finished chiming. School was letting out. Tammy and Mr. Salisbury would be arriving at the Gold Star training center for their second cruise. He dug more ice from the plastic bin in the freezer. Slivered some chunks with a steak knife. Wished he could afford to install an icemaker that would crush the cubes for him. He filled the cup, unwrapped a Werther's. Hard candy wasn't allowed on the Brace Watcher's Diet, but seeing as those damn things were coming out if Jerrell had his way, what was the harm in a little sweet?

A high sound drifted from the bed. Jerrell turned to see Ruth's arm arcing in a ballerina's flourish. Her back arched off the mattress. Her loose breasts rolled under her lacy housecoat. Blood soared down her chin, freckled her housecoat's scallop neckline. The broken wire must have cut her when she cried out.

Quickly, Jerrell buzzed the red button by the wall phone.

The response was prompt. With that practiced, bored efficiency, the young Assisted Living Staffer took in the arcing arm, the stiffened limbs, and arching back, the high pitched lonesome wail. "She's keening."

Jerrell moistened a cloth to clean up the blood. "Come again?"

"Keening." The young woman moved to the bedside. A real Morticia, with the pale skin and perfect ebony widow's peak. A lovely cloak on a ghoulish heart. She pressed the morphine-drip pump's button. A hiss, and Ruth's arm floated to her hip. Her legs shuddered, her back relaxed. The lonesome wail dropped to a low whistle, faded into the rosewater air. "It's a stage of this decline."

Jerrell squeezed the cloth to Ruth's chin. Rage bathed him, the source of which he didn't care to investigate. Might be the blood foaming around the brackets, a mark of his failure to fix and please her. Might be the way this Assisted Living Staffer, not much older than his teen drivers, viewed his mother's terrifying ballet as routine.

Might be Ruth, acting out just to scare him.

He wanted to pinch her wrinkled chin, get her to cut that shit out. Show her a thing or two now that she was down for the count. Didn't it stand to reason that after all those years of being slapped around he'd want to give her some of it back? What was his duty toward Ruth anyway, considering the mess she'd made of her duty toward him?

The Assisted Living Staffer moved to the bedside table. Her soft shoes hummed on the floorboards. She checked the pill box contents. Must have approved of Jerrell's organization because back the box went between the Sad Eyes puppy paws.

Well, no future in thinking about who owed whom, anyway. There his mother lay, and over her suffering body he would stand under Assisted Living's watchful eye. As Lydia would say, quit your brooding and do what you have to do. Which ended up being exactly what Lydia did. She was always complaining about his complicated feelings for his mother, but a woman didn't leave a man just for being a dutiful son.

"I have to go to work," he told the Assisted Living Staffer. "Can she be left like this?"

"The final stages could go on for hours. Or days."

Jerrell noted *stages*, plural. So there would be this stage, and then that stage. Assisted Living was likely to withhold from him the secrets and torments of the future, and anyway it didn't occur to him to ask what came next.

"We'll notify you of any change in your mother's condition." The young woman gave him what he supposed was meant to be a reassuring glance but appeared sly, a prompting, a knowing exchange. What was he supposed to know? His father had dropped dead of a stroke. Only one stage to that passing.

The Assisted Living Staffer checked the pump and left. As soon as the apartment door clicked shut, Ruth's eyes fluttered open. A flush rose to her cheeks, as if the blood the braces had drawn was rising to her skin. She flashed the hideous smile. The brackets glittered, the blood washed away, swallowed, or healed. Her hand flew to cover her mouth and her ugly puckered chin.

Both Jerrell and Ruth smothered mirth with their open palms. Crowding was their shared trait. Their narrow jaws stabled horsey teeth. Their canines jutted like rock outcroppings over the lower teeth twisting half-cocked. For all of six months in high school, Jerrell's braces had fixed the problem. He endured two years of painful adjustments. The old-style wrap-around bands pushed deep into his gums, ended up causing permanent recession. But after the suffering, he'd flashed a perfect grin. He'd broken the habit of slapping his hand to his mouth when he smiled. He laughed more often. He'd worn his retainer as directed.

But in the end, the teeth buckled back to where they'd always been.

The rage stirred again. Dr. Frank and his chintzy work.

"Don't worry about those braces anymore, Mom. They're coming out, I promise. Here's your Werther's. Open wide."

The mouth yawned open hungrily. White scales blanketed the tongue like unraveled lace. He tucked in the candy. Left his hand there a moment, tunneled back a bit to feel the warm soft pressure. Her eyes widened, flashed their flinty metal. Her jaw stiffened, snapped shut. Her teeth sank hard into the back of his hand.

Jesus! He grabbed her jaw sockets with his free hand, pinched hard, hard! Rammed his hurt hand down her throat, down, down, thrusting with all his might to the place where he began.

She gagged and let go.

Jerrell yanked out his hand. Goddamn *punctured*. Blood bubbled from the wounds. Her teeth and brackets imprinted his skin in a craggy oval. He wrapped the wet towel around his hand and stared at her. Was she out of her mind? Or was hurting him, even now, her natural reflex?

Was that a bruise rising along her jaw line, seeping through her wrinkles' waterfall?

She stared at him, clear eyed. He followed a movement of her throat. The butterscotch candy eased down the stubborn gullet.

His hand moved to the morphine pump, her gaze attached. He punched the button. His arm tingled with the machine's hiss. How much juice would it take to get her to quit staring at him? To assist her to sleep? To ease *his* pain?

"Do you feel like a zombie now, Mom?" *Come again.* He willed her to speak. Third time's the charm.

Her arm sailed. The keening rose from a low place in her throat. Jerrell pulled his finger from the button. When the machine fell silent, she looked right through him again, unruffled. No matter how strongly he came at her, she would always come right back at him stronger. He hated her with a searing hot flame. He loved her with all his heart. No decline would ever be *the* decline.

Jerrell had stepped away from the bed, pulled on his Gold Star jacket. He'd stop for Vernors on the training run with Tammy and Mr. Salisbury. He'd return to quench Ruth's tormented thirst, pour that butterscotch right down her hatch.

•　••••

"It's Dad's job to find fault because there has to be *someone* to sue. Although you can't really sue Kleenex for a freak incident, Dad says." Mr. Salisbury's face was level with the front headrests, his pale skin backlit with excitement over his old man's outlook on the freakish.

Tammy nibbled another nail.

"Both hands on the wheel, Tammy. Proceed through the intersection." Jerrell glanced at Mr. Salisbury with an uptick in the strict act. "Let's sit back in our seat, Ace. Your job right now is to observe."

Mr. Salisbury sat back dutifully. The next four-way stop, the last one before they arrived back in town, was a mile down the road. Traffic picked up, glided past at a fast clip. A Chevy Suburban passed Tammy with a roar. She jumped. "Never mind that, Tammy." Jerrell resisted the urge to pat her knee. "You're doing fine."

The glove box rattled on a gravelly stretch of pavement. Tammy fiddled nervously with the rear view mirror. "What *is* that noise, Mr. Jerrell? Is something wrong with the car?"

"Do you see a warning indicator lit up?"

Tammy's lovely green eyes flickered down to peer between her hands. "No."

"Then there's nothing to worry about. The cause of a dash rattle is notoriously tough to pin down. Could be a screw, or something with the wire harness. But it's not serious. Not if there's no warning light."

Tammy looked at him with the feminine doubt hardwired to assume that any niggling noise meant that something critical to the vehicle's operation was about to blow the car up. His reassurance speech had never worked on Lydia, either. She was always complaining that Jerrell never kept the Bronco tuned up, but a woman didn't leave a man just over minor lapses in auto maintenance.

Jerrell wadded up the bloody tissue and stuffed it in the glove box. Checked quickly for the rattle's source but found only the expected soft detritus. Vehicle manual and registration in the cheap vinyl pouch, some ketchup packets from the Burger King. The box of Band-Aids he'd left open had toppled over. His silver flask was stashed in the back, real silver, too, but filled with whiskey there was no way it was making that much noise. The car definitely needed a tune-up. Just in case, Jerrell stuffed the bloody towel he'd thrown on the floor mat around the flask.

"Knocks and pings are just routine engine sounds. Get 'em checked at the earliest convenient opportunity, is all there is to that. Turn right at the cemetery up there."

Tammy pulled the turn indicator. "You ever hold your breath, Mr. Jerrell?"

"Come again?"

"When passing a cemetery."

"I used to do that." Mr. Salisbury fidgeted with his lap belt.

"I still do." Tammy caught her breath the moment the Gold Star fender drew parallel to the town cemetery's iron fence. Her slender fingers gripped the steering wheel. Her knuckles, smooth, fleshy half-moons, flashed white.

"Let's breathe through the intersection, Tammy," Jerrell suggested. But Tammy held her breath through a roll past the stop sign. Her cheeks pinked. Her lips tensed in a pout. Her thighs flexed under her tight jeans. Jerrell fastened a stare on the windshield. No future in noting stimulating changes in a little girl's physique. He covered the instructor brake, checked for any cars barreling through the intersection, blessedly none. "That's called a rolling stop, Miss."

Tammy breathed, a moist whoosh that blended with the air vents' hum. "Sorry, Mr. Jerrell." The glove box rattled over the uneven pavement in front of the Brilliant Ford dealership. Tammy white-knuckled the center line to avoid the broken asphalt.

"You can't observe traffic safely if you don't bring the vehicle to a full stop."

"Especially if you don't *breathe*. Stupid little-kid trick," Mr. Salisbury muttered.

Tammy shot him a furious look in the mirror. "It's *not*. The souls of the dead can ride right inside you on your air."

"So, I breathed. Why don't I have dead people in me right now?"

"Who says you *don't*? Didn't kids ever hold their breath in your day, Mr. Jerrell?"

Somewhere along the way Jerrell's youth had become *your day* to the young people. "Proceed for a half mile. No, I never did hold my breath," he added when Tammy glanced at him, a brief, sidelong disappointment. He'd always felt something was dead inside of him, anyway. And the town cemetery, beautifully manicured, populated by regular funerals and cheery blossom sprays left by the adoring living, was a damn safe sight, in his opinion. He'd welcome in any dead so well loved.

"Aren't you religious?" Mr. Salisbury piped up.

Tammy chose to ignore Mr. Salisbury by keeping her gaze firmly on the gentle curve into downtown. Good call. "Start slowing down past First Lutheran," Jerrell instructed when the familiar gold-tipped spire glided into view. "The posted limit there is twenty-five. Take a left at the four corners."

"Your mom taught Sunday school, right?" Mr. Salisbury had decided on a persistence he never brought to bear on mastering his driving skills.

"So what?" Tammy flicked him a brief, dismissive glance in the mirror. Braked mildly at the four corners' stoplight. Lucky Drugs and the tavern stood opposite one another on Michigan Avenue. The home-decor shop where Ruth used to buy her Hull Collectibles was long gone. So was the Kresge. A bank and an optometrist occupied those storefronts now. Tammy eased into the left-turn lane next to a silver Volvo. The driver, a real Ozzie Nelson type, glanced doubtfully at the lurid Gold Star decals. The company mascot, a cartoon car with rubber balloons for wheels and a blubbery grin, filled the passenger door. Garish yellow stars splashed the side panel. A real carnival to announce the student drivers.

"Left blinker, don't forget," Jerrell reminded Tammy. She dutifully pulled the turn indicator.

"So, you believe that souls rise to Heaven. So, in that case, there wouldn't be any souls of the dead left on earth to get inside you. So, why hold your breath?"

"Not everyone gets to Heaven." Jerrell couldn't help defending Tammy's superstition, harmless and cute. Just the type of girlish habit that would make her a kind, spirited woman to love.

"So we're talking zombie souls here."

Jerrell's hand throbbed. Across the intersection, two men dressed in blue Con Ed overalls walked across the UAW lot on their way to Jackie's Tavern. With the workday shift finished, the drinking shift could begin. Jerrell used to be one of the Jackie's late-afternoon regulars, but the driver's training after-school schedule prevented him from joining in now.

"There's no such thing as zombies." The light clicked green. Although the oncoming traffic cleared quickly, Tammy's sneaker didn't move from the brake. "That's dumb kid stuff."

"Proceed cautiously through the intersection," Jerrell reminded her. With a swift, careful sweep of her slim neck, Tammy took the turn down Michigan Avenue.

"So all I'm saying is, if you believe in Heaven and you don't believe in zombies, why hold your breath?" Mr. Salisbury persisted.

"How do you know my mom taught Sunday school? You don't go to my church."

Mr. Salisbury clicked his tongue. "I just *know*."

"*How* do you know?" Tammy stared at Mr. Salisbury in the rear view mirror.

"Eyes on the road, young lady. I'm gonna have you parallel park up there at the meter outside Dr. Frank's office." Jerrell turned as if to check the traffic and instead fixed a warning glare on Mr. Salisbury to lay off. Unlike the tough guys he used to deal with on site, young Ace shrank into his seat. His turn next, was what he understood from Jerrell's glare.

Tammy slowed to a creep. Glanced doubtfully at the tight space between a tan Ford Expedition and a burgundy Dodge Ram. "Think there's room?"

The Gold Star sedan could fit into any dinky crawlspace. Jerrell ought to know. "Plenty, Tammy." Tammy relaxed a bit. Fatherly reassurance offered at just the right moment was the best part of the job.

Tammy positioned the vehicle just as she'd been taught. Rear fender aligned with the rear of the Expedition. She craned her neck backward, rotated the wheel, released the brake. Jerrell glanced back to check her aim. Saw Mr. Salisbury guiding her with a low flutter of his hand. *Keep coming, keep coming.* An unexpected kindness from the smart aleck. Jerrell tamped down a flicker of annoyance.

After the endless amateur jerking back and forth, Mr. Salisbury guiding every adjustment to her alignment, Tammy pulled the gearshift to park and beamed at Jerrell. She glowed with relief at the successful completion of what the student driver thought would be the hardest test.

But Jerrell was saving the real tough stuff for kind guide Ace back there, the maneuver that had quickly made Jerrell a legend. The dodgy turn, the one his former students always talked about, past Beech to Fuller where the road teed into State at the old train bridge. There the old bridge column completely obstructed the left sightline. The student driver had to nose out practically to the middle of State to see. Even for an experienced driver, the turn was a wing and a prayer. The kids always accused Jerrell of trying to trick them by taking them to the one impossible turn in the worst part of town, where no one ever goes anymore, anyway. Well, it was his job to prepare them for even the most unlikely scenarios, wasn't it?

"Well done, Tammy." Jerrell scratched some notes. Mr. Salisbury flashed a thumbs-up. "Tell you what, kids. Gotta run a quick errand here at Dr. Frank's."

"He was my ortho." Tammy's sculpted jaw and perfect grin was a damn testament to that.

"Mine, too," chorused from the back seat.

"Stretch your legs, why don't you, and switch drivers." Jerrell glanced into the back seat. "Ready for your spin, young man?"

Salisbury nodded, all contrite. Actually followed the affirmative with *sir*. We'll see about that, was Jerrell's reaction. Golf clubs and Kleenex would be the least of Mr. Salisbury's concerns this afternoon. Jerrell heaved stiffly out of the vehicle. Didn't mean to slam the passenger door so hard. The chintzy Gold Star corporate stars wobbled under the impact. The mascot flashed a perfect picket line of white teeth. The sedan looked real rinky-dink between the Detroit steel boxing it in.

Inside the car, Tammy had swiveled to face Mr. Salisbury. Her slim leg was slung over the armrest, swinging girlishly. She twined her golden hair between two slender fingers. Jerrell felt a sudden stab of longing. Not for the girl, no future in that thinking. He loathed admitting he missed Lydia, but she'd taken his soul when she left, no denying it. She could blame the recession all she wanted, but a woman didn't abandon a man just over money. Always more to it than a man's fortune.

Tammy nibbled the frizzy ends of her golden hair. Rinky-dink Gold Star clown car. Rinky-dink recession job. Jerrell would have to find his way to change, and soon.

• ••••

Frank's work on Ruth had been shabby from the start. The wires were always popping their sockets. Ruth's gums bled torrents when she was cut so Jerrell was forced to schedule frequent repairs between routine appointments. Dr. Frank insisted that Ruth must be *violating* the Brace Watcher's Diet by eating popcorn or hard candy. Dr. Frank was a real Snidely Whiplash, in Jerrell's opinion, and besides no way could the Werther's cause that much damage. Chintzy materials and poor workmanship were the cause, just like the construction shoddiness he'd spent his career mitigating before the whole industry went down the sinkhole. No one built anything like they used to.

Jerrell should have known the work would be a bust. Hadn't his own teeth shifted? His father, too, had asked Jerrell's orthodontist for a refund in his timid-ass way. The orthodontist was a real bully, not that it was tough to bully Jerrell's dad, a real Stan Laurel except Dad's wimp act wasn't funny at all. The doctor pointed out that to ensure sure-proof results Jerrell should have consented to have his jaw broken and rewired. Well, having his jaw broken once had been plenty for Jerrell. Ruth hadn't insisted he give in to the ortho, either, which was one of their covenants.

His teeth were a real shame, and so were Ruth's. She'd wanted braces her whole life. But she'd grown up with a stingy father and had married a pragmatic man with bad teeth who loved her the way she was and *so what* if in *their day,* prefluoride, preorthodontics, everyone's teeth were freak shows. Back then, teeth were a level playing field between men and women. Ashes to ashes, mouth to mouth. But Ruth carried the shame of her flaw like grief. Maybe because she was a woman, the shock to her vanity never faded.

In all other respects, she'd been beautiful. Had even modeled for a local designer once. A real knockout on the UAW hall velvet runway, with vivid upswept hair and perfect skin. All decked out in fancy skirts and tall slender heels skinny as pipe cleaners and wide brimmed hats with bright-pink polka dots. During the modeling stint, they'd all enjoyed a few months when Ruth was a stunning woman with a minor flaw, a flaw easily hidden behind her graceful hand.

But at the UAW benefit banquet, Jerrell had *acted out* when his mother was pirouetting down the red-carpeted platform. All he did was wave at her. Maybe he'd called out to her. He was a teenager, old enough to behave himself, not cry out like some baby startled to see his mother behind clown-red lipstick and white face powder. She'd pretended to smile but hadn't covered up with her hand in time because she was hissing at him to *pipe down*. Big horsey teeth, ugly puckered chin. Not runway material, not even for the local designer outfit. She'd never been asked to model again.

So when Dad dropped dead and Ruth, in Jerrell's view, had no choice but to move to Assisted Living, why not fix her teeth to ease the transition? A total waste of money, Lydia had called the gift when he'd dipped into their dwindling retirement to cover the work. The last straw, she'd called it. Well, a woman never left a man just over making his mother happy, and the gift had made Ruth deliriously happy. Her dream come true. Made all the crap he'd put up with all his life almost worth it. More to the point, the gift made her docile for the move to Assisted Living.

Jerrell cruised past reception to waylay the doctor. What a racket, orthodontics. In the midst of the downturn, Frank's waiting room was filled with the young and their antsy parents sipping big-portioned coffees and tapping at their smartphones and tablets as if there wasn't a damn recession going on everywhere but this office. The latest Disney looped on the play-nook's television, the screen level with the formative jaws awaiting expansion. In the second waiting room—business was so robust Frank needed two holding chambers—an entire wall was papered with video-game screens. A legion of gamers sat cross-legged on the floor. Indian style, Jerrell still called the pose. The good doctor kept the volume muted and the games mild. Eerily silent hedgehogs nimbly scaled bushes and streams to the low buzz of orthodontic tools wafting from the adjustment room. The young, too, kept their silence. Responding to conditions, Jerrell supposed.

The bank of screens sure did keep the kids calm for the painful adjustments awaiting them. Dr. Frank sure knew how to lash his clients right to the rails. The place was a far cry from the sepulcher office of Jerrell's boyhood orthodontist. Dr. Cannon the man's name, no joke. As humorless as his dull potted-fern waiting room, last year's *Reader's Digest* and *Good Housekeeping* the only stimulants. Hairy knuckles, a hard way with the appliances. Jerrell never much liked his mouth touched after Cannon. He never enjoyed necking, for instance. Another of Lydia's complaints, but it wasn't like he *wouldn't* lock lips under the right mood and circumstance, and anyway a woman didn't leave a man just over a mild aversion to kissing.

"Excuse me, sir?" The receptionist's lilt, an anticipated obstacle. The trick lay in figuring out which of the four young women behind the low counter was trying to detain him. Dr. Frank was actually hiring, then. On the last visit, a trio of beautiful grins had flashed Ruth as she shuffled past the play-nook, gums weeping.

"I have an appointment." A lie, but desperate measures for desperate times, plus, *Christ*, the man should return a phone call.

A click of the computer mouse, a flash from the monitor, and the smile vanished. "I don't see you on the calendar, Mr. Jerrell."

At least he was *known*. "Came up at the last minute." *Keep coming, keep coming.* Jerrell took the corner, landed in the adjustment room. Every station filled. Dr. Frank was bent over a teenage girl tipped back in the examining chair. Soft brown hair cascaded from the vinyl headrest. Frank was still tanned from the summer, or else the man actually drove to Ann Arbor to crisp in a salon. Glossy black hair, the crown just turning nude. The perfect teeth flashed the girl like a headlamp. A man just shy of Jerrell's age, whose childhood orthodontics had taken, all right. Not a picket out of alignment.

"What do you call a bear with no teeth?" The man had his hands lodged inside the girl's gaping mouth, so how was the kid supposed to guess? To the child's obedient gurgle, *ah-duh-no*, Frank grinned. "A gummy bear!"

Typical of the man's cruelty to crack a joke about a candy forbidden on the Brace Watcher's Diet. The kid winced under the pliers' methodical twist. The assistant standing by smiled brightly as if her job depended on amiable play-along. Jerrell rubbed his jaw. His hand throbbed. The doctor caught his motion.

"Jerrell." Frank snapped off the blue latex gloves. "Is Ruth due for an adjustment?" The man's straight-razor smile broadened. He glanced at Jerrell's seeping hand, then over his shoulder, seeking his mother's frail shuffle.

"Have a word, Dr. Frank?" Jerrell planted his legs in the practiced crouch that signaled the need for a serious re-tooling of the project plan. "Just take a moment."

The receptionist hovered at his elbow, the grin bloodless and fierce. "Mr. Jerrell insisted," she began.

Dr. Frank shifted his gaze to Jerrell. "Jenny in accounts is free to assist you."

"I'd appreciate a *private* word. Just take a moment." From the second waiting room, a triumphant gamer's howl pierced the office's low mechanical buzz.

Frank nodded in a confidential way to the receptionist, who was already manhandling Jerrell's elbow to deliver him to Jenny in accounts. "Be with you in a jiff, then." Frank rolled his examining chair to the next gaping mouth in the queue. The young assistant manning that station stepped back respectfully. "How can you tell a happy motorcyclist?" Frank flashed his incisors at the tipped head bobbing *no*. The punch line ushered Jerrell into the accounts office. "By the number of bugs in his teeth!"

Jenny in accounts, smile sheathed in clear plastic retainers, was firm on the refund policy, narrowly interpreted as no refund. She printed out terms of service on contracts Jerrell had signed and outstanding invoices Jerrell had ignored when Dr. Frank quit returning his calls. She called up his mother's vivid diagnostic photo on her oversized monitor. The whole truth yawned at Jerrell. Livid, swollen gums cresting golden crowns, the hideous crowding a lurid accusation of Jerrell's best intentions gone awry. The inkjet spit out Jerrell's obligations in a monotonous hum. A drop of blood splattered the mahogany desk. Jenny offered him an antiseptic wipe.

Behind Jenny's sporty pigtail, cherry floor-to-ceiling shelves displayed Frank's reference library, his degrees from schools both famed and obscure, family photos of his tanned, straight-toothed wife and sons. An examination chair stood in an alcove by the office's only window, the chair's headrest tipped down as if hosting a phantom patient. Outside, the traffic wove steadily down Michigan Avenue in the golden afternoon light. Tammy and

Mr. Salisbury loitered outside the Gold Star vehicle, shivering near the meter as they sipped gallon-sized soft drinks. They must have killed time by walking down to Lucky Drugs. Tammy was pointing her straw at Mr. Salisbury. *How do you know?* Giving him the business. Good for her.

Jenny stacked the sheaf of documents from the inkjet and pushed them across the desk as if settling the matter. Jerrell repeated the phrase he'd settled on as both firm and actionable. "My mother's braces are detrimental to her health and welfare. I'd like to discontinue treatment."

"Dr. Frank will have to assess, but he *is* assisting other patients. We *do* recommend scheduling an appointment." Jenny's cheery emphasis skated the boundary of professional courtesy.

"I've placed several calls." Hard to tell whether Tammy's posture had shifted from scolding to flirtatious. Mr. Salisbury's expression had certainly lit up, or maybe the sun was in his eyes. Jerrell shifted his gaze back to his mother's mouth. What wasn't capped in gold was black, or crimson. Not so much a mouth as a craggy, forlorn cavern. Well, his gift to her now would be to get those braces off, let her die the way she'd been born.

"I don't see a record of those calls."

"I called Dr. Frank's cell." A number he'd discovered though sneaky back-channel means during Ruth's last visit. Let Jenny hunt and peck for that record on her system.

"If King Midas sat on gold, who sat on silver?" Frank breezed through the doorway. The man never quit the corny act for a second. Jerrell's startled "I don't know" was pure reflex.

"The Lone Ranger!" Frank hovered over him. Grasped Jerrell's good hand with glad-hand bravado. The man's manicure gleamed like eggshell splinters. "A bit before your time there, Jerrell?"

"Not real interested in who sat on whom today, Dr. Frank." Jerrell curled his rough fingers into his palms. Winced when the punctures stretched and a warmth rose from the torn scabs. He pressed the antiseptic wipe to the top Band-Aid. "I'd like my mother's treatment discontinued for reasons of her oral health and welfare."

"Team Frank's on it, buddy." Frank turned to Jenny. "How much time is left on Ruth Jerrell's treatment plan, Jen?"

"Six months, Dr. Frank." Jen flashed her retainers at Jerrell.

"What I mean by discontinue is that the brackets need to come out," Jerrell clarified. "Now."

"Jenny has just reviewed the terms of your contract, champ."

"My mother has developed thrush. The braces are causing this condition. Which has become acute."

Frank's smile dipped. "Braces don't cause thrush, buddy." The man's effusive gaze turned brittle. The doctor wasn't sailing through the grim economy on the grin alone, then.

"My research confirms that metal complicates the mouth's environment, thusly leading to acute infections of my mother's sort."

Frank indicated the documents on the desk. "At the time we agreed to treat your mother at her advanced age, we also agreed we would not be liable for any decline in treatment effectiveness. Jenny can go over that agreement with you."

"It's part of the standard agreement," Jenny pointed out. The retainers' slight lisp promoted a smooth glide on the s sounds. "Regardless of the patient's age."

"Since the decline is being *caused* by the braces, well, there's your liability." Jerrell gave Frank the hard stare right back. Posturing was also part of the standard agreement, the one between men playing chicken at the wheel. He decided against standing up to confront the man. Sometimes staying seated was the best tough guy move. Showed you didn't need the physical advantage to prevail. "Which I can prove according to my research."

"No way the braces are causing the thrush, champ. But if you bring Ruth on in, we can put her to rights."

"My mother isn't able to be transported at this juncture of her health and welfare."

"I'm not Marcus Welby, buddy. No house calls."

"You'll have to make an exception. And I'll expect a refund."

Dr. Frank was smiling again, the grin of a winner with a signed contract on his side. "The refund policy is clear."

"I'm willing to accept a prorated reimbursement."

"Jenny has reviewed that policy with you, champ."

Jerrell's fists tightened on his lap. In fifteen years of construction work he'd only lost it once on a job site, so he wasn't about to overreact with a pill like Frank. His record of keeping cool was one to take pride in, considering the caliber of the men involved in building trades. Hard workers, mostly, but rough around the edges and drinkers or worse, some of them. After cold-cocking an electrician, Jerrell had been let go on that particular job, a renovation and addition to Brecon Corners, the local mall well past its prime. The episode was decidedly not the reason for Jerrell's chronic under-employment now, despite what Lydia claimed. The whole damn industry was in the shredder, and besides a woman didn't leave a man just over show-ing a wise guy a thing or two for once.

Jenny paper-clipped Jerrell's documents with a silver clasp. Outside, Tammy and Mr. Salisbury moved to the vehicle, impatient to resume the lesson. "I want those fucking braces out. Tomorrow."

Because he was all worked up, Jerrell's jaw was gaping a bit. Frank's gaze settled on Jerrell's mouth. "You know, Jerrell, I can fix that adult crowding for you." The doctor was squinting at Jerrell's lips in a way altogether inappropriate to a negotiation situation. "Jenny, pull the quote form."

"Not necessary, Jenny." Jerrell didn't mean for his tone to sound threatening. But Jenny hesitated. Looked to Frank for reassurance.

"You ever have braces?" The doctor advanced a step. "Back in the Stone Age, before jaw expanders? Or were you noncompliant during the retainer phase, champ?"

Jenny clacked away on the keyboard. Jerrell reoriented his position in the client chair to point his knees at Dr. Frank's shins. The man's brilliant smile flattened to a shrewd horizon. Strong arms, sculpted by years of unmerciful adjustments, crisscrossed at the chest. "I wore my retainer." Jerrell relaxed his shoulders, loosened up to engage. "Twenty-four seven."

"Just kidding there." Nothing about the steely copperhead stare looked like kidding around. "Wouldn't have mattered whether you did or didn't. Adult crowding was inevitable with the treatment available in your time. Especially with that narrow jaw. But I can put you to rights, same as your ma. Jenny, got that quote sheet handy?"

Jenny ceased clacking. "I'll get that from reception." She shut the office door firmly on her way out. The adjustment room's low buzz clipped to silence. The sun's slanting angle cast an orange oval on the beige rug by the examining chair. The headrest's dull shadow deepened like a lost patch of the night sky.

Frank slid a hand into his jeans pocket, pulled out a pair of powder-blue latex gloves. "How about a quick exam right here, Jerrell? Just take a sec."

With Jerrell's glance at the chair in the nook, Frank said, "Stay right where you are. Hell, I do these exams on busy housewives right in the Kroger aisle. Always carry my gloves."

Frank stepped forward. His knees brushed Jerrell's shins. His gleaming manicure vanished, wiggling, into the glove's blue casings. "Open up there for me, champ."

The office's quiet, warm air turned clammy. A gliding sensation along Jerrell's jaw tingled the nerves in his neck. A rage percolated. The windup was coming, like one of those spinning gyros Jerrell used to let loose with a string. He'd deck this asshole right in the pickets. He'd tear up the fucking contracts and wipe his mother's ugly mouth from the screen. He'd put that electrician square in the hospital, and a part of him got off on it, just as he was about to get off on seeing Frank's teeth skittle on the oak floor's polish.

Then the dry chalky latex was prying at his lips. Frank's knee pressed his shin. The doctor cupped his narrow chin, probed his jawbone with his thumbs, caressed the old breaks that had never healed quite right as if he knew exactly where Jerrell still hurt. Jerrell closed his eyes, straightened his shoulders, tipped his head back dutifully. A rubbery odor filled the tight space between them. A pressure on his jaw's socket, and Jerrell's mouth popped open like an obedient cork. The latex pressed his tongue, penetrated his throat. He gagged, and the fingers withdrew, pressed the swollen gums at the back molars, ran along the crooked line of the canines and incisors. Another sharp pressure to his socket forced his head further back. He opened his eyes, expecting to see the white-tiled drop ceiling. But Frank's mouth loomed close. His breath, musky-sweet, poured into Jerrell. A single filigreed wire glinted behind the perfect sentries of his bottom teeth. So that's how Frank thwarted adult crowding.

"Bite down, Jerrell." Frank slipped his fingers free. Jerrell aligned his teeth. Frank rubbed the inside lip, massaged the receding gum line with gentle circular pressure. Released Jerrell's jaw, snapped off the gloves. Saliva misted from the powder-blue latex.

The door glided open. Jenny kicked a doorstop into place and handed Frank a quote sheet.

"I can do the job for six big ones, Jerrell." Frank took a pen from his shirt pocket. "Minus the family discount plus a little consideration for Ruth's setback, that'll run you just under five grand." Frank leaned over the desk, scrawled the figures on the sheet, pushed the paper over to Jerrell. "Sign for your new smile with team Frank."

Jenny grinned. Her plastic retainers glistened behind her moist lips. "Oh Mr. Jerrell, getting fixed changed my whole life! You'd be such a looker if it weren't for those teeth."

The latex taste curdled on Jerrell's tongue. A real Sabrina, this Jenny, a wholesome mask on a cock-tease act. Not at all like his lovely straight-toothed Lydia who, for all her complaints about Jerrell, some of which he'd admit he deserved, never ever minded his bad teeth. He took the pen, signed *fuck you* in big script letters. "Schedule that, Miss."

Jenny backed away as if the heavy desk weren't between them.

"I'll take that, Mister." Dr. Frank slipped the quote sheet from Jerrell's grasp, folded it in two, ripped it in half. No jagged edges, clean as a razor blade. Jerrell made for the door.

"What promise did Adam and Eve make after they were kicked out of the Garden of Eden?" Frank called after him.

Jerrell swiveled on his heel, tossed the hard stare. "You're a real asshole, Frank."

Dr. Frank flashed the star-bright grin. "To turn over a new leaf, champ."

• ••••

Jerrell cruised into Lucky Drugs to snag Ruth's Vernors. When he eased into the passenger seat, Mr. Salisbury's skinny, leather-clad arms were already positioned at nine and three. The engine was humming, the rattle behind the glove box a soft, idle knock. The kids had tossed their empty cups and straws on the back seat's floor mats.

"Don't appreciate the litter in my car." The words, thick and sour, gelled in Jerrell's throat. His cut was seeping again. He pulled a Kleenex from the soft pack he'd stashed in the door's slot.

"Sorry, Mr. Jerrell," the student drivers said in unison. Friends now, were they? A few moments alone was all it took for the flirtation to begin. What had passed between them over Lucky Drug sodas and Jerrell's long absence? They knew they should have returned to the Gold Star facility by now. What wonders did they share about him? Jerrell resisted the urge to glance back at Tammy, hands thrust in her lap, lovely green eyes alert to conditions. Such a glance would be searching in a way altogether inappropriate to an instructional situation.

"Pull out when it's safe to proceed." Jerrell's throat felt bruised, sore, and swollen as if he'd vomited. Something about that garroted sensation made Tammy's presence unbearably arousing. All the more vexing since Jerrell's moral outlook did not allow for even the hint of hunger for the young. Jerrell unscrewed the Vernors's cap, tossed it into the cup holder. Took a big swig. Ginger flooded his mouth, a wretched chaser for the bitter latex. He hated Vernors. "Take a left up there at the Tastee Freez."

"You mean the Subway, Mr. Jerrell?" Mr. Salisbury eyed the soda as if he hadn't already chugged his own liter of pop.

"Well, it used to be the Tastee Freez." Jerrell should know. Tastee Freez was what he got as a kid instead of Dairy Queen Brazier because the Tastee Freez cones were a nickel cheaper. Only that one time Ruth had treated him to a Dairy Queen, the summer he was learning to drive, his first step toward leaving this crappy town and never ever returning. In the air-conditioned Brazier he'd ordered a soft serve in a cup. The twisty flavor, chocolate and vanilla ribbons joined like a snake-charmer's serpents. Nothing like the gritty Tastee Freez plain vanilla, ordered and eaten standing in the high hot sun at the cheap plywood stand, as if the Tastee Freez had been built from day one to be temporary. His jaw was wired after Ruth had fractured the mandible with one of her punches she referred to as exactly what he had coming for breaking her damn swans. For that entire summer, he couldn't eat a single cone.

"I remember when it was the Tastee Freez. We went there for Sunday school when I was little." Tammy's defense of his memory's ghost was gentle, sweet. A well-meaning young woman. Fair minded and considerate, as women, as all people, should be. Not a bit like that Jenny and Dr. Frank and the phony bill of goods they pushed on the cosmetically challenged. Jerrell sidestepped a swell of rage. He'd botched that encounter but good so he had only himself to blame. He took another swig of Vernors and gagged. The latex taste would never wash away until he could get his mouth around that whiskey flask.

"Your mom never took us to the Tastee Freez." Mr. Salisbury cast an accusing glance in the rear view mirror.

"Eyes ahead. Except to check traffic conditions." Jerrell made a note on the clipboard. Mr. Salisbury's hands maintained the correct position. Steady grip, no bleach to the knuckles. Yet the young man still couldn't track to the road. His weaving rubbed Jerrell's tire against the curb just past the stoplight at Maple. The car shuddered. The rattle behind the glove box and the cap in the cup holder clinked like pennies in a jar. Jerrell applied the instructor brake gently. "Easy there."

"Sorry, Mr. Jerrell." Mr. Salisbury corrected. Now he was riding the center line.

"She did so."

"Did not."

"She's *my* mom, so I ought to know what she did. Anyway, you never did tell me how you know my mom taught Sunday school."

The backseat defense was heating up. Guess the flirtation had flamed out. Jerrell imagined that if he looked at the young lady, he'd see delicate pinking cheeks, dismay's pretty flare. He decided not to look. "Let's simmer down, kids. Take a left at Redwood, Mr. Salisbury." Jerrell screwed the cap back on the Vernors and slid the bottle to the floor mat.

Mr. Salisbury glanced at Jerrell's boots. "My dad says the number one cause of crashes is unsecured beverages."

"How would you *know* whether we went to the Tastee Freez?" Tammy persisted. "You never even went to my church."

"That so? Left blinker, remember, Mr. Salisbury. I'm gonna have to start deducting for that."

Mr. Salisbury pulled the indicator. "Because your mom slapped me and then got me expelled from Sunday school, that's how."

Tammy paused. "That was *you*?"

The speedometer inched up past Redwood's limit. The Vernors collided with Jerrell's ankle. Mr. Salisbury's hand position on the wheel slid to seven and four. "Watch your speed," Jerrell reminded him. "Check the posted limit."

Mr. Salisbury eased up on the gas, settled into a cruise of thirty-five. "Yep. That was me."

"Oh. I forgot about you. Probably because you never came back, and then, well. But Mom did not get you kicked out." Tammy snapped off a nail with a plush nibble. The brittle sound of her mouth working the finger again drew Jerrell's attention to unproductive channels of desire. Before Lydia had left him, lust's lovely fulfillment was an obtainable mercy. They'd always been fine in that department, the kissing issue aside. When would such feelings again be mercies, not torments? Lydia had proven that staying in a place would always come to mean being left behind.

Although it was completely against instructor protocol, when Jerrell's cell phone buzzed he answered it gratefully.

"Yeah, well, who would want to come back after getting whacked by Jesus's babysitter?" Mr. Salisbury's eyes were—again—not on the road.

"Eyes forward, Mister. This is Jerrell."

"My mom was not Jesus's babysitter. She got *trained* in Sunday-school teaching."

"Your mother is asking for you, Mr. Jerrell." Whose voice of Assisted Living was this? The Staff never ever identified themselves.

"She went to school to learn to cut and paste for Jesus?" The passenger tire crossed Redwood's side line. "Takes lots of *training* to make a stupid diorama out of Daniel 12:3."

The shoulder's bumpy gravel rattled the dash, drowned out the voice of Assisted Living. "Correct to the center of the lane, please. Tell Ruth, *Mom*, I'll be over directly after my shift."

"She's past understanding, Mr. Jerrell."

Mr. Salisbury overcorrected. The Gold Star front fender angled over the center line just as a front loader rumbled by. The Vernors thudded against Jerrell's toe. From the backseat came a throaty creak. "Not *too* far. Gotta start deducting for that. Tell my mother we're making solid progress on the braces issue."

Assisted Living's voice garbled. "Accident," Jerrell made out through the reception's dead patches, and then, "Morphine."

"On my way. Tell her not to worry about those braces." Jerrell snapped the phone shut crisply. Secured the Vernors between his boots. Wondered if the moisture clinging to his socks was sweat or ginger ale.

"I remember that diorama." Tammy's voice trembled. "Did you do dioramas in your day, Mr. Jerrell?"

Mr. Salisbury sped up. Jerrell glanced back at Tammy. Her knees were pressed together, her knuckles pearly knobs on the door handle. A metallic-green Chevy Caprice crept to the rear bumper, a bit too close. "Ease up there, Ace. I was never a churchgoer, young lady."

Mr. Salisbury mashed the brake. Brought the vehicle to a dead stop in the middle of Redwood. The Chevy veered left, missed the Gold Star fender by a hair, roared past in a no-passing zone. The driver leaned over the passenger seat as he passed to flip the bird. Mr. Salisbury rolled down the window and returned the gesture. Tammy gasped, an adorable hiss.

"What do you think you're doing there, Mr. Salisbury?" Jerrell kept the tone mild.

"The fucker was *tailgating* me."

Tammy gasped again. Mr. Salisbury balled his fists in his lap, nerves jazzing a shoulder roll under the lofty leather padding. Joker at the wheel, the rare hard case in the Gold Star car.

Well, Jerrell should call it a day for Mr. Salisbury. But today was Salisbury's lucky day. Jerrell didn't have what it took to bust his balls. Had to conserve his energy for the next move with Frank. Had to figure *out* the next goddamn move. "OK, son. Never mind the asshole behind you honking or tailgating or flipping you off. *Never* flip them off back. Those types of drivers, those asshole types, they're just obstacles to your safety. To you getting where you want to go. Understand?"

Mr. Salisbury clenched his fists tighter. "Yes, sir."

"Look." Jerrell felt almost sorry for the kid now. Who was instructing small town men to keep their fists in their laps? When had *this* education become the norm? "You never really see how the world is full of obstacles until you start driving, Mister. You too, Tammy." He was bold enough, now, to address the pinking cheeks, the breath she'd been holding although the next cemetery was miles down the road. "You can't let those asshole drivers get to you. Understand?"

"Yes, sir." They spoke in docile unison, these kids. These student drivers. For the first time, Jerrell felt a measure of satisfaction with the Gold Star instructional environment.

Jerrell burped. Rubberized ginger misted his nasal cavity. "Good, then. Proceed, Mr. Salisbury. Hang a right at Beech."

Mr. Salisbury managed to remember the turn indicator. Progress was being made. "And they that are wise shall shine as the brightness of the firmament; and they that turn many to righteousness as the stars forever and ever," he recited cleanly.

"I can't believe you even remember that." Tammy sheared another finger. The pliant click of teeth on nail. A soft moue from her lips. Jerrell reached for the car's heat control. Clicked the temperature down a notch. Resisted the urge to dig out that flask. Stupid thing made him feel like crying. Lydia had given him the flask for his birthday, the last one she'd stuck around to celebrate. Embossed his initials. Filled it for him with Bushmills. Probably planning even then to leave him. Looking back on it maybe it was a sign, some statement that he was drinking too much, but a woman didn't leave a man just over the occasional after-shift drinks with the gang.

Mr. Salisbury kept the car dead centered in the road all the way through the turn. Grasping the basics, he was. A little deliberation, a little discipline, was all it took. The kid might end up passing driver's training after all. "Who could forget good old Daniel? All's I wanted to know was, how the heck do you build a diorama out of that?"

Jerrell couldn't tell if the young man was addressing him or Tammy. "I suppose it takes a little imagination, that's all. Follow the train bridge down about a mile."

"Why they'd put a train track in the middle of the road?" Tammy asked.

"There used to be a train." Sometimes the student drivers couldn't reason out the simplest detail of the roadway environment. "Why'd your Sunday-school teacher hit you?" Jerrell's question surprised him as much as it surprised the kids. An impulse, a crossing into personal territory he didn't usually undertake with student drivers. But maybe the boy had some feelings to work out. Feelings Jerrell was well-qualified to help him investigate.

Mr. Salisbury accelerated to the posted limit. "I asked her what a firmament was."

"She didn't get on your case for *that*." Jerrell didn't have to turn to visualize Tammy's exasperation. "You called Jesus dumb." As if that would justify hitting a kid.

"Did *not*. I called Daniel dumb. And the Bible." The speedometer ticked up five clicks. "And dioramas."

"Watch your speed there," Jerrell reminded him.

"Well, there you go." Tammy's smug tone masked a certain relief, the typical attitude toward a boy who had it coming. "Same dif."

The car approached the flashing light by the abandoned train station. A man in a felt hat, collar turned against the wind, stepped from the curb as if the train had just deposited him at home for the evening. Salisbury was speeding again. "Yield to the crosswalk, Mr. Salisbury." Jerrell covered the instructor brake as a precaution. The man on the street hesitated at the lurid gold stars and the clown car mascot that suggested exercising caution near a student driver. Jerrell flashed him a wave. *Keep coming, keep coming.* Like an old-time commuter to a Dearborn white-collar job. All the pedestrian needed was a chintzy fake-leather briefcase to be the phantom of Jerrell's dad.

Mr. Salisbury braked dutifully. No sudden jerking. Controlled movements. Maybe going a round with the lovely Tammy was focusing the young man's driving skills. "What, so Jesus is exactly the same dif as Daniel and the Bible and stupid dioramas?"

"You didn't learn much in Sunday school." Tammy crunched her nail between her teeth.

Mr. Salisbury soared through the crosswalk as soon as the man's coattail fluttered by. "Don't jump the gun there," Jerrell admonished.

The man's coat was frayed, grimy at the hem. The hat was stained, the brim speckled with holes. The pedestrian glanced back. Grizzled beard, gray teeth bared in a startled grin. Tired, sorrowed eyes met Jerrell's. The look his father had given him after Ruth brought him home from the ER, jaw wired shut, just what a smart-mouth wise-guy hoodlum had coming for snapping the bills off her swan collectibles because she'd given him the strap for ruining her stupid UAW hall fashion show. His dad was no crash-site investigator. He'd glued those damn bills back on while they were gone. Could hardly tell where Jerrell had broken them. His old man never asked what happened to his son's jaw. He never even asked why Jerrell had attacked the swans. Jerrell was old enough to know better, of course, but he'd read somewhere that swans were the only birds with teeth. Why not check for the Hull Collectibles' anatomical correctness, had been his thinking at the time. It was easier to think he was just investigating than hitting Ruth back. Jerrell should hate his father for his silent repairs, his caution to *keep quiet, keep quiet.* He should wonder at what point in his life a man's silence transforms from restraint into terror. But there was no future in excavating the secrets of a dead man's heart.

"Learned what a goddamn firmament was, didn't I?" Mr. Salisbury glared at Tammy in the rear view mirror.

The pedestrian stumbled past the abandoned tool and die, disappeared down Henry Street.

"All right, kids. Let's simmer down. Watch the language." Jerrell popped open the glove box. His hand was throbbing. Were those goddamn braces going to give him blood poisoning? Where had he stashed the Tylenol? "Lesson's over. Let's head back to Gold Star. Proceed to State and take a left."

"'The vault of the Heavens,' is what your mom said." Mr. Salisbury faked a falsetto. "'And by the way, it's not *a* firmament, when we speak about the Bible. It's *the* firmament. The firmament of Heaven.' All snooty, she was." Mr. Salisbury's cheeks blotched crimson. His eyes were suspiciously wet. "Remember?" As if what Tammy remembered, not what her mother did, was the real heart of the matter.

"Let's focus on our driving here, Mister." Had to do his job to keep the kid calm, but Jerrell had that number, all right. There was a reason he never attended Sunday school. Anyway, Ruth avoided church. Another covenant between them. She wouldn't expose herself to the charade of repentance. And he would not be asked to forgive.

"I mean, *the vault of the Heavens*. Who was she kidding?"

"Well, that's what the firmament *is*," Tammy said. Hard-edged, her faith no longer innocent and charming but as ancient and superstitious as believing in that vault. "Golly, remember that Misty girl, that weird girl, what she said after my mom slapped you?"

Mr. Salisbury's face cleared. His shoulders relaxed. "That retarded girl?"

"Let's not use that language about the disabled. Left blinker, remember." Jerrell gave up on the Tylenol, clicked the glove box shut.

"OK, differently challenged. Mentally unable. Whatever."

"She *actually* said, 'Thou shalt not kill.'" Tammy giggled.

"I *remember* she said that." Mr. Salisbury's expression lit up with the same happiness Jerrell had spied through Dr. Frank's window. "Remember what *I* said?"

"Wrong commandment!" the kids cried in unison. Tammy dissolved in laughter. Smiling with joy, Mr. Salisbury tried to catch her eyes in the mirror.

Jerrell's cell phone buzzed. He snapped it open, brought the lonely hiss to his ear. Another patch of dead reception. The train-bridge column might be blocking the connection. "Turn left ahead, Mr. Salisbury."

"Then she hit you again, didn't she?" Tammy ceased laughing so suddenly Jerrell wondered if she'd been faking.

Mr. Salisbury fell silent. The stop sign at the dodgy turn was coming up fast. Jerrell covered the instructor brake. Mr. Salisbury brought the car to a smooth stop in time but made no move to turn.

"Take a left, Mister."

Mr. Salisbury craned his neck to peer down State. Noted the column obstruction, how the cars appeared out of thin air, whizzed by. No way to see the traffic coming. How had it happened that the Big Boy was long gone but the dodgy turn was still here? Why hadn't the town laid this hazard to rest long ago?

Mr. Salisbury pulled the turn indicator dutifully and gave Jerrell the expected uncertain glance. "But I can't see anything."

The cell phone hissed. Or was it breathing? Jerrell squinted. As if that would improve his hearing. "You can see. Nose out a bit. Use caution before proceeding."

"Then *remember* my mom told you to cut out stars for the righteous or else."

It was breathing. *Her* breathing. How could Jerrell mistake that sound, and the blank-canvas feeling it raised in him? *Docile.* That's what Lydia had called it. Like riding out Ruth's black moods was a weakness, not a fortitude. Or a gift. Jerrell had always known that if he ever did raise a hand to Ruth he'd kill her, pure and simple. Their covenant depended upon his devotion to her nastiness. He'd never think of his confused feelings as tenderness, a gratitude that she'd *seen* the dark huddled thing he really was. Ruth always had ridden right inside him on his air, all the way to the place where he began.

A rasping plagued the phone reception that could be a last attempt to draw breath. Was she past the keening stage? Was Assisted Living standing over her? Goosebumps prickled Jerrell's arms despite the Gold Star heating vents pumping the everlasting hot air. He clicked open the glove box. Fished the flask from the bloody towel's swaddle. "Mom? Mom, is it you?"

"Is this a trick?" Mr. Salisbury gave him a look. Doubt. Fear, too. Even for an experienced driver, the dodgy turn was a wing and a prayer.

"So that's why you never got the Tastee Freez treats. You never came back to Sunday school." Tammy spoke like she was explaining the obvious to a dolt. But Jerrell recognized her tone as pure enjoyment.

"Your mom hit me!"

"So?" Tammy drummed her slender fingers on the door handle. "You were asking for it. Everyone knew you were a loser even back then."

Mr. Salisbury reoriented his gaze from the mirror to the dodgy turn. Gripped the wheel, nine and three on the dot. "Tastee Freez was dumb."

Jerrell couldn't agree more.

Through the phone came the chiming of the blue bird clock. Then the windup wail he'd heard all his life, *it was you! it was you!* As if he'd been cheeky although he hadn't said a word. To Ruth he would always be just a smart-mouth wise-guy hoodlum. A real Tom-Dick-and-Harry was the son his mother had wanted. A nobody. Not the troublemaker who only craved a cradle for his heart. No matter how strongly he came at her, she'd always come back at him stronger. Her decline could only ever lead to his decline.

Jerrell unscrewed the flask, took a swig. The Bushmills went down smooth. He wiped his mouth and handed the flask to Mr. Salisbury.

"Take the turn, goddamn it," he instructed.

Tammy drew in her breath and held it. Mr. Salisbury looked at Jerrell. Understanding flashed between them about the ancient ways of women, the commandments they laid down. The flesh they offered, the blossoming of their beautiful hearts, and then the bloom's vengeful withering that might take years, or only a moment. A repossession. A theft. Then they left, and the reasons they gave were never the whole story.

"Nothing to it, Ace," Jerrell said.

An Uneven Recovery

The downturn had come to this: Donder and Blitzen would be the Arnold family's sole source of income.

When the usual kid down the street couldn't pet-sit during the neighbors' Volunteer Vacation building schools in the Appalachians, Helen rather sheepishly asked if Arthur, Gina's thirteen-year-old, could do the job.

Gina rather sheepishly asked what the daily pay rate was.

"We usually pay Randy ten dollars a day for three visits," Helen replied delicately. "We can go a little higher for Arthur, since maybe you'd want to help out . . ." Hard to tell from the glissando of sympathy in Helen's frosty tone whether she knew of the Arnold's financial calamity.

"Fifteen a day and I'll be there every time." The words popped out, prompt and desperate. When she was growing up, her father had coached Gina for times like these with his own father's Depression-era slogans. *Any port in a storm* was one. *Pride won't pay the bills* was another.

Gina was willing to bet that feeding the neighbor cats wasn't the type of work Dad had foreseen.

She and Helen stood warily opposed on either side of the split rail fence marking the boundary between their yards that, at the beginning of that summer, had been in hot dispute. Behind Helen, Candy was mulching the row of sullen firs the neighbor women had planted to settle the spat. The dispute began when the women asked Red to move Arthur's play structure, which they claimed blocked their view of the subdivision's wetlands. When Red refused, the women produced a mortgage survey as proof the Sommer-ville-Smith property extended six yards past the Arnold side of the fence, right down the middle of the Rugged Rumpus's sandbox. Red parried with transit level and tripod to prove the Arnolds actually owned a three-yard strip of the Sommerville-Smith lawn. Gina wouldn't go so far as to say that Red's zeal had made the hostilities worse, but he'd treated the episode like gainful employment. He was hustling to replace the architecture work that had evaporated overnight in the real-estate crash. Gina's own bookkeeping job for Jim Price, a developer, had shriveled just as abruptly. Jim was a for-mer University of Michigan gymnast who'd been equally nimble in the Ann Arbor real-estate market, but when six major tenants folded in one month, Jim decided to perform his own stunts with the books. Gina was let go with ten minutes to gather her belongings and that pride Dad was always warning against. After months of searching, the escort now seemed like a ceremonial usher into long-term unemployment.

She couldn't exactly blame Red for his defense of their property line. The

Arnolds may lose their home, but in the meantime Red wasn't about to lose any yardage. Then, on the hottest day of the summer, Candy, who worked the counter at the landscaping business just down Wagner Road, had planted a line of young evergreens along the fence line right up the middle of the disputed green zone on the Sommerville-Smith side of the fence. A month later, the evergreens remained hunkered in their defiant adolescent slump.

Through it all, Arthur remained buddies with the neighbor women's kids, Colten and Priscilla. A thaw of sorts, for the good of the children, was underway at the fence.

"I don't want to put you out." Helen's sympathy might be genuine. Or merely curious.

Candy launched a pitchfork into the fresh mulch. "The kittens have a self-feeder," she said. "Nothing to it." She hefted the mulch toward the first fir in line. The sweet earthy odor of mushrooms and orange peel drifted from Candy's hand-fermented compost.

"Well, there's the vitamins for their coat," Helen said. "The litter box, of course, but Arthur knows how to clean that. Some daily TLC is a must. The kittens are so cuddly, can't stand it when we're away . . ."

Kittens, indeed. Donder and Blitzen were ancient. Arthur thought Donder was at least, improbably, twenty years old. Gina calculated two weeks at fifteen a day. Might cover the electric bill. "What a great responsibility experience for Arthur, Helen. Thanks for thinking of him."

Helen fanned her hair with slender fingers. Glorious hair, an auburn cascade that swept her shoulders with offhand glamour. She was in marketing for a private health system that catered to executives. Spin doctor for the criminal class, Red had described her job once to Arthur, bitterly, but that was soon after the property dispute. Before the recession, Red held an easy-going, big-tent heart toward clients, the sub-trades, neighbors, and family. He pursued contemplative hobbies like fly-fishing and nature photography. Lately his steadfastness had run off the rails in little ways, like his crack about Helen's job, or uncalled-for remarks to Gina like *grow up, honey.* Last week she'd caught him cleaning out his fishing vest, dumping his beloved flies into the trash. He'd claimed they were worn beyond repair. "Well, we love Arthur, and with all he's going through, maybe, who knows, Dondie and Blitz can provide him some comfort."

Gina had kept the details of their fortune's freefall fiercely private. Negotiations with the mortgage and utility companies and glum squabbles over the car payment she and Red conducted scrupulously out of Arthur's earshot. "With what he's going through?"

"With Red's old injury flaring up."

"Excuse me?"

"From the war. Arthur has shared with us. I hope you don't mind."

"From the war," Gina repeated. A field mouse scuttled from the mulch under the fir and darted into a crabgrass patch on the Arnold side of the fence.

Candy spiked another load. "Arthur is so open with us. I think we share a deep sense of trust." She fixed a disapproving squint as if Gina were a painful sunspot she wished to blink away. "Kids really have a radar about which adults in their lives are on the up and up."

"I don't know what you're talking about." Gina addressed Helen, who was watching the mouse rustle the crabgrass. Gina hadn't so much as plucked a weed all summer. The Rugged Rumpus sandbox was a riot of thistles. When Arthur and the Sommerville-Smith kids slid down the bumpy slide they flew squealing into doilies of Queen Anne's lace. Neither Red nor Gina could summon the gumption to do any yardwork beyond mowing. Gina would have expected that chronic unemployment would thrust the Arnolds into a single-minded determination to keep up with chores, if only to distract from the circumstances. But even dusting a shelf left her with an odd sense of shame.

"Gulf I," Helen said brightly. "The airdrop behind Saddam's Republican Guard. That hard landing in the desert. Of course Arthur couldn't give many details. It was so long before he was born. I may have the story wrong. But he does seem very secure on his Desert Storm facts. You'd never know, though, to watch him mow that Red was missing a leg. Although Candy and I always did think it was odd that he never wears shorts in the summer. Even on the hottest days."

"Jesus." Gina gripped the fence rail. A cluster of hornets rose from the clover, zigzagged to the play structure's tire swing.

"Don't come down on Arthur for telling us," Candy said. "Although I don't understand why your family feels Red's war service has to be a secret. Secrets are so *toxic* to kids."

"Arthur says Red's wound has been acting up." Helen appraised Gina's perspiration as if assessing a misfired PR strategy. "I know a very good infection specialist."

"I think we've got that infection under control now, thanks."

"Because I would feel terrible about imposing the kittens on you, if you had your hands full."

"No imposition at all."

Helen watched Gina's knuckles whiten. A satisfaction dusted her sympathy. She gathered her hair up to fan her neck. Gina's shaggy bob, long past any dignified hold on style, roped wetly at her shoulders. She hadn't purchased a cut since Red's final client skipped town to dodge his fee. "When we were bickering over the property line I had no idea I was haranguing a retired general."

"Who prosecuted a bullshit war." Candy parted the second fir's branches, piled mulch in a perfect ring around the trunk. Beyond her, the lawn's slow slope shone a perfect jade. No grub patches, no parched grass. Velvety, freshly showered dahlias lined the women's cherry-stained deck. Gina's shaggy yard was beginning to resemble the artificial marsh the girls were so bent on viewing.

Gina uncurled her fingers from the rail. "Arthur loves to exaggerate. Red's rank was colonel."

"Well. Colt tells some doozies sometimes." Helen's gaze flickered over the evergreens drooping in the heat. "Do you think you could water these guys for us, too? Candy says they need a bit of coaxing through these hot days."

As Gina hastened into the house to nurse anxiety over Arthur's latest lies—pathological or just imaginative?—she felt Helen and Candy's smug gazes on her back, the neighborly nosiness that she hoped hadn't guessed that the French doors Gina slammed behind her were the family's true infected limbs.

• ••••

Two days later, Gina lay sprawled on the neighbor women's spotless laundry room floor jimmying the self-feeder's jammed release. Fifteen minutes into the job and already a major equipment glitch. When she realized the cats hadn't been able to eat since the neighbors left the previous night, Gina hastily placed a bowl of EVO in front of their rheumy eyes. But the cats refused to eat. They doddered like old farts relying on a shared cane right back to the self-feeder. As Gina fiddled with the lever, a single EVO pellet disgorged and skidded across the polished bamboo floor. The cats bumped bony heads to snag it. Ropes of drool descended on the pellet. Gina wondered how on earth Candy maintained her floorboards' professional luster.

Dunderheads. The cats nestled close to lick each other's crowns. Whoever had won the pellet, the other certainly didn't hold a grudge.

Had Arthur had ever put two and two together to realize that Donder and Blitzen were the namesakes of his ritual Christmastime childhood blunder? He always mispronounced the final pair as *Dunder* and *Mitzie*. Arthur's error perfectly captured these old gentlemen. Their smoky Siamese markings were about as regal as a raccoon's. Some mysterious residue sluiced Blitzen's fur. Donder's favorite pastime involved licking the goo from Blitzen's back before coughing up spiny hairballs. OK, so she wasn't a cat person, but Gina found the tarnished pair ghoulish.

To her horror, the cats loved her.

Gina couldn't believe Candy and Helen starved the creatures for affection. Yet as soon as she'd disabled the garage security and unlocked the pass door, the cats had bolted to her. Glinting cataracts caught the brief twinkle of sunshine through the door like mewling little Havishams. Helen and Candy had drawn all the blinds for energy savings. The slit of light Gina brought with her would be their only glimpse of the sun.

Gina regretted scheduling this visit during Arthur's after-school fencing lesson. He was over here all the time playing with Priscilla and Colten. He'd know how to handle this pair. Gina had never even laid eyes on them, had never been invited into Candy and Helen's home. She suspected the women thought Gina was anti–gay rights, or at least, anti–gay marriage. Why they would assume this Gina couldn't guess. Her only parenting PC transgression had been to hand Priscilla a juice box to take home two summers ago. Fifteen minutes later, Priscilla returned to surrender the juice box, informing Gina that her mommies didn't allow her to drink sugar. OK, maybe she'd made some crack to Red later on, something about *the ladies* and *shame on them for sending the child* and *taking things too far*; and perhaps Arthur had overheard and repeated the fragments he'd remembered to Colten; and highlights like *ladies* and *shame* and *too far* had round-robined its way to the women. This would have been about the time they'd flown to Maryland to tie the knot. So, who knew what connections they'd drawn between juice and prejudice.

At last she maneuvered the feeder handle just so. EVO pellets poured cheerily into the dispenser. Relieved, she stepped aside to let the cats have at it, but now they refused to eat until she sprawled back on the floor with them, cooing and coaxing. She'd performed the same routine with old folks in the group home where she'd worked during college, scooping spoonfuls of soft mashed pot roast into aged caverns with the same gusto she'd once fed Arthur rice cereal at the other end of the life scale. As the cats ate greedily, Gina wondered at their neediness. Helen and Candy worked long hours. Who on earth gave Donder and Blitzen such pampering during the day?

Perhaps if the wretches could gain a few pounds before the girls' return, she could stretch this gig out a bit.

After the feeding, the cats set to cleaning each other's whiskers. While they were distracted, Gina scooped the litter box, skated to the patio door with the bag of dirty cat litter, and tossed it on the deck. She swept open the vertical blinds to let in the sun and left the slider cracked to air out the stale odor of ossified poo. She moved to the kitchen sink to wet a dishcloth, scrubbed soggy cat pellets from her bare legs, wrung out the towel, and hung it from the shining stainless-steel Jenn-Air oven pull. Did every surface in this house positively gleam?

Gina's own kitchen had turned as shabby as her landscaping; but then, she'd never indulged in trendy commercial-grade appliances and granite. *Keep your nut small* was one of Dad's sayings. As a kid Gina had no idea what he meant until he'd shown her a squirrel packing his cheeks with fallen acorns from the oaks bordering the car dealership lot. His jaw looked like a lumpy sack of potatoes. Gina had giggled. The sound sent the squirrel scampering and dropping his nuts along Jackson Road's shoulder. Dad had pinned that Depression-era look on her he'd inherited from his dad, survival pride masking a deep, exhausted unhappiness. *Look, Virginia. When you're greedy, you end up losing your nuts.*

Dad wasn't keeping his nut small now. He'd splurged on the Rugged Rumpus and then crowded the plastic swings and seesaw with a real tire, the spare to his Town Car. "Give the boy something genuine to play with," he'd said when Gina pointed out there wasn't *room* for the tire. Dad had watched Arthur spin happily under the coiled chains, his sand-dollar hair a silvery blur under the bright sun. This new attitude of delight Dad called revelatory and Gina called phony. His recent consorting with that phony psychic Madame Bozek had cultivated a late-stage joyful outlook that shone every bit as artificial to Gina's experience of her father as the neighbors' gleaming kitchen surfaces.

Gina had bit her tongue against reminding Dad that "something genuine" had once meant reselling tires to earn a buck for his struggling family. Dad, wading in the years just shy of golden, was determined to airbrush his own distant hard times.

A spiral-bound notebook was splayed open sloppily on the women's butcher-block island. Gina drifted over to leaf through the dog-eared pages. Brief notes in two different scripts filled the pages. One hand flowed in a schoolgirl cursive that might still dot an *i* with a heart. The companion hand formed terse, chunky letters. The uptight penmanship must belong to Helen, the schoolgirl script to Candy.

Donder sidled past, wheezing.

You make me high Sweetie-Pie!

And on the facing page, the stalwart response: *you rock my world every day every hour every moment*

On the next page the script announced *You are my sun and moon!* The block letters answered *and all the beams in between.* Candy lobbed exclamations. Helen tossed out punctuation with the trash. The lovey talk was sprinkled through with household chore reminders. *Don't forget! Recycling today! Grateful for your love!* or *picking up roast at sparrow babe do me tonight.* Nauseating.

From the living room, Donder unleashed a muscular hack. Blitzen, mewling, rubbed Gina's ankles. Gina nudged him and turned another page, this one smeared with something dark—chocolate, she hoped as her fingers landed squarely on the smudge—and saw single lines of script, centered perfectly on one page like parted lips:

I love you!

i love you

Blitzen snuggled stubbornly with her ankle. Gina didn't have the heart to push him away again. When was the last time she'd said those words to Red, or he to her? She always blamed money trouble for siphoning their affection, refused to do the math on whether they'd lost the habits of love before they'd lost their jobs.

She stepped over the tenacious Blitzen and trundled to the living room. A moist hairball studded with mysterious fibers hunkered on the midnight-blue carpet near the cherry entertainment center. At least Dunderhead still possessed enough youthful contrition to flee the scene. Gina trod off to fetch the carpet cleaner and towel, spritzed and scrubbed lightly. Although the mess reeked of EVO and sour goo, the ball cleaned up easily.

Gina pitched the goo in the stainless-steel trash canister in the kitchen and nursed a childish pleasure in hanging the towel on the Jenn-Air without rinsing it. She moved to close the patio slider. Calculated that the job had taken exactly twice as long as she'd planned. But Blitzen was in the way, tail drooping over the door track's grooves.

"Good way to lose that tail, Mister." Gina swatted the smoky rump with her sneaker toe. Blitzen squatted fiercely and raised a mirrored gaze. For once the blind look was not accompanied by a pitiful mewling. But Blitzen's silent appraisal, locked on Gina's eyes, was far creepier than the boys' typical noisy cavalcade.

Well, the cat must want something. Gina clicked through her list. She hadn't fed the boys their vitamins, but would Blitzen miss that useless supplement? *For their coats*, indeed. Then the silence tipped her. "Where's Donder?"

Blitzen flicked his tail crookedly. Gina followed the cat's blank stare out the glass. Old Donder emerged from the dahlia bed to limp purposefully down the sloping backyard. The scoundrel was cutting a jagged beeline to Candy's evergreens.

By the time Gina tore across the yard, Donder had lodged in the nearest fir's lower branches. When her coaxing raised only a baleful stare, Gina quit clicking her tongue and hauled the cat unceremoniously through bush and bramble. Mulch clumps clung to his clotted fur. A hairline cut razored down one side of the flabby neck. Blood puckered from the scrape. Gina tucked the cat under her arm like a football and ferried him back to the house. While she cleaned the cut with the hairball towel, Dunderhead ranted and Blitzen stared Gina down. Her last sight of the pair as she fled out the garage door was Donder sprawled on the bamboo floor, paws waving with unabashed pleasure under Blitzen's rough tongue massaging the cut.

• ••••

After fetching Arthur from his fencing lesson, Gina moped in the kitchen. Time to work up the nerve to place the weekly call to Dad. In hopes of glossing over how little he saw of her these days, Gina lately had established a routine of regular phone calls. Madame Bozek's transformation of her father from an emotional firewall to a peddler of joy only fanned Gina's anxiety. Now her aversion to the neighbor cat's dodder and slime felt unkind and troublingly instinctual, too close to her feelings over Dad's aging. That Dad deserved a lukewarm daughter did not ease her guilt. He was celebrating his age, while her mother never would have the chance either to love or suffer the twilight years.

She forced herself to place the call, which turned weird almost immediately. "It's important not to get rustly, Virginia."

She'd just told him Red had submitted his one hundredth job application, a federal architect position on a Dubai air base. For the building trades wiped out in the downturn, opportunity resided squarely in the Middle East. "Do you mean rusty, Dad?" Was it a bad connection or his new habit of jumbling his consonants that led her to hear made-up words? The land line filled with static. Dad refused to use his cell phone.

"Rustly, Daughter. Undisciplined energy will overtop your psychic stream."

"That doesn't make any sense."

"Wash dishes. Answer phones. Groom horses. Any job will do. Pride won't pay the bills."

"If only humiliation did," she muttered. *Rustly. Undisciplined energy.* Gina chalked such nonsense up to Madame Bozek's rhetorical flourishes. She still couldn't believe that the man who'd never trafficked in any spiritual creed was devoting all his time and God knew how much cash to sessions with a fortune-teller. This while he'd made no financial overtures to his own daughter to help with their predicament. Gina leaned against the counter. Under the cobwebbed window sill, dirty lunch dishes crowded the sink, the worn Corelle rims chipped like beaten-up teeth.

"Let me set something up for you with Steed," Dad was saying.

Barnard Steed Lincoln Mercury was in bankruptcy. Gina had heard the news from Steed's neighbors, who were tracking the foreclosure proceedings on the man's house. "I don't think Steed's hiring, Dad." The dish rack next to the sink boasted a spotless Toucan Sam cereal bowl. A spoon gleamed in the silverware holder. Arthur had washed his breakfast dishes again. That evening, when she came in to figure out the cheapest way to make pasta appealing for yet another night, Gina would find he'd cleaned up the lunch dishes, too.

Gina moved to the window. Beyond the fence, the loamy black mulch piled at the evergreen's trunks had turned a wan gray in the heat.

"You need to work the phones, Daughter. Resumes don't land jobs."

"I've made calls, Dad. So has Red. Many, many calls."

"Atta girl. I've got Madame working up some spirit lines for you. Keep you balanced until the breakthrough."

Dad insisted on calling the psychic Madame like the woman was some ancient village seer. Gina never could shed her irritation long enough to wonder whether Dad might be losing hold of his unerringly shrewd judgment as well as his wallet. A door slammed. Red appeared on the back patio swinging a spade and a pair of gardener's kneepads as if he were actually going to spruce up the yard. "Thanks. I guess."

"There always is one, sweetheart."

"Spirit lines? You know I don't believe in that stuff, Dad." Red caught her eye through the window, flicked a cheery thumbs-up, and headed toward the back fence.

"A breakthrough." Rebuke hardened Dad's voice, more like his old self. "Something will come along. Just make sure your eyes are open when opportunity falls in your lap."

"The impact should be hard to miss." Over the phone line's cottony buzz she heard the discreet clinking of Dad's china tea service. So Madame was there pouring out tea, no doubt diluting it with an elderly spinster's heavy hand with the milk and sugar. Once they hung up, the woman was bound to brush Dad's fingers discreetly when she handed over his cup and saucer, the china rattling bone on bone. Gina hoped these teas were a substitute for the exchange of more intimate fluids. Dad's wealth made him a prime mark for a rip-off artist looking to secure a more earthly gig. A murmured question flowed through the line, the clear, silky voice still clinging fiercely to youth. The mouthpiece muffled, and then Dad was back, tone brisk.

"Forces are gathering, Daughter. Have to sign off soon."

"That's fine. Got some spooks of my own to tend." At the fence, Red was strapping the kneepads to legs bunkered in long canvas pants. It was true Red hated shorts. And he did walk with a slight limp, a holdover from a serious bout of reactive arthritis when they were first married. No wonder Helen had been so quick to believe Arthur. Arthur must have based the fib on Red's limp, which Gina hardly noticed anymore but might be obvious to their son or their neighbors as evidence of an adventuresome past life.

"They hear, you know."

"Who, Dad?"

"Spirits. When you mock them. Your mother might be listening."

Some nerve. Her mother had committed suicide just before Gina and Red's wedding. Gina had discovered the body when she stopped by with the mother-of-the-bride dress she'd picked up from the local mall. The death came long after her parents' divorce, but Gina held Dad responsible. Any child would, she reasoned. After the split, her mother had struggled with depression and poverty. When her mother died, Gina couldn't bear to see Dad anymore. She broke off all contact until Arthur was old enough to ask if he had grandparents. By then, Dad was Arthur's only living grandparent. She'd reconnected, then, for her son's sake.

After fifteen years, calling him out on his unfeeling crap was misspent anger. "Yeah, well . . . I meant something else. Clients. I'm actually doing some consulting."

"Freelancing the bookkeeping?"

"Um. Pet care, actually."

"Excellent," he said approvingly. "Your uncle is mopping up that market in Florida, you know. I'll put you in touch for some pointers. Got a whole fleet of mobile grooming vans. *Joltin' Joe's Groom on the Go.* Shampoo, nail clipping. Even brush a dog's damn teeth."

DiMaggio should open a spirit line to his estate lawyers, Gina thought. Outside, Red sank gingerly to his knees and took up a spade. The emerald-green kneepads, brighter than the grass, disappeared in a thicket of clover. Was this stiffness new? Arthur had told the neighbor women Red's "wound" had been acting up lately. Maybe Red was having trouble with his joints. She pushed aside any guilt that her son was more in touch with Red's well-being than she was.

"Charges top dollar according to zip code," Dad was saying. "Make sure you do the same, Daughter. Swanky clients expect swanky prices for quality service. None of this fifteen dollars a day crap." He paused a beat. Gina swore under her breath. *Bull's-eye.* She hadn't mentioned how much the cat work was paying. "Any time you want Madame to meet with you, sweetheart, she's promised to make room. She's overbooked these days, but she'll fit you in. As a favor to me."

Gina had never met Madame and wasn't about to, either, unless it was to run interference on the woman's influence over her father. Gina kept hoping an intervention wouldn't become necessary. Dad's notorious suspicion of women's designs on his money was bound to triumph over the wiles of a woman no doubt draped in a paisley muumuu with wire-and-jade bangles twined around her bony wrists.

Madame Bozek was saying something to her father again. Gina imagined a flowing patterned scarf wound around a crimped nest of graying hair. Must be time to break out the cheesy crystal ball. But the charlatan's image Gina conjured at that drifting background voice didn't diminish one hard fact. Since taking up with Madame, Dad had divined, with eerie accuracy, every detail of Gina's misfortunes. He'd known about Gina's banishment from the Price office by the time she reached home in tears. He called the night of Red's disappearing client to warn her of "the dust storm," which, in the dead of winter, made no sense until Red told Gina the absconder's name was Dustin Stromberg. For a time, the land line threw him off. Dad had complained he couldn't get a "read" on her if she didn't visit in person. Now it seemed he'd scaled that barrier. Either that or Madame was coaching him.

She ruled out utterly the notion that the fifteen bucks was a lucky guess.

"Dad, you know, I'm real busy with Arthur."

"Bring the boy when you come tomorrow."

"I can't come tomorrow."

"The forces reveal a midmorning journey, Daughter. I miss the boy bundles. Signing off." The disconnection's flat drone rang in her ear.

Gina hung up, furious at the guilt trip that her avoidance was keeping Arthur from his grandpa. Red finished grooming one fence post and crawled to the next, sneezing. He must be wilting in the full sun, clad in those canvas pants. Why was he weeding by hand, when that flame-throwing gizmo stashed in the garage was supposed to make the chore a cinch? Gina's last gift to Red before the downturn had been the Weed Dragon, a portable flamethrower they'd laughed over at the local hardware store before the store manager demonstrated how to cremate a clump of dandelions to fine ash motes. Red could use it standing up, finish the job in a fraction of the time. That's what the store manager had sold them on, anyway.

Gina went to the garage and pulled the Dragon from between a stack of two-by-fours and the bird feeders they couldn't afford to fill this season. The whole outfit was bulkier than she remembered. She hefted the propane tank and tucked the wand under her arm. On the way out the back door, she remembered the store manager wore goggles. She also remembered the impressive radius of the blue flame zapping those poor dandelions. She dug out goggles from a box Red had labeled *Safety* and headed for the fence.

At the relief of her shadow blocking the sun, Red looked up at her. Gina plunked the Dragon down on the grass. "Why don't you use this? You look so miserable all hunched over."

Red stared at the flamethrower as if struggling to remember why they possessed such a contraption. "Seems like overkill, don't you think?"

"Worked great at the store."

"Yeah, well. We should have returned it when our pocketbooks went to hell."

Gina sympathized with the real reason he didn't want to use the Dragon, but she was sick of avoiding the gadgets and luxuries of their former life with the same buried shame that drove them to bail on the household chores. "Yeah, well. Since we didn't, might as well put it to good use."

"It feels good to be working with my hands." But Red rose slowly to his feet, his brow bright with sweat. The kneepads, streaked with dirt and grass, hung loosely at his shins. Red slipped them off and set the spade on a fence post.

Gina handed him the goggles. "Why do you wear pants in the summer, anyway? It's scorching out here."

Red pulled the goggles over his eyes and inspected the tank. "Call your dad?"

"How did you know?"

"You always ask weird questions after you talk to him."

"No I don't. But, as it happens, yes. I interrupted tea with Madame. Heard all about my uncle's lucrative mobile dog-grooming fleet."

Red fastened the tank to his back with the Dragon's wide black straps, toggled a switch. The wand's tip hiccupped softly, and the odor of propane swirled in the humid air. Red grinned, gray eyes shining behind the goggles. "Do I look bad ass?"

"Like you're out to launch a preemptive strike on a cockroach."

Red gave her a mock salute with the wand. A long blue flame shot from the tip. Red jumped. "Jesus."

"Be careful with that thing!" Gina took a step back.

"I'll say. Almost gave myself a permanent hickey." Gina rolled her eyes. Red laughed. "I know you can't resist a man and his fire stick. Come on over here and plant the real thing on me." Red moved to sweep her in a hug, one hand sliding to her thigh. The wand slapped her bare leg. The tip was still hot.

"Ow!" Gina pushed him away. Red stumbled back, thrown off balance by the tank, she thought. Or maybe his joints were stiffer than she realized. "Sorry. Didn't mean to knock you over."

"Of course you didn't." Red slid the tank off his shoulders and bent over a dial, not meeting her eyes.

"The guy at the store said to have water on hand." Gina rubbed her leg. "There's an idea."

She left Red fiddling with the dial. In the garage, Gina went right to a neat stack of buckets standing on a shelf marked *Medium Bins*. Before the downturn, Red had organized his garage meticulously, down to the smallest washer for a quick faucet repair. Now the cool, dim space felt like the last stand against the helpless disarray of the Arnold house and yard. Gina breathed in a momentary peace before fetching a bucket. Below the buckets was the *Recreation* shelf. Between Arthur's outgrown T-ball equipment and Red's high school practice football, the *Flies* bin lay empty, not yet re-purposed.

Gina filled the bucket with water from the spigot at the back of the garage. When she returned, Red was pointing the wand at a patch of clover near the fence post. The cheery purple heads incinerated in a flash of blue. The flame was smaller now, more precise. Red scuffed at the remaining ash with the tip of his work boot. "Wow. Nifty, don't you think?"

"Aren't you supposed to zap the roots or something? That's what the guy at the store said." Gina set the bucket down next to the play structure. "Should I be worried that Madame Bozek is exerting undue influence over my father?"

"I think that's the least of your worries." Red always thought she was overreacting to Madame Bozek. *If she makes the old man happy, be happy for him, Gina.*

"Not if she cleans him out. It says on her website that house calls go for five hundred dollars an hour." The website had scrupulously detailed prices, all of them outrageous. Rosy-cheeked fairy figurines perched on healing stones adorned the price list page. Gina hadn't seen a photo of Madame Bozek anywhere, only waterfalls spilling serenely amidst fern clusters. "The site said she specializes in grooming clients for future prosperity. I think she's grooming Dad for *her* future prosperity."

"Maybe you should visit more often, keep tabs a bit more. Might make you feel better." Red glanced at her as he pumped propane into the wand, his gaze shimmery behind the steamy goggle lenses. He seemed like he was having fun, for once. Score one for the Dragon.

"I feel better not visiting, actually. Now he's keeping his cell phone off all the time, so reaching him is a pain." She hadn't told Red about her suspicions that Dad might be reading her aura through the phone lines. She also never told him about Dad's dead-on predictions.

"He needs reminding to turn it on, Gina."

"He does it on *purpose*."

"He's just old, and not plugged in like we are. Remind him. A lot. That's what we do for elderly parents, right?"

Right. Before their passing, Red's spry parents thrived on farming the artisan winery they'd purchased from the returns on farsighted long-term investments. His parents lived a sensible, committed life. No goofy psychics laying hands on their grapes to predict the next harvest. No ghost of a mother who'd taken her life on the eve of her only child's wedding.

Red moved on to the next post. The crabgrass he zapped burned up and wafted away like an obedient signal fire. He'd gotten the hang of the Dragon fast, as was his way. "What puts you in such an energetic mood for yardwork, anyway?"

"I've been working on a lay out for some condos. Thought I'd take a break, tackle some of the stuff we've been letting go lately." Hope laced his voice.

"Who on earth wants to build condos now?"

"A Michigan football fanatic who wants to put his Chicago connections up for the home games in style. You'll be interested to know Jim Price referred me. I think he's hoping to revive the firm. We were supposed to meet up with the client this morning, in fact."

"*Supposed* to?"

"He had something come up at the last minute."

"You drew a sketch for a no-show client?"

"He *rescheduled*. Price thinks it's going to go ahead. Eventually. Anyway, nothing else to do but apply for computer-drafting work in the Arabian Peninsula." Red pumped the wand and moved down the fence. "By the way, Don Gammon landed a temporary job overseas."

Don Gammon used to be president of the state architects' professional society back when there was a state architects' professional society. "That's fantastic. Where?"

"Afghanistan. He's sleeping on his daughter's sofa until he leaves." Red torched the next patch of crabgrass. Now that the fence was looking manicured, Gina felt some unspoken pact between them eroding, that letting things go was their tacit way to face losing it all. Red had been right. Throwing flames at a bunch of plants was overkill. "I'll take my chances with Price," Red continued. "At least until Arthur is old enough to afford a sofa."

A breeze stirred, and sparks flew to the fence post. Flames lapped the pine. Gina made a move for the bucket, but Red smothered the fire with his sole. Flakes of blackened wood settled lightly among the weeds. The jagged scorch mark would be glaringly obvious to the neighbors no matter who owned the fence.

"Jesus, Red. How are we going to deal with this now?"

"Nothing. It'll give the girls something to remember us by."

Gina kicked at the post. "Next you'll light your pants on fire. Why *do* you wear them, anyway? Are you self-conscious about the limp?"

"What limp?"

"*The* limp. You know you hobble around when the weather turns."

"Do you consider this weather *turned*?" Red wiped his brow with his sleeve. "Why, after fifteen years of marriage, are you asking about my summer pants?"

"Arthur told the girls it's because you lost a leg in Desert Storm."

Red grinned. "Arthur learned about Desert Storm already? I didn't even get to Vietnam until AP History."

Gina folded her arms. "It doesn't faze you that our son is telling the neighbors you're a general who lost a leg in service to your country?"

"I'm honored he'd make me a general."

"Or maybe he feels he has to make up status for you." She bit her lip as soon as the words leaped between them.

Red turned away and launched a flame at a knot of dandelions. "Ginny, tell me what to do differently and I'll do it. It's natural for Arthur to feel that way. Just like it's natural for you to work out your frustrations by blaming me. I wish our reactions to this could be different. But it's all very . . . expected."

Sunlight flashed on his goggles. His thinning hair, pure silver now, ran sweat. When Arthur was two, Gina had suffered complications in her pregnancy's eighth month. The baby strangled on the umbilical cord. She'd had to deliver him stillborn. Another son. Overnight the brassy hair that gave Red his nickname leeched its color, turned gossamer. Now the silver strands were light-traps, especially in the sunshine. Quicksilver, as if all his bright energy had risen to the surface. She wanted to fly to him then, nestle her cheek to his chin's grizzle that sprang back from a shave like grass from a firm step, wrap him up in the playful hug he'd tried to give her.

"Red, I don't blame you for our . . . situation."

Red paused to roll up his sleeves, his ritual before concentrating on a design. "That's good, because it's not my fault. Ginny, can you ask your dad for a loan until this client signs?"

Her lovey impulse toward him evaporated. "I can't do that."

"You have to."

"Absolutely not. What do mean by loan, anyway? Is your phantom client the collateral?"

"OK, then, don't call it a loan." Red maintained a steady tone she could almost call professional. "Call it a gift."

"My dad doesn't give gifts. Look, I am not going to beg my dad for money. Even if I did, he wouldn't help. I promised myself a long time ago I wouldn't put myself through that ever again."

Red looked at her through the goggles, fogged over with sweat. His pants were etched with ash and dirt around the clean patch left by the knee-pads, his bony knees outlined like faces wiped clean of their topography. "Please, Gina."

Gina shook her head. A cluster of hornets darted from the tire swing's rubber rim. "You know better than to ask me that. And you better take care of those things before the neighbor kids get stung the next time they're over and there's real hell to pay from the girls." Gina pointed at the swing.

Red strode to the tire, aimed the wand and torched a hornet. The flaming body dropped into a patch of clover.

"Jesus, Red. What did you do that for?"

"It's what you want, right?" Confused, the hornets buzzed in a crooked spiral. Red launched another flame into their loop. Several bodies popped and sputtered to the grass.

"Hey." Gina retreated to the fence as the survivors regrouped and revved toward her. "Cut that out."

Red left her to duck and weave until the hornets swarmed past her into the neighbors' yard. He pumped the propane and aimed the wand at the Rugged Rumpus slide, incinerating the Queen Anne's lace with a smooth sweep of flame. The heat dimpled the slide's plastic lip. "You want to know why I don't wear shorts? Because you told me my knees were knobby. You said they were a turnoff."

"I did not!"

"You did." He paused. "At Ludington. On our honeymoon. I remember it because it was the first time you'd said anything even remotely mean to me." Like their wedding, their honeymoon had been delayed by her mother's death. The romantic ceremony at Cobblestone Farm was cancelled. Eventually they'd exchanged quiet vows at the new county courthouse on Main Street Red had designed. The honeymoon was an afterthought, Ludington chosen for the easy drive. Gina remembered lying on white, hot sand. One day she'd walked blindly with a group of tourists out to the lighthouse bisecting the bay. Lake Michigan stretched to the horizon, a brilliant accordion of every shade of blue. The tourists exclaimed over the lake's beauty, but the water's endless stretch struck Gina not as pretty, but sensible.

All that week she was surrounded by family picnics in the lakeside park. The aroma of smoldering brats mingled with the squeals of shaggy-haired kids, their wet swim trunks drawing shimmering streaks on shiny metal slides. The odor of charcoal had led her back to her mother's tiny bedroom on the day she died. The body splayed on the bed, flushed as if from the summer heat, was almost nude. Her mother was wearing her new lace support bra and Lycra hose, as if she'd known Gina was bringing the mother-of-the-bride dress and was simply waiting to try it on. But she couldn't know. The tailor had called Gina to tell her the dress was done early. This visit was to be a surprise. Two charcoal grills smoldered near the only window. The doorjamb and window casings were stuffed with towels. On top of the bookcase by the closet, a row of candles burned brightly, the only light in the dusky room. Flames licked the dropped tile ceiling. Gina remembered hanging the dress carefully on the closet doorknob. She remembered clambering on a chair to blow out the candles. She had to blow hard to extinguish the broad, bright flames, she remembered. Only after the black, curling wicks were trailing smoke did she throw open the window and douse the charcoal.

She never would understand why she hadn't immediately rushed to let in the fresh air, call 911, start CPR, scream her mother's name. Perhaps the fumes fogged her reasoning. Or perhaps she couldn't bear to touch the body, lurid with the legs sprawled, the arms thrown wide as if tied to the bedposts. Her mother bore the desolate, pleading pose of a violent death, not a self-inflicted one. Afterward she would carry a sadness that she'd blown out the candles at all. As she waited to die, her mother would have watched those flames graze the ceiling. The light would have been her mother's last glimpse of brilliance. Gina would always feel she'd smothered her mother's final comfort.

She remembered the harsh odor of charcoal in the state park, and Lake Michigan's stretch of blue, but she didn't remember Red's knees. "That's not fair. I wasn't exactly myself on that trip. Anyway, I would never say such a thing."

From the house, a door creaked. Arthur's sand-dollar hair bobbing across the brown lawn was the one reliable buoy to her spirits. He ran up to the tire swing, threw a deft parry at the swaying chain. "Hey, Dad. That flamethrower's neat."

"Does the job, buddy." Red ruffled his hair.

Arthur playacted a thrust at Red's tank. "Shouldn't we do the cats now, Mom?"

Red turned back to the weeds without countering Arthur's game. Arthur didn't seem to notice Red had cut him off. As Gina slipped through the fence rails after Arthur, Red's quiet *please* followed her, not, quite yet, a plea.

● ●●●●

When she opened the pass door into the back foyer, Donder and Blitzen crashed into Gina's ankles, mewling gratefully. "Pet them, honey. Quick," Gina pleaded.

"Kinda hard to do when they're fastened to *you*." But Arthur bent over dutifully to pass a hand over their bony skulls. The cats flashed him their baleful cataracts and pressed stubbornly against Gina's shins.

"You're over here all the time," she complained. "Why don't they run to you?"

"They only like girls." He scratched between their eyes and then bravely sledded his fingers down each lumpy spine. "Why is their fur always wet, Mom?"

"Just because they're old, I guess."

"Why does that make their fur slimy?"

"I don't fully understand the biology behind that. Isn't there a game you can play with Dunder and Mitzie here while I deal with the litter box?"

"It's Donder and Blitzen, Mom." Arthur threw her a look just shy of adolescent condescension. "You know. Like Santa and all that."

"I *know*, honey." Gina wavered between exasperation and an uneasy embarrassment that he wouldn't recall one of her favorite memories. "Don't you remember how you used to call Santa's last reindeer Dunder and Mitzie?"

"No." Now disdain flooded his expression. All that was missing was the eye roll, as if she were imagining the whole sweet story.

"Well, you did."

Arthur did roll his eyes then. "Well, I wasn't *wrong*. In my German language exploratory we learned that Dunder is the original German spelling."

"Oh. Guess you were just precocious, then." Gina tried to smile lightly at his scowl.

"We also learned that Dunder and Blitzen mean thunder and lightning."

Gina's smile froze. The doddering pair teemed unsteadily at her sneakers like fat earthworms on LSD. "Doesn't exactly describe this pair of dashing old men, does it?"

"They aren't men, Mom. They're girls."

"No, they aren't."

Arthur lifted Blitzen up by the front paws. "See?"

"Oh." Gina squinted halfheartedly under the sagging belly. "Why would Candice and Helen name girl cats after Santa's reindeer?"

"What do you mean?"

"*Boy* reindeer?"

Arthur frowned at her. "That's sexist, Mom. And dumb. Everyone knows Santa's reindeer are girls."

"They are not."

Arthur sighed. "Both girl and boy reindeer get antlers, but the boys drop their antlers in the fall. Only girl reindeer have antlers in the winter. Santa's reindeer *have* to be girls."

"I've never in my life heard that. You're making it up."

Arthur herded the cats toward the kitchen. "Look it up. I'll check their food. You do the box."

"We're switching next time." Gina headed south to the basement to perform the dirty work while Arthur corralled the old folks.

She puzzled over why she felt regret over bringing up the childish memory. Maybe her vague sense of shame had to do with his fastball into adolescence. Since the winter he'd sprouted dark, gangly hairs above his lip. He'd shot up five inches, his lanky legs still coated with a little boy's silky down. His voice was sinking fast under a restless Adam's apple. Thank God he wasn't towering over her yet, although by the end of the summer she might be staring at that bounding Adam's apple while demanding he clean his room.

Another child might have spared Arthur her chronic, anxious babying. After she'd delivered her stillborn boy, she suffered tender, leaking breasts through the memorial. For weeks afterward she was confused by an odd sensation of adrenaline that didn't feel like grief. She chased toddler Arthur around the house wrapped in a sensation of floating. Sometimes her ascent felt like being borne aloft by a pair of soft, sturdy arms. In those moments her breasts hurt as if her nipples had been bitten raw by pearly baby's teeth.

One night after Arthur was in bed and Gina roved the house, agitated and unmoored, Red sat her down on the den couch. He lit a candle on the sofa table and held her hand. He must have bought it just for her, since Gina never kept candles in the house. *I never wanted to tell you this. I was afraid it would upset you. But I know why your mother was burning candles.*

The flame was stunted, smoking. The wick was too short. A syrupy lavender odor filled the den, sickening sweet.

She hoped the monoxide would combust when it rose high enough. She was hoping to spare you the sight of her.

The smoke formed a silver filament she could almost climb, through the ceiling and Arthur's room and the attic to dissolve in the night sky's velvet. Gina was, suddenly, grateful for the vision she would forever carry of her mother splayed rudely on the bed. She'd seen her baby's final pose, too, the limp body blue and soundless on the table that for a living baby would have been warmed. These final glimpses of her mother and her son should be cherished, not mourned, she understood now.

If her first impulse hadn't been to blow out her mother's candles, Gina might have been caught in the explosion, but she didn't think of this. She let go of Red's hand. The candle on the sofa table sputtered out in the rising pool of lavender wax.

The floating ceased then. It was around that time that Gina contacted Dad for the first time since her mother's death. From the beginning, Dad loved Arthur with a gentleness Gina never thought he could feel for anyone. She never did tell him about the miscarriage, partly out of distrust of revealing anything personal to him, partly to protect the happiness Arthur and Dad shared that, although she didn't want to admit it, comforted her.

After a while, she and Red gave up trying for another pregnancy. They coddled Arthur fiercely. Nurturing his sweetness, they called it.

Gina scooped the litter box and tiptoed up the stairs, hoping Arthur's attentions would distract the cats. As she rounded the corner into the kitchen, they crashed into her ankles like kamikazes on their final run.

"Arthur," she whined. "What are you doing?"

From the living room the pump of the carpet-cleaner dispenser preceded his voice. "Cleaning up a hairball. Looks like vomit."

"Jesus." Gina waded through the cats to deposit the garbage outside the patio slider.

"There's pine needles in the vomit, Mom. And bark." The vigorous sound of spritzing wafted into the kitchen.

"Uh-huh."

"You didn't let them out, did you? They're too old to go outside."

"Of course not, honey." Gina nudged the cats away from the door and shuffled over to the kitchen sink to draw a drink of water. Through the window she watched Red head back to the garage. The low evening sun bathed the evergreens in a warm orange glow. She drank to a needy mewling chorus.

"I'm not petting you," she told them. "You're bad girls. Who left the hair-ball bomb?" Donder winked a glassy eye. "I thought so." No sign of matted blood on Donder's fur, Gina saw with relief. She could barely see the scrape's jagged line.

"What?" Arthur called out.

"Nothing."

"Talking just agitates them." Offered cheerfully, like plain-old helpful advice.

Were they agitated, or just plain addled? The cats set to licking each other's whiskers. Gina moved to the lovey notebook, opened it to the middle, eavesdropped on the snippets of affection, errands, and orders the girls swapped lightly like blown kisses. *Lick me like a lollipop*, the playful script suggested a few pages in. The block writing answered with a crude drawing of a sucker whose bold lines resembled the folds of the female anatomy. The couple was snug in the secure harness of dual incomes and dual kids and dual cats brimming with needs easily met. An unexpected crest of tears surprised her. Gina brought a hand to her cheek too late, and a drop landed squarely on Helen's scrawl. The babe in *it'll get better babe* bled into better until the ink cobwebbed.

What in Candy and Helen's life needed to get better? Gina rubbed her tears into the paper and flipped through the notebook's midsection, skimming. Clinical references to Monistat, Diflucan, and extra yogurt purchases populated the pages up until about the time the women had locked horns with Red over the property line. Was the neighbors' only setback during this downturn a stubborn bout of yeast?

The cats finished their shared bath and decided to clean Gina's sneaker laces. She suppressed a mean impulse to kick them away.

"Did you change their water, Mom?"

Arthur's deep voice startled her, as it often did these days. He was standing in the den doorway. She snapped the notebook shut. "Of course," she fibbed.

"We aren't allowed to look in that book." He studied her doubtfully. The bottle of carpet cleaner and the sodden rag he clutched reeked like a sterilized locker room. The cats mewled louder as if complaining of the fumes. "I don't think anyone's supposed to."

"Oh. I was just. You know, checking to see whether the *um* ladies had left any more instructions about the cats."

"It's not that kind of book." Arthur was giving her one those new unnervingly adult stares. "Colt got in big trouble when he looked in it once." He paused. "Is it true you don't like Candy and Helen because they're gay?"

"What? No! That's ridiculous. Why, did *they* say that?"

"Candy and Helen would never say anything mean. Which means maybe it's true?"

It was the first time you ever said anything remotely mean to me.

Red's knees. She did remember. His legs stretched in the sand, toes pointed at Lake Michigan, the kneecaps funny bald domes gleaming in the sun. She'd rapped the bone until he winced. Under her knuckle the cap felt like a skull. What had she said? Something about how bare they looked attached to his hairy legs, that was all. Better use sunscreen. She'd said that, too. Were those comments so cutting he'd carried them for fifteen years?

Arthur was still clutching the rag and dispenser, awaiting her answer. Wait—*did* she dislike the women because they were gay? She'd never considered herself remotely prejudiced. No, she'd liked them fine before the property dispute. Well, any high regard really dated from before the juice box affair, although the neighbors' showy, cultivated tastes and trendy helicopter parenting always had struck her as smug. Too, they'd always seemed so disapproving of her heterosexual, single-child, petless lifestyle as privileged, or at least, lacking imagination.

"Of course they wouldn't mean to be mean but it *is* mean to think that I would . . ." She let the words trail as she dropped her gaze to his T-shirt. Streaks of spit up, hair, and white stains spattered the fabric like the sloppy toddler art projects he'd once presented proudly to her. "Arthur. You're a mess." She paused, letting the fact of the white stains sink in. The locker room fumes came into focus. Her gaze slid to the bottle in his hand. Not carpet cleaner. Clorox with Bleach. "You didn't use that on the carpet, did you?"

He looked at the bleach as if seeing it for the first time. "No."

"You're holding the *bottle*, sweetie." She struggled to soften her accusing tone, coax the truth. "Is that what you used to clean up Donder's mess?"

He met her eyes boldly. "I didn't."

Donder bolted into the living room. She wouldn't have imagined that sack of bones could move so fast. She followed to see the old cat rubbing his—*her*—sagging belly against a softball-sized ring of bleached, frayed fibers glaring from the midnight-blue wool carpeting like a fallen moon.

• ••••

Before he left to meet with Price and the phantom client the next morning, Red delivered glum remarks he may have intended to be a pep talk about her dad and bridging temporary financial gaps. Gina burned her lip on the instant coffee he'd fixed for her. Red knew he was asking the impossible. After her parents' divorce, when the discrepancy between the caliber of lawyers each could afford had broken her mother and enriched her father, her mother's job in the Sears appliance department couldn't begin to cover the basics. As a teenager, Gina sparred with him over late support payments when her mother wouldn't muster the gumption anymore. Gina had even gone begging for groceries once when she'd broken her ankle and couldn't work at the evangelical home for six weeks. One of Dad's oft-donned aphorisms was about pulling yourself up by your bootstraps, and by God he'd stuck to that one over the years. She'd always viewed his stinginess as just another maxim, not as liberation from a depressed wife.

He *had* ended up buying groceries, though, that one time.

Gina trudged to cat duty not knowing whom to resent more—Red, Dad, or Donder and Blitzen. After changing the water and doling out the vitamins she'd managed to forget every time, she moped her way across the backyard. Arthur was parrying his foil with the tire swing chains. The foil had been his last gift before the recession hit. With an economizing impulse that in hindsight may have been her own future-gazing, Gina hadn't purchased the professional model Arthur had admired in the mall sword shop, but a cheap online knock-off. Arthur never noticed the difference. His lessons were the one luxury she didn't have the heart to take from him. She'd put the summer session on a credit card, nudging it over the limit.

She paused behind the evergreens to watch him practice his steps. He studied his canvas tennis shoes, streaked with grass stains and dirt, as they maneuvered into the lunge on a chain link. His lips moved silently with each thrust as if reciting the next step. It was like watching him learn to read, when his concentration had focused not on divining the meaning of the words but on the perplexing task of pronunciation. He executed a clean strike dead center through a link. The chain chimed merrily as the blade slid against the metal. Gina clapped.

Although Arthur was facing her as he sparred, he hadn't seen her behind the firs. He yanked the foil from the link. The rubber ball protecting the blade's tip popped off and plunked into the bucket of now-murky water, forgotten after Red's yard work.

"Mom! Look what you made me do!"

Gina bounded to the fence and hopped the rail. Arthur plunged his arm into the algae film the heat had shellacked on the water's surface. The sour odor of mildewed water mixed with his sweat's sharp musk. As a boy, on hot summer days he'd smelled of sugared milk. "Let's dump it out, honey."

Arthur withdrew his hand, cradling the ball in his palm. The smooth boyish skin and nubby fingers were adorably out of sync with his long body. With a childish cuff he kicked over the bucket. "What am I going to do now? My lesson's tomorrow!"

"I'm so sorry, sweetheart. I didn't mean to scare you like that." Gina's remorse burrowed deeper at the hard proof that she'd purchased a piece of shit.

Arthur examined the blade despondently. The tip had snapped cleanly off. "Can we fix it? Because we don't have the money to *replace* it."

She met her son's accusing gaze. *The forces reveal a midmorning journey, Daughter. Bull's-eye.* "We have to go see Grandpa now, honey," she sighed. "Maybe he can help us out."

Arthur grinned. "We're going to see Grandpa?"

"He . . . invited us."

Instead of demanding to know whether Grandpa would buy him a new sword, the thought that would have sprung to her own mind at Arthur's age, her son exclaimed, "I miss Grandpa. He's funny." He bounded to the van, broken foil aloft as if leading the charge.

The morning rush hour was winding down, but Jackson Road was stalled to a creep. A line of cars was backed up at the longest stoplight in town, where gas stations and car dealerships checkered the boulevard. Already the day's heat was oppressive. Through the open window an impatient horn blasted, and the smoky odor of gas and rubber clogged the breeze. Arthur cradled the broken foil on his lap like a wounded pet and stared out the window at the vacant lot where Diamond Ford, Dad's dealership, used to stand. A Subaru dealership had been planned for the site, but the recession hit after demolition on Dad's place. Concrete rubble and drifting piles of dirt stood abandoned. The demolition had taken out the old oaks lining the road, too. No more nuts.

A horn honked again, this time at Gina's rear bumper. She honked back. Sweat ran down her neck, pearled in the space between her shoulders and the upholstery. "Why did you fib about the bleach, honey?"

Arthur lodged a finger in his mouth. "I didn't."

"You were *holding* the Clorox. How could you look me straight in the eye and tell a fib like that?"

He looked her straight in the eye. "I didn't."

"Sweetheart," she began. He looked down at his foil. A flush seeped around his T's fraying neck. "Did you fib to Colten and Priscilla's mommies about your daddy being in the army?"

The flush flamed scarlet. "I don't remember."

"Did you fib about him being a general? Fighting the Iraqis?" She paused. His head sank to his chest. "Losing a leg?" Her voice rose impatiently.

Adolescent defiance surfaced hopefully at her change in tone. "Maybe."

The traffic eased through the light. Out of habit, Gina glanced at the hole in the earth where Dad's lot once stood. She used to spot Dad out on the lot no matter what time of day she happened to pass by. He was never one to sit behind a desk. "Come on, Arthur. Tell Mom. Why would you make up such a story?"

Arthur wiped at his nose with his wrist. "Colt was bragging on his dad. So."

"Candice or Helen?"

"His *dad*, Mom."

She sighed. "I didn't think Colten knew who his dad was."

"Well, he does. And he's cool. He designs software and plays in a rock band, I mean, not professionally or anything. Just for fun. He gave Colt some really cool video software when they met."

"Wow. That's pretty cool stuff. I didn't know the mommies kept in touch with . . . the daddy?"

Arthur picked up on the singular. "He's just Colt's dad. Cil has another dad. Anyway, Helen was making us PB-and-J sushi rolls and Colt's bragging, and his dad's . . . well, he's really rich and said he'd take Colt scuba diving in Hawaii over Christmas break when his band goes down there to play, and I guess . . ." He ran a finger over the foil's broken tip. "I guess I wanted to tell something cool about my dad."

"Your dad *is* cool. Architects are way cool. They build stuff."

"I *know*, Mom."

"Your dad designed many buildings in our very own town."

Arthur writhed, wiped his nose again. On the winding road to Dexter, the morning's sweltering tarry odor gentrified to rich, earthy leaves on a tolerably cool breeze. Arthur's hair ruffled in the wind. "I know he used to build cool stuff."

Used to. Gina glanced at her son's slouched body, tucked into the seat all angles and limbs. "Not rock-band cool, I guess. Not rich cool, either," she said quietly. "Right?"

"I didn't mean it like that." He stared at a point just past her shoulder, pleading with the empty space. "Are you going to tell Dad?"

"We have to work something out about the carpet."

"I mean about the other thing."

"Not if it's going to upset you." Her fib. Relief flooded his soft blue eyes. "Colt's a bit young to go scuba diving, you know." She rubbed his shoulder. "And you're a bit too old to be telling fibs."

"You can call them *lies,* Mom. Fibs are what kids tell."

Past the village's outskirts, Dexter's strip malls yielded gently to ginger-bread Victorian homes and wide-eyed bungalows. Gina turned down her father's street, lined with the oaks Jackson Road had lost. Whenever she pulled into Dad's circular drive, Gina always positioned for the getaway. She drove the car straight past the house around the horseshoe bend to park facing the street. A Honda Civic was perched in the turnaround near the garage. She noted the fresh paint, trendy tans and plums, on the Victorian's new siding. The home's style couldn't decide between modern and classic. Anyway he'd sunk a fortune into the renovation. He hadn't hired Red to do the drawings, either. Dad never mixed business with family. Gina cut the engine. Gripped the steering wheel. Stared at her knuckles' white domes. *Keep your nut small.*

"Are you coming, Mom?"

"Fine, honey." She stroked Arthur's hair, snagged a comforting touch of silk before he pulled away.

"I asked if you were *coming,* not how you *are.*"

"Oh. Guess I'm preoccupied." She smiled at him thinly.

He stared at her mouth warily as if the grin was a cover up. "Are you mad that I broke the foil?"

"That was my fault, sweetheart."

Arthur met her eyes squarely. "Then are you mad because I told those lies about Dad?"

"What? No." Gina caught herself. Disapproval felt like duty here. "Well, yes. A little. Not mad, honey. Just concerned, you know? Like maybe you're fibbing because you're concerned about our . . . situation."

"I am concerned about you guys not having jobs, but what does that have to do with lying about Dad?"

"Well. Kids fib when they're stressed. You're not born knowing how to lie. Kids develop it when they're faced with uncomfortable choices. Like having to fess up to something they're afraid to admit. Like breaking something." She paused. "Or staining something. Like the neighbors' carpet."

"I *said* I was sorry."

"I'm just saying, dear, that when all the choices are bad, kids fib. As a way out. Is this making sense?"

"You think I'm being mendacious because I want a way out of your guys not having jobs?"

A lacy curtain at the front window rustled, lifted, and fell. Dad, eyeballing their arrival. "Where did you learn a word like *mendacious*?"

"It was vocab last year, Mom." Arthur rolled his eyes. "Mendacious, mendaciousness, mendaciousnessly."

"Mendaciously," Gina corrected.

He frowned. "I don't think that's right."

Gina yanked open the van door. "Look it up."

Arthur dogged her heels to Dad's threshold. "Mendacity," he hissed into her ear.

Dad called out, "Enter, Daughter," through the door before she'd had the chance to tweak the bell.

As she cruised through the flagstone foyer to Dad's office, converted now into his "parlor," Gina worked to rearrange her expression from annoyance to an acceptable facsimile of good-to-see-you cheer. But her dismay took a hopeless plunge when she stepped into the parlor and saw the round table with the fringed tablecloth he used for séances groaning under the weight of a full tea service. The moist aroma of twigs and orange peel wafted over her. It was barely noon. She'd timed this visit to avoid teatime. Although Dad swore by the medicinal properties of the stuff, tea made her bloat.

"What a thunderpuss you bring today, Daughter." Dad drummed a wizened fist on Arthur's shoulder as her son bent over to hug his frail shoulders. His fingers shook, a tremor she'd first noticed on her last visit. Much worse now. Gina bestowed a light peck on his clammy cheek. Nerves, shame, a weird sort of subterranean gladness attached to her kiss, hanks of emotion she'd never unwind. "Good to see you, young man."

Arthur beamed. "Me too, Grandpa."

"I don't know what that means, Dad."

"That I'm glad to see the boy?" Dad winked at her.

"Thunderpuss?"

"The look on your puss." He motioned them to armchairs draped with the same lurid paisley fabric as the table. "You exude catastrophe and spilt milk."

"You're not making sense."

Arthur sprawled into the chair closest to Dad. "Grandpa means you look pissed, Mom."

"Righto." Dad grinned.

"And depressed." Arthur wormed a cucumber sandwich from a prissy bone-china plate etched with vines and roses.

"Thank you, Son. I get it now. Sit up straight."

Arthur stuck out his lip at her. Dad studied Arthur's slack posture approvingly. "Leave him be. A young man has to spread his aura."

"Whatever happened to *undisciplined energy?*"

Dad turned a rheumy gaze on her. His eyes' brittle lenses glittered like light glancing off dental mirrors. Cataracts? "The boy's energy isn't undisciplined, Virginia. It's expansive."

Arthur chewed away as Gina settled gingerly into the fussy chair opposite. She took in the room with the rising dread she always felt here. Her private spirit of dismay, and not come to reassure her of the joys of the next life, either. The parlor had the farcical look of a movie-set fortune-teller's den. The cherry bookshelves used to boast hardcover leatherette Book of the Month Club volumes, the Great Books series first through third, prized first-edition Sherlock Holmes volumes. Now clunky, mismatched tomes on spiritualism were stacked merrily in no particular order. Proof that, unlike the previous library's fastidiousness, these books were being read. Above the flagstone fireplace's granite mantel, the original Ansel Adams prints, Dad's treasures, had been replaced by grainy photographs of Houdini and Conan Doyle. She wondered again at how thoroughly the precious objects of his long spiritual slumber, as he now called the pre-Bozek days, had been cleaned out.

More fraudulent still was Dad's transformation from hale coffee-drinker to simpering tea-sipper. Every time she saw him, Gina was startled by what she could only classify as shrinkage. His broad chest had collapsed to a hollowed-out crypt. The lavender-scented shawl he'd taken to wearing accentuated the slack canopy of skin cascading from his jowly neck. His complexion, once tanned and thrumming with vigor even in the dead of rigorous Michigan winters, had thinned to a silvery translucence. Bright-violet veins throbbed in the cavern between his eyes and the bony knobs of his temples. He'd been an active man all her life. But while before his activity had been the product of a strong body in relentless motion—the man never sat down except to eat—the ceaseless pulsing of his flesh was now the forced by-product of inertia. There wasn't a single part of Dad that didn't throb, twitch, or distend. And the dowager's hump that had formed from his hunching over tea, blanketed by that ridiculous shawl, completed his transformation from a man of the world to a crone no longer quite in this world.

Unbearable. Gina folded her arms and locked her attention on the tea service, the finger sandwiches and scones, the clotted cream in a dainty bowl with a sterling silver serving spoon. The fussy chairs. The claustrophobia of clashing scents; tea, lavender perfume, the stale odor of sweat Arthur was exuding more fiercely now that they were cramped in this close room. And the overstuffed chairs made it impossible to sit up straight.

The empty one next to her seemed to be raised up off the floor. Maybe it was more comfortable. This chair sported a different slipcover than the rest, a lurid black-and-pink damask rose print. It slowly dawned on her that there were four chairs sidling up to the table. The empty one *was* positioned higher than the rest because the legs were resting squarely on Dad's spirit books. Like a damn throne. And the Civic in the driveway. Since when did Dad consort with Hondas?

Gina glanced up, collided with his eyes' inscrutable glitter. "Madame has just this morning opened up exciting spirit lines for you, Daughter," he preempted smoothly. "We have been waiting for you."

A young, lithe woman, smart in a tailored navy pantsuit, appeared in the doorway brandishing a silver tray loaded with tea cakes. The aroma of fresh pastry and roasted nuts sluiced the humid bergamot air. Arthur sat bolt upright.

"Those look great!" His gaze devoured the perfect double-decker rounds stuffed with almonds and fat whole raspberries, expertly topped with light pillows of icing. After weeks of eating nothing but plain, cheap cereal and pasta, Gina couldn't fault the eager spittle now peppering his lips.

"Cassie sure tinkles her tea cakes," Dad bumbled.

The young woman settled in the raised chair and set the tray on the table close to Arthur. "Help yourself, young man."

Dad pounced on the cakes, beating Arthur's snaking reach. The young woman handed Dad a china plate. Arthur snatched a pastry and bit it in half. Creamy icing skidded from the treat to his lips.

"Arthur." Gina glared at him. "Plate and napkin? And manners?"

"Here you go." The woman gave Arthur a plate. Arthur turned his admiring, hungry gaze from his cake to the beautiful young woman.

Gina's guilt over Arthur's almost desperate enjoyment of the treat was soothed by her irritation at this girl's easy flirtatious tone. Who was this, Madame Bozek's daughter? A niece? A sidekick? How many resources was the woman devoting to bilk her father? "Is this a family operation, then?"

The young woman gazed at Gina with dismayingly stunning eyes. "Excuse me?"

"Who are you?"

"I am Madame Bozek."

"Neat. I'm Arthur. Pleased to meet you." Arthur popped the rest of the cake into his mouth. "Are you going to tell my fortune?"

"At the right time, I will help you see your own future."

The woman's flirtatious tone had vanished, replaced by a level *for-an-additional-fee* drone. Jesus. The woman could not be a day over twenty-two. Far from the muumuued gypsy Gina had been imagining, Madame was not only practically a teenager, but remarkably beautiful. Her smoke-blue hair fell in a luxurious cascade down her back, fastened primly by copper barrettes at either trim ear. The barrettes' brassy color was matched by the scarf knotted at her throat and tucked in the collar of her business-casual blazer. Her clear skin radiated ivory as if backlit by the spirits she trafficked in. But it was her eyes, petal-shaped pools as absorbing as liquid tar, that swallowed the room. Under that gaze, Dad's wet slosh of a gulp was actually audible. Arthur squirmed in his chair. Gina had the feeling his fidgeting wasn't inspired by the sweets.

Madame again zeroed her luminous stare on Gina. Gina fired back with her own notorious look, the one that typically sent Red and Arthur scuttling for an apology over some unfathomed wrongdoing.

"You'll have to forgive my daughter's rudeness." Dad's chin was streaked with more cream than Arthur's. Madame tapped a manicured finger on her cleft. Dad grinned and wiped away the smear with the back of his hand. "These cakes are delicious enough to *wear*, my dear! Virginia's been dueling with some hard times. She's a real trooper, by gad. Pulling herself up by the bootstraps."

"Thriving, in fact," Gina snapped. There went Red's hope of bringing home a check from Dad.

"Started her own petting business."

"Pet care," Gina corrected. Arthur tented his brows at her quizzically. "Starting small. Cats, mostly."

Madame Bozek didn't so much as blink, but Gina got the uncomfortable feeling that the straight-arrow act meant that the woman saw right through her.

"Make certain you're bonded and insured, Virginia, in case those old fogies keel over on your watch. Just takes one unfortunate accident to rubble your business scaffold."

"Excellent foresight, Carl." Madame nodded.

Gina fumed. She'd never mentioned the cats' ages to Dad. "That makes no sense, Dad."

"Insurance, Daughter? A must!"

"*The rubble of my scaffold?*"

"It means if Donder and Blitzen kick the bucket your business is toast," Arthur supplied cheerfully.

"If I've taught my daughter anything, it's self-reliance. Gotta have the guts to start all over when the rustlies smack down. Shall I be mother?" Dad poured a cup for Madame shakily. Delicate golden drops splashed Madame's saucer.

"I can do it, Grandpa." Arthur took the pot gently, aimed a smooth amber stream into Madame's cup.

"I'm glad you arrived, Virginia. We have located some exciting energies for you." Madame's tone was once more brokerage brisk. Gina didn't know which was harder to take: Bozek's professionalism toward the psychic con or the fact that a woman closer in age to Arthur than Gina appeared so poised. And prosperous. Gina would have better traction against the village seer knock-off, whose fakery would eventually doom the charade. Madame Bozek's level voice oozed authenticity.

"Lighting the green candle every teatime for you, Daughter," Dad said. Gina glanced at the table and then, furtively, at the bookshelf behind Dad.

The top of the case was bare. No candle in sight, thank God. Only Red knew about Mom's candles. Apparently that secret was still lodged safely in the bunker of Gina's psyche.

"At the afternoon tea," Madame corrected gently.

"What's a green candle for?" Arthur asked.

"Money," Dad and Madame chimed in unison.

Gina put a hand over her cup as Arthur leaned to serve her tea. "Not thirsty." Madame Bozek finally broke her unnerving gaze to exchange a significant look with Dad.

"A fulsome cup of tea is the kit and caboodle of attainment, Daughter." Dad attempted an off-kilter sip. Tea splashed his lips. Madame rose slightly and discreetly slipped a napkin onto his lap. At least she didn't dab the man's chin.

"So, really, if you light a candle you'll get money?" Arthur asked eagerly.

"If it's green, works every time."

"Dad, please." Gina turned to Arthur. "Honey, that's not a proven fact or anything, OK?"

"Belief is not required for bestowal." Madame Bozek sipped her tea soundlessly.

"Now that my daughter is back in the saddle, time for the good news about my son-in-law," Dad announced.

Gina said, "As it happens, Red is doing fine."

"Daddy got a job?" Arthur's eyes shone with heartbreaking relief.

Gina tucked her guilt away. At least she was telling the truth, or some reasonable version of it. "He's meeting with a major client right now."

"The sands across the sea, then." Dad nodded with satisfaction. "Just so, Cassie. Hit another nail square on the head." Madame Bozek inclined her head modestly. Gina thought she could detect a girlish flush creep along the delicate jaw line at the sound of her name. And Bozek had called him Carl earlier. Could this girl, this *child*, be flirting with her father? Or worse?

"Do the Arabs keep cats, I wonder?" Dad continued thoughtfully.

"Cats were first domesticated in the Middle East, Grandpa." Arthur snagged another tea cake.

"What on earth are you talking about, Dad?" A globe of cream plopped on Arthur's lap. Gina handed him another napkin.

"Your petting business. Will the Arabs hire a woman, do you think? Red should factor in the cultural impact on both your livelihoods, Virginia."

"Dad's moving in with Arabs?" Arthur asked Gina.

"Dad! You're not making *any* sense at all, and you're upsetting Arthur."

"I'm not *upset*." Arthur swatted at his leg with the napkin. "I just want to know about Dad and the Arabs."

"Portability to the desert is something you should have built into the cat business plan, Daughter."

"Animal scientists traced the DNA of all the housecats in the whole world to the DNA of desert cats. Mostly in Saudi Arabia," Arthur said.

"It isn't Saudi Arabia we're talking about, is it, Cassie?" Dad turned to Madame Bozek.

Madame raised her delicate hand. "This revealing is premature."

"Cat's out of the bag." Dad winked.

"When the recession is over, can we get a cat?" Arthur asked Gina.

Madame gave Dad a fond look of mild disapproval. "Carl. Our task is to gift knowledge at the *right* time." She turned to Arthur. "There are adventures ahead, young man, and journeys, and good fortune."

"Neat," Arthur breathed. "Wish Mom hadn't broken my foil just in time for my adventure."

"I didn't break your sword!" Gina blurted.

"Goodness gracious." Dad set down his cup with a clatter. "What is this sword you are needing, Grandson?"

"A *foil*, Grandpa. It's a pistol grip. They sell them at the mall. They aren't *that* expensive."

"Well, that's a thing easily mended, at least." Dad bestowed on Arthur precisely the type of it'll-be-ok smile he'd never once parceled out to Gina. Buying the cheap knock-off was straight out of Dad's playbook. He believed in a child proving their commitment to an enterprise before investing in quality equipment. He never believed in replacing anything Gina had been careless or unlucky enough to break.

"There's the carpet, too," Arthur added.

"Arthur!"

"Well, now, Daughter, that's what insurance is for." Dad glanced at Madame Bozek, who nodded.

Bull's-eye. He divined everything, right down to the bleach stain. Gina should have stuck to the phone calls. "I'm sure the Arabs will spring for it. I thought this visit was all about doing a reading on *me*. How about we break out the psychic deck or the crystal ball or whatever Madame uses."

"They have already contacted me," Madame Bozek told Gina. "They are here with us now."

"Who?"

"Your mother and your son."

From the hallway, a clock chimed. Brassy, artificial notes stirred the air. Gina caught her breath. Rage, and then the old floating. The dull, feathery sensation was almost a comfort. Had she missed this grief?

Arthur crumpled his napkin. "Of course I'm here. But Grandma's dead. Both Grandmas are."

Madame gazed calmly at Gina. "Your mother tells me that the meaning of her passing became clear to her when you sent her your baby, for they are always together."

The floating sensation plummeted. A blackness seeped in, a shade being pulled. How could Dad have shared Gina's deepest wounds with this girl? For the moment she was forgetting that she never had revealed her miscarriage to Dad.

"Are you having a baby, Mom?" Arthur's hesitant curiosity was unbearable.

"What good news, Daughter! Cassie is saying your mother was driven by purpose when she took her life. Not madness."

By you! Gina wanted to scream. Tears sprung to her eyes. *She was driven by you!*

Arthur's voice again, high now, and very young. "Grandma committed suicide?"

"More good news! Before you leave the country, you can forgive me." Her father's certainty infuriated her, as if forgiveness came down to simple cause and effect, not a white-knuckle effort of the will.

Gina wiped at her eyes, bone dry now with rage. The clock's vibration had stopped up her ears. The tea's tangy aroma hung in the damp air. Dad was helping himself to another cup. "I want you to leave." She stared at Madame Bozek so she wouldn't have to watch her father's unsteady pour, wouldn't be tempted to make excuses for this lunacy.

Madame stood up promptly as if she'd been expecting Gina to banish her. She stacked the dirty plates and swept briskly from the room toward the kitchen.

"I meant, leave this *house*," Gina yelled after her.

"Did my grandma commit suicide?" Arthur repeated.

The expression on his face was one Gina had worked his entire life never to see. She reached for his hand. Forced herself to speak softly. "Grandma died of natural causes, sweetheart."

"There is some truth to that statement, Grandson, but the natural aspect of her passing was premeditated." Dad took up his cup again and sipped tea calmly.

From the kitchen the spray hose splashed hollowly against the porcelain sink. "Arthur." Gina handed her son his plate. "Please help Madame with the dishes."

"What about the *baby*?"

"Do the dishes, Arthur."

Arthur unfolded his legs from the prissy chair, grabbed the cakes and bolted to the kitchen.

The floating keeping Gina aloft now was quicksilver fury. There was a recklessness to this levitation she almost liked. *Keep your nut small*, she reminded herself. Anger at her father was a bad investment, one sided and corrosive. "Dad, I'm not sure how to say this."

"Madame B *can* leave one speechless, bless her. Never know to look at her that she is two years older than I."

From the kitchen laughter rose over the rattle of dishes. Gina couldn't separate Madame's light, friendly giggle from Arthur's, the only register of his voice that hadn't deepened. "That girl is barely in her twenties. Look, enough is enough. You can't have anything more to do with her."

"I must, Daughter. Twilight descends, and I crave the revelatory urge."

"That twilight is cataracts. I'm not even going to discuss what the urge is." Gina leaned forward, the nearest move she could make to drawing close to him. "I want you to see a doctor."

"I'm hale and hearty, Daughter."

"A mental health professional."

"Ah." Dad looked at her shrewdly, his old dealer's cunning. "It would be easier for you, wouldn't it, if I was unfit to forgive."

"We tell Arthur Mom died of natural causes. I don't want you telling him anything different. Ever." She tried not to think about the fact that Dad had just made it impossible for Arthur ever to believe this again.

Dad took up his teacup. "Do we tell Arthur about the baby? Your miscarriage was news to me. Thank God for Cassie. Did it ever cross your selfish mind that I might have wanted to know you had suffered such a loss?"

Gina snatched up a china cup and flung it. The handle grazed Dad's shoulder before the cup smashed against the bookcase behind him. A dog-eared *Infinite Intelligence* took a direct hit to the tattered cover. The splintering china was the most satisfying sound she'd heard in months. "Do we tell Arthur how his grandfather left his grandmother destitute? How he never gave his own daughter a red cent?"

Dad set down his cup. Drops of tea clung to his upper lip. He no more acknowledged the china shards lying at his felt slippers than he would acknowledge her tug at his sleeve on the car lot. "Did you know your mother embezzled from the dealership?"

Gina grabbed another cup from the silver tea tray and sent it soaring over Dad's other shoulder. Missed him this time, but nailed something called *The Secret Doctrine* right in the spine. Another satisfying burst of shards rained down on the carpet. "If that were true, don't you think that's something I *would* know?" All his gibberish, his bullshit slogans, his pride, and nuts. Now she understood why he spoke in loop-de-loops and banalities. She'd forgotten how Dad's straight talk was nothing but lies and malice.

"Would you? I never pressed charges, and she would never tell you the truth. Always *too depressed* to take responsibility for any damn thing."

More bullshit. Her mother's long days in bed, her repeated firings from menial jobs, her reliance on Gina for her stingy meals and abundant prescriptions, made her guilty of suffering, not lying. "Mom's condition had nothing to do with how you treated me."

"That woman wasn't going to get one more cent out of me by sending you to do her dirty work. She turned you into a slick little money-grubber, all right. You were such a happy, loving kid until she had her way with you."

"Shut up about my mother." Gina snatched up a rose-encrusted saucer and aimed it like a Frisbee at the loose knot on his lavender shawl.

"I was always terrified she'd hurt you. Really hurt you." Dad had warmed to the pitch. His shoulders squared with the old confidence. "Take you down with her. I thanked God when she died. My worst fears were never realized."

A sliver of truth arrested Gina's aim.

A row of brilliant flames, waiting for the gas to rise. Had Mom known Gina was coming that day? She'd always wondered why her mother had been wearing her new bra and hose. Had Gina mentioned she was bringing the dress after all? Because her mother relied on Gina for such things, Gina had told the tailor to call her when the dress was done. She'd never checked those last phone messages on the machine to see whether the shop had also called her mother.

Dad continued calmly as if he didn't see the saucer angled to shatter against his heart. "You will leave for Arabia unmerciful. This I have had to accept as the price for revealing Cassie's connection with your mother and your lost son, my dear little grandchild. And while you are away . . ." Dad took another swallow of tea. "I will pass to the other side."

"That freak better marry you quick, if she's planning to clean you out." But Gina's voice wavered. He'd succeeded again in making her feel like she'd lashed out childishly over things she didn't understand.

"Marry Cassie? The thought never occurred." Dad set the cup on the table. The china rattled with his trembling. When he removed his hand, the silence clashed with the quiet from the kitchen. "It would be like marrying my own self. I want you to know I have set up a trust for Arthur. You and Red can get back on your feet without worrying about the boy's future."

"Am I supposed to be grateful?"

"No more than I'm supposed to expect it. But know this. When I come knocking from the beyond, it will be to love you. I won't haunt you, Virginia."

Always the salesman, Gina fumed. It was all she could bear to think. At least he'd admitted that the parlor, the green candles, the beautiful fortune-teller were, like all successful pitches, both snow job and last bet that any future, even death, could be happily foretold.

Arthur ran into the room. Gina placed the saucer carefully back on the table. Arthur stared at Gina uncertainly, then at the china shards on the carpet. "What happened? Did something break?"

"Just clearing up," Gina said.

"Your mother dropped a cup," Dad said. "Or two."

Madame Bozek slipped past Arthur. Her eyes glided over the broken pieces. Gina would always swear she saw approval, even delight, light the woman's expression. Arthur sank to his knees to collect the slivers. Madame bent over Dad with a napkin. She brushed his lips dry, and then kissed him. Lingered lightly on his lips. An affectionate lover, a dutiful daughter, a loving mother of sound mind and body. The kiss could have been any of these women.

● ••••

As if obeying an unspoken command, Arthur kept the silence on the drive home. Perhaps he wanted to know the truth even less than Gina wanted to tell it. Or perhaps he was picking up on her lingering rage that Dad had confided to Madame secrets that rightfully belonged between a father and a daughter. She was convinced she'd been justified in not telling Dad about the miscarriage after they reconnected. At the time, mixed in with her doubts over whether reuniting with Dad for Arthur's sake was a good idea, Gina was battling terror that she'd never be able to bear another child. This was before she and Red decided to give up trying. Telling her father she'd lost a baby felt like admitting to a shameful weakness. Was it selfish to protect her grief from Dad's by-the-bootstraps attitude toward recovery?

And, if Dad didn't know about the miscarriage, how had Madame Bozek guessed, right down to the child's gender? As Dexter's leafy serenity changed over to Ann Arbor's steamy, clogged streets, Gina chose, for the moment, not to think about that particular bull's-eye.

All the way home, Arthur fiddled with his foil's broken tip. He lodged a finger in his mouth. As they pulled into the driveway, he pulled his finger out and rubbed his hand against his shirt.

"The cups didn't look dropped."

Red was back at the fence, working the Weed Dragon like an expert. He'd certainly taken to that contraption. He was wearing pants, boots, even a long-sleeve T-shirt. Had she insulted his elbows once? Dusky smoke puffs rose from the fence post. How many weeds could be left standing after his work yesterday? Gina said, "Bone china makes a hard landing."

"Madame does have some neat tarot cards. She showed me. Can I go back tomorrow for my reading?"

Did she say you'd be back? Gina almost let the words slip. "Honey. Grandma died a long time before you were born. OK? So there was never a chance for you to know her. So telling you certain things about her didn't seem . . . right to us. Because then all you would know of her would be that one terrible thing. Do you understand?"

"I guess." He picked at the foil like he was removing a splinter. Head hung low, hair sweeping his jaw, achingly beautiful. When they could afford the barber again, she might simply let his hair grow. "*Did* she die of natural causes?"

"No, she didn't." All these years later, finally telling the truth felt like a lie.

"OK." Arthur clenched his fist. "Did I have a brother, Mom?"

Where did the truth lie in any answer to that question? "I was pregnant. When you were still very young. I lost the baby before he had a chance to be born."

"Why didn't you ever tell me?"

"We did. You were still almost a baby." Gina paused. They had explained it all very carefully to Arthur when Gina returned home from the hospital. Arthur could have babbled something to Dad. That's how Madame Bozek would know. And how utterly typical of her father to keep secret that he knew, wait until revealing it would hurt Gina the most, and serve him best. "You were so young that soon you forgot. We wanted to forget. You know?"

"Yeah." She reached out to stroke his hair. He moved away from her hand. "It still feels like lying, Mom."

"I know. I'm sorry."

Arthur headed inside. Gina hiked across the lawn. She should be furious with Dad. She'd always sworn to give Arthur a happy history he could take for granted into his own future, the family bedrock Red possessed and she did not. Put Grandma in the category of an inevitable passing. Pass down to him a comforting myth of life's essential stability, death's arrival at the natural time. But under her lurking remorse over whether she'd been selfish not to tell about the baby, she wondered whether Dad was really in the wrong to have revealed the family pain without her consent. Had she, in the end, been wrong to fabricate a sensible rhythm to life and death, deny her son the right to ask the same unanswerable questions Gina had asked all her life?

She thought she'd startle Red, who was midblast when she approached. But he turned calmly at her tap on his shoulder. "Why are you out here firing away? The yard looks great."

"Just wanted to zap a few on the other side of the fence."

"Why not let the girls do that?"

Red reached over the rail and ignited a patch of crabgrass. "We own it, remember? How was your dad?"

"Let's just say the subject of money never came up." Odd how much she longed to tell him about her mother and their baby boy, that they'd found each other in the next life. Whatever the next life meant to a couple of non-believers. At this rate, she would end up as loopy as Dad.

"Doesn't matter now." Red straightened and rubbed his back under the tank.

"It went well with the client?"

"The client was a no-show."

An outcome Gina didn't need Dad to foretell. "What did Jim say?"

"Jim was a no-show."

"What? Jim wouldn't do that."

Red leaned the wand against a fence post and hoisted the tank higher on his shoulders. "Jim's in jail. Guess he got creative with the books after he let you go. Probably that's why he let you go."

"Oh, my God."

"No one to bail him out, either. He actually asked me to post the cash. Which I told him I'd be glad to do in a couple of weeks. After my first paycheck."

"You landed a job?"

Red nodded and took up the wand.

"That's wonderful, honey!" She wrapped her arms around his waist. Rammed her knuckles against the Dragon's tank. The propane's skunky odor clung to Red's shirt. "When do you start?"

"They want me to start as soon as possible. I fly out on Monday."

Gina peered into the goggles. "Where's the job?"

"Qatar."

Bull's-eye. Madame Bozek and Dad could boast a perfect record on foretelling the Arnold's fortunes. Gina's lack of surprise chilled her to the bone.

"We'll have to walk on the house, Gina," Red continued. "Start all over. I'm afraid it'll be on you to pack up and toss the key."

"I guess there's no scenario in which Arthur and I should . . . stay here." What she meant was not subject Arthur to complete upheaval until Qatar proved to be a going concern, as Dad would say.

Red's expression was inscrutable. "Well. At least that's out in the open."

"That's not what I meant, Red."

"Hard to know what you mean anymore, Gina."

Gina fought back tears. She looked over the fence at the neighbors' serene dahlias lining the bright, cherry-stained deck. She hadn't watered the flowers, either, yet they thrived under her lack of care, stubbornly beautiful no matter what she did to them. "It's not fair," Gina murmured, "that their worst problem is yeast."

Red followed her resentful gaze. "The cats have yeast?"

Gina shook her head. "Why on earth would the cats have yeast?"

"You're always complaining about spores on their fur."

Could the skin goop possibly be due to a yeast infection? The thought hadn't occurred to her. "I meant the girls. Helen actually recommends blow drying the crotch every morning to prevent moisture buildup."

"Good Lord, Ginny." Red was surveying Candy's evergreens. The trees looked more dispirited than ever in the glaring heat. The needle canopies drooped, lifeless and brown. "How would you know?"

Embarrassment at her snooping tied her tongue. She fibbed quickly. "Helen mentioned it once."

"Guess you two are real pals now." He hefted the Weed Dragon and prepared to move down the fence.

"Well, I had one, too, at the time, and it just came up. You know. Girl talk. Look, if we're abandoning the house, why bother with those weeds?"

"Just feels good to watch something else go up in smoke." Red torched a cluster of wild daisies on the other side of the fence. "There's a market niche for you. Mobile crotch grooming. You can franchise the vans from your uncle. That would really please your dad."

It took Gina a moment to realize he was cracking a joke. "We could call it *Joltin' Gina's Pussy Salon.*" She grinned.

"*Girl Time Groom 'n Go.*"

"*Clean Cunts.*"

Red squelched his laugh with a wince. "OK, that's nasty."

"What's nasty?"

"Referring to the girls that way."

"I wasn't!" Gina protested. "Anyway, you're not exactly one to talk. You don't like them either."

"At least I don't call them dykes."

"Helen uses that word!"

"You said it in front of Arthur." Red leaned over the fence to blast another daisy patch. The eyes and petals vaporized. Webs of ash floated in the breeze. "And you didn't use it the way Helen does."

"I did not." But Gina remembered a tart comment she'd lobbed after the property line squabble; Arthur's startled expression; her halfhearted attempt to explain the reappropriation of slurs. Not any worse than some of Red's postdispute jibes.

"When you're judgmental, Ginny, it's for all the wrong reasons. Not that there's ever any right reason to be judgmental."

"Wait a minute. What are we talking about here, exactly?"

Red faced her, wand pointed at her tennis shoes as if her feet were the next weeds in line. "At least the girls don't use their cunts for punishment." Behind the goggles, sweat had pooled below Red's eye sockets. His gray eyes swam before her, opaque and enormous.

"OK." Gina drew a breath. "Mind telling me what that means?"

"You haven't touched me in months."

"That's not true."

"Isn't it? When I tried to hug you yesterday you practically knocked me over."

"I did not! I was *reacting*. You hit me with the wand."

Red snapped off the goggles. Perspiration misted the air between them. "I haven't seen your cunt in a year."

"Hey." Gina stepped back. "Quit saying that word."

"Because you get to say what you want and I don't?" He dropped the wand and slid the propane from his back. The tank landed with a thud between them. "Because you get to decide whether you'll go or stay? Who deserves your love, and when?"

"That's spectacularly unfair."

A door slammed. Arthur's voice called for her, reedy and thin.

Red looked her up and down. Objectively, the way he sized up a dimension on a plan. "Take off your shorts, then. Show me your cunt."

"Jesus, Red."

Arthur called to her again. "Shouldn't we do the cats now, Mom?"

Red pulled the goggles over his eyes.

Arthur ran to the fence. His foil bobbed in his belt. Gina hurried over to him. "Leave that here, Arthur." She spoke more sharply than she intended. "The last thing we need is to stab one of those cats."

"Geez, Mom. We practice safety in class." But Arthur leaned the sword against the rail, the jagged tip safely tucked in the grass, before hopping the fence.

• ••••

Blitzen barreled out of the gloom like a ghastly tumbleweed. Gina snatched the cat up and deposited the slack sack of bones in her son's arms, told him to clean the litter box in the basement, and fled to the kitchen.

She wet the towel hanging from the Jenn-Air at the kitchen sink and mopped her face raw. Out the window, the jade-green lawn and the sky's metallic-blue canopy rippled under the brutal heat. Red was standing by the Rugged Rumpus, staring at the neighbors' perfect lawn. How could he accuse her of unlovey behavior when he, too, had barely touched her since the downturn? Was he out to prove that she had no heart left? That she was *unmerciful?*

Was this the man who had divined her mother's heart and then guarded her secrets until the moment Gina needed them revealed?

Arthur's sneakers pounded up the basement stairs and glided into the laundry room. Gina dropped the towel in the sink. Red was facing the neighbors' house, shading his brow with his hand as if searching for Gina in the window she was looking through.

Another thought struck her, then. Had Red known her mother might have meant to take Gina's life, too?

His professional expertise and instinct would be to avoid catastrophe. In her place, the first thought Red would have had that day in her mother's room was the monoxide, lighter than the air, rising to the ceiling. He would have guessed that while her mother was watching those flames lick the ceiling, she might not have been easing her own passing, but planning Gina's.

She tried to hold her voice steady as she answered the running commentary Arthur was flinging over the clack of the EVO pellets cascading into the feeder.

"Wonder where Donder's hiding."

"Mmm."

"I've never seen Blitzen without Donder practically riding on her back."

"Yes, honey."

"Do you think Blitzen's acting funny?" This remark rode on a stream of caterwauling. "She won't eat."

"Pet her."

"What?"

Gina wrung out the towel and replaced it on the Jenn-Air's gleaming handle. "She won't eat if you don't pet her."

The mewling was duly replaced by the prim clicking of frail teeth. Gina poured a glass of water, gulped a mouthful. A crystal decanter half-full of something amber stood next to the stainless-steel spice rack. Gina poured several shots worth of whatever luxury liquor the girls might store in crystal and drank it with one swallow. Scotch, naturally. She wandered over to the lovey notebook, turned over the leaves absently. A stash of blank notebooks must lie in wait somewhere to fill with future adoration. The women had turned every battle for equality and acceptance, from having kids to tying the knot against their home state's law, even disputing a property line, into a celebration of love. With so little to fight for, had Gina and Red failed to love long enough and hard enough to last until the recovery?

The words blurred. She was on the verge of losing it when her gaze lighted on the girlish scrawl. *Doc says Priscilla's yeast infection could = oral sex! Arthur?*

fucking clueless neighbors

Gina blinked away her tears. Arthur and Cil? They never spent any time together without Colt. She flipped through the notebook. The entry was one of the last, written after Helen had hired her to take care of the cats. Had they left the notebook out in plain sight, knowing Gina would snoop?

"Mom, there's green slime all over the carpet. Like, a whole ocean's worth." Arthur's deep voice rang from the living room.

Gina snapped the notebook shut. "Don't exaggerate, Arthur."

"No, Mom. For real." Alarm dusted his tone.

"Bleach turns fabric green sometimes."

"I don't think that's it. Come *here*, Mom."

"*You* come here a minute, sweetheart."

Arthur padded in, cradling Blitzen in his gangly arms. His throat's sweet apple bobbed as if already denying what she was about to ask.

"Honey. Are you and Priscilla . . . boyfriend and girlfriend?"

"That's gross, Mom." Arthur clamped a hand on Blitzen's squirming head.

"Arthur. This is important. Are you and Priscilla fooling around? Kissing, or . . . other stuff?"

"What? I really think you need to see this green goop. Come on!" He fled the kitchen.

Had his expression changed to guilt? *His energy is expansive, Daughter.* Was Dad's observation on her son's "rustlies" yet another prediction come true?

Through the patio slider, Gina saw that Red had strapped the Weed Dragon to his back again and was striding purposefully toward the fence. He hopped the railing nimbly, tank, wand, and safety goggles bouncing wildly. He pointed the Dragon's nostril right at the first evergreen in line and pressed the trigger. A burst of flame roared from the nozzle. The tree ignited as obligingly as kindling.

"Mom! Come *here*."

"Oh my *God*!" Gina flew to the slider, yanked the door wide, bolted down the deck stairs. Sunlight flooded her eyes as she ran headlong down the sloping lawn. She stumbled over a stick, regained her footing, limped the rest of the way to the tree line. Red stood with a hand at his hip. He was studying the flames with a tilt of the head she recognized from his working days, the affirming nod when all the dimensions on a drawing had fallen into place. A rogue clump of flames was dangerously close to jumping Candy's mulch ring.

Red nodded at the flame's progress, primed the wand, and took aim at the next evergreen.

"Red!" Gina shouted. "*Red*!"

With a sickening swoosh, the second tree lit up, flames arcing to the flawless sky. Another nod. Job well done.

Gina ran up, clutched his arm, gasping for breath. "Red! Are you crazy?"

"Yes." He shook her off deliberately and aimed the nozzle at the next tree in line.

"Stop that." She tried to band his chest in a tackle, but with the tank in the way she only succeeded in jiggling his arms. Ash and flaming needles rained down into the lush grass. She hadn't watered the lawn, either. The yard was bound to catch. She planted herself firmly in front of the Dragon's nozzle.

Red studied her blankly behind the goggles. "Out of the way, Ginny."

"No!"

"Out of the way, Ginny," he repeated in the patient tone he used to tell Arthur to pick up his socks.

Another pump, and a hiss. Red shot the flame deftly under her arm, and the third tree went up. Sweat poured down Red's cheeks. His eyes glowed behind the goggles' foggy plastic. The middle trees sputtered, their wiry skeletons burning themselves out. The shrubs on either end flamed steadily. As brittle branches snapped and fell, a breeze sprang up. Smoke wrapped lazily around Gina. A patch of grass sprang into flames. Coughing, Gina whirled around, took the fence in one bound, and snatched up the bucket by the Rugged Rumpus. Empty. She should have remembered Arthur kicking it over.

"There's a hose by the girls' deck," she cried to Red, who seemed not at all inclined to spring into action. "Red. Come *on!*"

Instead of running for the hose, Red primed the wand. Gina snatched up Arthur's foil. She leaped back over the fence and thrust the splintered tip at Red's wrist in time to prevent the next blast of flame.

"Cut it out, Ginny." He rubbed his wrist, parried the wand.

Gina jabbed the wand with the foil. "Did you *know* my mother was trying to kill me?"

"What the . . .?" Red smacked the foil near the tip, almost knocking it out of Gina's hand. "Did you *know* you'd turn out to be a lunatic, too?"

The slider jerked open. Arthur's long legs rolled over the deck at full steam. He leaped the stairs and raced down the slope, wielding a bright red tank and black nozzle as adroitly as a third arm. For a confused moment, Gina thought he'd unearthed another flamethrower and was hurtling downhill to finish the job. He skidded to a stop, pulled a pin, unleashed a waterfall of cottony foam.

The girls *would* keep a commercial-grade extinguisher on hand for emergencies. Within moments the trees were cooling under a soothing white coat as fluffy as an early snow. Smoke trickled from the grass and sputtered out. Arthur cut the spray. The foam retracted into the nozzle with a moist hiccup. Red gave a nod and pulled the safety goggles up to his brow. "Nice work, Son."

"Are you out of your mind?!" Gina shouted at Red.

"Are *you?*"

Arthur holstered the nozzle to the tank and laid the extinguisher carefully on the grass. He looked at his parents as if lunacy was just what he'd come to expect from the two of them. Wincing, Red wiped his wrist. Had she actually drawn blood? Gina snatched his hand and planted a kiss on the scrape.

Red looked at her warily, and then locked his fingers with hers. He dropped to one knee. The Dragon's tank lurched. The goggles' strap bunched his hair into a silvery haystack. "Gina, my darling, I'm down on my knobby knee for you. Come away with me across lawn and fence, across sea and sand."

"Get up, Red." Gina tried to yank her hand away, but Red held on tight.

"Mom. You've got to come *quick.*" Arthur took the foil from her other hand gently.

"I'll travel to the ends of the earth. I'll lay waste to any tree that stands in our way."

"Mom, it's Donder's blood all over the carpet."

"I love you." Red brushed his lips against her fingers.

"Red, *please.*" Drops of sweat tumbled down her cheeks, or was she crying?

"Say you love me, Ginny."

"It's *green*, Mom. And there's a lot of it." Arthur tugged on her hand.

Gina burst out, "God dammit, Arthur, I can't stand any more of your fibbing!"

"I've never seen anything like it," Arthur said wonderingly, as if he'd been alive long enough to have seen it all.

•　••••

The neighbors arrived home the next week to find healthy, well-fed cats—Donder's only sign of trauma was a neat seeding of stitches along his neck—a patch of fresh sod where the evergreens had once stood, and a note of apology from Gina, scrawled on the first blank page of the lovey notebook. Gina wasn't surprised to receive no word, and no payment, from the women. Arthur bolted to play with Colt and Priscilla the moment they arrived home, but on that score, too, not a word came from over the fence. Gina had written her note right after the entry on Priscilla and Arthur. The women would know she knew what they thought their children might be up to.

The morning Candy trundled a quartet of new evergreens across the lawn, the burlap-wrapped young roots bouncing in the wheelbarrow's tangerine bucket, Gina took a break from packing the kitchen and headed to the fence. Helen was digging in the sod Red had laid before he left for the Middle East. Arthur, Colt, and Priscilla were playing on the neighbors' swing set opposite the fence. Arthur wound Cil's swing chains in a tight corkscrew. Gina scrutinized the children as Cil whirled in a blond blur while Arthur and Colt cheered. Still acting just like innocent kids.

Helen looked up with more curiosity than resentment when Gina leaned over the railing. Gina decided this was a good omen.

"Sorry about this welcome home, Helen. We tried to save the trees, we really did."

Helen studied her blankly. "Sounds like you did what you could, Gina. We appreciate your quick thinking."

"Sorry, too, about the carpet stain. I didn't know Arthur was using the bleach to clean up after Donder."

"Our fault for storing Clorox right next to carpet cleaner."

"I'd like to help out with replacement costs."

"That would be appreciated." Helen's gaze flickered to Candy as she rolled up with the trees. "Must have been quite the storm."

"I've never seen anything like it. A direct lightning strike." Gina smiled weakly. Candy plunked the wheelbarrow down with a grunt. "Real fire and brimstone stuff. Felt like the end of the world."

"Huh."

"And it's been so dry. These guys just lit right up. Nothing we could do."

Helen's gaze eased to the scorched fence post. "Looks like your fence almost went up, too."

"It took some quick thinking to save the yard."

"So I hear." Candy took Helen's shovel and launched into a vigorous excavation.

Helen said, "Arthur tells us that Red left for his new job? In the Middle East somewhere?"

"Qatar, actually. We join him next week."

"Guess his Gulf service came in handy in the long run."

"Reaping the rewards from his bullshit war, right?" Candy hurled a load of dirt toward the fence.

Helen said, "We knew you had lost your job, Gina, but we didn't know Red was also unemployed. This must have been a very difficult time for your family."

"The losses all came about rather suddenly."

Helen cleared her throat. "You know, Arthur told Colt that his grandmother committed suicide and that his grandpa has a psychic girlfriend."

Gina blinked. "Well, she's not his *girlfriend*."

Candy said, "The term Arthur used was consort."

"Arthur did make quite the story out of it, didn't he, honey?" Helen said.

"He said that he saw Grandpa kissing *Madame* after Grandma and his baby brother found each other in heaven."

"There's some truth to that," Gina admitted.

"Arthur also said that Donder was covered in green blood because she was wounded in the yard when you let her out and you never noticed when it got infected."

"That's not quite accurate."

"And that Donder almost died at home because Red was burning down our trees with his dragon, whatever that means, and you were stabbing him with a sword and Arthur had to put the fire out himself before you would save Donder's life."

Helen swept her hair up to fan her neck. The fiery sun shimmered on her glossy russet streaks like an early peek at autumn's color. The jade-green lawn shone fiercely. The dahlias' bright pinks and purples glinted fresh and lovely against the deck's rich cherry stain. The kids' voices rang out, Arthur's giggles tuned to Colt and Cil's light, happy laughter. One last glimpse of brilliance on the other side of the fence.

Candy rested her shovel against her shoulder. Both women stared at Gina.

Gina met their gazes squarely. "Isn't it wonderful? Arthur's always had such a rich imagination."

Sole Suspect

The body in the road had become a reliable kindness. Tucked nimbly in the sharp dip on Judd Road just past the hairpin curve out of town, the body could be a trick, a blink, exhaustion's shadow. A chalky moon lit the curve. Beyond the light's rim, darkness poured into the hollow's bleak drop. Just in time again, Perry swerved off the road. He parked under the near-headless birch and aspen, canopies shorn wide for the power lines. The shoulder was choked so tightly with brush that Perry's rusted truck bed jutting into the lane became the obstacle the next motorist might see too late. Perry's door swung open almost to the head, which didn't, at first, flinch. Maybe this was the night someone else had finally hit the body.

A harsh wind cut through the bare branches. No buffer now against the chill. Perry's jacket might as well be his skin. Had the lying down begun before the cold set and the leaves dropped? Perry couldn't recall when he'd first come upon this body. After the girls had been discovered last month, this he knew. But he couldn't say when exactly these encounters became routine, and then, necessary.

The body wasn't waiting for him in that hollow every night. Perry never asked the questions he should ask; that if the body appeared on some nights, why not every night? What erratic calculus of despair determined a night's decision to lie in wait for collision's bliss?

• ••••

Perry was awaiting positive identification, which the authorities told him might come tomorrow. A foregone conclusion, since he and the Other Family had immediately identified the girls' clothes. Remarkably well preserved after twenty years underwater. Elsa's dressy blouse was laid out on the authorities' steel table, sleeves thrown out at right angles as if frozen in one of her impulsive hugs. Her denim cutoffs lay below the blouse, a strip of steel gleaming in the gap between hem and waistband like a prosthetic belly. The blouse's frilly scallops were fringed with mud. Dirt blotted the sleeves. Mud stains dotted the pearly buttons. Not a single button was missing. Not a speck of the mud on the blouse or cutoffs turned out to be aged blood, so the authorities finally knew to rule out foul play. A technician would have removed this blouse delicately from his daughter's skeleton. The cutoffs would have been pulled cautiously from her hips to avoid dislodging joints, shattering evidence. The silver glittering sandals with the Roman straps, now lake-bed brown with the buckles flaking rust, would have been carefully guided from each foot's frail bony accordion.

The clothes were pinned and air-dried to stiff, unnatural poses before Perry and the Other Family were summoned. The living knew that, like the DNA testing that would be compared against samples from their own bodies, identifying the clothes was a formality. The car, a '71 Mustang hauled up from the shriveled lake, was well known as the car Perry had given Elsa for her sixteenth birthday. The water level hadn't dipped so low in a century. Drought had dried up the wells on his out-of-town properties but had given Perry his daughter back.

He didn't know how the Other Family felt about closure, but he wasn't about to hand over last hope on a platter to the authorities. He'd studied the items as if he'd never seen these clothes, as if the unearthed car wasn't his well-known '71 Mustang with two female bodies strapped in the front seats, a mangled rear tire that must have blown and hurtled the car off the bridge. He told the authorities he couldn't positively identify this clothing. Hadn't too much time passed to be certain? Some items were missing, too. Intimate things. Were the authorities keeping Elsa's undergarments from his sight out of delicacy? The authorities hadn't recovered her cheap silver earrings either, but Perry didn't notice the baubles weren't among these personal remains.

He was not present when the Other Family identified their daughter's clothing, so he never would know if they'd given up their hope easily, even gratefully.

● ●●●●

Perry slammed the car door. The body stirred at the sound. Alive, still a man.

Perry helped him to his feet. Wrapped his coat around the man's gaunt shoulders, tucked him gently into the passenger seat. Hurrying for no good reason. If the man was in a hurry to live, he'd have risen on his own. If the man was in a hurry to die, he wouldn't choose to lie on a road rarely driven after dark. But Perry felt the urgency of their time together. Moving the truck out of the next motorist's way. Protecting the man from the cold and the country night's sticky ink. Perry thought that regard for this man's welfare made him hurry, but the rush was meant to beat the clock on Perry's dead heart. He could kill this man as easily as he could rescue him, because, given time, didn't reputation always become character?

This man was not yet Perry's age, but not young enough to be reckless, to have not thought things through. But, too, not ready to die. He would take to Perry's care, is how Perry knew. Put his fingers to the dashboard vents. Thaw out, smile a bit, relax into Perry's coat. He would never begin a conversation and he didn't tonight, either. Decisions could be made about what to find out and what to leave be.

Perry pulled onto Judd Road. The old F-150's engine rattled now like a lingering cough, but there wasn't a thing wrong with it. Tonight the man couldn't seem to get warm. He was fidgety, fretful. He kept rubbing his hands in front of the heater vents, then sticking his fingers between the seat cushions or in his lap. His smile was one of those Perry envied, radiant and straight. A few facts, released stingily, during their first rides together. The man lived with his parents. They did not know of the roadway roulette. The man would prefer Perry run him over than take him back home.

Perry nursed assumptions: an alcoholic, an unstable, a man diverted from the course of reason. But he did not reek of poisons, did not appear drugged. Perhaps he was one of those users who thrived on fooling his family. Once Perry had looked up the Marion Road address to find the number unlisted, no name attached to the property. He'd poked around a bit for the man's identity. Hadn't been too diligent. There were certain benefits to the man remaining a stranger.

Perry usually accepted the man's silences, which he interpreted as invitations to fill, but there came a point when he wanted to crowbar some answers.

—If you want to die, why not choose a busier road?

—I don't drive, the man told him.

—What's that got to do with it?

The man blew air into his cupped palms as if about to whistle.

—Out here, where else could I walk to?

The wind picked up, whistled through the F-150's aging window seals. Moonlight shimmered on the pavement like an early frost. The man pointed out the way home even though Perry knew the route, a left down Marion, one of those narrow, single-lane dirt roads. There the jarring washboards chiseled by long-ago summer rains would fragment their conversation, save Perry the burden of finding out why this man sought to die.

• ••••

Denise was the other girl's name. Perry didn't know what she was wearing the night the girls disappeared. He'd barely spoken to Elsa on her way out, which was why, he told the authorities, he couldn't say for certain about the clothes. Back when the authorities had questioned him—closely, Perry was the sole suspect—he described Elsa's glittery sandals, which he remembered flashing on the drab living room carpet. He didn't tell the authorities how he'd frowned over the cutoffs and dressy blouse. The clingy denim rode too high on her thighs. The Sunday Best top seemed like an insult to Sunday paired with those shorts, and she'd buttoned the blouse up tight to her slender neck. Not a trace of flesh until those long legs, as if she were lowballing the flirtation, and he didn't like her going to a teen party at the gravel pit in the first place. She was wearing earrings, silver dangling baubles that flashed like grins as she told him good-bye.

Should have driven the girls himself, he'd always suffer this guilt. A straight shot down Judd Road, across the bridge over the lake that had taken their lives. He'd have watched them walk up the gravel path to the ridge where the other kids were stoking the bonfire and pulling on beers, shadows against flames on a hot starless night. He'd have noted what Denise was wearing so he could keep tabs on both girls. Parked down the road within sight of the fire. All the way down the path, Elsa's silver sandals would have twinkled on her slender ankles. He'd craved this vision over the years, her glittering feet like sparklers' tails tethered to his vigilance. This vision sometimes relieved him from his doomed wonder about why she'd left, and where she'd gone, and when she might return to forgive him for some offense he wouldn't know to call a crime.

Maybe Denise knew, and that's why they'd grown close that year. Perry had known Denise only a bit, mostly by the loud laughing voice that overtopped Elsa's quiet murmur. He'd wondered afterward whether Elsa's soft voice was not her natural tone after all, but muted so he wouldn't hear what the girls were planning on that hot summer's night. Pretend to go to a party and just keep driving down Judd, which bisected Moon, which doubled back to Michigan Avenue to I-94. Once on the interstate, the girls could vanish before anyone knew to look for them. It was a good plan. It could be done.

Over time, Perry grew to love Elsa's flight as he loved her. So what if she'd never called? Showed her pluck. She'd made it to a better place, a place he wasn't meant to find.

The Other Family was convinced that a killer had snatched the girls on Judd Road. After Perry's arrest, the Other Family was convinced this killer was Perry. Maybe they'd thought him guilty right up until the moment the wheels unexpectedly crested the lake's murky surface, so near the places that had been searched so methodically, and then hopelessly. Maybe they needed to identify Denise's clothes and confirm the DNA match to see in Perry the father who had lost what they had lost, who suffered nightmares, spun wild stories, prayed, and raged and wept dry as they had. He wondered whether they preferred their beliefs about Perry to the truth, as he preferred the fates he'd concocted for Elsa. Perhaps he would turn out to have been their last hope. Perhaps his killing of the girls would be seen, now, as more sensible than this discovery; the girls' cruel suspension in gloomy waters, near to the bridge, near to their families, close and unfound until a freak disruption in the rainfall's seasonal pattern had revealed them.

The grieving should crave closure. The grieving should be grateful the drought offered up to the light their dear ones belted dutifully in their last pose.

Perry's daughter was thirty-six when she was found, had been dead longer than she'd been alive, and he did not want that corpse, he didn't.

• ▪▪▪▪

Perry asked the man straight out.

—Do you know who I am?

Shivering, the man looked him over carefully. Seemed to consider the question one he must respond to in just the right way, so he wouldn't be viewed as guilty, or stupid.

—I do not.

This could be evasion or it could be the truth.

The engine rattled, died away on a thin whine. Tomorrow the odometer would turn over to 300,000. The truck was new when Elsa went missing. He hadn't expected it to outlive his daughter. When he was the sole suspect, the authorities had dismantled Perry's truck. Stripped it down to the axle. Vacuumed the carpets and cushions. When they put it back together, the truck ran like it was fresh off the lot, had run beautifully ever since. Now he rarely drove it at all except on these night runs to a tenant call or the townie bar when he couldn't stand to be at home. During the day he didn't care whether the engine still turned over, but at night he liked to prove that he'd nurtured such stubborn longevity.

Just before the turn down Marion, the man reconsidered.

—You live out this way. Near the lake by the gravel pit.

By now the town identified Perry in many different ways. Always interesting to find out which identity a person attached to him. That night, he was associated with the lake. Another night the man might recognize him as the father whose daughter was recovered. On another, Perry might be remembered as the suspect in her disappearance.

The first time he'd saved this man, he'd asked the basics. Name, address, who should be called. The question of the authorities never came up. The authorities would never again be the ones Perry called. The man refused to answer for his identity, but when he pointed out Marion Road, Perry thought he had the guy's number. The road was nearly impassable. Deep furrows ridged the gravel like weather-beaten skin. But beyond the modest homes plunked close to the shoulder, a stretch of marsh formed a boundary between one type of family dwelling and another. Past the marsh stood a scattering of mysterious places. Brick walls enclosed sprawling complexes built for secretive, tight-knit clans who corralled the generations under a single roof. Gangsters, or drug lords. Foreigners, or the loony local militia. Crowded sheaves of aspen and maple protected the vast yards from street view. The crummy road, the overgrown shoulder, all natural riggings for fiercely guarded privacy. The man must hail from these secret clans. Such membership would explain both the need for escape and its impossibility. A hit and run under cover of night would be the best possible death, perhaps the only one.

But the house where Perry deposited the man was on the ordinary side of the marsh. A sturdy, well-painted ranch tucked into a pine grove. A broad gravel driveway, a lean-to carport, the porch light burned out or never switched on. A sensible home sheltering a family able and willing to ease this man's nighttime torments. Not a place of unkindness or neglect. Obliviousness, perhaps, caused by life's routine distractions, or perhaps the man was a brilliant sneak.

—But do you know who else I am?

After tomorrow's positive identification, Perry would need to become someone else, but the man would not answer his question.

* ••••

Perry hated the sight of Elsa peeking at him from all the familiar places. He'd have just convinced himself again that she'd found freedom in a place of sunshine and opportunity; and there she'd be, beautiful as ever, lobbing the lowball flirtation. In the high school parking lot he passed on his way to a property, she'd be leaning against some boy's Chevy sedan, one slender leg tented against the car door like an ostrich. Her dark hair would swirl in the breeze. She'd throw him a glance like he wasn't yet forgiven. *Keep driving*, she meant. *Keep driving*. Tough to pass her by without stopping to stare at her with that hungry grief. Allow himself to drink her in before reminding himself that this was another girl, because his daughter would not still be sixteen and hanging around the high school parking lot.

Sometimes, too, when he had to drive out to the rental near I-94, she'd be loitering near the cart rack at the new Walmart past the Industrial Park. This annoyed him, since how would she know this new place? When she left, the Walmart had been Wagner's U-Pik. Strawberry rows stacked to the horizon like lipstick smears. Kids gorged on fruit while their mothers filled their buckets for them. Once he'd sworn Elsa was smoking and eating strawberries from a Walmart plastic pint container. Leaning against the cart rack, staring at him. *Keep driving*. He'd pulled a U-turn right in the middle of Michigan Avenue, blown into the Walmart lot. Peeled over to the rack like a punk dragster burning rubber, only to find the girl's embers and nibbled strawberry hulls scattered at the carts' wheels.

Perry fell feverish with her ball busting, if that's what these sightings were. Accusations, her lack of forgiveness, but what had he done to earn her cruelty? He didn't know, or he couldn't remember, or what was worse, he'd done nothing at all. Children might count anything their parents did as a crime.

The Other Family's suspicion made sense, Perry understood this. Past a certain age, a man alone is always a sole suspect. His wife had left him without warning. Left her daughter behind with Perry, something others felt a mother wouldn't do. Once the Other Family thought of Perry as their daughter's killer, they'd suspected him of doing away with his wife, too. Ellen had, in fact, moved back in with her parents in upstate New York, a two-day drive from their town. He'd dropped Elsa in Detroit once so she could take the Amtrak to visit. When Ellen passed away from breast cancer, Perry hadn't run a local obituary. Pure spite at the time, his lust to erase her from the town.

After he'd grown used to being the suspect in the girls' deaths, it felt natural to become the suspect in his wife's fate. Denise and her family had been relative newcomers before the girls disappeared. They arrived in town long after Ellen's passing. They wouldn't ever know Ellen's friends, the few townies she kept in touch with before she died. Elsa would have stopped talking about her mother long ago. By the time Perry was a suspect, few if any remembered Ellen, except that he'd had a wife who vanished one day. After his arrest, two and two were put together. Even after he was cleared of official suspicion over the girls, the Other Family looked at him as a man capable of multiple crimes. They avoided him in the Farmer Jack aisle, and so did those others whom Perry used to get along with well. They spoke of him, said unkind things he could easily disprove, if he didn't rely so much upon this special regard.

Wasn't it better to be thought of as a killer than a man left helpless? Better to be thought of at all, not so lonely that way.

•   ••••

—One gets used to grief, Perry tried to explain on the turn to Marion Road.

The man sneezed. The car hit a pothole, dipped hard, jostled the man against the door.

—You don't think you ever will. It's like a change in altitude, a climb to a higher ledge. You know that down there you felt different. But now the difference is what's familiar.

Perry didn't know if any of it was sinking in. The man drew Perry's coat tighter around his shoulders and neck. Squeezed a hand between the seat cushion.

—There's no climbing back down, is the thing, Perry told the man.

Some nights Perry felt the impulse to take this man to his home, get him good and drunk, exchange frank talk about secrets that needed extraction. Except for his kindness to this man, in all other ways Perry had fulfilled the Other Family's special regard. He neglected his properties. He was slow to respond to his tenants' complaints. Some situations had teetered toward the dangerous. Threats to life, the tenants charged. An unplated electrical outlet shot voltage up a young mother's arm. A bat bit a little girl after the family had requested an exterminator. An elderly woman broke a hip stumbling over chipped pavement in the apartment lot. Perry wouldn't call his emotions over these mishaps satisfaction, but the incidents eased his grief in ways he didn't care to understand.

Perry achieved a dossier of complaints. He enjoyed minor run-ins with the authorities, the same men who had interrogated him during his arrest, who still believed him guilty, who, tomorrow, would not convert him back to innocence when his daughter's identity was confirmed. Perry became known to cheap lawyers and the Sixteenth District Court. Over time Perry learned how to win cases, avoid damages. He kept his rents and deposits low. Despite his reputation, his rentals boasted full occupancy.

The wind kicked up, worrying the aspen. Marion Road's trees had not been carved into horseshoes for the power lines. Marion was designated a Natural Beauty road, which forbade the authorities' shearing.

—I'm not grieving. It was the closest the man had ever come to arguing.

—You're not thinking this thing through, Perry told him.

—I'm perfectly happy.

This could mean anything, which irritated the hell out of Perry.

—Did you ever stop to think that if I do hit you, I will be your killer? What kind of guilt is that to saddle a man with?

—Quit pulling over, then.

Which was also beside the point. The man couldn't focus at all. Over the crest of a distant hill down Marion, a pair of headlights wobbled, rattled by the road's furrows. Nothing could hold steady out here. He never let Elsa drive these backcountry roads for fear she'd land in a ditch. The wide, sturdy bridge over the lake he'd considered perfectly safe.

No use reasoning with a crazy man's addled view of things, but Perry was wound up.

—What if it's not me who runs you over? I can stand it, probably, living with killing you. But what if some kid comes along? What will you be doing to their life?

—A kid would be absolved even more quickly than you for being inexperienced.

At times the man spoke like this. Formal, lucid, still guided by logical training he must have cultivated in a past life.

—You're not seeing my point.

The man shrank into Perry's coat.

—You aren't seeing *my* point. I don't care what happens to the driver who kills me.

• ••••

Here was something the Other Family and the authorities didn't know. Only he and Elsa knew the agony Perry could endure to save her life.

What father and daughter didn't argue at times, especially over the way a fifteen-year-old girl should dress? Those tight jeans with the lurid stitching on the back pocket, for one. A decorative element meant to draw the male eye, no other purpose to it. *They're in style,* she warned when he suggested a more generous fit.

Then, buried in the drawer under her flannel pajamas, he'd discovered a stash of delicate things from a local boutique. Expensive, impractical, all lace and peep. Either Elsa wanted someone, or she already had him. Which was fine, no problem, except she was hiding the boy as she was hiding these delicate things. Perry knew from Ellen that once a woman hoards one secret, she will be hungry to collect others. He suspected Ellen had lied about living with her parents, until she fell ill and then she died in that place, this he knew to be true. But he remained convinced she'd left him for another, whether he could prove it or not.

He couldn't have Elsa getting off on deception, so he'd suggested she invite the young man over to dinner.

She'd suggested he mind his own fucking business and stay the fuck out of her room. He'd missed this depth charge because she didn't look like a woman, not yet.

When he left the living room to give them both a moment, she snatched his keys and tore out of the driveway in the Mustang, which wasn't, yet, hers. He'd intended to let her blow off steam, but she'd laid a patch to goad him and the grinding of his specialty radials infuriated him. His first instinct was to overtake her on Judd, guide her to the shoulder. But a rainstorm made the Mustang a blur of taillights, and he was afraid he'd crush her in the new F-150.

She fishtailed the turn onto Marion Road. The gravel was soup. Mud splashed his cab and windshield. Aspen and swamp birch groaned under a boomerang wind. Ahead the Mustang's taillights bobbled. The car skidded, overcorrected, veered across the road toward the cattails clustered in the marsh. But Elsa recovered at the shoulder, peeled back into the middle of the road. Gunned it like she was afraid he'd overtake her, although he was hanging back, petrified she'd end up in the fetid water, sink into the long, dark grasses where he'd never reach her.

On the other side of the marsh, he breathed easier. The wind quieted, the rain lightened to a patter. *Keep driving, keep driving.* Then, at the first complex's driveway, the Mustang lurched violently to the left. Elsa threw on the brakes. She might have been all right if she hadn't hit a deep pothole. Water rooster-tailed from the Mustang's bumper. The tires lost traction, flung the back end ninety degrees. Elsa skidded straight into a bank of mailboxes flanking the drive's apron. A metal box flew up, thudded along Perry's hood, crashed into his windshield. Perry yanked the wheel. Stupid instinct. The F-150 threatened to spin out right into the Mustang's rear. Perry whirled his wheel, pumped the brake, finessed a stop just a foot from her bumper.

Elsa flew out of the car. Hair streaming, jeans soaked in blotchy dark patches. Perry kept his headlights lit. Ahead of the Mustang a metal gate stretched the length of the drive. A rusted chain braided the gate post. Elsa knelt to cradle a dark bundle in her arms. Perry glimpsed sharp ivory fangs, black grinning gums, a grizzled snout. One of those attack breeds, a Doberman, probably. Black fur glossy with mud and blood. Too wounded to bark.

A soft, bubbly gurgle mixed with the rain's gentle drum and the hum of the truck's idle. Elsa was weeping. Her blouse was ripped at the sleeve. The cuff was already crimson.

Perry took her elbow, hauled her up. *He'll bite you,* is how he explained his roughness.

I know.

Which made no sense, and she was wrenching away from Perry's hold to return to the dog. *If he's dying, biting is all he can do anymore,* Perry told her. It sounded like a plea.

On the other side of the gate loose gravel rolled. A figure hovered behind the gate on the edge of the headlights' glow. It didn't occur to Perry then that he hadn't heard footsteps, that the figure hadn't approached from down the driveway. Later he'd understand that the man had been watching them all along, but he dismissed the notion that Elsa planned to meet him. She'd had no time to place a call before speeding off in the Mustang. And her plunge into the driveway had been to avoid the animal, not a deliberate turn.

Elsa stopped struggling, alert to the man Perry couldn't quite see.

Suddenly the other side of the gate was populated. The original man made a muffled, bleak sound. Slowly other men slid into the shallow drainage ditch on either side of the gate, emerged into the headlights. Dressed in camouflage, soaked with rain. Men of indeterminate origin and purpose. Elsa stood perfectly still. A wail, thin as filament, seeped from the dog's throat.

Perry pushed his daughter toward the idling truck. *Go.*

Elsa ran, good girl. The F-150 roared, skidded backward. The headlights scudded down Marion Road. Perry's jaw exploded. A cracking below his ear numbed the side of his head and then set it afire. He hit the gravel hard, face down in the puddle. Boots swished near his shoulder, chucked water over his back. When he sat up and pushed the mud and blood from his eyes, he was hit again. Kicked in the belly, the knee. He opened his eyes once when he heard the dog moan. He couldn't have, it was too dark, but for a moment Perry thought he saw the gaping gash in the dog's abdomen. A constellation of purplish organs spilled to the gravel, or maybe he was seeing his own raw flesh oozing into the water.

He'd been allowed to crawl to the Mustang and drive away. He'd been watched on the drive down Marion, first by the men, then by Elsa, who was idling at the turn down Judd Road, waiting for him. He'd always wonder what her next move would have been had Perry never arrived at that intersection. It made of the episode a certain sense that Elsa never called the authorities for help.

When he became a suspect, he'd been tempted to tell the authorities about the episode. Prove he'd risked life and limb for his daughter. Suggest there were other dangers to the community besides Perry. But he hadn't. Loyalty to Elsa, he thought. He didn't want her viewed as rash or wayward, mixed up with the wrong crowd, when he knew for a fact that the incident marked the end of her association with Marion Road. Afterward she partied with the ordinary kids at the gravel pit. He wouldn't admit that his real motive was admiration for the clans, these men who would build compounds and beat back intruders and silence one of their own to protect what was theirs.

Years later he understood why her words about the dog hadn't made sense. She must have said *I know him,* and the *him* had been swallowed by the rain.

Elsa had told Denise of this incident. He knew because the Other Family asked him about it once. Wondered if his beating could be related to the girls' disappearance. They'd approached him angrily but warily, as if he were the brute. Elsa had changed a few facts, as kids will. Told Denise Perry had chased her down Marion, had made her drive too fast to see the dog in time. At the time, it irritated the hell out of Perry. But maybe Elsa saw it that way. Maybe what she remembered was the argument, not Perry standing his ground while she escaped, but wasn't it natural for a child to recall what had driven her to recklessness, rather than the consequences?

Wasn't quite her birthday when he'd handed Elsa the keys and title to his Mustang. The bruises along his jaw had healed by then. His nose had a battered stance to it, a bit off kilter at the tip, a crazy-fucker jaunt he grew to like. Elsa avoided looking at the damage. She'd lock her blue eyes directly on his or skirt his face altogether when they spoke. He'd noticed this same tendency in the Other Family, how they never were able to look at him straight.

Maybe he'd meant the Mustang as a gift and that was all there was to it. Maybe he'd meant to tell his daughter that the next time she ruffled the gravel in their drive he wouldn't follow her. If that's what he'd meant, he'd kept his word.

When it came to kids, keeping your word could end up being your biggest mistake.

• ••••

—Do you even know if you want to die? Perry asked the man, more out of spite than curiosity.

—I do, the man replied promptly.

Which was a confirmation of one sort and a denial of another. The man pushed Perry's coat off his shoulders, crunched his shirt collar up his neck.

Pointed out his driveway, still a quarter mile up the road, as if Perry had never been there before. Flashed that straight reliant smile, so odd, because what did a man have to smile about if he loathed being alive?

Perry slowed down over a riffle in the road. The truck listed and rocked. The tires thumped dully in the potholes.

—You don't know what this will do to the people who love you, he told the man.

The man held out his hand to Perry. Opened his fist, dropped something light and flashy into Perry's lap.

—Not a thought that ever comes to mind, he said.

Well, it was an agreement of sorts. Perry fished the object from his lap. Held it up as the oncoming car's lamplight cartwheeled through the windshield. A silver bauble, a flash like a smile.

Perry was trapped in a leap to an airless place. Vertigo rushed in, sour and noisy. How had this man come to possess Elsa's earring? He would have been no more than a child when Elsa went missing. But as with many men, his true age was hard to judge.

—Where did this come from? His voice was hoarse, hollowed out.

The other car's lights slipped away. Restored to their usual darkness, this was a man who could look at Perry straight on. His expression could be innocence. Or curiosity.

—Sorry, man. Can't feel the other one down there. The man slipped a hand between the seats to confirm this.

A swap, then. Something found for something lost. Was the other earring now at the bottom of the lake, a glinting, showy thing attracting the bottom feeders?

Or was this another of Elsa's sneaky leavings, like strawberry hulls and cigarette butts?

By whatever trick or oversight, for all they'd ripped his truck and his reputation apart Perry had in his hand what the authorities had failed to find. Elsa's last decoration, the part of her that would always be too young for secrets and gates and injury being the price of love.

Tomorrow Perry would hear the voice of an authority confirming his daughter's identity. The Other Family would receive the same call. They would lay their suspicions of Perry to rest. Someday, through a chance encounter with an old townie, they might learn that Ellen had died of cancer. They might even grow to understand how happy the father and daughter had been, once they'd adjusted to the mother's absence. How Perry had never missed Elsa's band concerts or bit parts in school plays. How he'd provided for her, granted her heart's desires when he could, suffered a beating for her. Perry would be restored as an ordinary man, who suffers as other men do who have lost their darling.

Once she was identified, Elsa would never again appear to him in their familiar places, always sixteen, dark hair ruffled by the breeze. She'd never again accuse him of driving her to search for a new life. Tomorrow he would receive confirmation that she'd never had any reason to forgive him, and even that crime would be taken from him.

Perry pocketed the silver earring. Pulled up to the tidy ranch house. The engine idled at a fast hum. The gear seemed sticky on the shift to park.

—Should I keep driving? Perry asked the man. It was still possible to do what his daughter had not. Drive past the clans' complexes that had multiplied over the years. Accelerate past the prison now standing on the county's outskirts, a federal penitentiary with prisoners of secret origins and crimes. Pick up the interstate, never take this man home.

The man shook his head.

—Thanks for these rides.

He folded Perry's jacket between them and opened the passenger door. The dome light clicked on and off, a brief, searing brightness. The man walked steadily up the gravel drive to the unlit porch. A man in control of his senses and destiny, who would again lie down in the hollow beyond the hairpin curve, and this he would do by choice, not madness.

On another night soon, care of this man would again be left to Perry, and because this man was the only kindness left to him, Perry would never walk the man to the porch, enter his home, wake his parents, and beg them to save their son.

The Lavinia Nude

He couldn't continue to stare at that girl staring right back at him, but there was nothing else to look at except the nude hanging above the young woman's left shoulder; and Marlin couldn't look at *that* without blushing. The nude wasn't the sort of painting that belonged on the wall of a family diner. It lacked eyes, for one thing. The formless nose was contoured from eddies of thick sun-colored paint. The hands were etched in messy black strokes, stumps without fingers, as if the artist couldn't be bothered with her details. And the exaggerated breasts, with enormous black areolae, were all out of whack with her slender body. No, he couldn't look at it without fire rising to his cheeks, and he didn't want the young woman in the corner to think he was reddening under *her* eyes. Because—unbelievably—she had looked at him first. Because she was very young, very pretty, and her gaze, deliberate and glowing, was an invitation.

Ridiculous. He was old enough to be her grandfather.

He couldn't go on just staring. Their connection had passed the brief point of accident, had turned nearly familiar. If it went on much longer one of them would have to cross the room, begin a clumsy conversation that would either sever or solder their shared gaze. Marlin reluctantly shifted his attention away from the girl's depthless watch on him to the art, and he wondered, as he always did, what Sarah was trying to say through the nude, and to whom.

He pushed the thought of his daughter-in-law away, decided that the girl at the corner table had to be looking at something else, perhaps at the painting on the wall behind him of a finch gripping a snowy birch branch. The finch was his. So were the other watercolors. His paintings weren't great art, but they were attractive enough. And they fit in, for God's sake. The chickadees in the pines. The snowbird on the fluted iron birdbath. The pair of mallard duck decoys on the shelves above the clock over the waitress station. He had carved those ducks. He had built and hung the polished oak shelves. In fact, the nude was the only thing in the place he hadn't made or worked on over the years.

After they'd gutted and updated the diner a couple of years back, Sarah's nude had replaced his watercolor of a cardinal perched on a rail fence. Sarah's fence in Sarah's backyard. He had painted her listing pear tree in the foreground, her patch of beetle-ravaged rosebushes tangled up against a fence post. Sarah and Ben, his son, were too busy to deadhead and prune. The roses never bloomed. The bird feeder he drew dangling from the pear-tree branch was filled with leaves and gray, clenched roly-poly bugs. He hadn't meant to be judgmental. He had only drawn what he had seen one day out their kitchen window. Sarah had liked the watercolor, or so she said. But after the renovation, the nude was hung in its place.

Just looking at the thing ignited an electric jolt of grief and guilt, and he dropped his eyes to glance—casually, he hoped—at the girl again. Those eyes were watching him still. Warm. Sexy. Impossible. What color were they? He couldn't tell.

Marlin blinked. The girl stared into him, her flat lips curving upward, the dusting of a smile.

The diner was unusually quiet for midmorning, so there was little to distract from their flirtation, if that's what it was. The gang of regulars who always sat at a row of tables to his right was depleted. Probably all out sick. Flu season was just hitting Michigan. A nasty strain this year was killing otherwise healthy people. An eleven-year-old in Illinois had died yesterday. Staph had piggybacked on the boy's illness, infected his lungs. In Ohio, a twenty-five-year-old Iraq War vet had succumbed after he'd been home from active duty for just two weeks. Every morning Marlin searched for grim health stories in the Brecon *Sentinel*. He read the obituaries, too, combing the notices for anyone he may have known. He skipped the lists of surviving relatives and career successes and civic-service highlights to mine the cause of death, digesting that information with the usual knot in his gut. With his illness phobia he knew he shouldn't be seeking out death notices, but he found he couldn't break the habit. Maybe it was natural at his age to indulge fear. That's exactly what Lily called it, too. Indulgence.

Now the flu was hitting their town hard, according to that morning's *Sentinel*. Only Sam and Al had shown up for their daily fifteen-minute break that always stretched to an hour or more. There was no way to join in on their conversations about the day's headlines, their supervisors, or their wives or kids or whatnot without interrupting them outright. Anyway, it would seem strange to the guys if he spoke to them first. Usually they butted into his business, not vice versa.

No, there was no easy way to avoid that beautiful girl's gaze.

Had Lily ever looked at him that way?

He didn't think so, even when they were happier and still making love. Days she had left behind too easily, so it seemed to Marlin, as she moved through the sex-sabotaging stages of a woman's aging. At first, her loss of desire made him feel guilty, as if he must be to blame for his wife falling out of love with him. His reserve during arguments that she mistook for lack of forgiveness. His harmless comments meant as compliments—on Ben, on a new hairstyle, even the colors she chose for a quilt she was sewing—that she viewed as disapproval. Why she had begun to misinterpret him so, he didn't know. When she had stopped loving him, he couldn't say. He understood only that it was down to him: his fault, his failing. When, several years back, they finally ceased making love, he figured it was probably him she wanted to avoid, not sex.

But when she lost interest not just in him, but everything else, he realized that their sexual life was forever over. As she tired easily and barely spoke to him; as she napped and watched television during the day when she never used to; as she quit sewing or crafting anything with her hands; as she faded and he did not, he grew restless. Not just restless. Horny, to use that ridiculous word from his youth. Suddenly his orderly life—up early, breakfast alone with the paper, midmorning coffee at the diner, then painting or puttering around until dinner and her early bedtime and his late nights with television and ice cream and cigars on the back porch—was steamrolled by lust. He found himself watching *G-String Divas* on the TV. He watched girls on the street or at the local mall as they shopped or ate salad and French fries or chirped into cell phones. He gazed at their bodies under their sloppy clothing, which these days resembled the old cotton pajamas Lily used to wear except for the writing across their butts—PINK, or CREW, or the University of Michigan's block M hitching a ride on each rounded cheek. Loose flannel slung low on their hips as if they might shimmy right out of their pants with every step. Tight under-Ts held their breasts firm. Bras were, apparently, out of fashion again. He saw girls nude, even in deep winter buried under heavy coats and snowy hair and the steam of sweet breath. He *watched* them in that disrespectful and public way he never could stand to see in old geezers. Now he was one.

He lusted shamelessly after these young girls, yet he reacted to Sarah's nude as if it were porn. He stripped girls in his mind yet he couldn't bear to look at that damn painting, that eyeless face, those ugly areolae like molasses cookies on the inflated breasts. How was that picture any more pornographic than the feelings he had right now for that girl in the corner?

Or than the feelings he had for Sarah, and what the nude had made them do?

And here came the waitress, oppressively ebullient, threading her way through the narrow aisle formed by a row of unsteady tables Marlin balanced by wedging sugar packets under the legs. He had been meaning to level them properly for weeks now, but kept forgetting his tools. Ben, of course, never had a proper wrench on hand. She held the coffee pot high as she descended upon him with resolute cheer. Her skin was yellow and smooth, like custard, and she was dressed casually in jeans and one of those tight Ts under an open cotton shirt. Her hair was loose. There was a hole in the worn knee of her pants. If Sarah was here, she would never allow such sloppiness. But her casualness turned Marlin on, like everything young girls did these days. He couldn't take his eyes off her breasts as she leaned over him.

"Let's warm you up," she said. Coffee splashed into the cup, coffee he did not want. He started, jerked his hand, bumped the cup. Coffee seared his fingers. The waitress reacted with predictably energetic dismay, dabbing at his hand with a towel already soiled with the morning's previous catastrophes. Marlin was shamed by this girl's tone of concern and the edgy movements it was bringing out in her; touching him on the shoulder and looking at him as if he were crystal, as if the translucence of his skin, the deep, loose ridges between his knuckles, the glassy shimmer in his eyes, meant that he would totter and fuss and buckle under the strain of a minor burn. When did he begin to inspire such anxiety in young people, anyway? The more he desired these young girls, the more like a hopeless old man they seemed to treat him.

He flushed and raised his hand. The skin was a faint pink where the coffee had scalded. "No harm done," he told her. "It wasn't too hot."

She flashed a fake, automatic smile and moved on to the regulars at the next table. He wished it was Sarah filling his cup. Sarah turning him on. Sarah, his beloved complication.

She used to flirt with him, even for a little while after that afternoon when everything should have changed.

Sarah was home with the baby now, and hadn't flirted with him in months. That's what had changed.

He picked up his cup and chanced a glance at the girl in the corner, but she was absorbed in writing something down on a legal pad. Marlin fidgeted when she turned suddenly to look over her shoulder at the nude. He felt himself blush as she stared at the thing. Did she find it grotesque, or sexy? A wave of desire strong-armed him.

Ben came out from the kitchen in a veil of grease and yeast, motioning abruptly to the waitress for a cup of coffee. The gesture was curt. Shy, not imperial. Ben wasn't used to being waited on. Before Sarah stopped working to stay home with the baby, he had never hired any help except the occasional teenager to wash dishes. He spent the hours before dawn alone baking, then cooked all day until the diner closed in the early afternoon. Marlin thought that schedule might have to change with the baby, but so far Ben was persevering in his old ways.

Today he looked drawn as he sat down across from Marlin. Ben had been a somber boy. Now he was a grim man, distant, with no pursuits beyond his business, which he would never grow, and his family, unexpectedly growing, neither of which seemed to give him joy. He and Sarah had been trying for years to conceive. You'd think he'd be happier about the baby, Lily had observed more than once.

"How's Sarah?" Marlin tried not to sound wistful.

"The baby's got the flu." Ben's voice was hoarse with fatigue. A cup of coffee appeared timidly on the table before the waitress flew away. "Her temperature's been climbing all morning."

"Well . . . did she get a shot?"

"You know Sarah. We all got the shot."

The mention of a day's headline, in this case the ineffectual flu vaccine, always invited a regular to butt in. Today it was Sam who took the bait. "Fucking vaccine." His blue Con Ed uniform was dusted with cinnamon-roll crumbs. Sam was a messy eater. He thrived on widespread mess—corrupt voting machines, the anticlimactic identity of Deep Throat, imprecise public-health policy. "That's what's killing everyone."

"You're taking a few sensationalized cases and making a big deal. Anyway, there's plenty of cross protection." Albert was a mechanic at the garage down the street. The ink of grease was permanently tattooed into his fingertips. Marlin liked Albert's optimism, even if it had taken him three separate repair appointments to fix Marlin's brakes last month. "It doesn't match the H5N1, but it's got an H6 variant, so there you go."

"That's bird flu, you dope. People get H3N2." Sam always had the facts straight. Maybe that accounted for his grim outlook. "Anyhow, some cross protection. Those kids who died in Colorado, some of them were vaccinated. What's your baby's fever up to, Ben?"

"One oh three," Ben said tiredly, but he smiled at Sam. The regulars were his customer base. He mustered the tolerance for them that he couldn't for his family.

"That's high." Marlin felt the familiar bubble of anxiety. He swallowed hard. Nothing like illness to smother lust. He didn't even want to look at the girl in the corner now.

"You better take that baby in." Sam popped the rest of his roll into his mouth. Flecks of cinnamon peppered his chin.

"I'm going to close up in a while and go home early," Ben told Marlin.

Al said, "Business isn't going to be worth much this afternoon. Most of my crew is home sick."

"I can go over to the house," Marlin said to Ben. The offer wasn't sincere. There was his anxiety, and there was Sarah herself. Sarah in the diner was a different creature altogether from Sarah at home with the baby, with her chronic fatigue and endless worry turning her by excruciating degrees into Ben, exhausted, unsmiling, preoccupied.

"It's OK. Wouldn't want you to get sick. But you never do, do you? Lucky you." That pebble of anger in Ben's voice.

"I don't know, if it's luck or not." Marlin didn't want to discuss his devilish immunity to illness. But it was the time of year when Ben, susceptible as he was to colds and viruses of every strain, always brought it up, and with such resentment Marlin always wondered what his son really wanted to say to him. As if there weren't plenty to say.

"So, Benny, if your wife isn't coming to work anymore, how about taking that lady home?" Sam nodded to the nude and grinned. Marlin glanced over at the corner. The girl was writing again and seemed oblivious to the comment, although Sam's voice filled the dining room. "Gives me a stomach cramp every time I look at it."

"It's not so bad." Al gave the painting an appraising look. Al was the only regular who didn't mock the nude. The regulars also made fun of the scruffy artist who had painted it, although he was famous around Brecon for having shown his work in New York City. But any kind of long-hair fame was fodder for the regulars. "Except for the digits being chopped off. Wonder what the guy has against fingers."

"Fuck the fingers. What does the guy have against nipples?"

Marlin winced. Making fun of the nude always made him cringe. Sam's coarse language in earshot of the beautiful girl made the whole thing unbearable. Why didn't Ben take it down, anyway? He knew Ben disapproved of it even more than Marlin did.

Ben shuddered, a subtle twitch of his shoulders that only Marlin noticed. "Think I want to have to look at it at home?" he said. "Plus I wouldn't want to remove such a vital conversation piece."

"Looks like she was hacked to bits," Sam muttered. "How're you supposed to eat corned beef hash looking at that?"

"It's Lavinia." Ben's tone wasn't lightened-for-regulars anymore.

"Oh. OK." Sam turned away. A line of crumbs on his shirt lifted like a regiment of fleas. He wouldn't brush himself off until break was over. Nor would he ever admit he didn't know who Lavinia was.

"Explains the fingers," Al said. Marlin was surprised. He wouldn't expect Al to know his Shakespeare.

"Well, whoever it is, it's fucked up," Sam said loudly.

"Hey," Marlin said. "Watch the language."

"I think it's lovely," the girl in the corner said to them suddenly, and she was looking at Marlin again when she spoke.

Of course her voice was beautiful, too. Of course it shut Sam up.

Marlin should have been the one to answer. She wasn't looking at anyone else. He could have agreed with her, even if strictly speaking it was a lie. The nude was hideous. But the girl was lovely, so agreeing with her was instinctual.

Which Ben did before Marlin could stammer anything out. "It's a fine piece," he said to her in his neutral business-owner's tone. "Maybe just a bit too challenging for our space."

Her gaze shifted to Ben. "Can I quote that?" She smiled. Marlin felt a ridiculous pang of jealousy.

"Better not." The waitress was passing him on the way to the kitchen. Ben stopped her. "Bring the lady a piece of apple pie," he said quietly. "On the house."

"Who is that?" Sam said, for once lowering his voice to a whisper.

"A reporter," Ben told him. "From the *Sentinel*. She asked me some questions before you came in. Guess that artist has a show in Paris now. Guess we own one of the only nudes that hasn't been bought up by some rich art collector."

"Guess Sarah knows a good buy," Sam said.

"Guess she knows good art," Al replied.

Ben rose abruptly. "Dad, I'm going to close up."

"Well, hey—let me go over," Marlin said. "Or I'll send your mother," he added, a better idea by far. He disliked seeing Sarah at home. He disliked her worry. He was on the verge of disliking the baby.

"Mom pressures Sarah to give the baby a bottle whenever she's over. She insists the baby's crying because she's starving when she's just nursed. It's driving Sarah crazy."

Lily. Always saying exactly what she thinks, and doing it, too. No doubt baby's had a few bottles on the sly.

Marlin watched the waitress take the pie over to the girl. She smiled briefly and raised her coffee cup for the waitress to fill. So she was here for the nude. He wondered if Ben had mentioned the watercolors were Marlin's. Maybe that's why she had been looking at him. When the waitress left her table, the girl returned to her pad without glancing up. She twined a neck-lace of hair in her slender fingers. He watched her, those lovely fingers, the way she squinted at the paper.

He rose to leave and saw that Ben had hesitated by the kitchen entrance to stare at the girl. Marlin walked over to him. "So she interviewed you about that thing?"

"I wouldn't call it an interview. She seemed to know all about it already. I think she's just here to look at it."

"She's pretty," Marlin said without thinking. Eager, like some old geezer.

"I'm thinking of selling that thing. Sink some real money into this place.

Hire skilled labor this time around."

Ben was staring at him, hard. Expecting him to be offended by the skilled-labor crack. Expecting him to care about the nude one way or another. Well, he did care, but he wasn't about to let on to his son. "Sarah won't like that."

"Sarah won't care."

A customer entered the diner, snapped for a menu. Ben walked one over, patient and grim. Marlin stuck his hands in his pockets, nodded at Sam and Al, and crossed to the door. As Marlin walked past the girl, he watched her out of the corner of his eye, but she did not look up, not even at the squeal of the heavy glass door as he pushed it open into the cold air and riven walkway Ben couldn't afford to repair.

• ••••

Lily had the flu; he could see it at once. Her gray eyes glittered with fever. Swollen blood vessels on her cheeks inflated her veil of wrinkles. He still wasn't used to it, the way the fine lines of her skin had withered to an alarming tangle of folds and creases that left only the soft crescents under her eyes smooth. Lily had aged rapidly in the past two years. Her hair had thinned, her eyes had narrowed and hardened, her joints had stiffened so that she did not walk like herself anymore. All at once, although it could not have been so quick, her body had turned unfamiliar.

Now the fever made her unrecognizable. Her flush was watermelon pink. Drops of sweat beaded on her brow; pearls pulled taut. He crossed to the couch, where she lay enfolded in the old pinwheel quilt she had sewn right before they were married.

"When did it start?"

She didn't, or couldn't, answer him. She was trembling. He tucked the quilt more snugly around her fallen shoulders and caught sight of her night-gown. She had not even dressed. When he left that morning, she had been nursing her coffee. Marlin felt a prickling of fear. He knew how it would go. She would lie in bed, shivering violently as if she meant to throw the fever off, watch him with hard, shining, practical eyes while the fear gnawed at him. The days would crawl. They would both be waiting, each certain of different outcomes. Lily had not been vaccinated, a bad decision at her age. Neither had he, but then, he didn't need it.

"It's the flu, you think?" He sat balanced on the sofa's edge so that they barely touched.

A rasp rose from her throat's deep hollow. "For heaven's sake. Don't start hovering."

"Let me check your temp." He was pleading, as if quantifying the body's struggle would solve anything.

"Don't bother. Some ginger ale, all right?"

Marlin looked down at her withered hand bathed in sweat, shrinking like the rest of her. A year ago she had her wedding ring adjusted down a half-size. The band of white gold still spun easily around the finger's delicate spindle, barely secured by the bump of her knuckle. "Baby's sick, too."

"I spoke to Sarah. She's talking about going to the emergency room."

"Ben's going home early," Marlin said, but they both knew it would do nothing to calm Sarah down. Lily couldn't understand Sarah's chronic anxiety over the baby. Lily had never worried over Ben. Marlin had mistaken her bravery for some kind of innate feminine utility toward children. Ben's frequent fevers had sparked dismal fear in Marlin, but Lily had taken care of every health emergency with her usual practicality. Sarah's worry over baby seemed unwomanly to them both, but, to be fair, she and Ben were late parents. They had tried everything. Fertility treatments. Talk of adoption. Then they had conceived unexpectedly, and with the baby had come the seismic ripple of anxiety. Lily, too, hadn't become pregnant until many years after they were married, but she had never wanted children the way Sarah had.

Lily was radiating heat. Marlin went to fetch the ginger ale.

After he had held the glass for her to drink, Marlin escaped upstairs to the bedroom to confront the latest unfinished watercolor. A junco nestled deep in a fir tree, half-concealed by a cylindrical pine cone. Marlin had matched the brown patch under the bird's wing to the color of the cone, but the exact shades made it look as if the cone were a big brown wing. Sloppy work. Anyway, he had no reason to make the scene more complicated by placing the bird behind the cone, except that's what he'd seen out his window one day. Painting exactly what he saw all the time was poor craft, a lazy habit he should work harder to break.

He lay down, closed his eyes, saw the girl in the diner. Saw the slender fingers curled around the coffee mug, the eyes piercing the space between them. He undressed her, and the body was slim, sprinkled with tiny blemishes on the shoulders and above the breasts, pepper on cream. Not perfect. Not impossible.

What was wrong with him, fantasizing about a little girl with Lily so sick? And what made him think that girl was looking at him anyway, really looking at him and not a pair of blue eyes that reminded her of someone else—her dad? Her grandpa?

He opened his eyes and stared up at the ceiling at a webbed crack in the plaster he'd patched some time back. He had done a careful job with the spackle, but last winter the patch had cracked with the expansion of air in the narrow room that was almost an attic, tucked as it was between steeply graded eaves. He hadn't tried repairing it again. He got up, returned to the easel to fix the junco. No way was he going to nap the afternoon away like an oldster.

He never had the same energy for fixing things around his own house as he had for fixing up the diner. He'd supervised the diner renovation, even when Sarah told him that she wanted to replace a watercolor or two with a local artist's work after the diner reopened. His feelings weren't hurt. He offered to recoat the walls himself, to save on contracting costs. His pictures weren't anything great anyway. He never took the whole thing seriously. Painting was just a way to relax. But he had to admit he was dismayed when, a few days before they were due to close the diner for those two weeks, the new leatherette booths already delivered and crowding the kitchen, Sarah brought in her artist. The artist brought with him the Lavinia nude. The guy was messy and dour, his face hidden by an untrimmed beard and oversized eyeglasses, a real long-hair. He looked as if he hadn't cleaned up for a woman in years. Marlin didn't approve of the way the man swept Sarah to a back table to huddle together, speaking in whispers as they studied the nude. Her admiration. His flattered attention. God knows how she had even met him.

She had purchased the nude on the spot.

Of course the damn thing turned Marlin on. The fat, sexy breasts. The tantalizing curve of the thighs. He hadn't even noticed the missing fingers until after the renovation, when Sarah hung it and the regulars started their teasing.

It drove him crazy to imagine what Sarah would do in bed if she'd buy a painting like that.

He had never felt the way he was supposed to feel toward her, and she had never acted the way she was supposed to act toward him. He could never say for certain whether her flirting was a kind way to tease an old geezer.

Until they'd gutted the diner. Until she'd bought that nude.

Sarah. A whistle of syllables, like the silk of young skin. How absurdly deceptive a woman's name could be. He had said this to Lily once, during one of those marital hiatuses when their sex life was halted by illness or kid care or just because she was tired of him, and he couldn't seem to repair it; couldn't do or say anything right; could only hope she'd get over it yet again. He was mad, and lonely, and so he said to her, *You're nothing like your name says you should be.*

Of course she was amused, not angry. *How so?*

You're tough. You hate yellow.

Lilies are tough, and plenty aren't yellow. She was knitting something, something with stripes—a scarf, or a sweater for Ben. The needles clicked efficiently. She was spinning out fabric as he watched. *Mama named me after the Easter lily. They're white.*

You don't seem like any kind of lily to me, he had answered, like a jerk. It was a mean thing to say. Why would he say it? But he couldn't stop himself, that impulse to hurt her.

Of course she wasn't hurt. *Easter lilies are tough to grow,* she had said. *You need just the right soil. But the bulbs will make it through anything. They're only a hassle after you plant them.*

He looked up lilies after that and read that lilium bulbs are scaly and unprotected. Exposed flesh.

Nude. And never dormant.

Although his door was closed, he heard Lily cough violently from the couch downstairs. Fear soured the lingering taste of coffee in his mouth.

He set down the brush he hadn't even dipped into the junco-colored paint yet, and he couldn't remember what that girl at the corner table looked like anymore.

• ••••

The *Sentinel* didn't appear on his doorstep the next morning like it should.

"The carrier must be sick," Marlin said to Lily. She was worse, much worse. She wouldn't drink the ginger ale he brought her, wouldn't get out of bed. She also wouldn't put up with his worry.

"Go get some breakfast at the diner. Help Ben out."

"I'd better not leave you."

"You're making me worse just looking at me like that," Lily said.

So Marlin drove to the diner, anxious, not thinking about that girl at all, and so it was a shock when he creaked open the door and there she was, seated in the corner by the front window under the nude, looking straight at him. Her hair was pulled back and up. Loose strands floated about her neck. The morning sun lit her, bright, glaring, and whole. She kept hold of him, her gaze traveling brashly from his hairline to his chin. A slow blush beat the same path down his face.

Could he cross the room to her? Could he sit with her right now, face the nude, and see *her* nude? Lace her fingers with his, bring them to his mouth as she entered his gaze, brushed his irises with lashes and lips until she was all inside, filling his eyes and throat with her sweet mist?

He blinked, kept his eyes briefly veiled. His blush was downright shameful. Not hard to see what trend his thoughts were taking.

He walked unsteadily down the line of tables to where Sam was sitting alone. He was plowing through his cinnamon roll as if eager, for once, to finish his break. A couple playing hooky from their jobs was ordering eggs from the teenage boy who usually washed dishes. The waitress must be sick, too. Two insurance agents whom Marlin recognized as cheap tippers were drinking coffee in a booth by the front door. Marlin tapped Sam on the shoulder as he walked by.

"We lost Al," Sam grinned. "I'm the last man standing."

Marlin found Ben in the kitchen, piling shredded potatoes on top of a yellow mound of fat. The grill was stifling. The hood fan whined ineffectually as it struggled to draw out the heat. Ben was ill. A sick flush matted his cheeks. His eyes glittered with fever. His arms trembled as he nudged some eggs over easy. The teenager ambled in with the order, stuck the slip into the slot above Ben's grill, and began crashing dishes together in the sink. When the toaster popped, the young man wiped his hands on his suds-soaked apron and plodded over to butter the toast. Ben must be really sick to let the dishwasher handle food. Marlin's gut burned with alarm. He should offer to fry-cook, and Ben should accept his offer. An emergency like this should lead them back to the normal state of affairs where the father pitched in to help the son. Anyway, the whole family knew Marlin was the better cook. But Ben barely glanced up at Marlin's worried hover.

"Bad night?" Marlin settled on the safe bet of asking the obvious.

"Bad enough." Ben wiped away a sweat slick on his brow. Marlin caught the glimmer of pallor under his flush. "Baby's real sick. Hard breathing, you know, that awful rasp."

"Your mother's sick, too."

"She OK?"

"She's fine, nothing to worry over. Did you go to the emergency room last night?"

"Sarah decided to wait. Afraid it would be too crowded, too many germs. She's going to the doctor today. What time is it? Maybe they've already been." He reached over for a plate, slid the eggs onto it, potatoes, the toast the kid had left teetering precariously on the sideboard, before giving in to a fit of painful coughing. The kid left the dishes to run the breakfast to the dining room.

Marlin took up a cloth to wipe crumbs and grease from the sideboard.

"Leave it, Dad." There it was, the sharp, suspicious tone that cast a shadow over every bit of help Marlin had ever given his son. Ben was right to suspect that any work Marlin performed at the moment would be a selfish distraction from his own ridiculous immunity. Ben and Lily both knew how wrapped up he was in the notion that when he did at last fall ill—and someday he would, he would have to—it would take him quickly, catastrophically. There would be nothing to distinguish illness from accident, unanticipated and unlucky.

It was the way his father had been taken. He had been robust for his age, perfectly healthy, as Marlin was now. Then a sudden bolt of sickness, some devilish, seemingly minor cold, whisked him away. The fact that Dad was elderly and it was quick should have been a comfort to Marlin, especially after his mother's horrible wasting from liver cancer. During her excruciating slide, he'd come to believe that no other death could be as frightening. The tumor growing palpably day by day, bloating her abdomen. The sleepless agitation near the end as, despite the morphine, she battled nights of terrorizing pain by attempting to hoist herself from the bed and fling herself to the floor, desperate to be free from the mortal trap of lying prone.

After Mom, Dad's quick end should have seemed merciful. Maybe once it had seemed that way, when Marlin was younger and not yet his father's age. Now he was that age. Death's sudden, unprovoked snatching frightened him more than ever. Marlin had never seen his father nude until the afternoon he died in Marlin's bathtub. The water was still warm. The folds of white, withered skin floated gently around his skinny body like nesting doves. Dad had complained merely of a stomachache. He had taken the bath merely to be soothed. He hadn't even had time to run a fever.

Ben rattled out a cough. Marlin dropped the towel onto the sideboard and peeked into the dining room at his girl. She was absorbed in a book now and didn't see him gazing at her. She seemed completely uninterested in the nude. The couple waiting for their eggs was openly gaping at it. Even the insurance guys, who were regulars, were studying it. No matter how regular a customer was, everyone always ended up staring at the nude. Not his girl. Not today. Guess she had written her article.

Her fingers curving and smooth. Her hair with shavings of gold. She was beautiful, but not hopelessly so. Her lips thinned when she smiled, and the bridge of her nose was broad and angled slightly, as if it had been broken once. She was not perfect. It was not impossible.

"What's she doing here again?" Of course his voice was too eager.

"Who, Dad?"

"That girl. The reporter."

"How should I know? Maybe she likes the coffee." Ben staggered as he broke an egg onto the grill. Grease spattered his cheek.

"Hey, come on. Let me cook. You need to go home." Marlin resisted the impulse to take Ben's arm. Ben didn't like his dad to touch him. Never had, not even as a kid.

"No, I'm OK. Go take the coffee pots around, why don't you. Fill everyone up. Cash them out. I'll close up after these folks are done."

A détente of sorts. Maybe the flu would do them both some good. Marlin went to fetch the coffee. Sam had the pot of caffeinated and was filling his own cup.

"I told Ben I'd warm up the customers." Marlin reached for the pot.

Sam clowned clutching the carafe to his chest. "No way. I'm gonna warm up the fox in the corner."

"Hey," Marlin protested, but in a flash Sam was down the aisle and leaning over Marlin's girl. Marlin fumed as Sam aped the waitress's trick of splashing coffee into the cup from a foot above the table in an amber cascade. What an idiot.

"There you go, Miss."

"That's nice of you," she said. Her clear voice carried across the dining room. "But I'm leaving. I didn't want any more coffee."

"I'd like some," one of the insurance guys called.

"Cool your jets," Sam told him. Then he said to the girl, "So you like that painting? The nude?"

Even saying *nude* out loud to that beautiful young woman would cripple Marlin with embarrassment and desire both, and here Sam was, making a joke of the word. But the girl was unflappable. "I think it's his best work."

"Well, I'd hate to see his worst," Sam said. "What does he do, lop off the heads?"

"How about that coffee?" The insurance guy snapped his fingers.

Sam walked over to his table and banged the pot down. "Here you go, buddy."

"For heaven's sake," Marlin said. Sam grinned at him. Ben emerged from the kitchen with the couple's order. Marlin crossed the room to fetch the pot from the agents' table and nudged Sam hard as the jerk headed back to his table. The girl in the corner stood up, gathered her coat. Marlin wanted to cash her out, but by the time he had returned the pot to the burner Ben was already at the register taking her ticket.

"Everything OK?"

"Marvelous," she said.

"Thanks for the article." Ben handed her the change. "Great publicity for us."

"Oh, was it in today's paper?" Marlin stammered. He was standing next to Ben. Because the register stand was narrow, it meant he was also standing close to the girl. Too close. She was looking at him again, and he saw her eyes were brown. Deep, almost black, like the nude's darkest lines.

"Front page of arts and entertainment," the girl said. "My favorite artist. And my first byline."

"Why don't you take it?" Ben said.

It took both Marlin and the girl a moment to figure out what he meant. "The nude?" she asked.

"Yeah, why not? Dad, go take it off the wall." Now it wasn't a young girl's gaze piercing him from across a room, but his son's hard look a breath away.

"Thank you, but I can't accept it."

"Go get it, Dad." Ben's voice rose. Marlin flushed and looked away.

The girl rested her hand on Marlin's arm as if he had made a move to get the painting when in fact he hadn't moved a muscle. It was all he could do not to smother her fingers with his own. "Please don't. I appreciate the offer, though. I understand you painted the watercolors. They're nice."

She looked at him warmly as she complimented his hobby. It was the same gaze as ever, deliberate and glowing, but its core was friendly, not intimate, a look bestowed on an old geezer who painted pleasant pictures of birds.

He refused to imagine what his son saw.

The girl pocketed her change and left. Sam grabbed his coat, nudged Marlin hard and winked on his way out the door. Ben disappeared into the kitchen, scraped at the grill, although there were no more orders. One of the insurance guys refilled his coffee at the burner. Marlin followed his son reluctantly. No choice now but to confront the accusation Ben had lobbed with the nude, but when he saw his son's sweat-drenched flush, his tottering movements over the hot grill, he hesitated. They couldn't talk now. Ben was sick. Nothing would be said in just the right way. They'd have to wait until this flu had passed.

• ••••

Marlin drove home to find the *Sentinel* on his stoop. He took the paper into the kitchen, leafed through it to the arts and entertainment section, found the article on the artist's big Paris opening and the related box feature on the nude in the diner. He read the byline. Olivia Bell. He closed his eyes, saw again her friendly gaze, felt the wince of embarrassment. What a fool he'd been to think she could possibly want him.

But Sarah had wanted him. He hadn't been wrong about the meaning of her gaze across a room.

He'd been attracted to Sarah ever since she'd married Ben, but after his retirement freed him to spend his days at the diner, Marlin had fallen in love with her beyond all reason. He loved her so much that he came to resent that Ben had her, when he, Marlin, was so much the better man for her. Marlin never ignored her as his son did. He could even cook better than Ben, he'd proved it to her. When Marlin took over the home cooking from Lily, Sarah used to compliment his food in the bright, teasing way she had that made him flush and want to say something fun, meet her eyes, and hold them and then do it, just do it, walk over as if she belonged to him already; take her arms, brush her lips with his, and from there it would happen without restraint or misgiving. All in a moment, everything would change.

He thought about kissing her for years until he realized he had to stop it, and the only way to stop was, in fact, to kiss her. By that time, he and Lily rarely made love, and when they did, his thoughts of Sarah were so intense and lovely, made Lily feel as he knew Sarah must feel, tight and vital and—he had to admit it, old geezer—young, that he would lose himself, move hard. Eventually he would hurt Lily. He had to have Sarah, the vast safe cloak of sex, where nothing happened suddenly and nothing was ever taken away.

So he waited. Eventually the greasy buildup of endless fry-cooking forced them to close for cleaning, and why not update the place while they were at it. They shut the diner down for two weeks to work. Marlin and Ben installed new flooring and fixtures while Sarah cleaned. Her efforts were mostly in the kitchen. The nude she had just purchased stood propped against the sideboard, where Marlin could see it on the frequent trips to the restroom coffee and his fussy prostate were causing lately. By then the marriage was clearly strained. Sarah did not want to be in the same room with Ben much, was even avoiding Marlin. The sun of her flirtation had cooled a bit. Marlin found out later that the fertility treatments were failing, that they were on the brink of divorce. But he was ignorant of this as he removed his watercolors from the walls and stripped grease from the paint in fussy black balls that stuck to his nails. He was relieved that she was out of view when Ben was around, because he could hardly control himself anymore. He was glad for the strained relations. He liked to think that she'd come to realize he was the better man for her, and he felt no qualms about his wishing this were so. He even ceased to think of Ben as his son, but as a man standing in the way, refusing to accept what everyone else knew to be the truth.

And finally came the day, when the sluggish sun burned hot and the space, although air conditioned, was as steamy and close as tiles firing in an oven, that Ben took the afternoon off to pick up new tables for the dining room. Sarah did not go with him. Marlin read much into this. He was more encouraged when she abandoned the kitchen work to paint with him. By then the grease was stripped, the walls spackled and primed. It was just a matter of coating with the eggshell color Marlin had chosen, a rich echo of her skin. They did not speak, did not look at each other. The space was completely private. Ben had papered the windows for the renovation. So easy to lay his roller in the tray and wind his arms around her before she had a chance to push him away, if that's what she was going to do. She stood close to him, bending to dip into the paint tray, and it was as if she had the same impulse, because she straightened with a queer, tense smile, came up empty handed, arms at her sides, and she was looking at him.

He couldn't believe it. He had thought all along that he would have to wait until she wasn't expecting him, but here she was, sweating with the heat of the room, brilliant and soft and no longer as young as she had been when he first loved her. It wasn't graceful or even very loving. He was too rough, although he knew he didn't have to be. He may have hurt her. He would never know, she never made a sound.

● ●●●●

It was only one time. Afterward they were never alone again. Sarah worked in the kitchen for the remaining week of the renovation, hung the nude when the place reopened, packed Marlin's painting of her bleak backyard away in the back with the boxes and mops. She still flirted a little, but she avoided being alone with him whenever he tried to engineer it.

Maybe he had hurt her. Maybe she just came to her senses. Nothing changed in either of their lives, except to make him want more. More of her. More sex. It was the start of his obnoxious horniness. At first, when he was hurt and lonely for her, he wondered if she really had loved him. Eventually it occurred to him to wonder if she was hoping to become pregnant by him and spend their lives hiding it. But he didn't believe it of her, not really, considering the irrevocable disorder it would have created. It wasn't Sarah's way to risk everything and emerge messy. But if that was her plan, it had not worked. She didn't get pregnant for at least another year.

They had shared one moment. Now they shared worry, and it was all they shared. Perhaps, afterward, Ben became more distant, more preoccupied. Perhaps Lily was wise to it. She fell ill more often, spent more time away from him, and finally ceased to make love to him altogether, like the tightening of a faucet head after a prolonged leak. And then the baby was born, and that one reckless, lovely time with Sarah felt like the ghost of another life altogether. Fading, almost able to be forgotten, if only Marlin could stop thinking about her when he looked at that nude.

Until his son's angry command to give the damn thing away.

Marlin folded the paper and went upstairs to check Lily. Her eyes were closed, her chest's rise and fall a dreadful shudder. The easel stood close to the bed's foot. The junco watercolor cast a shadow over the slope of her legs under the quilt. He'd pulled the easel into the west corner by the wardrobe before bed the previous evening. He was certain it still stood out of the way when he'd left her that morning. Had she moved the junco to a viewing place, picked out each glaring amateurish flaw as a distraction from the struggle to breathe?

Now that she was so deeply asleep he could fold back her quilt without waking her. He could ease her fragile limbs from her soaked nightgown, peel away the flu's terrifying cloak. Pose her like a nude. Tuck her legs to expose the curve of her thigh. Prop up a shoulder, a hip, arrange her hollow breasts and loose belly. Would he paint her as if he were looking out the window at a natural scene, render exactly what he saw? Or would he exaggerate her fallen limbs, her flaccid breasts, and the faint silvery gashes on her belly? Would he make her nipples ugly brown moles, chop off her fingers, gouge out her eyes and mash her nose?

Which of the two nudes would be more familiar to him?

Lily opened her eyes; glossy, distant, almost gone.

Marlin moved the easel back to the corner, turned over the junco to its blank side. He touched her brow and then fetched the thermometer. He stood over her and watched her wince with her breathing. He felt his clear, untroubled breath as if it had a scent and a taste of its own, tidy, pure, and free. It was shameful how well he felt.

If she noticed he'd removed the easel she didn't say. She shook her head at the glass wand he tried to slip between her lips. "Don't bother."

"I think we should know how high it's gone."

"It will pass."

"I'm calling the doctor." His voice was thick with fear. Lily would hear, as she always had, the selfishness behind the worry. Her chest constricted as she pressed back into the pillows. Her gaze at him wasn't right.

"Don't." She coughed, her shoulders bearing the brunt of spasms, and he backed away despite himself. "Marlin. If I die in this bed there's not a damn thing you can do about it. So quit worrying. Give Sarah a call. Check on the baby."

"Ben's sick now." Another selfishness. No point to the comment other than to prompt Lily to reassure him.

"He'll be fine." Lily soothed him dutifully. "Go call Sarah."

"Why? Ben will be there soon."

"You two can worry yourselves sick together. Do you both some good." She reached for his hand. He moved closer to take it. Her fingers were dried petals in his palm, powdery and fragile. She coughed violently again, the force of it bending her back off the bed. "Go on," she said, and her gaze was distant, and her powdery hold on him was no longer so weak. "You can't avoid her forever. She's your grandson's mother."

Then it wasn't the flu dimming her gray eyes.

He swallowed hard against the lump of fear in his throat that should be shame. "Let me wait," he pleaded, "until you're well."

Lab Will Care

Neither scientist nor trainee, Emily managed others' inspiration. She oversaw the care of the lab equipment and animal husbandry. She conditioned mice and recorded results. During the boom in Alzheimer's research funding, she sorted out the need for space, and she just as efficiently managed the lab's recent sharp downturn. For a decade, the Abel lab's steady gains in the understanding of the hippocampus, the ruler of memory, had nurtured new Alzheimer's therapies. The same decade of the war on terror had steadily siphoned Abel's funding. Now Emily fit scarcity to discovery, square peg, round hole.

The lab's survival now depended upon the conquest of fear. Abel's latest grant supported post-traumatic stress research. Emily instilled, and then extinguished, fear in mice. In the lab such feats were systematic products of biological prompts. The *why* of the fear response was the concern of the neuroscientist, Abel, and the postdocs studying under him. Although fear had chiseled the rules of her life, Emily would only be an adjunct to its cure.

In a Spartan room adjacent to the conditioning lab, she used a computer monitor to observe the freeze response. Her presence in the lab, even out of sight, would disrupt the mouse's instinct. So Emily positioned a camera above the test cage and watched the isolated mouse scamper in a black-and-white video frame. She programmed a tone to coincide with a wave of electrical shocks conducted through the cage floor's metal grid. One or two rounds of shock were all it took to imprint fear. When she played the tone without the shock, the freeze response ossified the body in its last pose. A tail curled in curiosity and a neck craned in casual investigation were captive to an exquisite stillness until the tone ceased, the threat passed.

After the fear response was ingrained, it was time to decondition. For two days, she would chime the single note without the shock and record how long it took for the mouse to become unafraid. With time, learned fear could be unlearned. But the mouse retained a shadow terror that could be measured neurologically. Original fear never leaves the subconscious. If fear of a musical note couldn't be erased, Emily didn't hold Abel's hope for erasing the psychological pain of war or trauma. Anyway, she didn't want to think about what might be left exposed in the memory if terror's linchpin were removed.

The animal-husbandry staff was in charge of feeding the mice, filling water dispensers, cleaning cages. But the cage room across from the conditioning lab was reserved for Lab Will Care. Only the researcher cared for these mice, who matured without ever being touched. Successful conditioning required them to be handled for the first time as adults. Once acclimated, mice behaved like cats. Rubbed their bodies to her skin, eyes glittery, drunk on her touch. Ten days was enough to train the mice to come to her open palm, rely on her by sight, by smell, by sensation. Today Emily was halfway to acclimation with her current subject. After five days, the mouse still skittered restlessly under her methodical stroking of his back and belly. Like the observation room, the acclimation lab was designed to be neutral. White walls, white tile, white plastic shelves overflowing with equipment. From the far wall, a clock's second hand slid quietly from moment to moment, the hushed tick the only sound besides Emily's breathing and the click of the mouse's claws on the steel tabletop when she set him down. Emily scooped him up again, a soft bundle of brown with a white belly. She was practicing the motion of delivering him to the conditioning cage and removing him again, training him to accept without fear the sweeps of changing altitude. In a few more days, the mouse would trust her hand as he would trust a flying carpet's spell.

She carried the mouse back to Lab Will Care, set him gently in his cage. Soon her essence would bedrock his sense of security, and then the fear conditioning could begin.

Emily crossed the hall to another cage room that housed the mice who had completed their conditioning. Imprinting fear had altered their neurological patterns. These patterns could now be recorded. Fear would have substance as waves on a monitor, the effects on the hippocampus as visible as a web of veins under the skin. Emily pulled on a pair of gloves, scooped up her subject, carried him to the euthanizing table. She snapped his neck and from there worked quickly to preserve the animal's brain, the hope of peace it might reveal.

• ••••

After she packed the brain in dry ice, a grayish ball no bigger than her thumb, Emily peeled off her scrubs, threw them in the hamper by the security door, and made her way through the basement hallway. She rode the elevator to the Life Sciences Institute's top floor and entered the walkway crossing the lobby's lofty glass atrium. Through the curtain wall at the building's entrance, traffic wound down the street, glittering metallic under a high sun whitewashed by the cold. Smokers huddled around the building plaza's concrete planters as if the frostbitten remains of azaleas were warming fires. Ash trickled from bright scarves and heavy winter coats. Below Emily, a crew wheeled banquet tables on squealing dollies to the atrium's center. The screech echoed in the ceiling above her. The soaring, glassy space amplified disturbance like a touchy microphone.

Emily stored the sample in the sub-zero just inside the lab's door, washed up, went to her desk in the last bay cut from the lab's countertop. Out the window, the university's unglamorous power-plant roof, a dense thicket of pipes and valves clustered around a chimney, blocked the view of the ivied graduate library and the heritage-brick dorms rimming the Ann Arbor campus. The Life Sciences Institute was a model of green efficiency, but when the power blinked off, the power plant kept the lights on as reliably as it had for a half-century. There had been talk recently of closing off parts of Life Sciences, mothballing whole corridors, abandoning the south wing. Fifteen years ago, the University of Michigan had driven deep stakes into biomedical research. Life Sciences coaxed top researchers to modern labs, encouraged risk, all but guaranteed reward. Now the Abel lab was a holdout in independent science's losing war. Many labs had folded, the researchers absorbed into corporate labs. In hindsight, Life Sciences could be considered a reckless gamble with public funding, but who could have foreseen that an endless war on terror would divert the public's fear of disease? The courage of conviction would soon be all that fed the Abel lab.

Two bays down, Abel was speaking quietly into his phone. His daughter Amelia perched on a stool, coloring. Amelia, an epileptic, must have a medical appointment. Tom, one of the postdoc trainees, stood over Amelia, waited for Abel to end his phone conversation. Tom's study of mesial-temporal-lobe epilepsy was personal to Abel, one he still insisted on funding out of the dwindling PTSD grant. Abel hoped to eradicate the need for lobectomy surgery on the worse cases so that Amelia would never be laid out in a white theater, swathed in blue surgical sheets, brain yawning to the theater's chill.

Temporal-lobe seizures were hard to detect. Until Amelia was three, Abel himself hadn't spotted his daughter's quiet recessions from motion and sensation, like being suspended in a wave's backswing. Emily witnessed a seizure only once, when she picked Amelia up from daycare to help Abel out of a scheduling jam. She'd had Kurt and Kristin with her, so she decided to treat the kids to ice cream. She'd gone for more napkins to clean up the creamy rainbow streams the waffle cones wept in the heat. When she returned to the bench, her kids were ringing Amelia like a protective fence. Amelia was sitting stiff, expressionless, as if encased in a shell. Ice cream bubbled mildly from her lips. A lavender-and-pink slurry had pooled in her lap, soaking her sky-blue shorts.

Did she turn into a doll, Mommy?

Kristin had described Amelia's transformation perfectly. The soul's flight left behind waxen skin, stiff limbs, a doll's lifeless eyes. When she'd come out of it, Amelia blinked and resumed lapping at the cone as if the moments had never been lost. She watched Emily mop the mess from her lap with a distant curiosity. After Emily's shock calmed, she'd felt a jealousy at the easy erasure of time Amelia would never miss. Anything could be done to her during her release, and she'd have no memory of the damage, nothing at all to fear.

Amelia offered Tom a blue crayon. Tom glanced impatiently at Abel. Back when Emily started her career at Worcester Polytech, before she had kids of her own and understood how impossible it was to staunch the bleed between work and family, she'd resented Cameron Jeffers's domestic life spilling into the lab. A spat with his busy scientist wife over missed child responsibilities. The call from the kid himself, sick or stranded or otherwise marooned. Emily's own family had bottled their emotions. She would never dream of calling her father at work. She'd never approach him with a problem at all, and her mother suffered from *chronic sinusitis*, the diagnosis her father preferred over *suicidal drunk*. But at her stage of life, divorced with two kids, midthirties, lodged between outgrown insecurity and middle-aged authority, Emily could easily join in Amelia's drawing or wait out Abel, either course a natural one.

Tom finally took the crayon and bent reluctantly over Amelia's drawing. Kate, one of the undergraduate trainees, entered the lab carrying a parcel. Plain brown paper, twine gathered in a perfect square knot at the top. She slipped past Abel to hand the package to Emily. "This was delivered for you."

No shipping-company labels, no name on the package. Flat, a box the size of an egg skillet. For security reasons the lab didn't accept unmarked packages. Not that the Abel lab drew the attention of extremists. Research on neuronal function and behavioral output was, for the mice's welfare, uncontroversial compared to the oncology research she used to perform. The oncomice she'd made for the Jeffers lab were bred for tumor growth, engineered to be gruesome, perfect propaganda specimens for the animal-rights activists. The Abel lab's transgenic mice were designed to lack behavioral genes, the animals more tool than subject. But Emily couldn't ever again risk a breach. "You shouldn't have accepted this. Who delivered it?"

"I'm sorry. It was a woman." Kate spoke as if women were a safe bet. "She was looking for a name on the building directory outside. On my way in, I asked if I could help her find someone. She said she was a friend of yours but didn't want to disturb you. I thought it was OK to bring this up."

Abel snapped his phone shut, answered Tom's question. Tom moved to the scope in the next bay. Abel looked over Amelia's wave, *look, Daddy*, to rest a gaze on Emily. His long reliance on her to carry out his imagination's practical applications had cultivated a shorthand sympathy between them. Emily had shared a version of this sympathy with Jeffers, but back then she'd been a promising researcher, still untested. Jeffers's job was to test her, train her to move past her natural aptitude for discipline to invention's messy play. She'd failed Jeffers's test, all right. Abel had hired her not as a researcher with promise, but as a sidetracked career scientist who had chosen lab management for family reasons, or temperament. Not everyone was suited to the tedium of discovery or the funding chase. Abel respected what he assumed was her choice.

When she proved her ability to anticipate the lab's needs, their connection matured to signals. A glance caught her attention. A slight dip in her expression caught his. *We're better than married*, he'd said last year after they'd managed a grant cancellation efficiently, as if bad news was merely another project launch. No layoffs, no interruption to the work, accomplished with no collateral tensions springing up between them, the managers of catastrophe.

By the expression in Abel's eyes now, Emily knew that the phone call had not concerned Amelia. She reassured Kate it was OK that she'd accepted the package and placed it on her desk. Kate moved to join Tom at the scope, took up the computer keyboard to record results. Abel stroked Amelia's hair, *great job honey, sit tight*, pulled a stool to Emily's side.

"The DOD cancelled." The next modest grant in their slim pipeline, the only grant in that pipeline after the current funding ran its course. "Tried to get through just now. They won't even take my call."

"OK." News she'd received so many times over that past year it was pointless to react.

"How long?"

He meant the budget, operations, staffing. She'd made all the cuts she could, and he knew it. "Operating as we are, a few weeks."

"We won't hear from the CDC until January."

"I can't tell you what you want to hear, Mike."

Abel tucked a finger into the palm of his other hand and made a fist around it, his nervous habit. She referred to it as holding his own hand. His black hair, speckled now with gray, curved at the temples. Narrowed blue eyes stared past her to the window, the billowing smokestack, the glittering cars on the road below, but he wasn't seeing a thing at the moment. Emily waited. Behind Abel, Amelia crouched over her drawing. Six medication adjustments in two years. None had controlled Amelia's seizures without also rendering her nearly catatonic.

Abel was going to have to give up the temporal-lobe research. Emily thought through how much operational time this might buy, was startled to see Abel was again gazing at her as if he were the one waiting for Emily to finish brooding.

Abel spoke before she could. "We'll have to cut husbandry."

She'd faced last resorts before. The drastic never resulted in a long-term solution. "I'm not going to do that."

"We'll have to trim anyway to make it through this round of results."

Cut. Trim. Euphemisms she couldn't stomach even after years in the profession. "I'd rather explore alternatives."

"Like closing down?"

"Like prioritizing what we get paid to do. Which at the moment is not epilepsy research, Mike."

Abel glanced back at Amelia. She was meticulously filling in her drawing's blank spaces with a fiery-amber crayon. The picture could be a sunrise, or a ring of fire. He opened his fist, clamped it closed again. "If we euthanize half, how long can we hang on?"

Managing death was her job, but for what ends mattered to Emily. Of course she'd made cuts before. For the Abel lab, when the downturn started, but that operation was small scale, one she could fulfill with the older mice who would die anyway within a week or two. For the Jeffers lab she'd had to perform large-scale euthanizing on rats, dogs, chimps that were too sick to offer for adoption. It was the one task she couldn't view with the scientist's detachment. She couldn't help but feel she was betraying her subjects. The animals had given their bodies. She felt beholden to those bodies and the consciousness behind the eyes. What Abel was suggesting, and it would only be a suggestion for a few moments more, involved euthanizing the young. The choices of which subjects would live and which would die would have nothing to do with age or physical condition, everything to do with their queue in the research process.

"Come on, Emily." Abel met her gaze. She saw the determination she expected to see. She wished she could see regret.

She also saw the results of the reduction as if the accounts were before her. "We could operate until January, yes."

"We've got a solid shot at the CDC funding." Abel spoke as if he were confirming the plan's success. He rose, walked back to his desk to help Amelia put on her coat. Amelia left her drawing to hug Emily, *bye-bye Emmy*. She returned the hug, drew in Amelia's candied-apple aroma; missed, for a moment, her own daughter's scent, an appalling strawberry-kiwi shampoo being the current stinky favorite. Amelia skipped away. Abel didn't look at Emily as he swept Amelia up toward the door over her squeals that she was *too big, Daddy*. Abel's avoidance was their rarest, and their most powerful, signal.

The security latch on the lab door buzzed Abel into the hall. Emily stared blankly at the parcel she'd set out of the way. She took the package by the perfect knot, snipped the tweedy threads with scissors, tried to remember the last time she'd seen a package wrapped with twine.

Inside an old Bering cigar box, wrapped in white tissue, was a glass vial capped with a rubber stopper filled to the rim with cherry-bright blood. Shaking, Emily set it aside carefully to unwrap the flat object nested underneath. She tore at the tissue, not careful now. A foam tray thudded on the desk. After all these years, the bones were still perfect. Bleached white, a meticulous design of scissoring limbs and curved rib cage. From the spiny feet's angle, Emily saw that this frog wasn't hers. She'd dissected Dinah's, too. She'd arranged the legs differently so at a glance they could tell them apart. In eighth grade, Dinah was already squeamish about mutilating animals, no matter if they were long dead and reeking of formaldehyde and born, anyway, for the purpose of study.

But for the first time in school, Emily felt drawn to explore. Running the scalpel down the belly, peeling back and pinning the skin, seeing that the organs were arranged exactly where she'd learned they would be, sparked a rush she'd later come to realize was joy. Dissection proved a death could be useful. Some harm in the world could make sense, was even for the good.

Dinah, with her flair for deception, had received an A for that unit. Mr. Bartley had given Emily a B-plus although she'd prepared both frogs exactly the same.

Emily flipped the tray over to confront Dinah's handwriting, the off-hand scrawl, the fat bellied a's, the l's loose loops, as if the lines existed only to corral the generous empty spaces.

"What's that?" Kate was leaning over her shoulder. Emily flipped the tray right side up.

"Don't you remember middle school biology?" Remarkable how she tamed the bobble in her voice. But the tray was shaking. Emily set it on the desk, folded her hands in her lap.

"I never dissected a frog," Kate said. "That's cool."

"I had to bleach the bones." Tears scarred her vision. "The teacher was very particular. It was a big part of the grade." Of course Dinah wouldn't record Bartley's name. She never made a record of any man. She didn't understand anything about Emily's feelings for Bartley. The teacher was the first man she'd trusted after *him*. By then Dinah knew about *him*, although Emily had held back many details. She didn't think Dinah would understand being trapped and doing what you were told without putting up a fight. Was she afraid that Dinah would say what she always said in answer to Emily's surrenders? *You're so provincial, Em.* Or maybe she'd been afraid Dinah would make an altogether different statement. *You were raped.* A confirmation of one thing, a denial of another, neither of which felt like the truth.

"Well, you did a good job." Something in Emily's voice must have betrayed her. Kate's tone was a tentative approval. "I didn't dissect anything until high school. The fetal pig. So gross. But, some part of me must have liked it. Because here I am."

Emily wiped her eyes with the back of her hand. "What did she look like?" She almost added, *now.*

"Who?"

"The woman who gave you this."

"About my height, long dark hair. Kind of heavy. Your age. But pretty. She had her head covered. One of those bright cashmere scarves with the paisley squiggles."

Your age. But pretty. "What did she say?"

"Not much. Just asked me to put this in your hand. She said it like that. *Put this in her hand.* She had a funny way of speaking. Kind of formal. I asked if she wanted to see you. But she said no. I'm sorry. I didn't think about security or anything."

"It's OK." But the thought of Dinah so close to the lab was terrifying. "Did you see where she went?"

"No. God, is that *blood*?" Kate snatched up the vial, popped the stopper. The blood wobbled. A fake-cherry scent trickled into the air. Kate pressed a finger to the filmy surface. "Jell-O. Weird. Some sense of humor, right?"

Emily didn't answer. The last time she'd seen Dinah was in Moynagh's, a bar near the Worcester campus, over whiskey shots. Several days had passed since Dinah had broken into the Jeffers lab with Emily's ID. Emily was promptly fired, a consequence Dinah may not have yet known in the tumultuous wake of her organization's so-called rescue operation. Emily was determined to be civil. The damage done, Emily simply wanted to know why

Dinah had used her when she could have found another way. For resourceful Dinah, there was always another way. She must have wanted to send Emily a message, teach a lesson, pay her back. When Emily asked point-blank and Dinah started in about animal rights and liberation, it dawned on Emily that she and her goons had not taken the animals to a safe house, as she'd assumed, but had released them in a field on the outskirts of town.

Freed them to die.

She'd said it aloud, sick on whiskey and the thought of her hobbled subjects, some with advanced-stage tumors *for God's sake*, abandoned to the wild. When Dinah looked at her with incredulity, *you know you have killed them already*, Emily's old feelings about Bartley flooded back.

How could you fuck him?

Dinah had met her fury with disbelief. Then she'd laughed. When Bartley was transferred to teach advanced-placement biology their senior year of high school, Dinah had slept with him and made certain Emily knew. During their affair, Bartley's passionate attention to Emily's scientific aptitude blinked out. Dinah ruined her belief that men who could be trusted around girls did exist.

The man. Not the animals. This is what upsets you. Dinah approved of her outburst, as if putting the man first was—finally!—a show of gumption.

Emily still felt stupid for blowing up over Bartley that day, who hadn't mattered at all, or so Emily had trained herself to believe.

Kate handed Emily the vial and returned to the scope. Emily wrapped the tray up carefully, pulled the cigar box toward her. Saw the note there, not folded, the loose handwriting plainly in sight. She wondered how she'd missed it.

Release them.

The words could be merely a reference to Dinah's goons. "Release" was her organization's name. But the note could be a warning. Emily stood up and quickly retraced her steps to the atrium walkway. Dinah couldn't invade this lab, no way. In the years since the Jeffers stunt and similar high-profile incursions, security had become every lab's top priority. But Emily had to view any word from Dinah as a threat. She took the elevator down to the basement, scouted the corridors around husbandry. Asked the techs she met if they'd spotted anyone unauthorized, felt an absurd impulse to laugh at the word. Then a conviction seized her, that at the moment she'd gazed at the traffic's brilliant snarl while carrying the mouse brain, Dinah was huddled with the smokers, wrapped in her bright scarf, willing Emily to see her.

Emily took the elevator up to the lobby, emerged into the great glass atrium feeling foolish and angry that Dinah would, as always, drag Emily out into the open. Of course she wouldn't still be on the street. It was all a tease, the bones, the Jell-O, the words that were half-command, half-taunt. Release them. Had nothing changed in all this time?

Nothing had. There Dinah stood on the other side of the glass, breath frosting from her bright scarf, loitering patiently in the cold as if Emily were only running a few minutes late.

•   ••••

In the café at the north end of the atrium lobby Dinah sat silently across from Emily sipping a watery herbal tea. The young man behind the counter knew Emily, asked her if she wanted the usual, didn't identify what the usual was. Emily had refused to order. Making the statement about not breaking bread with a traitor.

"You didn't need the theatrics. Those stupid old bones."

For all her reserve, Emily never could stand silence between them. That much hadn't changed. Dinah knew the Jell-O and the note would make her furious. Emily needed to be picked at like a stubborn scab. You had to carve chinks in her so real feelings could seep in.

But she had thought Emily would like the bones. "The frog wasn't for show."

"You put Kate in a terrible position."

"Kate?"

"The young woman you used. Our postdoc."

"She approached me, Em. She offered to take it." No need to point out how lax security could be, how easy it was to insinuate into any place. Dinah took another inventory. Emily looked happy, she'd bloomed. Her fragility had toughened, she had meat on her bones, she smiled now. She'd grinned all right when she caught sight of Dinah through the glass, grinned with joy until she swallowed her reaction, adopted the shock and caution she assumed Dinah would expect from her. The flash of brightness made Dinah wonder if she was no longer so angry, which would defeat the purpose of this visit.

"*Release them*? Is that some kind of threat?"

"That was the theatrical part."

"Some stunt. If you know where I work, you also know where I live. I'm in the damn phone book."

"This is a beautiful space." Dinah set down her cup, looked over Emily's shoulder at the glass lobby. The brittle winter sun reflected harshly on the directory kiosk and chrome waste cans. A crew was setting up tables for some sort of event. Emily flinched when a metal chair leg scraped the tile. The squeal shrieked into the atrium, lingered in the vast ceiling. "So much light and air. Is your lab also so open, so *humane?*"

"Why wouldn't you just call me, Dinah?"

"Do you remember how gloomy your Worcester lab was? Those wicked basement cages. I remember thinking you could feel comfortable there, hidden away. But it was a stepping stone after all, or else things have changed a lot, your people are letting the light in now."

"Disrupting research isn't exactly letting the light in."

"There is still something in you that doesn't want to find an alternative to killing, Emily."

"I shouldn't have let you in the building." Emily glanced at the security guard standing at the building's entrance. When she admitted Dinah into the lobby, the guard had swept them both with a practiced scrutiny as tactile as a pat-down.

Dinah set aside the tea, it was too hot, too gingered, laced with a bitter aftertaste like the root's bark had snuck in with the tea leaves. Behind Emily the crew was setting up a podium. A tech wrestled a microphone with a testy stand. The tripod splayed out no matter how he positioned it. "What's the occasion?" Dinah nodded at the tables, now draped in flowing white skirts. The banquet crew was setting out water glasses, rims pressed to the cloth.

"Did you appear out of thin air to ask me about the evening's entertainment?"

Furious, but curiosity lurked behind the exasperation. Emily would never kick her out until she found out the reason for dumping those bones on her. For Dinah, *why* was the least interesting part of any endeavor. *Why* got in the way of taking action. "I'm just asking, Emily, that's all, it looks so fancy."

"It's a hospital benefit for Alzheimer's treatments our lab developed. Care to donate?"

"You must be proud of that work."

"Cut the bullshit. What are you doing here?"

"You know I am up to no good, Em. Why not alert the guard?"

There it was, a chink. Emily almost smiled. "Would Nan have any reason to kick you out?"

"Are you curious to find out?"

Emily's smile flattened. "Something wrong with your tea?"

"Not a thing." Dinah smiled. "It's delicious."

Emily sat back, waited her out. Dinah kept the silence. Emily would be expecting her to ask about her life, a husband, children, her mother and father; but, too, would not be surprised to know that Dinah had learned of her divorce, the ages of her children, the dates her parents had passed, and exactly when she'd joined Abel after staying out of the field for years.

The tech succeeded in propping the microphone on the portable stage and murmured, "*Check*." He motioned to an elderly woman waiting at the riser, elegantly dressed in a black pantsuit with a maroon scarf knotted at her throat. A man in military dress uniform escorted her tenderly to the microphone. The tables gleamed with silverware and china. Dinah felt the heat rise under the coat she'd kept on to hide her weight gain from Em. She looked old and fat, felt old and fat. Emily hadn't changed. Timid Emily, not tentative at all when it came to killing. It was like that, Dinah had found. Those committed to cruel acts preserved their zeal and devotion, while those out to stop them burned out. But the moral was never ascendant, this was natural law. Being moral must mean going against some instinct of self preservation, she'd decided. Dinah arranged her expression, keep it neutral, keep it friendly. The heat of the day Emily had shot at that asshole came back. Who would think Em of all people would lug that old war trophy clear across town to take a wild shot at *him*? Then shoot that can clean off old Socks's back as calmly as swiping a gnat?

The elderly woman grasped the microphone's round head. A shrill electronic screech grated and faded. The military man—her son?—removed her hand gently. She looked at him, her lack of recognition translating as utter fear. "What am I supposed to say?" Her amplified plea echoed through the atrium.

"I'm going to speak, remember?" The soldier-son meant to soothe, but his low voice rumbled harshly through the speakers. "You don't have to say anything."

The dress rehearsal wasn't going very well, then. Emily was struggling to ignore the booming voices, her effort so familiar in her tensing shoulders, the way she had of shrinking into herself. Dinah felt the old urge to take her hand, *pull* her out into the open. "So Alzheimer's is your life's work now?"

"Was." Emily was watching the soldier-son pat his mother on the shoulder. "I'm studying the fear response now."

"Why?"

"We're researching PTSD treatments."

"But what am I supposed to say?" the woman cried into the microphone.

"You're doing great, just great." The man nudged her away from the mic stand. The feedback whined, fell silent. Emily clenched her hands on the table.

Dinah said, "Fear is suppressed anger, Em. You of all people know this."

Emily unclasped her hands. "It's the other way around, actually. But there's a bit more to it than glib psychology, Dinah."

Her voice was calm, Emily-prim, but she wasn't even attempting to hide her fury, never could. But Dinah hadn't sought her out to pick at the same old scabs. No more underground, no more useless symbolic rescues, no more bullshit.

"You want another shot, Em?"

"I don't drink anymore."

Dinah laughed. "At *him*."

Emily froze, her expression blank, her old slipping away. That's how she remained merciless, by this brief flight of her soul.

• ••••

After she left—*fled*—Dinah, Emily drove home to cower in her bathroom, retch into the toilet. When they returned home from school, Kristin and Kurt hovered outside the door, tentative. Their mother was never ill. When she emerged, they were fearful, unbearably clingy. She was helpless to fix dinner, tuck them into bed. She couldn't even touch them, for God's sake. Was some revulsion toward her children lurking deep in her that *he* could surface? She finally called Collin to take them for a few days, didn't tell him why. The good-bye hugs felt like welts on her skin.

He was the first thing she'd checked before moving back to Michigan from Worcester. He moved away years ago, her still-clueless father had told her. His house had been razed for a new subdivision.

What happened to the bees? Her question popped out, as if the insects were what mattered.

Her father didn't remember that his friend had kept bees.

At the time, she'd convinced herself that his erasure was some justice, some safety. Now his return was an intent to finish with her. If he *had* returned, if this wasn't another of Dinah's games. Something catastrophic was turning inside of her, a compulsion to call Dinah's bluff. Their friendship had always held a sadistic undertow that Emily both hated and craved. After two days battling sickness and a baffling feeling of shame, whatever impulse drove Emily to punch in the number Dinah had given her, it wasn't trust in her motives.

Dinah picked her up in a rusted silver Jetta. The engine growled on the idle like a complaint. They spent the brief drive in silence. When Dinah pulled up to the Asian grocery store in the slummy part of town, a cramped market where Emily often shopped, Emily stared at her. "Why did we come here?"

"He lives here." Dinah pointed to the second floor. Burred cedar shingles dangled from the battered siding. The landing of an old iron fire escape clung precariously to a cracked window. Traces of that morning's frost still dusted the sill.

"That's not possible. There's no apartment." Ang's shop was a cherished local secret, tucked away in this run-down residential neighborhood south of campus. The block building was a rude outcropping on a three-sided curb, as if tossed by accident onto a street of rented bungalows and subdivided Queen Annes. Before the recession, the shop was a tea house for the Russian and Eastern European immigrants seeking work with the university and a peaceful life on a quiet tree-lined street. Now the neighborhood housed Asian university students destined to take their education back home. Ang's was the transient community's bedrock. Emily bought star anise and the rice threads the kids loved here. She'd never even noticed the upper floor. If she had, she'd have assumed the space was storage for the shop.

"*Apartment* is a loose term, but yes."

Emily studied the second floor window. No shades, no sign of life. The glass pane reflected the sun back to her, shimmering and fierce. "How long?"

Dinah maneuvered to the curb between a rusty pickup and a Buick missing a wheel. Ang's triangular lot didn't have room for parking. Dinah pulled in too tight, rolled up on the curb. Emily felt the lurch as another wave of illness. "I didn't ask."

"You've been . . . in there?"

Dinah cut the engine. The winding street was deserted, a midday calm. Across from the Jetta, a power line sagged from the listing poles like a playground jump rope. How could Emily have failed to sense him? That she could have run into him anytime on this street made her shudder. More troubling was the thought that she had seen him and hadn't recognized him. That he would no longer be a familiar, after she'd held such terror of him for so long, was unthinkable.

"I befriended his sister, she leaves him in my care sometimes."

"He has a sister? How can he have a sister *and*—" *And do what he did to me?* But she couldn't say it aloud. Was this woman a monster, had she belittled him, abused him, made him hate young girls? Or was it Emily who'd been different, nothing at all like the sister he loved?

"He's got a sister. He had a mom and dad. He got married and divorced. He moved to Indianapolis, became a teacher of industrial arts. He has lived an ordinary life." Emily leaned against the passenger door. Dinah added gently, "Nothing about him has ever been extraordinary, Em."

"Except what he did to me." Emily covered her mouth with her hand, swallowed hard against the nausea. "You wouldn't call that extraordinary?"

Dinah reached for her hand. "Yes, dear. I would."

They held on for a moment in the old way. Palms pressed tightly, fingers curled to form one fist. How many times had they clasped hands while running through fields or horsing around on the playground? Such easy contact then. This habit lasted into adulthood. As late as Worcester, just before the Jeffers raid when Dinah had appeared on her doorstep, she'd taken Dinah to the seaside thinking the ocean would help soothe her latest heartbreak. They held hands on the beach, shared whiskey straight from the bottle. Emily had wondered then why they weren't lovers, and then chalked up her wonder to her usual confusion of affection with sex. *He'd* conditioned her to experience any touch as sexual. On the beach, with the waves caressing their ankles, their toes girlishly painted pink and tucked into the soft sand, Emily knew that if Dinah meant them to be lovers, they would be. Drunk on whiskey and the thin salty air, Emily didn't trust herself to question what she wanted.

But that day on the beach had proven to be the usual bullshit, Dinah's broken heart a ruse to steal her lab ID. This sudden appearance out of thin air, too, must be a lie. *He* must be a ruse. Emily would always be an operation to Dinah, had been since the days Dinah had used her to earn her grades, fuck her favorite teacher, invade her lab, destroy her career.

Emily yanked her hand away. "Why are you really here?"

"The single time I hold pure motives, you think to ask this question?"

"You're a liar. He doesn't even live here, he can't."

A woman holding a plastic bag pushed open Ang's door. Chopped spiky hair, a nose ring studded with steel beads the size of ball bearings, flowing leather coat. Green shoots poked from the top of the bag, scallions and chives. During the day, Ang's attracted the alternative set. Emily shopped in the evening, when the Asian students stopped by the market to gather the evening meal.

Dinah caught Emily's brief stare at the nose ring. "You're still so *provincial*, Em."

"Fuck you, Dinah. Take me home."

Dinah gave her that appraising look. Approval, affection, like Emily was rising to a dare. Emily still couldn't read her. Under the bright scarf, her gray hair tumbled to her shoulders. A yellow undercoat shadowed her skin. Dark pouches rimmed her eyes. Age and fatigue only highlighted her loveliness but the old ferocity still made her beauty a deterrent.

"I don't mean that as an insult. You're reliable, Em. Consistent. I must turn to you when I need someone. After all this time, I still have only you."

"When you need someone to fucking *use*. What is it this time?"

"This time, it's *him*. I owe you another shot."

"Got a gun?"

That snide smugness. She'd think she was calling Dinah's bluff. Dinah stared out the window at the nose-ring. Just the type of woman Emily would stare at, someone with the guts to display who she was. But poke Emily and she'd shake off her conventions, this Dinah could count on. After the Jeffers operation, she'd gone bonkers in that bar. Yelled at Dinah for fucking Bartley, as if the lab raid didn't matter at all. *I told him all about the frog*, Emily had cried. *I told him you were a cheat.* This ridiculous outburst had summoned the fat bartender to throw them out. Dinah hushed him with a stiff tip. *There's no one even in here,* she'd told the man. The tweed-and-elbow-patches scanning student papers over spectacles and a Bloody Mary looked up then. The two utility guys in blue canvas jumpsuits drained their ale, studied Emily curiously as they passed the women, break over, back on the job. Typical Yanks surrounded by Yank bar kitsch. The bar made from Babe Ruth's bowling lane, polished, glowing in the gloom. Colonial blacksmith tools sharing the walls with cheap mirrored Samuel Adams ads. What did Emily see in these dark places, her labs and bars with their patriarchal bullshit? For a girl who mistrusted men, Emily sure barricaded herself with them.

Emily could have turned Dinah in to the police after she stormed out of Moynagh's, but she hadn't. By keeping quiet, Emily ensured that the raid was Dinah's first and best success, the one that had made Release a movement. Emily would think Dinah owed her for the break-in, but the real debt lay in her silence. In the bar that afternoon, Dinah could have revealed they'd only released the animals who couldn't be saved, filmed the least-gruesome subjects vanishing into the tall grass and wildflowers for a recruitment video. The rest she'd delivered to animal care experts. When Emily had cried out *released them to die,* Dinah should have reassured her that only a few met with that fate, but fuck it, Emily was the one who'd mutilated them. She didn't deserve, did she, to know what was only for show?

Seeing Emily now, shrinking against the passenger door, clenching her hands together, Dinah still didn't regret the omission. Emily's fear had always struck Dinah as artificial.

The nose-ring walked to the rusted pickup parked in front of Dinah's sedan. She glanced at Emily through the glass before stepping quickly up into the cab. In this temporary neighborhood of strangers, everyone earned a quick glance, a hurried avoidance. Unpunished crimes could languish here. Secrets could wither away into past lives. But forgetting was not forgiveness. "What if I did have a gun? Would you use it, or forgive him this time?"

"Take me home."

"Get out, then. Call a fucking cab."

Emily didn't answer. The pickup pulled away from the curb. When the motor faded, Dinah said, "What happened to you was meant to shape your genius and your compassion. You maim and kill animals for pleasure, for authority. You were meant to be better."

Emily said, "I hate you." Childish, to believe those words would hurt.

Because this belief would make Emily expect it, Dinah replied, "I hate you, too. I really always have."

Dinah opened the car door, slipped outside into the cold. She wrapped her scarf around her hair before heading around the back of Ang's store. Emily caught up to her at the cheap plywood door behind a row of dented aluminum trash cans. She meant to have it out with Dinah, say everything she should have said in Moynagh's. But Dinah slipped through the door into a cramped foyer, where a raised voice could bring anyone to witness. Later Emily would wonder whether she'd followed Dinah in silence because she needed to matter to *him* again, or maybe she was lonelier than she would admit.

The foyer was freezing. Wind whistled through cracks in the doorjamb and siding. Black scuff marks slashed the cheap white tile. *His* name was written on a smudged paper scrap stuffed crookedly in a mailbox name-slot. *Bill White.* Ordinary, a name of no significance. A flyer from the local Kroger flapped in the mailbox's lip. Someone had bothered to find this door, stick an ad in this solitary box. A phone book, still shrink-wrapped, lay on the floor below the box. *He* had no use for a community of names.

The women climbed a listing flight of pine stairs flanked with an ornate carved banister. Light from the upper landing's cracked window shone on the polished wood. The staircase was missing treads. The rotted boards shuddered and creaked, but the elegant banister glided up to the second-floor landing like a velvet rope. Emily couldn't imagine who had thought to decorate this shabby entryway with something so lovely. Also how the staircase bore the weight. With every step's shrill whine, she expected to tumble down to the foyer, shatter a bone, embrace the pain that would pierce her numbness. She told herself that Dinah was playing with her. Emily would follow her through the door at the top of the landing, find Ang's overstock of exotic cans neatly stacked on shelves, and Dinah would grin, *I really had you going.*

At the landing, Dinah rapped on the only door. Behind them, cold air hummed through the window pane's jagged crack. The sharp aroma of star anise and wild mushrooms filled the landing. Ang heaped the mushrooms high in raised rectangular bins, the moist, sticky stems laced together like raw tentacles. When she untangled the long stems from the caps, Emily would plug her nose against the raw dank odor that reminded her of basements. Although she hated the smell, she loved their earthy taste. Her kids wouldn't touch mushrooms; she ate them alone.

Dinah opened the door without waiting for an answer. By this Emily knew how often she'd visited. Emily slipped in behind her. The apartment was as cramped as the foyer. An efficiency, with a kitchenette on the far wall, a neatly made cot lodged in the nook where a dining table should be. Sealed mover's boxes made a corridor to *him*, reclining in an easy chair by the room's only window. The reek of iodine and, faintly, urine reached her before she saw the stand looped with dangling tubes and an IV bag next to his chair. A cup and saucer rested on a box top near his feet. A spoon stood upright in a Ball jar filled with honey. A handwritten label, *Wildflower*, curled around the jar under the lip. On a water-stained love seat, a cobalt-blue silk robe was folded neatly on a bright granny-square afghan. A beekeeper hat lounged near the afghan. Black mesh curled around the hat's white rim like a lacy nest of hair.

He lay deeply unconscious. Another of Dinah's tricks, not warning her of his illness, but Emily's numbed wade closer to him felt like curiosity, not shock. Under a thin, faded nightshirt dotted with orange—old yolks or iodine—a Hickman port wormed from the sallow chest. A growth below the waist poked at the nightshirt's loose fabric. Angry purple veins popped from the drooping hands like rain-swollen crawlers. Thickly ridged nails curled toward the palm like branches sloping toward sunlight. One of her terrors, the memory of how he'd slashed her with them.

How could she have ever thought she wouldn't know him? But he wasn't anything like he'd been. Swollen purple pouches under his shuttered eyes and plump bleached lips bloated his most familiar features. The mustache had been weeded, the round naked head a faint mustard color. She should have recognized jaundice right away, but she was disoriented by a swooping feeling of flight. She blinked, stepped back, brushed against Dinah. Dinah must have thought Emily meant to touch her. She slid an arm around her shoulder.

"Where's the sister?" Emily whispered. She was terrified of waking him, witnessing his slow dawning recognition. A lack of recognition would terrify her more.

"She is often out at this time, grabbing a smoke and coffee. He is usually out cold, easy to leave."

He didn't react to their hushed voices. Emily watched for a flutter beneath the eyelids. He might have been dead except for the pulse at the throat's hollow and the chest's uneven rise.

"His liver?" Emily's voice registered high, unfamiliar. The room *must* be cold. The iron radiator behind a tattered sofa was steadfastly quiet, but a prickly warmth seared her back and neck. No goose bumps on *his* bare legs and arms, either. They shared this dream of heat.

"A sarcoma. Rare, I am told."

He stirred. A hand curled into a fist. The nails dug into the yellowed palm. Had he meant to cut her back then, or were his nails so long he couldn't help it? She'd been pinned to the concrete floor, her shirt twisted around her neck. The furnace fan whirred in her ear. Hot air fanned her back. Wonder seeped through the numbness, *if the furnace is broken, why is the fan working?* It would take her days to understand he'd lied about needing to fix the furnace. Stupid, she was so *stupid* to have let him in when her parents weren't home. But he wouldn't have had to lie. He was her father's friend, a man she'd flirted with, even held hands with once when her father couldn't see. He used to call her sweetheart. She loved hearing him say it. Shit, she'd loved *him*. She would have let him in no matter what he said, with her twelve-year-old rash craving to find out if he loved her back. The lie proved he'd meant to hurt her. She was too stupid to realize he possessed this intent all along.

He still didn't trim those nails. The sister didn't groom him, either.

The yellowed hand relaxed. Blood rose to a crescent notched in the palm. A sour taste tickled Emily's throat.

Dinah pushed her scarf back. Her hair spilled out over her coat. Dinah's weight struck Emily then as it hadn't before. Her lips were pinched red slashes, her eyes slits snipped from the fleshy pillows plumping her cheeks. A musky odor clogged the air. *His* wasting, or Dinah's sweat, or the worn oak floorboards steeped with mushrooms and spice.

"Val will be back soon. You have to decide what to do. Emily?"

Emily stumbled to the kitchenette and vomited into the sink.

The radiator clanged. A hiss spiraled from the valve. Emily wiped her mouth with her hand, wouldn't risk touching the stained towel draped over the faucet. Dinah was moving around the room. Emily hoped she would have the sense not to come near her. "What do you mean, decide what to do?"

She turned to see Dinah placing a gun on the box next to the dirty cup and spoon, a chunky revolver straight out of some cheap Western. So Dinah's glib comment in the car had been the truth, but Emily knew this was a fucking kid's toy, just another jab at Emily's provincialism. Dinah was the last person to carry a weapon. Self-defense wasn't nearly as colorful as martyrdom, and besides, Dinah wasn't afraid of anything.

"What are you doing to me?" Not what she intended to say, and why was she pleading? Words slipped out of her sloppy, all out of order.

"I promised you a second shot." Impatient, as if explaining it all to Emily *for the millionth time*. "Or if you prefer, euthanize him like one of your animals. Look in the cupboard there, you'll find his medications. You must know which drugs you can use. You have this skill, right, you know what to do."

"Fuck you, Dinah."

Dinah went on as if all Emily needed was to see reason. "Look at him, you can see this is for mercy. The gun is licensed to me, I will be blamed, and I will say I did it. But if you use medical means, no one will know his death is not natural. Your choice. Revenge on us both, or just on him."

"That's ludicrous."

"Or you can forgive us both. Decide quickly." Emily's gaze flickered from Dinah to *him*. Incredulity and anger softened to thoughtfulness. Or curiosity. Reliable, ruthless Em. Dinah relaxed. How little Em had changed, how easily she slipped back into the child who had swiped her grandfather's war prize, determined to kill her rapist. Emily would never for a moment believe how much the memory of her gutsy move kept Dinah from giving up. But Emily needed to quit picking the wrong weapon for her targets. "We can always just leave, if you don't think you can."

Emily would never simply leave. Dinah watched her approach the chair, then stop near the box holding the gun. For a moment it appeared she would snatch up the gun, take aim. But she seemed frozen in place.

"Show him to me," she said.

"What?"

"Show me." When Dinah didn't move, Emily pointed to his waist. "The tumor."

Emily *would* want to observe him, that was her training, her way to courage. Dinah knelt heavily at his slippered feet, rolled up the nightshirt's frayed hem. She leaned into him to ease the bulk past his hips, coughed at the odor of urine and mildewed cotton. Under the wafer-thin eyelids, his eyes fluttered.

When she had arranged the fabric above the belly, Dinah sat back as if Emily had merely asked her to fetch a glass of water. Dinah's calm always felt like teasing. The stained underwear was frayed along the seams, Emily saw. The crotch was hollow, squished and emaciated, but she didn't want to see his sex. The tumor was a tight balloon of flesh protruding from the rib cage. Patchwork veins laced the skin like leather stitching. A new body, nourished by his failing one.

Dinah said, "Just think. If you'd stayed in cancer research you might have been his cure."

Emily lunged for the gun. Heavier than she expected, not a fake at all. She pointed and squeezed the trigger, realized too late she was aiming too close to Dinah, *at* Dinah. She screamed.

His eyes snapped open. "Leave me alone!"

Dinah was on her, fist closing around the barrel. "Shut up, Em, Jesus Christ."

"Jesus Christ! Leave me alone!" He tipped forward, struggled against the jutting leg rest. The IV tubes rattled on the stand. A gurgle rose in his throat. *Had she hit him?*

She must have said this aloud. Dinah took the gun and hissed, "Jesus. I keep it chambered on an empty cartridge."

"Jesus! Oh Jesus!"

Emily pushed past Dinah and ran to the sofa. She rammed the beekeeper hat on her head, covered her face with the black netting. Lunged at him, wiggled her fingers in front of his marbled bloodshot eyes. The mesh shrouded him in a shallow gloom but he saw her, he *did*. Those marbles bore through the mesh as if he'd never stopped seeing her. "Boo, you fuck! Boo!"

"You fuck!" he cried.

"Fuck you!"

"Boo!" he screamed.

"Em! Stop it! He doesn't even *see* you."

"He sees me all right. Come *back*. Come *back* you fuck!"

"Em, calm *down*." Dinah caught at her shoulder.

"Get off that monkey machine, Jesus! You're an addict!" He rattled the tubing as if swatting at her. The IV stand tipped, hit Emily in the back.

Dinah grabbed Emily by the arm, peeled off the beekeeper hat, tossed it away. The gun clicked and was in Emily's hand again. "Just don't shoot at *me* this time, you numbskull."

"You numbskull!" he shouted.

Stripped of the mesh's curtain, the room oozed glare and heat. Her arm steadied. His babble and bullshit were no barrier at all, with one shot she could slip through his stupid noise. Emily felt a revulsion too close to grief, squelched her pity just as she quashed mercy in the lab, pointed the barrel at his plump pale lips.

He moaned and opened his mouth. His throat worked as if he were swallowing her aim.

She lowered the gun and moved toward him.

Dinah groaned. "Christ, Emily. You're close enough."

Emily didn't hear her. He quieted down as she knelt at his feet. "Hand me his robe," she told Dinah.

"Emily." But Dinah fetched the silk robe from the love seat, shook out the folds, handed it to her.

The silk was genuine, light and smooth between her fingers. Emily tucked the robe around the tumor, the belly. She drew the collar gently around his slack neck, taking care not to disturb the port. The deep hue lit up a rich blue under the irises' calm surface. She'd never been close enough to his eyes to see they weren't really black. He burrowed his chin into the robe. Touched her hand with his mouth briefly, a kiss, or maybe he'd mistaken her flesh for silk.

Emily plunged a finger into the honey jar, sticky and warm. Perfectly smooth, no crystals. Fresh, except it couldn't be new. Did the stuff spoil? She didn't think so. Perhaps this everlasting purity was what had drawn him to tend bees. She leaned over and smeared his lips, daubed his chin, his cheeks, painted him tenderly with sweet. His eyes blinked slowly into focus, shrewd, *back*.

"Sweetheart," he murmured.

"I forgive you." She tried the words on. Hated how they scraped the surface of her numbness.

"I forgive you," he whispered back.

Emily licked her finger clean and nestled the barrel in the notch above his lip.

"Don't!" Dinah moved quickly to pull her hand away.

"Get off me, Dinah."

"Get off!" he cried.

"She's here." Dinah pried the gun from Emily, broke the cylinder open, tapped the bullets from their chambers. Slipped the revolver into her coat pocket like she was stashing a joint. "Clean him off, for heaven's sake."

Emily mopped the mess with the robe's collar. The silk stuck to the honey, draped his chin and mouth. She jumped back when the apartment door swung open. A woman impeccably dressed in wool slacks and the type of glossy mink coat Emily had only ever seen in vintage magazines slipped into the room on a wreath of smoke.

"You're an addict, you numbskull!"

His shrill muffled voice stopped the woman in her tracks. "Oh, Christ. Not again."

"Oh Christ! Oh Christ!"

The woman took a long drag, held the smoke in her lungs, aimed a gray vapor at the ceiling. The faint caustic odor of mothballs wafted under the smoke. The woman took in the silk robe stuck to the chin, the shrunken lap and bared legs, the IV stand toppled against the box. "Oh, Bill. How *indiscreet*."

She threw the mink on the sofa back. The lining was moth eaten, the coat's luxurious sheen matted under the arms and collar. Some ancient relic from a shabby closet. She crushed her cigarette out in the cup next to her brother's chair. Untangled the IV line that had looped around his wrist. Tossed the silk robe on the love seat, pulled his nightshirt down, tucked the loose ends around his legs. "Bill, you're all sticky. Have we been after the honey again? Hand me a blanket, would you, Dinah?"

"Sure, Val." The beekeeper hat had landed on the floor. Dinah replaced it carefully on the sofa cushion, took up the granny-square afghan, bent to wrap his legs. His eyes fluttered closed. He became as lifeless again as Emily's first glimpse of him, the throat's pulse a faint restless skitter under the brittle skin.

"There we are." Val frowned at her brother, as if his peace were more troubling than his agitation. "I'm a nurse, so you'd think I would have seen it all. But these fits are so awful."

Emily couldn't breathe. Her skin was scorched crimson like a drunk. Dinah saw her distress, shook her head, *keep it together*. But Dinah too was pale, for once as rattled as Emily. "I'm sorry, Val. We must have upset him. He was sleeping soundly when we got here."

"Oh, bosh, it's not your fault. No rhyme or reason to these episodes, he just explodes. It does reach the point when you just wish him gone. Anyway, it's not Bill anymore, is it?"

Emily's eyes filled with tears.

"Oh, I am sorry." Val clasped Emily's hand. "Of course, seeing him this way is a shock. Are you all right?"

Val's clammy palm slid against hers. Emily pulled away. "You should call hospice." Remarkable, her steady voice. "They can manage this." She didn't say *better*, but from Val's sharp look Emily guessed her meaning was plain.

"You should, you know, Val." Dinah smoothed the blanket around his knees.

"Oh, I know it. But Bill never liked strangers touching him. He was always so private. And one can't let him get the upper hand."

Emily couldn't have heard right. "The upper hand?"

Val glanced at Dinah as if sharing a private joke. "Bill has a bit of the devil inside. In this condition, there are things he might say that he ought not to. People who don't know him wouldn't understand."

The radiator's hiss crawled along Emily's skin. "What might he say?" She stared at Val. Not a hint of him in her steely gaze, no family resemblance in the features. Shouldn't his healthy ghost lurk in his sister, or had Emily lost all memory of how he used to look?

Val met her gaze coldly. "Things he ought *not.*"

Over Val's shoulder, Dinah touched him. Showing Emily how he didn't move, how he couldn't feel. Val's firewall stare waited her out. Was it a warning of some sort that she hadn't asked her name, or questioned why they hadn't removed their coats? Val must have overheard the commotion on her way up the stairs. She was managing the women as warily as she was being managed.

Emily took a step back, bumped into a box behind her. Val relaxed. "Better to have a quiet passing, and I am perfectly capable of seeing to *that.* But how nice that you came in time. How do you know Bill? Were you a student, like Dinah? Bill insisted on moving back home here to pass. A few of his former students have managed to find us and send condolences." She smiled brightly. "Dinah said Bill was her favorite teacher."

Of all the ruses Dinah could have used, she chose Bartley as their cover. Dinah removed her hand from his shoulder. Smiling a little, but exhaustion lined the crescent wrinkles at her mouth. She waited, as she always used to, for what Emily might do next.

"Yes." Emily's voice was distant, but normal. "He was our favorite teacher."

Such a cool liar, Dinah noted, ruthless to the core once she was poked. Interesting that Emily had aimed at Dinah first. Likely a heat-of-the-moment slip, but they never would be certain, would they?

• ••••

When Emily returned to the lab the next morning, Kate asked if she'd recovered from her stomach bug. Abel overheard her quiet yes, took in her pallor and evasive brush past him to her station; chose not to ask what was really wrong. The frog bones still lay loosely wrapped on her desk. The Jell-O was propped against her lamp's blue circular base. She felt Abel watching her as she gathered up the bones and the vial and pitched them in the wastebasket.

"Did you ever catch your friend?" Kate must be watching her, too.

Emily glanced outside. A film of frost dusted the window's glass. The iron chimney billowed white steam against the gray sky. "Yes. I did catch her."

Kate turned her attention back to the scope. Abel approached with a sheaf of bills he'd corralled in her absence. "We OK?" he asked quietly.

"Perfectly."

"I can assign Tom to cull if you'd rather not do it."

He was blaming her absence on the work when he should know her better. She'd never convince him she hadn't been avoiding the task. But he hadn't ordered the euthanizing done in her absence, either, and he hadn't performed the work himself. Abel wasn't squeamish. He was ruthless about the priorities of discovery and the imperative to cure. Some reason particular to her must lie at the core of his delay.

Abel hadn't pulled up his stool, as was his habit when they spoke. He was avoiding her eyes as she was avoiding his, worrying his hand with the familiar anxiety. Emily shuffled the papers in her hand and laid them aside. Amelia's drawing from the other day poked from the stack. The amber circle was a ring of fire after all, not the sun. The empty space within the flames was colored a bright, cheerful blue. Beyond the ring a roller coaster's skeletal frame loop-de-looped around a single empty car on the track. On the other side of fire, Amelia knew to draw what she one day hoped to experience.

Better than married.

Well, she knew what Dinah would say; that the wedding's proof lay precisely in Abel's waiting for Emily to carry out the killing.

"I'll take care of it, Mike." Emily handed him the drawing. "How was Amelia's appointment?"

If he felt relief, he didn't show it. "What controls her symptoms best is what zonks her out the most. Nothing's going to change that. Except us, right?"

Even if Abel's research led to new drug development, Amelia would be living with her soul's flight for years, fragments of her life forever missing. "Right."

Abel watched her leave the lab as if observation could be intimacy.

In the basement, after suiting up, Emily stepped into the cage room on her way to Lab Will Care. No stickers had been mounted on the cage's identifying cards indicating which mice would be euthanized. Every detail of the cull had been left to her.

And every opportunity.

Release would put up the initial funding to seed the lab's migration to chips and scans on human subjects. *Who can afford to maintain it?* was Emily's first unspoken reaction to Dinah's offer. Dinah would think it immoral to compare technology and human trial costs, not to mention efficacy, to animal subjects. What Emily had said was, "I'm nobody. Not a leading researcher, not even a scientist anymore. What use would my conversion be to your people?"

Dinah had laughed. "Your conversion is the only one that matters, Em."

Dinah would insist on molding her into the scientist she always believed Emily would be. Emily told her the effort was wasted. The lab was Abel's, not hers, to convert. But Dinah viewed Abel as another of the tasks Emily could manage if she chose.

Dinah left *him* up to her, too. She'd noted the times Val was likely to be out, but Emily wasn't about to have anything more to do with that stunt. A stunt blessedly interrupted by Val, but perhaps the interruption, too, had been part of Dinah's grand design. Of the hours Dinah had written on a scrap of paper, she hadn't included the time of their visit.

Now Emily would have to *decide quickly* to kill these animals or release them to Dinah. Something sadistic had always lurked in Dinah's treatment of her, but the same impulse was rooted in Emily, she couldn't deny it now. She wasn't dreading the cull at all anymore. She'd spent her career ensuring she would be the one to perform such deeds methodically and conscientiously. This was what Dinah and Abel both recognized in her and sought to use, her daily devotion to extinguishing life. Each hoped to find lodged in her heart different strains of mercy. What she'd almost done to *him* had shown how far beyond mercy she really was.

But Dinah was wrong about one thing. Emily didn't need to make a quick decision. In the lab, one takes time to consider.

Emily clicked off the cage-room lights and entered Lab Will Care. After two days away from Emily, the mouse scrabbled from her handling. In the acclimation room, the needling claws clicked on the metal table, fought for a grip on the cool steel. Emily scooped him up gently, imitating the arc that would soon carry him to fear. Before long he would reacclimate to her scent and then to her touch, give her his faith in a safe journey down.

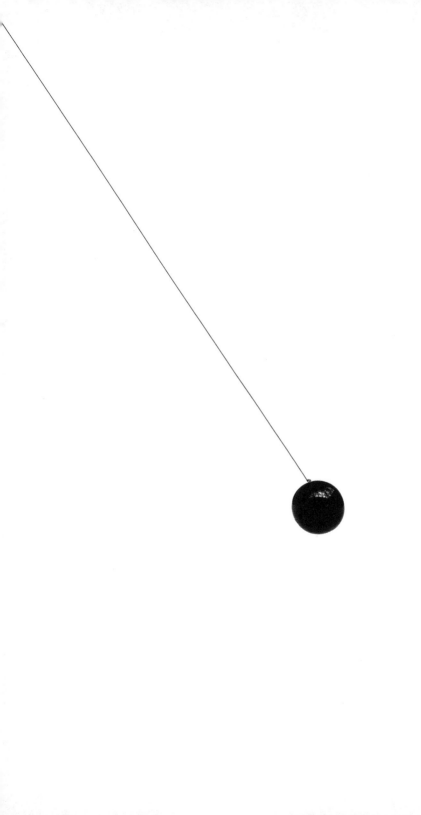

Photo by Ron Thomas.

About the Author

Laura Hulthen Thomas's short fiction and essays have appeared in a number of journals and anthologies, including *The Cimarron Review, Nimrod International Journal, Epiphany,* and *Witness.* She received her MFA in fiction writing from Warren Wilson College. She currently heads the undergraduate creative writing program at the University of Michigan's Residential College, where she teaches fiction and creative nonfiction.